GW01090526

CEL.......

SEÁN KENNY was born in Dublin in 1956. He gave up his
high-earning, high-pressure job in California to write his first
acclaimed novel, *The Hungry Earth*, which was published by
Wolfhound Press in 1995. His novel for children, *Fast-Wing*,
was published by Wolfhound in 1997. He is married with two
children. A UCD engineering graduate, he currently works in
the computer industry.

Reviews of *The Hungry Earth*

'Turlough's journey of self-discovery in both the past and present is a strikingly original one, at once haunting and enlightening.'
IRISH ECHO, US

'... transcends mere reconstruction and in doing so attains a chilling contemporary relevance.'
BOOKS IRELAND

'... an engrossing read. Seán Kenny brings the horrors of the Famine to stark and shocking life while showing how its consequences reverberate through 150 years of Irish history and still affect the Irish mindset in the 1990s.'
IRISH VOICE, US

'... a must for readers with any inkling of interest in that tragic period of Irish history, and you're guaranteed a thriller-like read.'
IRISH GLOBE

'An intriguing story about famine times in Ireland.'
IRISH CATHOLIC

'... a dramatic first novel by Seán Kenny ... which will jolt readers out of any complacency they may have about the Great Famine and how it may have affected all our lives.'
TALLAGHT ECHO

'... a very entertaining novel.'
NORTHSIDE PEOPLE

'... combines the Famine with the contemporary malaise of materialism and discontentment and the mix actually works, resulting in a fine well crafted novel.... Highly recommended.'
TUAM HERALD

'An excellent read.'
IRISH AMERICA MAGAZINE

Celtic Fury

Seán Kenny

WOLFHOUND PRESS

First published in 1998 by
WOLFHOUND PRESS Ltd
68 Mountjoy Square
Dublin 1, Ireland
Tel: (353-1) 874 0354
Fax: (353-1) 872 0207

The Arts Council
An Chomhairle Ealaíon

Wolfhound Press receives financial assistance from
The Arts Council/An Chomhairle Ealaíon, Dublin, Ireland.

British Library Cataloguing in Publication Data
A catalogue record for this book is available from the British Library.

ISBN 0-86327-607-5

10 9 8 7 6 5 4 3 2 1

Cover photograph: The Slide File, Dublin
Cover Design: Slick Fish Design
Typesetting: Wolfhound Press
Printed in the Republic of Ireland by Colour Books, Dublin

*To Molly Ahearn, Doll Kenny and Nell Keogh
for their memories of a simpler, harder life*

Acknowledgements

Thanks once again to my patient family, Kate, Justin and Helen; to Joe O'Sullivan and all at Apple Computer for the time off and the support; to Emer Ryan and all at Wolfhound for the priceless input on the draft; to Dan and Bill for their usual merciless help; and to all the Irish women whose guile and charm inspired the characters in this story.

O luxury! Thou cursed by heaven's decree,
How ill exchanged are things like these for thee!
How do thy potions with insidious joy,
Diffuse their pleasures only to destroy!
Kingdoms by thee, to sickly greatness grown,
Boast of a florid vigour not their own.
At every draught more large and large they grow,
A bloated mass of rank unwieldy woe;
Till sapped their strength and every part unsound,
Down, down they sink, and spread a ruin round.

Oliver Goldsmith, 'The Deserted Village'

Chapter One

Jack Amonson leaned forward, resting his forearms on the iron railing of the small balcony. Below him, the people of Guadalajara went about their business in the old city centre, fragments of Spanish conversation drifting up to him from passers-by. He swirled the ice in his glass, raised it to his mouth, and looked up at the slowly darkening sky as he drank the day's first tequila.

Across the street the stucco façades and stone window-frames of buildings like his own blocked the view of Plaza Liberacion, but the yellow tiles of the cathedral spires held the last of the sun's light. If Aaron had left the Hotel Mendoza immediately he would now have walked past the Teatro Degollado and crossed the plaza.

The intercom buzzed. Jack straightened, walked back into the gloomy living room and pressed the button on the wall.

'Si?'

'Jack, it's me, Aaron.'

Jack stared at the small speaker for a few moments. Already, welling up in him, he felt the pain of reason fighting disbelief. Aaron was here, so Aaron was real. And Aaron had been there, at least for some of it. He pressed the button that released the solenoid lock below and just said, 'It's open.'

For a moment he stood there, the realisation dawning on him that with this simple act he had broken the promise he had made to himself, and the child, never to reopen the past. But she was no longer a child. Seventeen years had passed, and he had failed to distance himself from any of it. As fast as memory faded, the reality grew steadily in front of his eyes, to the point where he had wished for blindness, and more.

The sound of Aaron's feet rising in the stairwell came to him through the fanlight over the door, and then a change in the rhythm announced their arrival on his floor. Jack reached for the handle and swung open the apartment door. For a second neither man recognised the other; then both saw through the years and they smiled.

'Jack,' said Aaron quietly, taking the slowly proffered hand in both of his own, 'it's so good to see you again. My God! After all these years, just to know that you're alive!'

'You're looking good, Aaron.'

There was just enough hesitation to imply that the compliment could not be returned.

'And so I should be,' replied Aaron Rothberg. 'Life's been good to me.'

'No thanks to me.'

'No, no, no. Don't say that, man.'

Jack smiled weakly again. It was a better start than he had hoped for.

Aaron was tanned, with neat white hair, a well-cut suit and that unmistakable poise that comes only with success. He was still overweight, but he had kept that earlier trend in check. Jack knew that by comparison he was a gaunt shadow.

'Are we going to stand out here all night?' asked Aaron.

'Jeez, no, sorry. Come on in.' Jack gestured with the drink he was still holding and led the way inside. 'Have a seat.'

He turned on the lights. 'Can I get you a drink?'

'Sure.'

'Tequila?'

'Hey, what else?' Aaron smoothed his suit as he lowered himself into one of the armchairs.

'Don Pedro, Herradura, Dos Amigos or Commemorativo?' Jack opened the cabinet where he kept his frequently replenished stock, then turned to the other man when there was no reply.

'I'll have whatever you're having.'

There was a pause while Jack made his selection. 'Still wondering why you ever took me on as a client, Aaron?' he asked, before turning back to his visitor.

'Just trying to remember what age you are, Jack,' said Aaron softly.

Jack snorted as he brought a bottle, another glass and an ice bucket to a low table in the centre of the room, now lit by a couple of standard lamps, the light outside giving way fully to night.

'Fifty-four,' he replied, sitting down.

'Yeah, I guess that would be right.' Aaron nodded.

Jack poured the Mexican liquor into two glasses filled with ice cubes. 'Thanks for coming,' he said.

Aaron took the drink. 'I'd have come any time if I'd known where you were all these years.'

'Well, you're here now. *Salut!*'

'Cheers!'

Both men leaned back in their armchairs. Jack knew that Aaron was waiting for him to say something, but he had no idea where to begin, had not thought this through at all, other than that he needed Aaron's help.

'I asked you to come for her because I couldn't think of anyone else,' he said.

'My God, Jack, you should have called years ago!'

'I just wasn't ready to let her go. And I guess I feel I owe you too much already, Aaron.'

'I took you on as a client because you were hot. You don't owe me anything. Hey, the world is full of unfinished scripts.'

They sipped their drinks in silence at this painful memory until Jack said: 'Do you remember the night Maeve introduced us?'

'It ... doesn't stand out.'

'Ah well, lot of people since then.'

'Yeah, but I'm not an agent any more, Jack.'

'Oh. That's a pity. You were the best.'

Aaron smiled and shook his head. 'Don't you even read the fucking newspapers down here? No? I'm the head of Excalibur Studios now.'

'Wow!'

'Yeah, who'd have thought, all those years ago?'

The drone of people and engines went on beyond the

open door to the balcony. Now it was Aaron's turn to break
the silence within the room.

'Where's your daughter, Jack?' he asked.

'Deirdre?'

'Right, Deirdre. Noreen says it's an appropriate name. You
said she was here with you.'

'Yes. She's at her music lessons.'

'Do we need to pick her up?'

'No. She'll walk home across town.'

'Is that safe? A teenage girl out on her own in this place at
night?'

'One of the reasons we live here.' Jack watched as Aaron
shook his head in disbelief. 'It's true. I don't know how long
it will last, but this city is somehow different....'

'Sanctuary?'

Jack leaned forward at this and refilled his own glass, then
topped up Aaron's. The word brought back a conversation
seventeen years earlier — perhaps their last conversation
before now. 'No such thing exists, Aaron. Believe me. I've been
searching all this time. Twelve different places before this.'

'Well, it was all Maeve's idea if I remember right.'

The two men eyed each other, unsure where Aaron's remark would lead.

'Yes, it was.'

'So why go on torturing yourself, Jack? It was an accident,
a terrible accident, but it's all in the past. And you have the
girl to think about.'

Jack covered his eyes.

'I meant Deirdre,' Aaron added, clenching his teeth at
Jack's misinterpretation. 'Sorry.'

'Don't be. No, really. You've done me a big favour by coming down here.' Jack paused, then fixed his eyes on the other
man. 'You know I can't really tell the difference between the
past and the present any more. I wake up in the mornings and
I don't know where I am or what to expect, and the more I've
tried to escape the memories, the more they fill up my life.
There is no sanctuary, Aaron. Not from this anyway.'

The Hollywood executive took a deep breath. 'Come back
to the US, Jack. I'll find you something to do.'

Jack shook his head, then smiled weakly back at his old friend. Yes, he had summoned Aaron here to bring Deirdre back to Ireland, to the one place where he could not follow her, but there was another reason too — if any man knew the dividing line between fact and fiction, between reality and fantasy, it was Aaron Rothberg, who had spent a lifetime, and made a fortune, exploiting this very subject.

'You still don't know the half of it,' said Jack, shaking his head.

'Then tell me.'

Jack smirked at the cue, the invitation that must have been given a thousand times over the years to someone to pitch their story. 'You remember the day Maeve and I left Los Angeles?'

'Yes.'

'You came to the airport to see us off....'

Jack pushed the tickets into a pocket of his hold-all and left the check-in counter to rejoin Aaron.

'So you're really sure you want to do this?' his agent asked.

'For the last time, I'll be in touch — they have phones there.'

'Okay, okay. Such a deal. No tax. We should all move there.'

'Only applies to creative artists, Aaron, not the whole industry.'

Aaron Rothberg looked at his watch. 'Gotta go. I have an eleven a.m.'

They looked around one more time for Maeve. Then both raised a hand and waved as they saw her stride quickly across the shiny floor of the terminal. She beamed back at them, waving an envelope.

'Sorry I'm late. Bloody IRS. But it's official. We don't live here any more!'

Maeve kissed her husband on the cheek then turned to Aaron. 'Tell me you've given up trying to talk us out of it and you're here to wish us the best.'

'You got it, Maeve.'

She reached over with both arms and hugged the agent,

not quite as tall as her in the heels she was wearing, so that her glistening dark hair fell forward as she kissed his cheeks.

'Thanks for everything, Aaron.'

He nodded, backed up to leave, pointed a finger at her and said, 'Make sure he stays at the typewriter. We're all waiting for this one.'

'But that's the whole point.' She linked an arm with Jack; they both waved a last goodbye and were gone towards the metal detector.

Aaron stared after the couple — actress and screenwriter — for a few seconds, looked at his watch, and fled towards the parking lot.

The plane left the gate on time, then queued for almost an hour before finally roaring into the blue California sky towards the west, out over the Pacific, to bank south over Long Beach, then back inland. Jack and Maeve looked down at the view below their window. It was early in the year and there was no smog. The San Gabriels held some snow in their rocky creases, and the lower hills had a hint of vegetation. But for both of them it was still an alien picture, a vast sprawl of malls, tracts and freeways about which it was impossible to become emotional. It was all a giant facility for transacting business. Leaving it — he after two years, she after seven — was like going home from some interminable day's work.

When they reached New York it was already dark, and raining. They ran for the inter-terminal bus and Maeve laughed and hugged Jack as he clung to the pole. He put an arm around her and looked at both their reflections in the side window. It had been his idea to get out of LA, but she had come up with the idea of moving to Ireland.

He knew that by agreeing to this he had given her something priceless: a way back home. And even if it hadn't been a lucrative tax-avoidance scheme he would have done it to see her this happy again.

She nuzzled in against his shoulder. They were the same age, but her career had already come and gone. A few horror movies, a brief stint on daytime TV, and idle periods in between that had all but killed her with depression, and now

she was unmarketable — still beautiful, but relatively un-
known, and tainted by her earlier unreliability.

The bus swerved into the awning of their terminal and
hissed to a stop, opening its doors. They ran to the Aer Lingus
desk and the ground staff held the plane for the two First
Class passengers.

'You take the window seat,' Maeve insisted as they
handed their jackets to the green-uniformed flight attendant.

They had seen the movie before, so they read and dozed
through the night, Maeve curled up in her seat with her head
on Jack's shoulder. He thought she was still asleep when they
began the slow descent into Shannon, but as he peered out
the window she began to speak quietly.

'For me this is always the best part — the idea that the land
is down there, below the clouds, the way it's always been.'
Her chest rose and fell as she let the thought roll through her.

'I think,' she went on dreamily, 'that's what keeps the Irish
going, no matter where we are. We know this island will
always be here for us.'

The aircraft sank into the cloud cover, droplets formed on
the windows, the overhead racks creaked from the buffeting,
and then the mist shredded away.

'I suppose that's Galway,' said Maeve, frowning slightly at
her own questionable geography as a dark landmass with a
jagged horizon came into view beyond the grey ocean. Then
there was the thump of the landing gear locking into place, and
wet fields of green grass slipped past, with white-painted
houses here and there, tiled roofs glistening darkly with dew.
Jack heard his wife sigh, and though she wanted him to watch
the view, he shifted so that he could see her face instead —
her huge blue eyes — and share her joy at this homecoming.

The jet pressed down onto its wheels and immediately
slowed. Maeve fell back against her seat, closed her eyes, and
gasped for air.

'How was it for you?' she asked, squeezing his wrist.

'Can we try this in bed?' he replied, and she laughed,
reached over, and pulled him into a kiss that lasted all the
way through the taxiing.

Maeve drove the rental car, but still they had to stop several times at signposts to consult a map. After a couple of hours they rounded a bend and she made a fist and shouted, 'Yes!' seeing a sign that said 'Rathbrack'.

The ocean peeped from behind sand dunes to their right, while the road curved around a low hill on the left. They passed a right turn that led away towards a cluster of slate-roofed houses by a small stone harbour, and then a second turn that also led into the same village, and here Maeve turned right, then left again past a church and school that shared a concrete yard.

Now they were on a straight road, barely wide enough for two cars, but there was no other traffic. On the right-hand side, tall beech trees grew in a line just beyond the brambles, with rookeries exposed in their bare branches. This was a shallow valley; the hill they had passed earlier was now on the left, beyond the church, and fields sloped up to end at what must be a sharp drop into the ocean on the right.

'From here on, the land between here and the sea is ours,' said Maeve, then added, flatly, 'Well, Owen's land now.'

They had met perhaps a dozen vehicles all the way from Shannon, and Jack had become used to the curving roads, so that this last laneway, with a dry wall of round granite stones on one side, and along the other a drainage ditch, over which arched a dense line of grey tree shoots — ash plants, Maeve would later tell him — no longer seemed unusual.

They slowed, and the brambles blocked the view of the fields on the right.

'It should be just here,' said Maeve, peering out as if she doubted herself. And then, as quickly as they saw them, two pillars marking an entrance had slipped past. Maeve jammed her foot down on the brake pedal. Preoccupied with the search for her childhood home, she forgot that this car was not an automatic and it lurched to a standstill.

Laughing, she restarted the car and reversed it past the gateway, then drove in between the two square gateposts, old structures of cut stone, the gaps heavily mortared to preserve what must have been crumbling away, and even that done so long ago that great tufts of moss had once again taken hold.

They ground slowly up an unpaved avenue, weeds taking over between the wheel ruts, which, here and there, held long fingers of muddy water, splattering the lower reaches of their rental car so that it would resemble all the other cars Jack had seen parked in the villages along the way.

'Here we are,' Maeve proclaimed. 'The house I grew up in.'

There was a thrill in her voice and just for a moment Jack, unable to share the feeling, felt not just left out, but as if there might be facets to Maeve about which he still knew nothing. But she turned to him, smiling, and the moment passed.

They rolled down a short incline that gave way to a wide, cracked and uneven concrete slab. On the left stood some ruined outhouses, then a barn, a simple metal structure filled in with block panels, the green paint of its corrugated sheet-metal roof giving way to rust. In front of them now was a building in better repair, whitewashed, with windows, coiled hoses and tubular steel gates and fences at each end.

Maeve turned the car sharply to the right, stopping next to a Mercedes with the 'D' for diesel suffix at the end of its insignia, nose in to a low wall that bounded a lawn and flowerbeds. Beyond this was the farmhouse itself, single-storeyed, with a major addition to the left that looked no more than about ten years old.

They stood out into the cold air and slammed the car doors. Behind the house the land rose gradually, ending in cliffs about a mile away. To the south, beyond the building that Jack now realised was a dairy parlour, the fields went on and on in an endless patchwork, with glimpses of the dark sea just before more mountains that peeped up in the distance.

The iron gate squeaked on its hinges as Maeve swung it open and beckoned to Jack to follow her up the pathway. She pushed the doorbell, but it made no sound, so she led the way around to the back. There, through a window, they saw a man sitting at the kitchen table, reading a newspaper. She rapped on the glass and shouted, 'Owen, are you deaf or what?'

The man, started, looked up, then beamed and got to his feet. Maeve pushed in the door to the outer back porch, a repository for rubber boots, coats, bales of peat briquettes and crates of empty bottles. She opened the kitchen door bounded up the two steps, crossed the kitchen and hugged her older brother.

'Christ almighty,' he said, 'we weren't expecting the pair of ye at this hour of the morning!'

'Well, here we are.' Maeve pulled off her jacket and hung it on the back of a chair. 'Jack, this is Owen, who you've heard all about.'

'Very pleased to meet you, Jack,' said Owen, offering a brawny hand. They were about the same height, but the Irishman did not look tall, with his broad face, a neck fore-shortened by jowls, and a gut that pulled at his shirt, defying it to stay tucked into his dark trousers.

'Maeve's told me a lot about you, Owen.'

'Oh God, you can be sure it's all bloody lies,' Owen replied. 'Here, take off your coat and sit down. The pair of you must be exhausted by now. I'll make a fresh pot of tea.'

'Where's Olivia and the boys?' Maeve asked, taking in the room, then perching herself at the sink with her arms folded. Jack watched, smiling, as his wife so easily slipped into the movements and mannerisms of the girl who had grown up here twenty years before.

'I don't know what's keeping her,' said Owen. 'She dropped the younger two up to school. Went round to check up on that bloody horse of hers I suppose. Sure I thought ye were her.' He reached past Maeve to fill the kettle with water. 'You're looking well,' he said to his sister.

She gave one of those winning smiles that had first drawn Jack to her. But her brother did not return it. Instead he added, 'A lot better than last time anyway.'

Maeve moved away. 'That was four years ago,' she said. 'Before I met Jack.'

'Ah, well, aren't you the lucky girl then?' He lit the gas and placed the kettle on the blue flames.

'Oh, I think I'm the lucky one,' said Jack, sitting down. 'Not only did I get your beautiful sister to marry me, but now she's spirited me away to this really fabulous place....'

'Sure, maybe she only married you for your money?'

Maeve shook her head and laughed. 'There was no money then. And how were any of us to know that *The Steel Blade* would make a blind fortune?'

Owen brooded on this for a few seconds. 'Then you might have thought he could get you a part in it?'

'Will you give over, Owen. Did Olivia marry you for your money?'

'Oh-ho, she did not. She married me so she could get what she was getting in the back of the car on a Saturday night every night of the week!'

'God, you're the same as ever.'

'Aye, well, what reason would I have had to change?'

They heard a car pull up outside. The front door opened and closed.

'Owen is that them?' a voice asked as a pair of heels clicked along the hallway and a woman in a wool coat with a silk scarf around her neck stepped into the kitchen. 'Maeve!' she exclaimed.

'Hello, Olivia,' said Maeve, crossing the kitchen to embrace her sister-in-law.

Jack stood up again. Owen's wife extended a hand. 'And this is Jack? Oh, we've all been dying to meet you!'

'Well, we did invite you to the wedding,' said Maeve.

'Oh for goodness sake, Maeve,' said Olivia, shedding scarf and coat. 'We're not millionaires, you know. We couldn't just go flying off to California like that.'

'Couldn't you have come over here to be married again?' Owen was now seated, looking up at the three of them.

'Owen!' said Olivia, slipping past him to tend to the kettle. 'You're so incredibly tactless.'

'Now, that's an understatement,' said Maeve, glaring at her brother. 'Where are the cups, Olivia?'

'Not at all. Sit down out of that, the pair of you.'

They did as they were told and Olivia went about the business of laying out four complete place settings, with knives and forks.

They protested that they weren't hungry, that they had eaten on the plane, but it was useless. Sausages, rashers, black pudding, white pudding, fried eggs, fried tomatoes,

fried bread, all appeared in front of them. They heard that
two of Maeve's nephews were doing well as boarders at
Rockwell College, and the two younger ones were holding
their own at the local primary school. The weather had been
abysmal all winter and they had had no summer worth
talking about in Rathbrack the year before.

'But then again,' said Owen, stirring the last wedge of to-
mato around in the egg left on his plate, 'as long as the grass
grows, the cows will eat it, and that means we get milk out of
them, and that's all that bloody matters.'

'How long are you over for?' asked Olivia.

Jack exchanged glances with Maeve.

'Well, actually, we have no plans to go back,' he heard his
wife reply, hesitantly.

This was not just news, he noted, but news that might not
be embraced wholeheartedly.

'And what are you going to do here?' asked Owen.

'Write,' Jack replied, catching a plea for help in Maeve's
face.

'Jack has been given a very large advance to write a sequel to *The Steel Blade*. And when he has that done there are
plenty of others lining up to get him to do scripts for them.'

'I see,' said Olivia, riveted by this world-class gossip.

'Well I don't bloody see,' said Owen. 'I mean, fair enough,
if Jack can command that kind of money, but there's no one
round here with big sacks of dollars to throw at making
movies. Do you not think you've flown about five thousand
fucking miles off course?'

'Owen, don't be so vulgar,' snapped Olivia. 'And what
does it matter where he writes it?'

'Exactly,' agreed Maeve. 'And in fact it's a much better
idea to be here, because it's all tax-free.'

Her brother threw back his head and snorted. 'Oh, now I
see, another Frederick Forsyth here, is it?'

'I think Jack and I should try and get a bit of rest,' said his
sister, rising to her feet, unwilling to pursue the conversation
further.

'Let me show you your room.' Olivia led the way out of
the kitchen. 'Stay here as long as you like. With the boys

away at school, we've no end of space.'

'Jack, I'll give you a hand in with the bags,' Owen offered, and they went out the front door as the two women entered the newer part of the house.

'Back to stay, bedad. How long do you think that'll last, Jack?' asked the dairy farmer.

'Oh, we're serious about this.'

There were four suitcases and various other smaller bags in the car. 'So I see,' muttered Owen.

'Look,' he went on, 'there's no point wasting your money on that rented car while ye're here. Sure ye can borrow one of ours any time.'

'Oh that's very kind. I hope we won't be here too long.'

'And why would you be?' Owen removed the first case, then the next. 'All you have to do is find a house and buy it, right? And God knows, with the state this country is in, that won't be hard.'

They ferried the luggage to the bedroom, and Jack and Maeve were left alone, to rest until dinnertime.

'Are they always thinking about food?' he asked as Maeve unzipped one of her bags.

'I suppose so,' she laughed, kneeling down to search. 'Either that or money.'

'Emmm, I didn't want to say the wrong thing, Maeve, but it kind of seemed like they didn't know....'

'Tonight,' she declared, eyes wide as she looked back up at him. 'Honestly, I'll sort it all out.'

'Sure, but I thought you had already talked with him about it, the way you sounded so certain.'

'Oh, Jack, you've met him now. Don't you see I couldn't do that over the phone, or in a letter — it would just all have been misunderstood.'

'I just kind of thought....'

Maeve stood up and wrapped her arms around his neck. 'It'll be fine, Jack. Really it will.' And she gave that winning smile again.

Chapter Two

Jack awoke before Maeve. It was still light outside, the patterned curtains backlit by the uniform light of an over-cast sky. For a few moments he was confused, the thought persisting, as though he had been dreaming about it, that it was he who was back home. He swung out of the bed and used the drawstring to open the curtains partially.

Even before he saw the scene outside he realised why he had thought he was back in Iowa. He had been listening to the sound of cattle, and now, there they were — a herd of black and white beasts slouching by outside, heavy with milk, all trying to cram into the pens at the near end of the dairy parlour.

This was Owen's livelihood and, as he had said, all it took was for the grass to grow. He turned from the window. He had not lived on a farm in Iowa, but the business of farming was all around, as it would be here. Jack began humming to himself and rooted for more warm clothes to wear.

'What's the weather doing?' Maeve mumbled.

'Well, it's not raining.'

She sprang into a sitting position. 'I'll give you two choices,' she said. 'Either you take me for a long walk up to the top of the cliff, or you get back in here and use up the same number of calories on me.'

Jack straightened up. 'Jeez. Sounds exhausting. I mean, I'm still sort of jet-lagged....'

He loved to watch her response to any hint of rejection like this. Perhaps it was cruel, since she was so predictably unclear whether he was serious or not, but this was the only vulnerability she had ever shown. And he knew she had perfected her armour of self-assurance long before he had met her — and probably it was this, this Irish pride, that had kept her going through all the disappointments and depression and left her as whole as she was.

She fixed him with a wide-eyed stare, and in this half-light there was an angelic purity to her face — a pale oval, blue eyes framed by dark lashes and brows, lips parted as if to speak, but unsure what to say next. She was wasted on Southern California, a bleached ghost who could barely survive an hour at the beach, and then only to freckle up, burn and peel. But here she was perfect.

'If you're not up to it....' She shrugged and leaned forward on her knees.

Jack ran his hands through his hair and frowned. 'What are my choices again here?'

'Ooooh!' She bared her teeth up at the roof.

'Both!' he shouted, startling her.

'Jack, be quiet!'

He ignored her, lunged forward and clawed away the bedclothes.

'Jack, stop it. You'll have them all in to see what's wrong. Let's go for a walk.' She recoiled to the far side of the bed, but he caught her ankle and pulled her back, sideways across the bed, then sprang up on his knees over her. Maeve burst out laughing, the more so when he tickled her ribs to force her to shriek even louder, pushing her face into the pillow to muffle the sound, and flailing uselessly until he tugged her panties down by the back elastic and she gave up her feigned resistance. Then she turned to him, back in control now, and grabbed forcefully at his crotch. 'All right then, get down here on top of me,' she said, 'and warm me up!'

It was a windless evening, but the grass was wet everywhere and as they traipsed up the peninsula their hiking boots could not prevent their jeans becoming sodden up to the knees. Maeve led the way over another rusted gate. Jack steadied it for her, amazed that it stayed upright at all.

'Here we are,' she told him as he followed her. 'This is the place.'

'What about a road?'

'Oh, there's one just down there.' She pointed and Jack saw a double row of hedges, suggesting a road of sorts between them, which followed the course of the bay. On the right, it led back down to Rathbrack — dull slate panels between stone gables and chimneys, and on to a pier that divided the bay's sandy beach from the rocks that grew higher and more jagged further west.

They walked on into this uppermost field of the Fitzgerald farm, stopping when they were far enough up to get a good view back over the low hills to the east.

'Well, what do you think?' Maeve asked quietly.

Rathbrack's beach curved away below them, lapped by white surf. Between the beach and the road by which they had arrived was a maze of sand dunes, while further inland was all rolling grassy hills. He swung around to look south at more of this pastoral countryside, Owen's farm the nearest of dozens of similar dwellings. And from this height more of the indented coastline, battered incessantly by white surf, was visible, leading away to the far mountains.

Being from the Mid-West, he tended to be mesmerised by all seascapes, but there was more going on here. It was not just the vista that captivated him, it was the idea that, through Maeve, he was connected to this world. She was descended from the people who had shaped this place, who had depended on it for their existence; she was literally the stuff of Rathbrack.

'It's really magnificent,' he said.

She smiled at this, dug her hands deep into her pockets and pulled up close against him. 'Come on, let's walk on to the top.'

They slipped down to the road, clambering over a stone wall onto it, then followed it up to where it gave way to an ill-defined parking area with a 'No Dumping — By Order' sign in one corner. A last short walk over hard sheep-eaten sods brought them to the brink. The drop was not quite sheer, rather it slid away in angled slabs, so that in places the cliff was undercut and the ocean swell rolled in out of sight and growled back up at them.

The daylight was almost gone. A few shipping lights stood out like stars on the horizon, and somewhere far to the south a lighthouse beacon blinked slowly on and off.

'It has a kind of end-of-the-world feel to it,' said Jack, still looking out to sea.

'Yes it does,' Maeve agreed. 'You know, as a child I had really no concept that there could be something beyond the horizon. Or perhaps it was impossible to think of another Rathbrack out there. It was much easier to imagine magical places and sea monsters and the Spanish Armada being blown away.'

'This *is* a magical place,' said Jack, looking around in all directions again. 'This is fantastic. It'll be easy to work here.'

It was fully dark when they got back to the house. Jack met the two younger Fitzgerald boys and answered questions about America until they were banished to the kitchen to do homework while the adults sat down to eat in the dining-room: potatoes, cauliflower, carrots, peas, huge portions of lamb, a salad, three different cheeses, bread, crackers, and Olivia had even mentioned that she had made a dessert.

'Iowa? Now there's a place you never hear much about,' said Owen, pouring out the last of the first bottle of wine, and thus signalling Olivia to get another one from the kitchen.

'That's because there isn't much to tell,' said Jack. 'It's flat, boring, and a thousand miles from any ocean.'

'Ah, now, Jack, I thought it was very picturesque when we visited it. Really friendly, middle America,' Maeve countered.

'Will you listen to that?' said Owen. 'Coming from the very one who couldn't wait to run out of this boring dump.'

'I didn't say I'd like to live in Iowa,' Maeve retorted, frowning.

'No, and you don't want to live here either,' said her brother, accepting the full bottle of wine from his wife and going to work on it with the corkscrew.

'I certainly do!'

'Will you get away out of that! The pair of ye are here

hiding from the taxman in America, and when it all blows over you'll be back in Hollywood flashing your tits in some stupid film again.'

'Owen! Will you grow up and stop trying to embarrass Maeve? You're just making a fool of yourself.'

Owen raised surprised eyes to his wife. 'A bit bloody late for her to be embarrassed when you can rent videos of her in any town in the country....'

'I'm not bothered by any of that, Olivia. Don't you go topless on the beach in Spain?' Maeve turned to her brother. 'I really just wish Owen would make some effort not to let Jack see what a thick eejit he is on the first day he meets him.'

Owen put his head back and laughed. 'Ah, sure he may as well get used to us if he's going to be living around here. Isn't that right, Jack?' He began to refill their glasses.

'Just don't become like them,' said Maeve.

'You could do worse, Jack. I suppose our humour is a bit over the top, but at least we're not short of a few laughs, are we?'

'We're serious about living here.' Jack twirled the now full wine glass and looked at Maeve.

'And would you not rather live somewhere a bit closer to Dublin?' asked Owen, causing Jack to fix a stare on Maeve that he knew she read as an order to get on with it. She cleared her throat as she might do at the start of an audition.

'We happen to know exactly where we want to live,' she said slowly.

'And where's that?'

'Owen, I'd like you to sell us a site.'

If her brother had any inkling this was coming, he didn't show it. A silence descended, and the other three fixed their gaze on the dairy farmer as he put the wine bottle down on the table with a slight tremble to his hand.

'What?'

'We want to build a house on a piece of the upper field.' Maeve's words carried just a hint of haughtiness.

'The upper field? That's the biggest field on the farm!'

'We don't want to buy the whole field, Owen — just a half acre or so that fronts onto the road, that's all.'

'And when did you come up with this bloody hare-brained idea?'

Too quickly she replied, 'Why do you think we came straight here?' She winced as soon as the words were out, but it was too late.

'Oh, is that right?' asked Owen, leaning over towards her. 'And there we were thinking you were coming to visit your closest living relative to introduce your new husband!'

'Oh God, Owen, what I meant was....'

'I know what you meant.'

'No! No, you don't. What I meant was I wanted to come here and discuss this with you in person, which is why I didn't bring it up over the phone before now.'

'You mean you didn't want to give me a chance to think about it!'

'What is there to ... think about?' Maeve smiled and blinked nervously.

'Aye, there's nothing to think about. I'm not going to sell you a bit of the farm. Feck off and buy somewhere else!'

'Owen, be reasonable,' said Maeve, in a voice that Jack knew was genuinely pleading. 'You have two hundred acres here, which, by the way, you didn't have to buy from any-one....'

Owen jumped to his feet. 'Is that right now? Is that fuck-ing right?'

'Owen, please. Sit down,' urged Olivia.

'You stay out of this!' He approached his sister and grasped her shoulder roughly. 'Listen here, miss high-and-mighty. All those years you were gadding about all over the world, all expenses paid, I was here, up to my arse in cow shite, working on this farm. And I didn't get it free and clear. It came with a lot of debts, which I still have, by the way, not the least of which was death duty itself, which meant I had to sell off the fields down by Kilmarnock, and I'll be damned if I'll sell off any more of it!' He let go of her, sat back down and folded his arms.

Jack watched as Maeve tried desperately to remain composed, unable to make eye-contact with any of them.

'So, how about this,' he began. 'You sell us the site up

there with a view and use the money to buy a few more
fields?' No one seemed to hear. 'I mean, cows don't give
more milk just because they have a view of the sea. Trust me,
I know these things — I'm from Iowa.'

'That would be far too logical, Jack,' said Olivia.

Maeve straightened up and stared at her brother until he
looked back. 'Listen, Owen. I had no more choice in the way
things worked out than you did. There was no place for me
here. You were always going to get the farm. I could either
marry another farmer's son round here, or leave. And I still
love this place. I've never stopped thinking about it. I've
always dreamed of coming back to Rathbrack — it just always
seemed impossible.

'But now, with Jack, I have that chance. And we'll pay you
a fair price. We want to build a house up there because it has
the best view and we know that's worth something.'

Owen drank back some wine and chuckled. 'It has, but
God, it's bloody windswept at times. A couple of bad winters
and you might run out of the place.'

She had won him over. Jack marvelled at her. 'Maybe we
should all sleep on the idea and talk again tomorrow,' he
said, anxious to consolidate the gain they had made.

Olivia lit a cigarette, signalling an end to the half-eaten
meal. 'So tell me,' she said, blowing a long stream of smoke
up at the ceiling, 'is Burt Reynolds really bald?'

Jack and Maeve arose late the next day to bright sunshine,
and Jack resolutely refused Olivia's offer of a cooked breakfast, opting instead for a mug of coffee while he waited for
Maeve in the kitchen.

'He'll come around,' the farmer's wife told him as she
handed him his coffee. 'He's too stubborn to admit it, but we
could use the money. He borrowed a blind fortune from the
bank to build up the herd, and we're spending a ton of
money on fertiliser.'

'I guess stubbornness runs in the Fitzgerald family.'

'Oh, don't talk! There are times....' She left the thought

unfinished, saying instead, 'You know, we do have four boys of our own to think of now.'

'Of course.'

'I'm an outsider myself, you know.'

Jack raised his eyebrows at this.

'Yes, I'm from Kilcashel, less than twenty miles away, but I might as well be from America.'

Jack smiled. 'So, you're new blood?'

She chuckled at this. 'Oh yes, very much so. I'm Protestant, from way back. Owen saw me as a good catch....' She paused, and Jack thought that again she would not continue but this time she went on: 'I know he went after me as much to prove to Maeve, or to himself, that he was different from all the gobdaw farmers around here....'

Olivia trailed off as they heard Maeve coming down the corridor.

'Tea?' Olivia asked.

'Ooooh — I think I smell Jack's coffee!'

'Coffee coming up.'

'And tell me about this horse,' said Maeve, wrapping her hands round the mug to warm them as she might have done when she was a child.

'Oh, he's just an old point-to-pointer. But, for God's sake, don't bring that up! That's a sore point with him too: hay and vet's bills.'

No one spoke after this, and Jack felt it was as if neither of the women could think of anything that they could be sure wouldn't involve Owen's disapproval.

'Maeve is taking me on a walking tour of Rathbrack today,' he eventually said to Olivia. 'Do you think she'll remember her way around?'

Both women laughed at this suggestion and Olivia replied, 'Oh now, if she does get lost, you'd want to be seriously worried about her. Nothing changes around here. Right, Maeve? You come back after fifteen years and everything's the same. Except those of us who are still here are a bit fatter and our husbands a bit balder....'

'Ah now, don't be putting the place down before he's even seen it!' Maeve shook her head. 'And there have been a few changes. There's some big new bungalows around. And they've repainted the church.'

'Isn't it a ghastly colour? Salmon-pink! That's that new priest, Fr Byrne, trying to make his mark.'

'Olivia, we'll go while the weather's fine.'

'Right then. Be sure now and show Jack the old monastery.'

They were at the door when Maeve turned to ask: 'Is Gladys still living in her cottage?'

Olivia nodded. 'She is, and not a bother on her. But sure, she's pickled altogether now with the vodka.'

'We might see if she's in then.'

'Oh, do.'

They picked their way around the puddles in the drive-way, out past the gate pillars onto the road, and turned left, sauntering hand in hand along the deserted road.

'Isn't Owen an awful bastard?' Maeve began.

'Is that what's been on your mind since we left the house?'

'No. Yes. I suppose so.'

'And you had to wait till we were clear of the farm to ac-tually say the words.'

'What?'

'You've been itching to say something bad about him all morning but you waited till right now, till we passed the end of your brother's land.'

She withdrew her hand. 'So what are you suggesting?' The dark eyebrows gathered into a frown.

'Nothing. Just an observation.'

Maeve folded her arms. 'Oh, Jack, I hope I haven't read this all wrong.'

'Hey, don't worry about it. If you have, we'll just buy some other place.'

'No, no! I want us to live there. I want you to have that view to look out at in the mornings when you're starting to write. It's by far the best location in Rathbrack, and he knows he should sell it to us.'

As they walked on, she folded her arms and looked to the left over the fields that swept up to where she wanted to build their home.

It was early spring, the sun, even in the middle of the day, casting long shadows so that all of the land's features stood out in dark relief. They followed the floor of the valley with the cliffs that dropped away to the Atlantic on the left, Rathbrack and its bay ahead of them, and rising again on the right, inland, a series of small hills.

Dark hedges divided up the fields, as if some giant had thrown a net over the grassy hills, and here in the deep lowland soil the big beech trees stood sentinel over the blackberry bushes and the road that passed beneath their boughs.

'I wonder if she's in,' said Maeve.

'Who?' Jack was pleased that she seemed to have stopped brooding about her brother.

'Gladys.'

'The lady you mentioned to Olivia?'

'Yes, old Gladys Clery. She used to do the washing and ironing for my Mam. That's her house there on the left.'

They were coming up on a small cottage of red bricks on the left. Its two front windows had granite sills and lintels and the door was set into a brick-edged porch with its own small slate apex matching the main roof. The metal gutters and downpipes were rusted through in places, but otherwise it was in good repair. Maeve walked in off the road by an open gate, held forever ajar by the weeds and grass that had used its lower rails as a trellis for many years.

'She used to keep hens,' said Maeve, 'there in the back.' She pointed to a tarred wooden hut, with tiny windows, set on block piers to give the poultry a fighting chance against the rats. 'And I was sent down here for eggs.'

'Ah, now I see.' Jack nodded sagely.

'You see what?'

'Well, it's obvious. You left town, and the egg lady had no one who wanted her eggs, and you've come back because you can't bear the guilt any more.'

'Hah! Save that for Hollywood.'

They reached the front door and Maeve rapped twice with the heavy doorknocker. She looked at her watch. 'This is the best time to get her. It's late enough that she's up, and early enough that she's sober.' She shook her head. 'Poor old sod.'

There was a shuffling inside and the door swung open.

Gladys Clery's face was not a welcoming one. Her brow, framed by short thinning curls, grey at the roots, was deeply furrowed at this unexpected call. Her eyes too were full of suspicion.

'What do you want?' she asked flatly, stout legs planted apart, left hand still holding the door.

'Gladys, it's me, Maeve!'

'I don't know any Maeve.'

'Maeve Fitzgerald!'

For a few moments Gladys hovered there, the small sunken brown eyes seeming to focus on some point between them. She had no eyebrows, having plucked them away at some earlier time, and when at last she recalled the name she had just heard, her mouth spread into an open smile to show some brown teeth.

'Ah, my God! Maeve! Sure I wouldn't have recognised you!' Gladys flung the door wide, held up both her arms, and Maeve stepped forward to be hugged, as she must have done a hundred times as a young girl.

'Oh, sure I should have known the minute I saw you that you weren't from that bloody social welfare crowd. Ah, you're only gorgeous looking, more beautiful than ever. I hear you have the sun out there in America all year round.'

'You're looking very well yourself, Gladys,' said Maeve, stepping aside so that the elderly lady could examine Jack fully.

'And is this your husband?' she asked, her face quite different now that she was at ease. Now the small nose and twinkling eyes told of a woman who might have been quite pretty herself once upon a time.

'Yes, ma'am. I'm Jack.' He held out a hand which she clasped in both of hers.

'Oh God, he's very handsome. Come in, come in!'

She closed the door behind them. 'God, if only I'd known you were coming. I haven't a thing in the house. Sit down, sit down and I'll make a pot of tea.'

'Oh now, Gladys, really, there's no need. We just stood up from our breakfast.' But Maeve's protests were useless, as she knew they would be. Gladys left them in the main room of her house, which had a window onto the front and one onto the back, and strode into a small scullery that extended out beyond the back wall, where she clanked about out of sight.

Maeve winked at Jack. 'Can I be of help out there, Gladys?'

'No, no, I'll be back in now in a minute.'

Maeve sat down in a faded brown armchair with lace-edged linen cloths on the arms and headrest. The fireplace had a small pile of ash on the grate, but the brass poker, tongs and shovel on the tiles in front of it looked unused, and Jack noticed that a second iron poker and beaten-up shovel stood next to a metal bin of coal on the right.

The mantelpiece held a variety of brass ornaments, and on a small cabinet to the left there was a reading light with a tasselled shade. The top of this cabinet also held a square of lace and a framed photo that caused Jack to bend forward to see it more clearly. In the dim light from the two windows it was still hard to see, so he picked it up.

It was an old sepia print, now faded, and it showed a soldier, looking up at the sky and saluting, posing side-on so that the sergeant's stripes on his left sleeve were to the fore. Behind this dashing young warrior was the nose of a plane, with a three-bladed propeller in evidence. Looking back at the uniform, Jack now saw pilot's wings on the right breast and a rounded wing-tip just beyond his saluting arm. Maeve stood up to see what he was looking at, and immediately took it from him and replaced it exactly where it had been, just as Gladys came towards them with a tray.

'Jack, sit down there and rest your legs. God, it's not often I have a man in this house. Oh, you did very well for yourself there, Maeve.'

'Oh, I did indeed.'

Gladys distributed the two cups and saucers and Maeve poured for her.

'You know who he reminds me of, Maeve?'

'No. Who?'

The old lady clasped her hands in front of her and smiled down at Jack. 'Gary Cooper.'

It was all Jack could do not to splutter into his teacup, the more so when Maeve tilted her head and stared at him as if she were looking for the resemblance.

'Really?' she asked. 'Do you think so?'

'And sure I can tell, you know, I can tell,' Gladys went on, 'that the two of you are madly in love.'

'Oh, we are,' Maeve agreed, mischievously.

'And are you a movie star too?' the older lady asked Jack, clearly hoping the answer would be yes.

'No, I'm afraid not. I just do a bit of writing.'

'Oh, I see.'

This was such awful news for Gladys that Maeve added, 'But he does quite well at it.'

'Oh, I'm sure. But then there's others has no luck at all, like that unfortunate Fletcher woman.'

Before they could ask who that was, Gladys moved on to another concern.

'All that talk down in Sweeney's,' she said, with a slow shake of her head, 'was a load of old rot, and sure I knew that all along.'

'What talk, Gladys?' asked Maeve.

'About you, well, you know ... ah well, people around here have little enough to be talking about. Scandalmongers, the lot of them. Sure I knew there was no truth in it. About you being divorced and all. I said that all along. Little Maeve, that used come up to me for the eggs for her mother? Not at all!'

Chapter Three

They walked on towards Rathbrack, coming to the end of the road not far beyond Gladys's house. Another road cut across in front of them. On one side stood the houses of Rathbrack with their shared walls; on the other side, the school and newly painted church; and ahead of them a very old ruined church surrounded by a field of tombstones.

'Come on,' said Maeve. 'I'll show you our only real historical monument!' She took his hand and pulled him across the road to a gap in the wall, then led the way through the maze of graves, some with upright headstones, some with large inscribed slabs lying flat above their occupants.

It seemed they were headed for the church, but close in to its wall Maeve turned right, and the trail led them to a large free-standing stone cross. Jack had seen these in guidebooks about Ireland. It was a Celtic cross, an elaborately carved crucifix, with biblical scenes in panels on the lower part of its upright, perhaps twenty feet high, the stone crosspiece strengthened by an inner circle integral to this part of the structure, each quadrant hollowed out, so that there was no ambiguity — this was a cross and a circle combined.

'They have a plaster cast of this in the National Museum in Dublin,' said Maeve. 'Isn't it fabulous? Over a thousand years old!'

Jack nodded agreement and they stood in appreciation for a few moments, looking at the west face of the cross, clouds rolling by behind its four windows. The horizon seemed, strangely, to be pulled upward directly behind the main stone pillar, until Jack realised that the cross was positioned be-tween them and the hill-top beyond the main coast road.

Again, Jack felt a powerful connection to the past.

'Are any of your ancestors buried here?' he asked Maeve.

She shrugged. 'I never really thought about it, but I sup-pose it's quite possible.'

It was a matter-of-fact response. But she was from here, and if the air itself was magic she had been breathing it all her life. It was he who was from a strange place where he had no past of his own.

They turned away, leaving the centuries-derelict monastic site by a gate out to the other road leading into Rathbrack, and walked back into the village towards the only building between the road and the sea, Sweeney's Bar. There were no fishing boats in the harbour now, and the L-shaped pier, its stones polished smooth by the chafing of ropes, was just a perch for the gulls, gathered in close groups as if awaiting the return of the missing fleet.

As Maeve had predicted, Sweeney himself was behind the bar.

'Back for awhile, Maeve?' he said, nodding, as they ap-proached the counter.

'Is there anything that happens in Rathbrack that you don't hear?' she asked, and then introduced her husband.

Jack wondered whether Sweeney too was of the impres-sion that he was her first, but this was a person who would reveal nothing by face or body language. He offered a limp hand to Jack, his neck apparently not much stiffer, to judge by the way his head lolled about. Having mumbled a wel-come, the bartender withdrew to adopt a servile stance.

'Have you anything in the way of food, Micko?' Maeve asked.

'Eh, no, sorry now, Maeve. Not at this time of the year.' He clasped his hands together and leaned forward in a slight bow as he said this.

'Anything hot at all?' she asked next.

'Oh, aye, I could do you a hot whiskey.'

'Well, no, not at this hour of the day. I meant like soup?'

This seemed to amuse him. 'Oh now, Maeve, this is not

America. Not much call for that in this establishment.'

He had a good point. They were the only customers. Outside there were a few parked cars, and the only traffic they had passed was an old man on a bicycle, who touched his cap to them.

'Fine,' said Maeve flatly. 'Pour a pint for Jack, please, and I'll have a glass of any kind of mineral water.'

'Right you be,' the publican replied and set about this task.

The bar was a shabby mixture of old and new. And it was not evident that it had ever seen better days. The shelving behind Micko Sweeney was simple planking that had been painted a glossy cream, over and over, along with the wall. The bar itself was topped with the red marbled formica of a diner, the pattern worn away on the customer side; the stools were similarly polished from their original black vinyl to a neutral grey; and the carpet, certainly more recent than these, its pile and flowery colouring still in good condition where it was unused, was matted down into a web of dark trails that led around the tables to the booths along the walls.

'What line of work are you in, Jack?' asked Micko.

'I'm a writer.'

'Oh. Books is it?'

'No. Screenplays.'

'Ah, right. And have you met Noreen Fletcher?'

Jack shook his head at this name for a second time.

'We just met up with Gladys Clery,' said Maeve. 'Is she still your best customer?'

'Aye, well, she comes in here now and again, all right.'

'And are you still watering down her vodka, Micko?'

Again, that faint twisting of the mouth, which could be amusement or anger, appeared on Micko's face, but as he delivered the two drinks he looked very seriously at Maeve and said, 'A thing like that would never happen here.' He took her money, then excused himself and disappeared.

'Jeez, that was kind of harsh, Maeve,' said Jack.

'Oh, listen, enjoy your drink,' she replied, voice lowered now. 'The Guinness here is not exactly legendary, but you'd better get used to it. And that old miser really does keep a special bottle of watered-down stuff for poor old Gladys. That way she stays sober longer, which means she spends even more.'

'So who was that in the photo you made me put down?'

'Back in the cottage? The pilot?'

'Yes.'

'He was her fiancé back before the war.'

'The war? Which war?'

'Emmm, the Second World War, I think.' Maeve's history was about on a par with her geography.

'But that was forty years ago ... more....'

'I know. He was a local boy who had gone to England and joined up. He was shot down, pretty early on, I think. Maybe the Battle of Britain — would that be right? Anyway, she never got over it.'

Jack drank some of the black beer and thought about this. Maeve watched him over the rim of her own glass.

'Are you wondering would I end up like that if something happened to you?' she asked.

'Jeez, no. Obviously you wouldn't. I mean you're not stuck here raising chickens the way she was, with no way out.'

She leaned into him, her hand on his leg. 'But, Jack, in a different way I am. I've been out there. I made it all the way to Hollywood, and whatever it takes to be a part of all that, I know I don't have it. I don't know if life would be worth it at all without you, Jack.'

He tried to speak but she went on, her voice forceful now. 'In fact, without you, I think that for sure I would never leave here again. Oh, maybe someone else would come along and sweep me off my feet, but I doubt it, and I wouldn't go looking.'

It was one of those revelations that just come from no-where, the kind of thing she might have told him much earlier on if they had met here and sat on these stools and thought about their futures from this viewpoint. But then it would have been a free choice; now it seemed somehow unfair that she had linked their future together to this place.

He leaned in close to Maeve's face. She was oblivious to this aspect of her statement. 'Well, this is a dumb conversation,' he said. 'I'm here because you're here, and I'm not going to get shot down because I'm not going to fuck up this next script.'

'You're right,' said Maeve, sliding a hand round his neck. 'I've had so much better luck than Gladys. I brought my hero home with me.'

She pulled his face against hers and kissed him. Rathbrack was as good a place as any to live, better than most, he thought, since it had produced Maeve.

Dinner was less formal than on the night before. Jack had driven the fifteen miles into Kilcashel to get a few bottles of wine, leaving Maeve to help her sister-in-law. What they finally served up was a rehash of the previous night, aug-mented with cold meat and a more varied salad.

'How do you find driving on these windy little roads, Jack?' asked Owen as they ate.

'Hey, I enjoy it. Changing gears all the time. Great scenery. You never know what's round the next bend.'

'But you wouldn't want to be going to and from work every day like that?'

'No.'

'Well, obviously,' said Maeve. 'That's why no one lives here. Only the lucky few who can work from their home can do that.'

'You mean like farmers?' asked Owen.

Jack caught Maeve's eye. She continued sawing up food as if not completely concentrating, but he knew she was and that now they had once again broached the dreaded subject.

'Well, yes, farmers. But I was referring to Jack. All he needs is to wake up in aesthetically pleasing surroundings....'

Her brother laughed loudly. 'Bejasus, you couldn't wait to get away from these aesthetic four walls.'

Maeve stared blankly at her brother. 'I don't disagree. But now I'm back.'

He grunted at this. It was not what he was expecting and was hard to follow up with a new jibe.

'Go on, Owen,' said Olivia. 'Tell her your idea.'

Owen glowered at his wife for prompting him, then nodded slowly and began. 'That upper field, you know, is a very valuable bit of land. Great views. Walking distance to Rathbrack Beach. Wouldn't be much trouble to sink a well, put in sewage, and the electricity's not far away either. All things considered, cheap enough to develop.'

'Well, that's all good news,' said Maeve.

'Oh, it is right enough. So much so that I thought I'd develop the whole lot of it. Put in about ten houses, maybe twelve. What do you think?'

Maeve looked at Jack who shrugged, unconcerned by this property-development proposal.

'This is a total surprise,' she said. 'When did you come up with this notion?'

'Ah, we've thought about it on and off. Right, Livy?'

Olivia nodded and reached for her cigarettes.

'Fine then,' said Maeve. 'We'll be your first customer. We want the site between the gate up from here and the road up to the cliff.'

Owen frowned for a moment. 'That would really be two sites.'

Maeve flicked her hair back. 'Okay then, we'll buy both of them. How much?'

Jack nodded his support for this idea, but Owen held up his hands and said: 'Oh now, steady on. What I'm really looking for here is more of a partnership to develop all of it.'

'How do you mean?' Jack asked.

'That you'd invest in the thing....'

'You want us to put up half the money?' Maeve asked.

'No. All of it.'

'What? Why would we do that? And what would your role in all this be?'

'The land, Maeve. I'm putting up the land.'

Jack watched his wife's face darken.

'I suppose you can do whatever you like with the place now, Owen,' she said very quietly, 'since it's yours. But we won't be drawn into some scheme that might drag on forever. Just sell us the site.'

'Isn't it well for you,' Owen replied, 'that you needn't be drawn into anything you don't like? Hah? You just fuck off around the world and do what you like and then you come back here when the fancy takes you with your rich new husband, and build the house of your dreams.'

'And aren't you living the good life here too?'

'I've worked my arse off to get where I am!'

'You have not. You had a two-hundred-acre farm handed to you!'

'Jesus, you little bitch, I'm not listening to that again. Didn't Dad ask you to stay here after your mother died? But no, you had to go off again.'

'I had commitments.'

'Yes, commitments to yourself, elsewhere. And you weren't here for him at the end either.'

Tears came into Maeve's eyes. 'Oh Christ, Owen, please, let's not go through all this again. You could have left too. They said they'd pay your way through college, but you didn't want to leave your yobbo friends. You stayed because you wanted to, so don't give me this martyr routine of yours.'

'Yobbos? Culchies? Rednecks, you'd call us, Jack! None of us good enough for Maeve's company....'

'I think we're getting off the point here,' Jack intervened. 'Look, why don't you just sell us our site, then you can use the money to finance the next one, and so on?'

'Ah well, as Maeve so rightly points out, it's not so simple. It might drag on forever, and I'm a bit over-extended right now, with borrowing the money to build up this herd. That's why I can't finance it myself.'

'So sell the field to someone else to develop!' Maeve shouted at her brother.

'Don't try giving me advice on how to run my affairs, Miss Failed Actress!'

'There's no need to insult her like that,' said Olivia.

'Listen, buddy, she's your sister,' said Jack, his tone changing, 'your only sister.'

'Isn't that the whole point?' Owen yelled. 'Where has she been all these fucking years, when she wasn't looking for something for herself?'

'How much?' Maeve shouted, rising to her feet. 'Just tell us how much you want!'

Owen's eyes swivelled up to meet hers. 'All right then. One hundred thousand pounds.'

'What? You're insane, Owen. Mad!' She stepped back from the table, clasped a trembling fist over her mouth, then lowered it again.

'Jack, get out your cheque book,' she said softly.

Jack reached into an inner pocket of the jacket he had slung over his chair and produced a long, thin book of cheques and a pen. 'I opened a bank account in town today,' he said, 'but it'll be a couple of days before you can actually cash this.'

For a moment no one spoke. Owen eyed the cheque book suspiciously. Olivia gazed on implacably from behind a curtain of her own cigarette smoke, and Maeve watched her brother's face. 'Write out a cheque,' she said slowly, 'to Owen ... for ... twenty thousand pounds.'

'What are you talking about?' Owen physically jerked back on hearing that they were not going to pay even a quarter of his asking price.

'You heard me. That was my inheritance — at least that's what I got out of the will anyway. You might be long dead before you get anyone else to pay that kind of money for a site around here. And I'll bet Dad would have given me that site as well if I'd asked him.'

'I don't owe you anything, Maeve.'

'Oh? We'll see about that. My God, Owen, if you don't sell me that site, if it's the last thing I do, I'll overturn Dad's will!'

Owen now rose to his feet, so quickly his chair toppled over behind him.

'Is that right? And how are you going to do that?' He walked over and prodded her. 'Do you think anyone's going to listen to the whining of some returned yank, three years after the death of her father? And by the way, if they do, it won't just be me you'll be up against, because the bank who gave me the mortgage will have to defend the fact that they were sure I owned the place.'

The two Fitzgeralds glared at each other. Jack and Olivia

watched in silence. Again Jack was seeing a new side to Maeve, but this was not a complete surprise. He had long suspected that the source of her ambition, her willingness to weather all those setbacks, to keep going against the impossible odds of Hollywood, was this anger at her brother and the inevitability of her inheritance.

'I'm giving you all the money Dad gave me,' she said, 'in exchange for that piece of a field. It's more than it's worth. Take it and let's move on.'

'Well now, I'll rot in hell before I'll do that.'

'You bastard!' She raised a hand so quickly and hit his face so hard that she stunned him. Then, without pause, she pummelled his chest and as he tried to back away, the loose fireside rug twisted under him and he fell backwards. Maeve picked up her dinner plate and flung it down to smash against his raised elbow, and was reaching for another when Jack bounded around and caught her arms.

'Maeve, Maeve, what are you doing?' He shook her, but she was already trembling. He turned to Owen. 'Are you okay?'

'I'm far from okay!' Owen sat upright on the floor and pointed at his sister. 'I'll bet that's a side to her she didn't show you before she marched you down the aisle!'

'You pig!' she retorted.

'Christ, that's a right bloody mess she's after making.' The farmer pulled himself to his feet and sat down heavily in his own chair again.

'It's just a few plates,' said Olivia, reaching for her cigarettes. 'Can't you both calm down. None of us can change the past, so why don't you just let it be.'

'Look,' said Jack, walking back around the table, 'let's settle this thing. Maeve says she'll pay twenty thousand. You said earlier you saw it as two sites. So why don't we pay you forty thousand and get started on the right foot as neighbours?'

Olivia nodded enthusiastically at her husband, still scowling up at his wayward sister. Maeve shook her head at Jack, her face still a high colour, locks of her black hair breaking away to fall in over her cheeks. 'No, no! Jack, it's far too much. I don't want you to do this....'

He ignored her. 'So what do you say, Owen?'

Owen looked sullenly at him. 'Fifty thousand and you can have it.'

Now Jack looked up at Maeve, unsure how to react to this counter-offer. His doubts lasted only seconds. She lunged once more at her brother, both hands outstretched. But he was ready this time and pushed her aside, so that she fell against a standard lamp that toppled over, sweeping china ornaments from the sideboard on its way to the floor.

'No!' she screamed. 'I'm not spending the rest of my life with this extortionist as my next-door neighbour. Now I know what really drove me away from here — it was the shame of having a thick, ignorant brother like you for family!'

'Oh, and where did I get it from?' Owen barked over at her. 'Didn't I come from the very same parents as you — and theirs before them?'

Maeve's eyes blazed at him. 'Come on, Jack,' she rasped, steadying herself. 'Let's get out of here. Some day you'll get yours, Owen. You just wait. You won't always have all the power, and then you'll see what it's like to be on the receiving end of some heartless bastard like yourself!'

Fifteen minutes later they were gone, the rental car filled with their bags and loose clothes. Jack reversed away from the building, sped up the lane, left onto the road and into Rathbrack past Gladys Clery's cottage.

Maeve spoke for the first time since cursing her brother. 'Jack, I'm so sorry.'

'Nothing else you could do,' he said, reassuringly if not convincingly.

'I never wanted you to see me like that,' she continued.

'Hey, I'm on your side, remember?' He put a hand on her arm, but she shrugged him off and stared out into the dark.

'So, where to now?' he asked.

Maeve rubbed her hands along her face. 'I noticed a sign for a B&B up the road when we visited the monastery.'

Maeve rang the doorbell, which chimed melodiously inside. They heard a door close further back and the dull sound of footsteps. The front door opened and a stout lady wearing a white cardigan over a dark dress looked them up and down and said, 'We have a very nice room with its own shower if you'd like to have a look at it.'

'We'll take it,' Maeve replied.

'Oh. For how many nights?'

Maeve looked at Jack. 'A week?'

He nodded. They had no other plans now. And he might actually get some work done.

Chapter Four

They awoke to a clear blue sky, the dunes, the surf, the village and the harbour all picture-postcard perfect. It was as if the weather was mocking them; as if Rathbrack was saying to come on out and see what they could not have. They were the only guests, and if it was past breakfast time when they rose, their landlady made no mention of it.

Maeve knew, once she had been reminded, who the owners were — Sonny and Maura Mulcahy.

'I would have been a good five or six years ahead of you in the nuns, Maeve,' said Maura Mulcahy, bringing tea and toast to the smaller of the two tables in her dining-room where they were brooding over their predicament.

'Yes, that would be right.' Maeve nodded and painted on a polite smile.

'Of course, all the old nuns are dead now. But my Margaret had Sister Ann for the first two years.'

'Oh. She's your oldest, isn't she?'

'We only had Margaret.'

Jack sensed that if he had not been not there, a long and detailed medical explanation would have been forthcoming.

'She must be a teenager by now,' said Maeve, absently.

'Oh, stop! Sure she's nineteen, finished school and no idea what she wants to do. Maybe a bit of your ambition will rub off on her now, Maeve.'

'Well, we won't be here all that long.'

'Oh. I heard you might be building a house.'

Maeve shook her head. 'We were thinking about it, but

there's nothing here that would really suit us.'

'Oh, I see.'

'Her husband's a fisherman,' Maeve explained when Maura Mulcahy had left them. 'And she runs this place. He does some building work too.'

Maura carried the plates on which she had served their fries back into her kitchen to find her daughter pouring herself some orange juice.

'Oh, you're up,' she said to her daughter, who didn't reply. 'Well, we have a couple of interesting visitors out there.'

'Who?' asked Margaret, folding her arms over her dressing gown and the oversized cotton shirt she used as a nightdress.

'Maeve Fitzgerald, the actress, and her husband. He's some sort of big-shot movie writer.'

The girl's eyes widened at this. 'And what are they doing here in this dump?'

'Margaret!'

'I mean Rathbrack. Why would anyone come here, especially if they could afford to go somewhere decent?'

'Don't you know she's from here?'

Margaret shook her long uncombed hair free and swept it back behind her.

'Of course I do. But she must be crazy to bring him here, even for a holiday.'

'Well now, Miss Know-All, what I heard is that they're looking to live here. They arrived late last night, coming from the brother's, no doubt, so I'd say she had a fight with him....'

'My God, Mam, do you have to poke your nose into everything?' Margaret made for the kitchen door as she said this.

'And where are you off to?' her mother asked.

'Back to bed.'

Maeve took the car and went into town to spend the day meeting estate agents, to satisfy herself at least that Owen was a bloodsucker. Jack set up his typewriter on the larger unused table in the dining-room, consulted his notes for a while and settled down to a day of plot weaving and dialogue. It was afternoon before he was interrupted, but it had been a productive few hours.

'Sorry,' said Margaret when he turned to see her standing at the door. 'I was just wondering if you wanted anything — tea, coffee?'

'What? Oh, no, maybe later.'

'Right, well, it's just that I'm going out, so there won't be anyone here.'

'Oh, hey, no problem.' Jack flashed her a smile, but she did not return it. She was an attractive young girl, thin, long-legged in her tight denims, and could be beautiful if she did something with her hair. Or perhaps even if she just smiled.

'I'm Jack Amonson,' he said, standing up and offering her his hand. She took it limply, not expecting this attention. 'And you are?'

'Oh ... oh, I'm Margaret. I'm their daughter.' She waved a hand at the house.

'No school today?'

'Oh, I'm finished with that, thank God.'

'Ah, so you're helping out with the family business?'

She threw him a look of teenage horror at this suggestion.

'I can't wait to get out of here,' she said.

'You should talk to my wife, Maeve, then. She felt the same, I guess, at your age.'

The girl brightened up at this. 'She did?'

'Hey, ask her about it.'

'I will.' Now there was a trace of a smile. Jack realised that the girl had come into the room in the hope of finding Maeve there, not him.

'Can I get you anything down at the village?' she asked, and when he insisted there was nothing he needed, she left.

Margaret had only to walk around the front of the house to see that her father's fishing trawler was tied up at the pier. She set off on foot around the bay to find him, hands dug deep into her jacket pocket, eyes squinting against the bright, low sun.

He was in Sweeney's, with his crew, all of them talking loudly, which usually meant the catch had been good.

'Hello, Margaret.'

It was Eddie O'Shaughnessy, blocking her way around the

bar counter. She didn't answer him, or look at him, but when she stepped to the left he got in her way again and winked at her.

'Can I buy you a drink?' he asked.

'No.'

'Will you go to the pictures, Saturday?'

'I don't know, Eddie.'

He was her father's youngest crew hand. He had been to the national school over by the church with Margaret, but had dropped out without finishing secondary school.

'Why? What else would you be doing?'

She frowned at him. 'It's none of your business.'

'Ah, Margaret, don't be like that.'

She wanted to push him out of the way, but her father and the others had already noticed her and might jeer if she made a scene. Besides, she didn't want to touch his filthy greasy sweater, all full of holes and smelling like diesel and fish and sweat.

'I'll see,' she said, and pushed her way towards her father.

Sonny Mulcahy was a bull of a man. A life of physical endurance had left his face weather-beaten to a tanned hue; his hands, lacerated and healed over and over, were a purplish leather; and his throat and arms had their coarse skin coated in frizzled grey hairs.

'We have famous guests,' said Margaret.

'Oh, I know. I heard,' Sonny replied. 'What'll you have?'

'A glass of Carlsberg.'

'Oh, indeed. A glass of lager, Micko!'

Margaret felt Eddie watching her, but he wouldn't come over and pester her because her father didn't like him being around her.

'Here you are now, Maggie,' said Sweeney, sliding the drink over, then leaning forward after it to add, 'I hear Maeve Fitzgerald is going to build up there on the cliffs.'

Margaret shook her head. 'No. The brother wouldn't let her. That's why she's staying with us.'

'Oh. Oh, I see.'

Sweeney backed away and busied himself with other tasks. Sonny Mulcahy glared at him. 'I've been sitting on this bar stool for twenty years, Maggie, and I can read that little gombeen man like a book.'

The men around the bar were creating enough of a buzz to prevent anyone else from hearing.

'So what are you saying?' asked Margaret.

'Never mind. Drink up and go home and tell your mother, when she gets home from Fr Byrne's jumble-sale committee meeting, to make dinner for our guests — whatever they want. I'm going to have a little chat with Mr Sweeney here.'

'But....'

'I'll explain later.'

Jack and Maeve were easily persuaded to stay and eat a dinner of fresh pollack, filleted, poached and served with a perfect white sauce. Margaret and her mother came and went while Maeve narrated her meetings with a dozen estate agents, or auctioneers, as she called them.

Beside her on the table were piles of photos and specs, maps, business cards and pieces of newspaper with listings circled. She had been busy and had formed an outline in her mind of the market, such as it was, in this part of the country, and it had done nothing to brighten her mood.

'That bastard!' she hissed. 'My God, Jack, he was really trying to take us....'

'Jeez, calm down.'

Margaret burst into the room with a pot of tea and placed it nervously on the table. Maeve ignored her, lost in last night's fight and all the family arguments of her life. Jack mumbled thanks and Margaret left again. It was difficult to believe that Maeve was closer to Maura Mulcahy in age than her daughter, a fact presumably not lost on the girl.

'There's about six places up and down the coast road that we could look at tomorrow,' said Maeve without much enthusiasm.

Jack was still trying to think of a cheerful comment when Sonny Mulcahy entered the room and shook their hands.

'How's everything?' he asked.

'Fine.'

'Terrific!'

'Ah, good. Anything else we can get you? More towels? Is the water hot enough all the time? By the way, are you interested at all in deep-sea angling?'

Before they could respond to this barrage of questions he turned his head around to look at Maeve's papers.

'You're looking for a place to build a house, is it?' he asked.

'We were,' said Maeve.

'Well now, to be perfectly honest, I'd actually heard that earlier today. Down in Sweeney's. Did you know he owns the field behind here, the far side of the main road?'

Maeve thought for a few seconds. 'You mean the hill?'

'That's right.'

'No, I didn't.'

'Maybe you should ask him about it.'

Sweeney's was busy for a week night, and Maeve was relieved to see that her brother was not there. She and Jack slid into one of the vinyl booths, and she fiddled with a beer-stained coaster until Sweeney came over.

'A pint and a mineral water, is it?' he asked.

'No, I'll have a vodka and tonic,' said Maeve.

'Right you be,' he said and left again.

'Exonerating him of vodka tampering, are we?' asked Jack.

'I suppose so. Look — there's his victim.' Maeve raised a hand and waved across the room. Beyond, in the corner, beneath a television mounted on a large triangular shelf, wearing a black fur hat, sat Gladys Clery, erect, coat buttoned up to her neck, handbag firmly clutched in her left hand. She lifted her right hand and gave Maeve a child's wave in return, her mouth spreading into a near-toothless grin that caused her eyes to squint closed.

Sweeney returned with the drinks.

'Micko, we hear you might have a bit of land for sale,' Maeve began.

'Oh aye, I'd always be interested in an offer. Wouldn't say

no to the right one.' He leaned low over the table, at an odd angle, so that he nodded in a circular motion as he said this.

'Sit down, please,' said Jack.

He did so, but this seemed to cause him extreme discomfort, as if he were breaking some taboo of his trade.

'Yeah, that hill the far side of the road ... I bought it about ten years ago,' he mumbled.

'And is it suitable for building?' Maeve asked.

'Oh, it would be.'

'Does it have planning permission?'

'Well now, that could all be sorted out.'

'Aaah....'

'I'd be willing to give an undertaking to resolve that as part of any, eh, transaction.'

'I see,' said Maeve, putting on an intensely interested voice now, 'And did you have any sort of a price in mind?'

Micko smiled involuntarily. 'Oh now, that would be hard to say.'

'Would we be talking in the region of ten thousand?'

'Oh God, I couldn't let it go for that. It's very big, you know. Oh now, I'd say it's worth maybe twice that. But sure why don't you go up and have a look tomorrow?'

'And it's the whole field, is it?'

'Aye. Down to the road and out to the hedges.'

The next day was again dry, but a westerly wind carried banks of white clouds as they drove out of Mulcahys'. Maeve turned right, taking this road to where it merged with the bigger road, then swung around to the right, and drove slowly along until she came to the gate that gave onto Sweeney's field, and pulled in close against it.

'We might as well have walked,' she said as they left the car.

Jack was surprised to find that this gate actually worked; when he pulled the bolt out of the opposing concrete pillar, it swung noisily towards him.

They slipped in, closed the gate, and began walking upwards. This was a small hump-backed hill, so that the summit was not visible until they were nearly there, but it levelled out at the top into an area perhaps fifty feet wide. When they reached this, their first view was to the east, inland, over a landscape of similar rolling hills, mostly grassy fields, recovering from the winter, green pushing up through pale straw, broken in places by fields tilled back to dark brown soil, a diversification from the uncertain world of cattle.

To the north, ridges of poorer land sloped down to meet the sea on their left and, whether it was the light, the weather, or their new position, they had a view now that Jack had not noticed from the peninsula cliffs — purple mountain-tops were visible across the northern horizon.

And then there was the ocean, surging against the rocks at both ends of the bay, and breaking into white fans that ran in over the sand and vanished into it all along the beach, sea-birds probing for whatever the tide might disturb, or screeching as they took to the air and flew along the length of the deserted shore.

The view to the south was also better from here. Instead of Owen's farm below them, the land dropped away into a thicket of small trees and bushes, which in turn met the road at the point where it passed the parish church on the far side. Beyond this were larger trees, walled fields, and then the same rich countryside that spread all the way to the distant spine of the next peninsula.

'Well?' Maeve asked quietly.

'It doesn't get any better than this,' Jack answered, now looking at their more immediate surroundings. 'And you could build a house here. In fact, I think you'd have to build it on top, because the slope is too severe on all sides, except at the bottom.'

'Of course we'll build it up here!' She beamed at him when she said this, the widest smile since they had landed at Shannon. 'I had no idea the view from here was this magnificent. I haven't been here since ... since I was a child. But I can see it now, Jack. We'll put the bedrooms and kitchen on the east, for the morning sun, and have plate-glass windows with a view of all this ... and a library for you to work in with a window onto the bay....'

'Hey, steady on! We still have to get this guy to sell to us!'

'Oh, I think he will.'

They strolled across the top of the hill until about halfway, where they encountered broken stones, hidden by weeds, and then came up against an obstacle about two feet high.

'What's this?' Jack asked, standing back to look in both directions at what now appeared to be a curved section of some long-tumbled and overgrown wall.

'I remember this!' Maeve declared. 'It's the old fairy fort. See, there's another piece of it over here.' She walked towards this other small bump. There was enough at least to imagine that this might at one time have been a continuous wall, making a small 'fort', perhaps twenty feet in diameter.

'We used to come up here after school,' she said, pointing down to the school beyond the church, 'and play all sorts of games about being kings and queens and soldiers attacking each other. Then Owen and his friends, who got out later, would chase us away and we'd run down into the woods by St Brigid's Well....'

'Where?'

'Down there.' She pointed into the leafless bushes below them. 'Come on, I'll show you.'

She ran down to the south, laughing, then stopped, put her fists in the air, whooped like an Indian in an old Western, and took off again.

Jack followed, through a maze of prickly gorse, then down a slope so steep there was no stopping, and on through a group of small trees whose branches whipped him, until finally he caught up with her. Breathless, they leaned together for support.

'There!' she said, pointing, and as he followed the line of her finger he saw that there was a small spring flowing down from an undercut of rock. It had washed all of the soil away in its steep path, so that it actually seemed to emerge from a cleft in the hill, and flowed out over a ledge into a stony pool, itself the result of a concrete lip that had been added long enough ago that it was now the same green as the natural stones around it.

The water trickled over the edge of this pool and flowed the last few yards down the hill to meet a larger stream that vanished into a culvert under the road.

'Is this part of Sweeney's field too?' Jack asked.

'I don't know. People come here all the time, so there's certainly a right of way.'

'Is this some sort of magic wishing well?'

Maeve laughed at the way he had put it. 'I suppose so. You're actually supposed to pray to St Brigid. She's good at cures, and not just people, mind — cattle and sheep too.'

They stood watching the water for a while, recovering from the dash down the hill. Then Jack put his arm around Maeve and said, 'Let's go talk to Mr Sweeney.'

'This way,' Maeve answered, and led the way to a stile in the wall that gave onto the road.

They decided to leave the car and cut across the church-yard on foot, but halfway across the parking area Maeve stopped and her face clouded over.

'What are we doing?' she asked. At first Jack thought she was having misgivings about the location, or perhaps now about the whole project. Behind her, between the church and the school, there was a large rockery. Near the top of this was a painted statue of the Virgin Mary — blue and white, as they all were — and at the bottom was a kneeling area, with a box for donations.

'Here we are,' she said, 'being idealistic fools for a second time, playing right into the hands of these cowboys.'

'So we shouldn't look so enthusiastic?' he suggested.

'We should play the bastards at their own game. Come on. To hell with Sweeney, let's go back to the car.'

'It's an incredible site for a house....'

'Yes, it is. Priceless. And right here in Rathbrack! Oh, and we're going to buy it and build the house of our dreams on it!'

Again they dined, at Maeve's request, at Mulcahys'. Maeve had shopped for wine, and tried to persuade the family to join them for dinner, but they declined. It was only when Margaret arrived with the inevitable pot of tea that they finally coaxed at least her to sit down and talk to them.

'And would you like to go to the States, Margaret?' asked
Maeve.

'Who wouldn't?'

'Well, you never know. If we build up the road there in
Ballylacken, we can stay in touch and might be able to help
you out.'

'Yes. We found a wonderful old farmhouse up there.
Where's the photo, Jack?'

'Oh, I thought you were going to build,' said the girl. Her
eyes drifted towards the wall and a charcoal sketch of the
local Celtic cross.

Jack rummaged through the pile of promotional photos
and produced the one they had agreed on earlier. Margaret
looked at the ivy-covered Georgian building, and then back
at Maeve. She had no interest in the house. What she wanted
to know was how you ended up getting all of these things.

'I was thinking,' said Maeve, looking first to Jack then to
the girl, 'of going up to Dublin some day next week, just to
do a bit of window shopping. Maybe you'd like to come with
me, Margaret?'

For the first time, the girl's face broke into a smile. In that
moment of hope, Jack saw her potential beauty radiate
through. The rest was just clothes and cosmetics — they
could be bought anywhere.

When she left, Jack shook his head and said, 'I'm not sure
she'll remember about the house, you've got her so excited.'

'Oh, don't worry, they'll ask!'

Next morning, as they passed the kitchen, they caught
sight of Sonny, pacing around, and when Maura served the
mandatory sausages and rashers, she wasn't her usual self. It
was as if she couldn't wait to get out of the room, and when
she did, the door opened again and Sonny greeted them. He
was an incongruous sight, a man who should not be indoors
— too big, too reddened by the wind, and dressed in layers
of clothes to defy the elements.

'Did you get a chance to take a look at that hill?' he asked.

They nodded.

'And what do you think? Isn't there plenty of room for a
house up there?'

'But you might not get planning permission,' Maeve replied.

'Oh God, you would. Have no fear about that!'

'And then we'd have to go through all the hassle of building....'

'But that would be no problem.' He waved a hand in the air as if making this problem disappear, then pulled out a chair and sat down. 'Listen, you don't want to be buying old farmhouses round here — all full of damp and rats and no insulation. No, no. Look at this house here — warm, dry, every comfort, and it's all my own work. I could build you a grand house up there, and you could stay here, at a reduced rate, of course, while you're waiting.'

'Sounds kind of risky,' said Jack.

'And there are loads of buildings on the market,' Maeve added.

'I tell you what,' said Sonny, slamming a palm on the table. 'Why don't we all sit around a table and see what we can work out? Now we have you back in Rathbrack, Maeve, we don't want to lose you again.'

'To Ballylacken, you mean?' she asked slyly.

'Aye, well, whatever.'

Sweeney might well have been in bed when they called to the pub. They heard him descending the stairs to let them in by the side door not used by his customers, and he blinked in the morning light that poured through the front windows as they gathered to sit in a booth.

'So tell them, Micko, how you'd get over this fear they have about planning permission.'

'Ah well, now, yeah.'

'Go on!'

'Well, maybe, you might be better at explaining that, Sonny.'

The fisherman frowned. 'Have you made your mind up about the price?'

'Yeah, yeah, I think so.'

'You're sure?'

'Ten and fifteen. Yeah.' Sweeney's head bobbed up and down in agreement with himself.

Sonny Mulcahy sucked in a deep breath. 'This is a very good deal, very good,' he said. 'What Micko is saying is that you'd agree to buy the land for ten thousand pounds, and then we'd put in for permission, with the drawings for the actual house, and then, when we get the go ahead, you'd pay him another fifteen thousand pounds.'

'Cash,' Micko interjected.

'Cash?' Jack repeated.

'Well, eh, you could wire the money to the Channel Islands, but that would be another five per cent for handling.'

'Handling?'

'Yeah. That's only fair. I'd have to go over there and get it.'

'Wait a minute,' said Maeve. 'Whatever kind of a scam this is, we're not getting involved. You two sort all this out and then get back to us!'

Sonny drew in more wind. 'Oh now, that could take a long time. Months. This way is much better, for you two, because there's no delays.'

'And I suppose you'd want to be paid cash for building this house?' asked Maeve, narrowing her eyes in a reprise of one of her better roles.

'Either way,' Sonny grunted. 'But it'll cost a lot more if the taxman gets his cut.'

Maeve, backlit by the low sun, folded her arms. 'Jack?'

The light caught the sides of the other men's faces — Mulcahy's bright eyes shining from two craters of wrinkles, Sweeney's shifting about in a face aged indoors, more subtly, by smoky air and the endless calculation of the night's take behind a nodding mask of bonhomie.

'If we do pay you this first ten,' asked Jack, 'and things don't work out, will you buy the place back from us again?'

'Ah, well, now....' Sweeney began.

'You will!' said Mulcahy. 'Say you will, because I'm damned sure that won't happen!'

'Fair enough, so.'

Maeve nodded to Jack, who stood up and reached a hand across, first to Sweeney, then to Mulcahy.

'You won't regret this,' said Sonny. 'This will work out very well — for all of us!'

Chapter Five

Over the next two weeks Maeve saw to the details of purchasing the site from Sweeney, both sides careful to avoid any publicity. Jack got into a routine of writing in the mornings and walking the area in the afternoons, if it wasn't actually raining.

Yet it was this very sense of being in a place that was endlessly scrubbed by rain, wind and ocean that defined Rathbrack for him. He walked one day to the north-western end of the beach. Here it did not rise into cliffs, but long black fingers of rock reached out into the sea, and when he scrambled up onto the sedge above the highest reaches of the waves, the trail led along the coast past small coves until the way was blocked by a narrow river that had found a way out between the layers of rock.

He turned back, and now the sharp fractures of rock faced him, a natural defence of the bay. From here the hill on which they were about to build their home rose behind the only friendly piece of shoreline for miles up and down the coast. Maeve was right — it was a priceless view; and the un-predictable weather had the highly desirable effect of hiding that from the casual passer-by. It was necessary to be here for a prolonged period of time to know the bay in all its moods and so to appreciate it to the full.

When he returned from this walk, the rental car was in the driveway. In the dining-room he found Maeve poring over her growing collection of books and magazines on home design.

'What do you think of that picture of the cross?' she asked, indicating the charcoal sketch.

'It's the only actual piece of original art here,' he replied. 'I think it's pretty good.'

'Well, according to Maura Mulcahy, the fellow who did it is an up-and-coming young architect who stayed here last summer. They have his phone number in their guest book.'

'Ah ha! So when do we meet him?'

'Tomorrow. He'll come down from Dublin, and spend the night.'

'Does he have a name?'

'Ó Murchú. Cathal Ó Murchú.'

'Well, that's pure Gaelic anyway.'

Maeve looked up quizzically at him, then said, 'Yes, it is, I suppose. But in fact it's just the Irish for Charlie Murphy.'

✦

They waited in their car in the empty car park of the church next morning, occasionally turning on the wipers to clear the drops of rain that grew on the glass out of the fine drizzle that descended from a low blanket of grey cloud. With each cleansing swish, the Virgin Mary appeared brightly on her rock perch in front of them, untroubled by the elements or the absence of any faithful at the prayer rail.

After half an hour a small, red, French hatchback splashed in off the main road and pulled up beside them. Jack rolled down his window, as did the other driver.

'Are you Maeve Fitzgerald?' asked a man with long red dreadlocks and a matching beard.

'Hello, Cathal, is it?' asked Maeve, leaning over Jack.

'Yes! God, sorry I'm late.' Cathal extended a hand, but the window blocked his elbow, so he opened his door, which banged into the side of the other car. 'Sorry, sorry.' He drove forward a few feet, allowed his car to lurch to a dead stop and stepped out into what was now a fine mist.

They shook hands and Cathal returned both of his to the deep pockets of a huge, green, woollen trenchcoat. 'You're hardly going to build a house right here,' he said, looking around disapprovingly at church, grotto and school.

'No, no, of course not. That hill across the road there is where we'll be building,' said Maeve, pointing, and then leading the way back towards the main road. 'It's probably too wet to climb up by Brigid's Well, but the main gate's just up to our left.'

'We're walking?' asked Cathal in his flat Dublin accent.

'It's not far,' said Jack.

'Just need to get some things.' Cathal loped back to his car.

Jack stared wide-eyed at Maeve.

'Let's just wait and see what he comes up with,' she replied to his disbelieving look.

The architect returned with a tripod in one hand, a camera bag over his shoulder, and a battered leather valise in the other hand, which Jack concluded was a remnant of his student days. He said very little on the way up the hill, answering Maeve's questions in monosyllables, and looking around as they walked.

'You're going to build right up here on the top?' he asked when they reached the flat summit.

'Do you think there's any alternative?' Maeve asked.

'No, not without serious excavation of the hillside anyway. But I'm surprised you'll be let put something up here.'

'It is possible to build here, right?' Jack demanded, fearing that the architect had already noticed some obvious defect in the land, invisible to amateurs.

'Oh, Jesus, I'd say so. We'll take a few core samples, but I don't think that'll be a problem. What I mean is, well, this will sort of be a landmark forever more, won't it?'

'But Cathal,' said Maeve, 'that's why we want you to come up with a plan — one that fits in, or blends in. We could have had Sonny Mulcahy throw up a bungalow without any architect at all.'

Cathal sucked in his moustache and glowered at her. 'You'd be willing to use some unusual materials then, not just concrete blocks?'

'Oh, of course!' Maeve waved an arm over the bay. 'I want a living-room with a vaulted ceiling and wrap-around picture windows, wood panelling, a huge granite fireplace —

gas-fired, of course — all open plan, but with lots of nooks and ledges and places to hang art, the master bedroom down here where we can catch the dawn, a study for Jack to work in over here, three more bedrooms on this side....'

'Hold on, Jesus, slow down!' Cathal fished in his bag for a notebook and tried to scribble down some of her ideas. 'Let me just walk around the top here a bit and get a feel for the place.'

He took off towards the southern end of the summit and when he was out of hearing Jack leaned in close to Maeve and said, 'I guess he must be good, because he sure doesn't win any clients with his personality.'

'He's an artist, Jack. We're entitled to be odd. I think he's just nervous.'

'What's this?' asked Cathal, waving his notebook at the ground as he walked back towards them.

'It's just some old mound,' said Maeve. 'They say it's the remains of a fairy fort.'

Cathal stepped up onto the raised grass and walked along its length, then across to the smaller second piece, and traced with his eye the route of this wall that must once have been a complete circle.

'You know it's supposed to be bad luck to interfere with these things,' he said.

'And does that bother you?' asked Maeve.

Cathal snorted. 'It does my arse. I did a bit of work for a builder up in Dublin last year and he had to plough away about two hundred graves, and sure nobody gave a fiddler's fuck. But is this listed in the sites and monuments record?'

'I don't know,' said Maeve.

'I'll have to check that. There's no actual preservation order on this, is there?' persisted Cathal.

'No....' said Maeve slowly, looking at Jack. 'How would someone go about doing something like that?'

'Round up public support,' said Cathal. 'Do you think that's likely around here?'

Maeve shook her head. Cathal pulled out a camera and took a quick photo of them, then turned his attention to the rooftops of Rathbrack, barely a blur in this mist. 'You go on to wherever we're staying and I'll follow you in an hour or so. I want to have a good look around here.'

'It's that bungalow there,' said Jack, pointing to the right of the old monastery, at the back of Mulcahys' guesthouse.

'Oh, I know,' Cathal replied with an odd smile as they began their descent.

The rain stopped long enough for the architect to get a good view of the surrounding countryside, and to set up and take photos in all directions, but the cloud cover descended again as he was sketching the contours of the hill, and even his beard dripped onto the paper.

'Ah, fuck it!' he announced to himself, then crumpled up the sodden drawings, packed the remaining pad back in his valise, shouldered the other bag, grabbed the tripod, and laboured at collapsing its legs as he traipsed down the wet hillside.

It was far too soon to meet up with the American and his opinionated wife yet, so instead of going all the way to the car, he walked on between the school and the monastery, with its Celtic cross, the one he had drawn that summer afternoon while the Mulcahy girl had leaned over his shoulder. He marched on past, following the low wall that separated road from beach until he came to the front door of Sweeney's Bar.

'Soft day out now,' said the publican by way of greeting.

'Great weather for ducks,' Cathal replied.

'Aye.' Sweeney bowed and waited.

'Emmm ... a pint. Have you anything to eat?'

'No. Don't do food at this time of the year.'

'Come to think of it, when I was here last summer you didn't do food either.'

Sweeney twisted his head in a silent chortle. 'I thought I remembered you. As you can see, we get very few tourists at this time of the year.'

Cathal didn't bother to point out that he wasn't a tourist, and occupied a booth under the large front window. By the time Sweeney placed the Guinness in front of him he was already on a second elevation of the hill, which he could see out the window when he rubbed away the condensation.

Eddie O'Shaughnessy and a couple of the other younger
locals were drinking quietly at the bar, watching a televised
horse-race from some other part of the country that was also
being rained on. From time to time, they eyed the progress of
the bearded artist whose work gradually covered all of the
surfaces in the booth and required him constantly to search
for more pens and pencils in his bags and coat pockets.

Cathal looked up momentarily when a new customer arrived and guffawed greetings to the racing fans. He was a big
farmer in muddy wellingtons, with a raincoat turned up at
the collar, and a soft cap pulled well down onto his ears.

'The usual is it, Owen?' asked Sweeney.

The farmer nodded and walked over to where he could
take a look at Cathal's work.

'Ah Jesus, don't drip on it!' said Cathal, pulling back a
finished concept sketch.

'Sorry,' said Owen and turned back to the bar. He sat up
on a stool and frowned at Sweeney. 'Have Maeve and her
Yankee husband been in much?' he asked.

'Aye, well, a bit.'

'It usually doesn't take her this long to come to her
senses.'

'Ah, well....' Sweeney's voice trailed off and he moved
away, busying himself with wiping ashtrays.

Owen sat back, looked at the artist, then back at Micko,
who turned now to watch the horse-race with the others. The
boys were shouting, urging some horse on. Someone had bet
a few pounds ... and then it all fell into place. Owen jumped
to his feet, strode over to Cathal's drawings again and picked
up a handful of them.

'Take your hands off those, you fucking gobshite!' shouted
Cathal, but Owen ignored him and sifted through them. Then
he held one up towards the bar and roared, 'Sweeney, you
fucker! You sold them the fucking hill, didn't you?'

The publican's face displayed a rare moment of emotion.
His eyes widened and his mouth opened as if he wanted to
answer this but couldn't.

'Well, that fucking explains it. That's why she didn't come

crawling back with a new offer. The bitch!'

Cathal got to his feet, and for a few moments Owen did nothing. Then he threw the papers back on the table and said, 'Be sure you get paid cash in advance for these, Sonny, because they won't be building any house up there.'

'Why not?' asked Cathal.

Owen leaned forward. 'Because that little weasel back there had no business selling them that field.' He pointed to Sweeney, now nodding involuntarily.

'Do you know where you are?' he continued, menacingly

'What?' Cathal did not understand the question.

'What this place is called?'

'Rathbrack.'

'That's right. Rath. Brack. The fort of the trout, I think it means. And the rath in Rathbrack is the mound on the top of that hill! That is Rathbrack and she's not going to build some Hollywood mansion on it, so don't you spend that money yet, Sweeney!'

Owen crossed the room as he yelled the words and on the way out banged the door hard enough to rattle the window panes.

'Aye, well, he's barred now anyway,' said Sweeney.

Jack and Maeve were enthused by Cathal's initial sketches. They chatted on through dinner, then returned to the unused dining table with cups of coffee as soon as they were finished. Margaret came to clear the table and Maeve called her over for an opinion on roof colours.

'Forest-green tiles or just dark slates?'

Margaret shrugged. Cathal smiled up at her. Jack caught a look between them, almost of hostility on her part, and with Cathal he couldn't say. It reminded him once again that the subtleties of the Irish were still lost on him.

'The tiles,' said Margaret, turning away and continuing her chore with a noisy, uncharacteristic efficiency.

Jack looked to Maeve for her response. She too was aware of Margaret's strange mood. 'Tiles it is,' she said.

Cathal added this to his notes. 'I think that's a good decision,' he said, following Margaret with his eyes, as if wanting not his clients' approval, but hers. But she ignored him and left the room with lowered eyes.

'We can give the roof a lower pitch,' he continued, 'which means it can be bigger and overhang where we have the big windows.'

'We seem to have more or less defined the structure then,' said Jack. 'So when do you think we could see detailed drawings?'

Cathal tugged on his beard. 'End of next week?'

'Yes, that'll work fine,' said Maeve. 'I'll go up to Dublin with Margaret and get them.'

'With Margaret?'

Maeve nodded at the architect.

'Right. Emmm, I'll meet the two of you for lunch then?'

'Could you have them done by Thursday?'

'I'll try.'

'Cathal, we want to get this through the planning process as fast as possible.'

'I can understand that.' And only then, with his assignment in hand, did he tell them about the altercation with Owen earlier in the day.

The following Thursday Maeve and Margaret left for Dublin while it was still dark, speeding through the main streets of the chain of towns and villages that mark the way from one coast to the other.

'Oh, this is great, Mrs Amonson,' said Margaret as the sky paled promisingly ahead of her. 'It's just fantastic to get away from there for a while.'

'You can call me Maeve.'

'Are you sure?'

They sped on through the midlands, chatting about clothes, films, California, the weather, music, and about the schooling they had in common.

'Not much has changed over all those years,' said Maeve.

'We're just so backward,' moaned Margaret.

'You'd be amazed how backward everywhere else is too.'

'Seriously?'

'I'm afraid so.'

The girl absorbed this unwelcome revelation in silence for a while, then asked, 'Maeve ... why did you come back?'

Now it was Maeve's turn to drive on without speaking for a while.

'I was just like you, Margaret,' she began eventually. 'When I was your age, I couldn't wait to get away from Rathbrack. So I left and went to London. That was the sixties, remember, and I got in with an arty crowd....'

'Like Cathal?'

Maeve looked at her, caught a dreamy look on the girl's face and laughed. 'I think he's a bit more serious than most of the people I knew.'

'Well, what's wrong with that?'

'Nothing at all, Margaret!' At last the truth began to dawn on the older woman.

'Anyway, go on,' Margaret urged, as if sensing that she had revealed too much.

Maeve sighed and went on with her own story. 'Somewhere along the way I made up my mind that I wanted to act — and that I actually could act. My parents paid for a couple of years of drama school and I got a few minor parts in plays around England. But it was all very depressing. There was no money to be made, and I just stuck at it because it was either that or back to the farm.

'Then I met a guy who really knocked me off my feet. He was a brilliant actor, really witty, and gorgeous looking. And he was into movies. He was into a lot of other things too, but I didn't know that at the time. So we lived together for about a year — and then he got the chance to go to California!

'Looking back on it, it sounds really stupid, that I really was just a thick eejit from the bog, but I went with him, not realising that I wasn't a part of that plan at all. We were there about a week when he decided I was in the way, so he made it very clear that I wasn't wanted — with his fists.

'So now I was in tinseltown, along with thousands of

other redneck girls who do the rounds of every agency and any audition they can get, but at least I had some sort of portfolio, which I embellished, and eventually I started getting small parts and making a few contacts. And that's how I met up with the crowd making *Tomb of the Undead, Part Two*, and they liked my shrieking and gave me the part!'

'And then you met Jack?'

'Oh no, there were a few more years of disastrous mistakes before that. I got married. To a movie producer. I thought he would really make me — that's what he said — but, fool that I was, I didn't see that I was further along in my career than he was, and that really he was using me! All very ironic looking back now, but it really messed me up, and when it all fell apart I took to the drink in a big way, and it took me another few years to get it together again.'

Margaret was clearly aghast at all of this, so Maeve leaned conspiratorially towards the girl to finish by saying, 'But that's actually not a bad thing over there, because it means you know what you're up against. I managed to get back into shape — well, minimise the bags under my eyes and tone up. And then a really sharp agent — Aaron Rothberg — got me some work. And then I met Jack. Two years ago.'

'But you're so famous....'

'Yes, I know, and I still haven't answered your question, have I? So now I'm in my late thirties. I wake up in the mornings and look back over my life and I feel this awful sense of failure — a longing in the pit of my stomach for what might have been. Oh, you're right, I made it. I could go on acting indefinitely. I'll never open a movie, but I'll always get work.

'But I couldn't do that. I can't look ahead over the years now and see myself at the end and be happy that I would never have faced my demons, that I would have run away from all the pain of my childhood, and lost all the good of it too. And so, I'm back here, trying to reconnect all the threads of my life, because now I know, after all, that there isn't some ideal out there worth chasing, because I've been there.'

Margaret stared out the windscreen and sighed. 'And did you think you were very lucky to find Jack?' she asked.

Maeve nodded and smiled. 'You mean a man who could flesh out my dreams — and was willing to do it?'

'Oh, well, I just meant....'

The actress realised that she had read too much into the girl's question. But now she didn't like to leave the answer hanging. 'Jack had even worse luck with women than I had with men. I think he'd just about given up on American women when I came along. We're both really in love, at least right now, but sometimes....'

She felt Margaret's eyes fixed on the side of her face, trying to absorb this priceless wisdom from the real world, and she knew she should stop — was saying too much to someone who couldn't possibly know what it all meant. But again it was unfinished.

'Sometimes what?' Margaret asked quietly.

A mist hung over the flat bog on either side, and the coming of day merely retinted the browns and greys of winter. Perhaps Margaret did have some insight beyond her years and life's experience. Maybe it was wrong to judge her, having seen her only in the cocoon of her home and Rathbrack.

'There comes a time, I think, in every relationship, when we wonder what it is we see in each other. For me, it's Jack's innocence — the fact that he's still a boy at heart, writing adventure stories, going along with this adventure ... but I worry, well at least I wonder, if I'm not just some sort of exotic heroine to him, and if I am — I mean, if that's my appeal — well, will it last? Or will I destroy it just by bringing him here?'

Maeve shook her head, determined not to say any more, sorry now that she had burdened the girl with all of this. But a quick smile over at her passenger revealed a young woman lost now in thoughts about her own life. 'So you think Cathal is cute?' she asked by way of changing the subject.

Margaret seemed almost to wince, then pulled up one of her knees under her chin and leaned on it. 'I thought maybe we had something going last year.'

'Aahh, so that's why you recommended him!'

'Oh, he is really talented, Maeve.'

The actress shook her head at the younger girl's discomfort.

'And has he shown you just how talented he is?' she asked. It was a mistake. Margaret stared out the window, unable to respond to this teasing.

After a while, Maeve said, 'I take it you don't want it to be over with him?'

Margaret cast a glance back over at her and replied, 'Well, he doesn't exactly have a lot of competition in Sweeney's, does he?'

Maeve grabbed the girl's knee and shook her. 'And neither do you, Margaret,' she said, drawing a fresh smile.

'No, but you'd want to watch out now, Maeve, the way Gladys is giving Jack the eye!'

They giggled together at the thought of this, and overtook a slow-moving car pulling a little trailer of milk-churns, and sped on towards their day's shopping in Dublin.

Jack stretched, twisted and made fists in front of his typewriter. At this rate he would easily beat Aaron's deadline. He was about to launch into a new scene when the door opened and Maura Mulcahy came in, looking agitated.

'Are you busy, Mr Amonson?'

'Well, I am, but if you need something....'

'Oh, no, it's not me. No, I was just wondering, could you spare a few minutes to meet with our parish priest?'

Jack shrugged. 'Sure? When?'

She leaned in over him and said in an exaggerated whisper, 'He's here.'

'Where?'

'You're sure it's not an imposition?'

'No, no....'

'I'll send him in so.'

She left and was replaced almost immediately by a wellgroomed Catholic priest with thick wavy hair. The landlady hovered behind him uncertainly.

'Good morning,' said the priest. 'I'm John Byrne. Hope I'm not interrupting anything too important.'

'Not at all. Pleased to meet you.'

'I was hoping to meet your wife as well, but I hear she's out of town, taking Maura's daughter shopping.'

'Can I get you another cup of tea, Father?' asked Maura, but Byrne shook his head.

'No, thanks. I really can't stay long,' he said. 'I just wanted to have a quick word with Mr Amonson.'

Maura Mulcahy waited, but when this quick word was not forthcoming she backed out of the room and closed the door.

'Very protective of her guests,' said Byrne.

'We're certainly enjoying our stay with her.'

'I see I'm interrupting the work, so let me tell you why I dropped in,' the cleric went on. 'You're a writer of sorts and, well, we have another writer here in Rathbrack, and she would very much like to meet you.'

'Sure. Tell her to drop by.'

'Ah, that's it you see. She's not able to get out much. So we were wondering if perhaps your wife and yourself might join us for dinner at her house — maybe tomorrow evening?'

'Yeah, hey, sure, we'd love to. What's this writer's name?'

'Noreen Fletcher.'

'And what does she write?'

'Poetry.'

Byrne explained where Noreen lived and said they would expect them at about seven.

Chapter Six

'Divil a bit of it is recorded,' said Sonny on Friday morning as he gathered up the rolled-up drawings that Maeve had brought back.

'Well, that's one less complication,' Maeve enthused.

'All the same,' said the fisherman, 'I'll bring these plans in myself to them just to be sure there's no misunderstandings.'

It was a sunny, windy day, with a forecast of warm, dry weather for the weekend. Maeve had returned with more books, fabric samples, kitchen brochures and catalogues of light fittings, and when Sonny had left, she and Jack spent their time mulling over endless combinations of these possibilities for the interior of their house.

Only as it was growing dark did Maeve tune into their dinner invitation and begin readying herself. But at this she was a pro, and by five to seven, as Jack straightened his tie and combed back his hair one last time, she was by his side, her dark hair clasped back from her oval face, eyes made up to accentuate perfectly the blues in the designer cocktail dress that had lain dormant in her luggage till now.

'Now that,' said Jack, running a hand around her waist, 'should inspire a few lines from any decent poet.'

'If she's gay....'

'Hardly likely when she's got the local man of the cloth as her ally.'

'Well, who's to say he's not a bit of a deviant himself?'

'Come on. We'll be late.'

They were tempted to walk, but Maeve was wearing high

heels, so they drove through the village, to where the only choice after Sweeney's was to turn right onto the pier, or left onto the road leading to the cliffs, by way of the upper reaches of Owen Fitzgerald's farm.

Here, on the left, was a terrace of old houses, the first two with small windows upstairs, the remainder with only one floor. Ascending the hill away from the harbour, each was in a worse state of dilapidation than the one before it, the last tiny window seeming to have been built into the dry stone wall that bounded the road as it rose into the fields.

'A red door, he said,' Jack muttered.

'There,' said Maeve, pointing to the door of the last house with its roof intact.

They parked and walked up to this small, red door, Maeve carrying roses, Jack some gift-wrapped wine. There was no bell, or knocker, so Jack rapped on the timbers with his knuckles.

'Come in!'

It was the kind of latch you press down on with your thumb. Maeve swung the door open and preceded Jack into the main room of this cottage. In the centre a table had been set for four, and beyond a small coal fire burned. The chimney at first seemed flush with the wall, but that was because the alcoves on each side were entirely filled with books, from floor to ceiling.

A thin woman with close-cut hair, brown eyes and fine features sat on the far side of the table, facing them.

'Hello, Noreen, is it?' Maeve asked.

'Yes, and you must be Maeve. I've heard all about you.' She extended a hand from where she sat, and Maeve grasped it. 'And I take it you're Jack?'

'Hi!' He moved over by Maeve to take the woman's hand and saw then why she had not stood up — she was sitting in a wheelchair. Noreen smiled up at him and held him there long enough to study his face.

'John's not here yet,' she said. 'Actually he was around earlier to help me get things ready, but he should be back soon. Oh, flowers, beautiful.'

'Can I put them in a bowl for you?'

'No, no thanks. I can manage that.' Noreen took the flowers on her lap, wheeled herself towards the kitchen annexe and said over her shoulder, 'Jack, you may as well open some of that wine. There's a corkscrew on the dresser.'

'Have you been in a wheelchair long?' asked Maeve.

'Oh, about five years now. I can still get out of it — barely — to wash and go to bed. And my arms work fine, so I can dress, and cook, and write!'

'Do you mind if I ask...?'

'What's wrong with me?'

Maeve nodded at the question, sitting awkwardly now on the edge of one of the three chairs.

'I thought someone would have told you. I have MS — multiple sclerosis. It affects different people in different ways. I'm just gradually going downhill — chronic progressive.'

'And can you take anything for it?'

'Not really. I'm not in pain, if that's what you mean. But for MS there is no known cause, no prevention, no treatment, and no cure.'

'I'm so sorry.'

'Yes,' Jack concurred.

'Don't be. That's why I came here, to be away from all that. Maeve, would you put these flowers on the table for me?'

She handed the roses, in a tall hand-thrown pottery vase, up to Maeve. Jack tried to guess the woman's age. Her face and neck were still supple, but there were laugh-lines leading away from her eyes; and her lips, which might once have been fuller, were drawn now. Perhaps she was not in physical pain, but Jack suspected that she had suffered in other ways. Somewhere in her forties?

'Please, sit down. Make yourselves at home,' said Noreen, in an accent that, though it was Irish, had no trace of being from this part of the country.

They were about to resume their conversation when Fr John Byrne pushed in the primitive front door, ducked his head warily, and stepped into the room.

'Oh no, sorry, Noreen, I got tied up down at the school with Confirmation plans. It's the same every year.'

'Not at all, John, you're in plenty of time. We're just about to have a glass of wine. Sit down!'

The priest shook Jack's hand and took the remaining chair. He took in Maeve's appearance as they too exchanged greetings, looked back to Noreen and said, 'Very brave of you, Noreen, to invite two celebrities to dinner. I'm surprised I wasn't accosted by newspaper photographers outside!'

'They'd want to be pretty desperate for news,' laughed Maeve.

Noreen filled the four stemmed glasses with wine. The table had been carefully laid with white linen napkins and an eclectic mix of china, pottery with a metallic blue glaze, assorted glasses, a large wooden bowl of tossed salad, a wicker basket of bread and a black wrought-iron candelabra.

'Cheers,' said Byrne, 'and welcome to Rathbrack.'

'Thanks,' Jack replied.

'It's good to be back,' Maeve added.

'Yes,' said Noreen. 'You grew up here, of course. The rest of us are just blow-ins.'

'Rathbrack could do with some new blood,' said Maeve, cheerfully, smiling at the other woman. 'It's hardly changed since I was a child.'

Jack caught a look between Byrne and Noreen at this remark, but couldn't connect it to what Maeve had said.

'So, let's eat!' Noreen gestured to the bread and salad. 'John would you just check the salmon in the oven?'

'Of course.'

The four of them filled the living-room, with possibly room for another person to sit crouched on the one armchair beneath the back window. The cottage itself had only one other room — Noreen's bedroom — and a flat-roofed extension to the rear gave the building a small kitchen and bathroom. An old stripped-wood dresser against the centre dividing wall was stacked with books and papers. Jack guessed that these were normally spread over the table they were now using for dinner, the only possible writing surface in this quaint clutter.

Byrne busied himself in the kitchen for a few minutes, then returned and lit the candles, added some coal to the fire with a tongs, and reseated himself.

'John's a great help to me,' said Noreen. 'He's convinced that he'll lead me back to the path of righteousness by his personal example.'

'You're hardly leading a life of sin here in Rathbrack,' Maeve suggested. 'And if you've found a way to do that, could you let the rest of us in on it?'

'True,' said Noreen, 'but it's my soul he's after, which he's sure I've sold to the devil.'

'Oh, and why's that?' asked Maeve, turning to the priest.

'Ah well, I'm in the business of saving souls, and it's not up to me to pick and choose. You're a Catholic, aren't you, Maeve?'

'Not a very devout one.'

'Well, God forbid, but if you were struck by a car and dying by the roadside, would you want a priest to hear your last confession?'

Maeve frowned at this. 'I suppose I would. I mean, who knows? Why take chances?'

Noreen laughed. 'And do you really think it would make any difference to some cosmic being whether you managed to whisper a few words in this fellow's ear before you went?'

'I don't know. That's the whole point.'

'At least she's open-minded about it,' said Byrne.

'And what about you, Jack?' asked Noreen.

'Hmmm? I guess I'm a lifelong agnostic.'

'Do you mind if I ask,' said the priest, 'what persuasion you were originally?'

'Episcopalian.'

'I think you had him worried there that you were one of the chosen people,' said Noreen. 'You know — Amonson.'

'No, no. Scandinavian.'

'And what part of the States are you from?' she asked.

'Iowa. The heartland.'

'A bit like here then?'

'Without the hills or ocean. And,' he added, without knowing why, 'without the same history.'

'The Church has nothing against the Jews,' said Byrne.

'No,' Noreen replied. 'Why should they? We stole their ideas and then tried to exterminate them. It's the other way round. The existence of Jews is an affront to Christianity. Very bad prospects for your brand of soul-saving.'

'And are you a Catholic?' Maeve asked Noreen.

'Well, I grew up one, and they say once they baptised me I'm theirs forever unless they' — she pointed to Byrne with the crust of her bread — 'decide to excommunicate me, and they're very stingy with that honour these days.'

'Especially,' Byrne replied, 'when it's a ploy to sell books of poetry.'

Noreen shook her head. 'He really doesn't get it. It's amazing how someone who's able to read books and speak in complete sentences can be so brainwashed by Maynooth.'

'Rubbish,' said Byrne, as he got to his feet, then squashed past Maeve to the kitchen. 'I made a free, well-informed, choice to follow the teachings of Jesus, to take the path of the light of the truth.'

'The vegetables are in the pot in the bottom of the oven,' said Noreen.

'Can I help?' asked Maeve.

'No, no,' said Byrne. 'We're all organised here.'

'Just watch him to make sure he doesn't bless the food or anything.' Noreen winked at her two new guests.

'How can we get a copy of your work?' Jack asked.

'I'll give you one when you're going. What do you like to write yourself?'

'Oh, I've just tried a few screenplays. Thrillers.'

'And how did you get started on that?'

'I was a highschool teacher. English. Just got so bored I did it to fill in the evenings.'

'He turned his hobby into a full-time job,' said Maeve.

'Only in America.' Noreen shook her head.

'Are you sure I can't do anything?' Maeve asked, ill at ease as the priest placed her dinner in front of her.

'There isn't room to swing a cat in this place, Maeve, and sure I know where everything is.' In two quick trips he was finished and seated again. For a while they ate in silence, then Noreen picked up on Jack's earlier remark.

'You mentioned the fact that this area has a history,' she said. 'And that is a big difference between here and the

United States. Of course, the Indians were there, but they weren't very numerous, and there's a big discontinuity between them and America as we know it.'

The aerial view of Los Angeles from the plane flashed in front of Jack — imported water, imported vegetation, the vast majority of it all built in the past thirty years — no history. But the people had all come from somewhere, from places like this, like Ireland, like Rathbrack.

'And here we have somewhere that's been continuously inhabited,' she continued, 'possibly since the end of the ice age, but at least for the past five thousand years. Isn't that amazing, to think that the gobshites down in Sweeney's can trace their heritage all the way back to the beginning of civilisation?'

'And very proud they are of it,' said Byrne.

Maeve now saw where the conversation was going and stopped eating. 'I'm sure you know we're planning a house here,' she said softly.

'I had heard about that, yes,' said Byrne.

'In fact, there's even a rumour that you're going to build it on Rathbrack Hill,' Noreen added.

'Rathbrack Hill?' Maeve repeated. 'I've never heard it called that.'

'Well, it is the hill with the rath on the top of it.'

'Yes, but it never had that name.'

'*Rath Breac*,' the priest added. 'The fort of the trout.'

'Or at least that's how the muck-savages in the civil service translated the English back into Irish, but the original name could have been completely different,' said Noreen. 'There isn't any river; there aren't any trout. I've looked in the county library and the national library and I can't find any reference to any legends or folktales from around here with trout in them.'

Maeve sipped her wine, eyed the other two and said, 'It's true. We're going to build a home up there. Don't worry. It won't be more bungalow blight, and in fact I think it'll fit in very well. It's going to have a dark green roof and a lot of stained timber.

'So your plans are quite advanced, are they?' Noreen

asked. The way she said this held some challenge, and Maeve and Jack simply nodded in reply. 'I see.' Noreen lapsed into silence and continued eating.

'Well,' said Byrne, 'we were hoping you wouldn't say that, because one of the reasons we wanted to meet you tonight was to talk you out of building, at least on the very top of the hill.'

'Why? Who cares?' Maeve asked.

'I do, for one,' said Noreen.

'And a few people have been to see me,' said Byrne.

'A few people,' Maeve repeated slowly. 'And would one of those be my brother, by any chance?'

The priest was seriously put out by this direct question. 'It was,' he said. 'And I realise he has a vested interest in getting you to buy from him. But all the same, he makes a good point.'

'Which is?'

'That you don't have the right to destroy the landmark on the top of the hill.'

'Or to plonk some monstrosity on top of it!' Noreen added.

'We'll show you the plans,' said Jack.

'It's not just what you're putting up there that matters,' said Noreen. 'It's what you're taking away. Forever.'

'Really, Noreen, I think you're taking this way too far,' said Maeve, in her voice of perfect reason. 'There's nothing there — just a couple of lumps of dirt.'

'You know, Maeve,' said Noreen, pointing an accusing finger at the actress, 'that that's a fairy ring.'

Maeve gasped up at the ceiling then fixed her eyes on Noreen and said in an agitated voice, 'Every hill and half the fields in this country have rings and stones and ruins of castles....'

'Oh don't exaggerate!' the poet interrupted. 'But yes — we have a lot of relics of the past, and we should be glad of it. They're reminders of a time when the people — we — believed that the land was sacred.'

'Fine,' said Maeve, raising her voice now so that it filled the room, 'so it's sacred. Surely that doesn't mean we can't build on it. All the more reason to live there.'

'You don't get it.'

'No, sorry, I don't!'

'Now, ladies,' Byrne held up his hands. 'There's no need to become so emotional about this! Maeve, you're a native of Rathbrack. I'm sure you'd be the first to object if someone wanted to bulldoze away the old monastery and build a hotel or something on it.'

'Absolutely. In fact, when I get time I'd like to organise some effort to clean that place up. It was embarrassing showing Jack the cross, with no decent path, or explanation. The monastery really is a thing of beauty, worth preserving.'

'And what makes you the judge of what's to be preserved or not?' Noreen asked.

'I'm just expressing my view, as a native of Rathbrack.'

'A convenient, self-interested view.'

'I don't believe this,' Maeve shouted, slamming down her glass in indignation.

'Look, I'm sorry if you feel we've tricked you,' said Noreen. 'Obviously I don't get around much, and I wanted to tell you my position, before we did anything else.'

'What?' Maeve looked from the poet to the priest, then back to Noreen again to fix her yet again with her well-developed icy stare.

'Whoever put that fort up there did it for a reason,' said Noreen, unaffected by these theatrics.

'Fort?' said Maeve. 'That wall is less than two feet high. And the whole thing couldn't have been more than twenty feet across. You think there was a race of midgets here, *fadó, fadó*?'

Noreen shook her head. 'I shouldn't have said fort. Obviously that's not what it is. Either it was a dwelling place, presumably of some tribal chief or king, or...' — she paused and looked at all three of them in turn, finishing with Maeve again — '...or, and I think this is the most likely explanation, it was a burial mound that has since been washed away.'

For a while no one spoke. Jack was surprised at Maeve's silence, unable to second-guess what she might be thinking. 'But it could just be some ruined shepherd's hut, right?' he suggested.

'Or a lookout post,' Noreen added. 'At one time this area would have been thickly wooded, and, as you've seen, that hill has a great view in all directions.'

'Ah, then you don't really know,' Maeve quipped.

'Oh, I know. I just can't prove it,' said the poet.

'I'd be glad to act as an intermediary with your brother, Maeve,' said Byrne, leaning forward.

She scowled at him. 'Don't bother!'

'We've already bought the site,' said Jack.

'That can all be sorted out. Sweeney won't go against local opinion,' said Byrne.

'That's it. That's just fucking it, isn't it?' said Maeve, rising to her feet now. 'Between the pair of you, you're going to drum up the superstitions of the parish and write cute little essays for the papers. We've given you one more cause to fill up your empty little lives. Well, go right ahead then and we'll see you in court!'

'Ah now, Maeve....' Byrne, who saw himself representing the views of absent followers, was still calm, but Noreen took the threat personally.

'Just watch me!' she shouted up at her guest. 'You know they have laws against this kind of pillage in other countries? This is the very same as stealing antiquities, and I mean to stop the two of you!'

Maeve picked up her bag and slid around between the table and dresser to the door.

Jack stood up to follow her. 'Quaint custom you have here,' he growled, 'of ambush over dinner.'

'Just one more question,' Noreen barked, causing both of them to turn back as they opened the door, baffled as to what she might say now. 'Why do you think the monks didn't build their cross up there?'

'What?' asked Jack, bewildered by this seemingly pointless aside.

'You heard me,' said Noreen. 'Think about it.'

'Superstition,' said Maeve. 'Sheer, stupid, medieval superstition, that's all!' And she vanished out into the night, followed by her husband who pulled the door hard onto its latch.

Chapter Seven

On Saturday morning Jack awoke from a fitful sleep to find that, for the first time since they had moved here, he was warm — and not just under the blankets. When he sat up he felt no chill at all. At first he thought the Mulcahys had made some mistake and left their radiators on all night — something they never did — but when he reached over to the one under the window, it was cool to the touch.

He stood up and pulled back the curtains. Outside was a clear blue sky over a deep blue ocean, untroubled by any breeze. Maeve moaned and squinted against the brightness, made fists and propped herself up on one elbow.

'What time is it?'

'Late,' Jack replied.

She sat bolt upright. 'I still can't believe those two last night!'

Jack just smiled. He loved to see her worked up about things. Her dark brows, lowered over her eyes, accentuated the light burning in them, and her face, framed in the locks of uncombed dark, dark hair that hung forward over it, hid its oval softness, showing only the finely chiselled features. Her real passion was far better than her best acting and now she sat there in a cotton nightdress, fuming, like some empress betrayed, ready to order the destruction of whole cities to avenge this slight.

'So, what can they do?' he asked.

'They could hold things up.'

'For how long?'

'I don't know. Maybe forever. You have no idea how strong the whole begrudger mind-set is in a place like this.'

'So maybe we should go back to Owen and try to cut a deal?'

'No! Never!' she hissed, conscious that they might be overheard.

Jack shrugged. 'Hey, okay. I'd just like, some day, not to be living out of a suitcase.'

Maeve sighed and reached a hand out to him. 'I know. Me too.' She smiled, and he thought she was going to pat the bed next to her, meaning he should get back in, but she didn't and said, 'See if you can get them to organise something quick to eat. Then let's get out and enjoy this weather.'

It was long past the time breakfast was served, and when Jack walked into the dining-room Margaret was stacking crockery on a tray. Though there were seldom any other guests during the week, a few couples would usually over-night here at weekends. The girl gave him a glance, then ignored him, and for a few seconds he watched her in her tight jeans as she bent over the table, but that just made him want all the more to hurry back to Maeve before she could finish dressing.

He too was concerned by the events of the night before. He now legally owned the land and doubted that Sweeney would buy it back. It wasn't a great amount of money, but it was a commitment, and he didn't want to have to abandon it. Like the parting with Owen, it would also leave a bad taste, so much so, he doubted he could become enthused about any further adventures in Ireland.

'Mam's down at the church,' said Margaret as she moved around the bigger table. 'And I don't think Maeve would eat anything I'd cook.'

'Hey, no problem. All we need is juice and coffee.'

'Oh.'

She left with her tray, and Jack pondered her remark. What about whether he would eat it or not? He knew she meant nothing by it, but there it was. Maeve was like a big sister to her now, while he was the exotic outsider that her heroine had brought home.

He was still pondering this when the door swung open, and both Maeve and Margaret appeared, laughing. Margaret led the way with a small tray of breakfast for two, while Maeve swished around her holding the coffee pot.

'Cheer up, Jack, the sun is shining!' Maeve declared. She had on a polo-neck that clung to the outline of her upper body, a long corduroy skirt, and ankle boots. As Margaret placed a coffee mug in front of him from one side, Maeve bent in close from the other to pour. Her fragrant hair rubbed gently against his face, he felt her breast push in on his shoulder, and then she was gone around the table to seat herself.

'Jack,' she said, 'we need a man's advice here.'

'Maeve, don't,' Margaret pleaded.

'Nonsense. Jack's paid to dream up plots.'

'Go on,' he said, suspiciously.

'Right, Margaret thought she had something going with Cathal last year. He did that sketch on the wall for her — you know, of the Celtic cross. And I could tell on Thursday he was walking on eggshells, but even when I left them alone he didn't say anything, did he, Margaret?'

The girl shook her head. 'He's very nervous about getting this house right for you.'

'Well, I guess he's hired now,' said Jack.

'Right, so how do we get the two of them back together?' asked Maeve.

Margaret looked away, clearly embarrassed. Maeve tilted her head and eyed Jack coquettishly.

'Can I have some time to think about this?' he asked, then took his first sip of coffee of the day.

'How long will we give him, Margaret?'

Jack saw that Maeve had overestimated Margaret's willingness to play along with this seductive intrigue. 'Give me a few days,' he said to the girl, winking up at her as she backed away to the door and left the room.

'I think they're both just shy,' said Maeve as the door closed.

'You're in an amazingly good mood,' Jack muttered, 'given the situation.'

'What can ah say?' said Maeve, tilting back her head and biting a tiny corner of toast as she mimicked a southern belle, 'but frankly mah dear, ah don't give a damn!'

'What?'

She ignored him, watching while he finished his coffee, then jumped to her feet, came around and pulled him by the arm out of his chair.

'Come on, come on, mustn't miss out on this glorious weather. Let's go walkies!'

Jack barely downed his cup before she dragged him from the table and led the way out the front door.

'The beach?' he asked.

'No, no. Let's tour our own country estate!'

Gulls soared lazily overhead, while smaller birds chattered in the hedges. New, bright-green fern leaves rose up on both sides of the road to take over from last year's dead ones, and even the grass in the fields was now a thick, new carpet over firm brown earth.

'I'm sure I know how to get around Byrne,' said Maeve, arms folded as she walked.

'So that's why you're in such good form?'

She linked an arm with him, and once again he was aware of her breast bumping against him.

'It's a pity you're not a papist,' she said. 'But anyway, you don't need to be bothered with all this getting in the way of your work. I'll see him this afternoon.'

'Be sure to thank him for the little soirée.'

They reached the gate.

'I'm not climbing that thing dressed like this,' said Maeve. 'In fact, I'm not going to climb over it ever again.' She walked up and kicked it with her boot, but it rattled and remained in place.

Jack laughed, vaulted over the rusty gate and dragged it into the field over the spring growth.

'The way is open!' he declared, bowing and flourishing as Maeve strode past, holding her skirt up from of the grass. They mounted the hill directly up its steep front slope.

'We'll have to put a curve in the driveway to get past this bit,' said Maeve, panting as they reached the shallower slope.

Jack did not reply, already lost in the vista that opened up to the east as they took the last few steps to the summit. If there ever was a Camelot, or a Tír na nÓg, or any place where the people had made the land into their own peaceful, prosperous garden, it must have looked just like this. This hilly country did not lend itself to huge fields, so instead it remained here a patchwork of stone walls, hedges, iron-red barns, and herds of black and white cattle in the luxuriant grass.

North and south the mountains seemed closer and higher today, so clearly lit that individual stones and sheep stood out on them. They turned back the way they had come up, and saw Rathbrack, its slates and walls dry, its granite pier glistening, and beyond, the sparkling bay, bright blue behind the waves that ran up the dazzling sand, blending into the darker blue of the infinite ocean beyond.

They sat down.

'It's fabulous,' said Jack.

'I don't ever remember it being this perfect,' sighed Maeve.

'It's almost worth the money just to be able to sit here and look at it,' said Jack quietly. Maeve's arm slipped around his neck and he turned to meet her lips, and as they kissed she fell slowly down onto her back, pulling him with her.

Now he could press in against those hidden breasts, and he slid onto his side to search for some opening to her skin. She clasped her hands behind her head and smiled as his hand rubbed past her navel, up over her ribs, and pushed her bra out of the way.

'More, Jack, more,' she pleaded and arched her back and raised her knees.

All of the morning's little temptations went to his groin as he realised that this was what she had in mind all along. He slid the soft skirt material up over her knees, then followed the smooth skin, feeling it grow hotter as he reached the top of her thighs. Now he knew why she didn't want to climb the gate — she was not wearing any panties.

She clasped his wrist, saying, 'Jack ... just do it. Right now.'

He didn't make his usual offer to go at her pace, just dropped to his knees and pulled down his jeans and underwear in one quick movement that caused his penis to spring painfully back. He fell between her silky knees, feeling her wriggle a little at the first push into unprepared flesh, and then she was wet everywhere.

She gasped, eyes closed and tossed her head to one side then the other, so that as he looked down on her she appeared to be lying on a pillow of her own hair. A harder look came over her face, as if there was some deeper thought behind all this than just the fine weather.

Jack watched her, willing a significance into this union here, and then, just for a moment, it was as if the world beneath them ceased to exist and they were both floating, so that he was powerless against her. As quickly as it came, that feeling went, and Maeve's body now felt so firm it was as if she were a part of the hill. Now an even stranger thought overcame him — that it was not Maeve behind those closed eyelids, but the hill itself, aware of them, knowing what they were doing here.

He clasped her shoulders and she wrapped her knees around the backs of his legs and he drove home into her, coming in long hot spurts each time he flattened her buttocks against the wind-dried grass of the hilltop, then fell on her, spent, and gave a gasp of laughter in her ear.

She turned her head towards him and opened her blue eyes, and, as if he had just awoken from a strange dream, he was relieved to see her staring back up at him.

'This is our hill now,' she said, 'forever.'

They brought Margaret with them to Sweeney's that evening, a night so perfect that they walked on past the pub and out to the end of the pier.

'Which one is your father's boat?' Jack asked as they stood looking back at the village under the stars.

'That sort of reddish one in the middle,' she answered. 'He keeps saying he's going to sell it, that what's the point hanging on to it when he just has a daughter.'

'Just a daughter?' Maeve chided.

'Ah well, he knows I have no interest in it. I wish he'd hurry up.'

They began back towards the pub, the voices within travelling over the still air to meet them. Inside, they jostled through a standing crowd, but found half of one booth recently deserted, its table covered with empty pint glasses, and Maeve slid into it, followed by Margaret. Jack sought out a way to the bar and squeezed in close to a lone customer at one end.

Next to him sat an old man, hard to tell how old because he had an enormous, unkempt grey beard. He was wearing a huge, dark overcoat, with another jacket beneath that. Sweeney came towards him with a pint of lager, and the man leaned forward to whisper something.

'Ah no,' said Sweeney, placing the drink in front of him, then picking it up again. 'No. Sorry now. Come back when you have money!'

The stranger glowered at Sweeney from beneath huge eyebrows, but said nothing.

'What'll it be, Jack?' asked the publican, ignoring the other man now.

'Look, I'll pay for that for him,' said Jack. 'You have it poured now.'

'Oh, well, fair enough.' Sweeney slid the drink across to the tramp, saying, 'There now. You're very lucky. This kind man is buying you a drink. Now get up off that stool and sit over there in the corner! That's for paying customers.'

When he stood up, the bearded man was taller than Jack, heavily built, with a shock of white hair that stood out at odd angles. He was evidently homeless, or at least, to judge from the smell, came from somewhere with no running water. He picked up the drink, saluted with it to Jack, and moved away with big powerful steps to sit on a small stool by the side door.

'One of them is more trouble than a whole bloody trainload of tinkers,' said Sweeney, surprising Jack with his sharp tone. Then he leaned forward conspiratorially over the bar. 'That one Fletcher is writing letters to Dublin. We'll have to get moving fast now.'

'And what about Fr Byrne?' Jack asked.

Sweeney backed off, once again his most obsequious self. 'Well now, that's a different problem.'

Jack gazed around idly while Sweeney prepared the drinks, to find Gladys Clery waving her little-girl wave back at him. He smiled ingenuously back, and she blew a kiss at him. Then when he unguardedly nodded at this, she beckoned him over, and he could see no way out. There were several other older people sitting with her, but she was at the near end and they did not acknowledge him.

'I just wanted to say,' she half-said, half-sang up at him, 'how gorgeous Maeve is looking tonight.'

'Oh, well, thank you, Miss Clery. I'll pass that along.'

'And I always knew she'd find herself the handsomest man for a husband.' Now she grabbed hold of his hand. 'Oh God, you're the most beautiful couple....'

She swayed around on the seat and began to hum a tune, eyes squeezed shut. 'Oh and I remember Maeve in her little pinafore, coming to get the eggs for her mammy ... a little dote, so she was.'

'I'd better get back to her.'

'Oh, you'd better, before some other handsome man sweeps her away!' The old woman laughed at this, picked up her vodka tumbler and used it to conduct the orchestra playing in her head.

Jack returned to the counter and, as he scooped up the three glasses, saw Owen at the far end in discourse with some other men of about his own age. They looked at each other for a few seconds, and something in the way that Owen turned away told Jack they were talking about the hill.

Returning to the others, he found that Gladys had been partly right. There, at the edge, next to Margaret, was Eddie, who might indeed be handsome if he combed his hair and made some effort to get the grime out of his wind-blown face and hands. Jack checked his desire to say that they made a poor advertisement for the rest of him, saying, 'I thought the fleet would be out taking advantage of this weather, Eddie?'

The youth leered up at him. 'Ah, I won't be doing much of that for a while. Sure I'll be helping Maggie's da with your house.'

'Don't call me that,' said Margaret through clenched teeth. 'And that's Mr Amonson's seat.'

'What? Well, slide up a bit and make room for him.'

'Get up,' she insisted.

'Oh, right so, I'll find a stool.'

He left and Jack slid in.

'Is he coming back?' Margaret asked.

Jack picked up his pint and looked around to see Owen Fitzgerald towering over him, leaning in to talk to his sister.

'Listen, Maeve,' said her brother, 'we've both said some harsh things. Now you know there's going to be trouble if you go ahead with what you're doing — a lot of superstition about those old fairy rings. That's why the things are still there. So what do you say we go back to the forty you offered, and that acre is yours?'

So confident was he of this offer that he held out a hand to her across the table, but she just smiled up at him and said, 'I take it you still go to mass?' He nodded. 'Then I'll see you at ten o'clock mass tomorrow.'

'Right,' he replied slowly, backing away. 'Mass. Tomorrow. Right.'

Eddie had failed to find a free stool, but he was now in some kind of negotiation with the tramp, who was pointing to his empty glass. Eddie shook his head and pointed to the door. The old man put down his glass, rose slowly and stared at the young trawlerman. Then he took a long look around at the people of Rathbrack — the farmers huddled together to exchange small secrets; the publican scurrying back and forth, unwilling to pay an assistant; the old people seated around the walls, saying little; Gladys, lost in her own romance; and the younger men looking up at a chat show on the television — and shuffled out into the night.

Next morning, Maeve took some pains readying herself for mass as Jack watched from the bed.

'You're sure I can't go?' he asked yet again.

'I haven't the foggiest idea what the rules are any more. But anyway it might look as if we were just parading ourselves about if you did. Better this way.'

'Oh, and you'll be so devout you'll stare at the ceiling with your eyes rolled back in rapture, will you?'

'Very funny. It's a social thing, you know.' She adjusted a wide-brimmed hat in the mirror, stood up, smoothed down the sides of her skirt again, viewed herself from both sides, checking the alignment of the seams of her tight jacket, made a kiss for him with her brightly glossed lips, picked up her bag and left.

Maeve timed her arrival for minutes before the mass started, strode two-thirds of the way up the centre aisle, excused her way in past a young family and sat, then knelt, exactly six rows in front of the wooden lectern. She was more or less where the old pulpit had been; the polished oak reading stand that had replaced it stood where the communion rail had been when she was a girl.

Fr Byrne arrived from the sacristy in the purple vestments of Lent, preceded by two altar boys.

'In the name of the Father, and of the Son, and of the Holy Spirit.'

'Amen.'

She had almost expected to hear the words in Latin, as though she had stepped back into her own childhood, but it was all in English, and after the first prayers were chanted back and forth between priest and faithful, someone from the congregation walked up to the lectern and coughed politely into the microphone.

'A reading from the Book of Deuteronomy...' he began, and droned on through the responsorial psalm and the second reading, losing the attention of the congregation because he had not read through it in advance, and was not putting any feeling into it. And then, as he mumbled his last words, the listeners all reawoke with a chant of 'Thanks be to God', which rippled through the church like some huge, deep gong, and he was gone and was replaced by the parish priest who boomed out the gospel with much greater authority in his voice.

Then there was a pause, with a few coughs from around the church, while Fr John Byrne gathered his thoughts for the homily. Maeve sat perfectly still, shoulders back, feet together under the kneeler, a credit to the nuns who had educated her, and fixed her eyes on the priest. All of Rathbrack was at this mass — the Mulcahys, Owen, Olivia and their boys, the louts from Sweeney's standing at the back, Gladys, Sweeney himself and most of the three hundred or so families whose fields Maeve would see from the windows of her new house.

'Today, I want to talk to you a little bit about the subject of superstition,' he announced with some gusto. 'As we all know, Ireland has a sad history of the forces of light and the forces of darkness confronting one another. Its people have suffered like no other Christian nation, have been given good cause, in every generation, to doubt whether indeed the one true God was on their side or not.

'And yet, not for one moment in all that time have the Irish people swayed from the faith that was brought to this island by St Patrick fifteen centuries ago. And just over a year ago, when the Holy Father himself came here for that historic visit, we witnessed just how alive that faith remains in the hearts and souls of all of us today.'

He paused, looking down at his notes. He was younger than the parish priests she remembered, probably not that much older than Jack, and she wondered whether Jack's hair would thin and recede like that too. But Byrne had more the look of someone who had long since given in to the good life, soft around the chin, with a paunch spreading to love handles, well hidden by these flowing vestments. She hadn't noticed it at Noreen Fletcher's in the gloomy fire and candlelight, but yesterday at his house she had. Still, he had an easy smile and a voice that didn't grate or bore.

'Here in Rathbrack we are graced by what remains of a monastic settlement from the tenth century, right in our midst, with a beautiful example of a well-preserved Celtic cross, an utterly priceless work of art, no less than any Italian fresco. And, we here in this parish can rightly speculate, when we stand in those ruins, that these very monks were among those who set out to re-convert a barbarian Europe back to Christianity.

'And yet, time and time again,' he said, so loudly that the sound from the wall-mounted speakers reverberated around the church everywhere, 'I am confronted by questions and stories about piseogs and fairies, and about trees and stones with magic powers and ghosts that have been seen and banshees that have been heard and some cow that won't give milk because of it all, and I have to ask myself, dear people ... to ask myself whether I should be out and about converting heathens ... whether the sight of all of you here today is just some apparition ... or ... or whether some of you have two religions and lapse into some pagan darkness when you're not within these four walls.

'There is only the One True God! He is the Father Almighty and he sent his only Son down among us to atone for our sins! That is the creed we all recite every Sunday, and it is the first commandment that was given to Moses — I am The Lord thy God, thou shalt not have strange gods before me!

'So, let us refocus our energies on our rich Christian heritage.' He paused, and for the briefest instant when he looked up again, his gaze passed over Maeve. 'For as long as I have been fortunate enough to live in this lovely parish of Rathbrack it has been a pet project of mine to try to do something about the deplorable state of the old monastery and cross. Now, a donor, who wishes to remain anonymous, has come forward and initiated a fund to be used for that very purpose.

'What we now need are volunteers — people who are proud of their real treasure here in Rathbrack — to do some of the actual work of restoring the pathways around the graves. And let me assure you that this will do more for the community than any idle speculation about fairy rings and the like ... and it will encourage tourists passing by on the coast road to stop off and get out their cameras' — he smiled briefly — 'while at the same time showing the world that we in Rathbrack have been practising the one true religion since we first heard the word and saw the light!'

As he finished on these words, it was all Maeve could do not to smile too, or even applaud. Yes, she was back in tune with how this place worked. She felt her brother's eyes on her and felt an enormous satisfaction at having finally broken free of — no, of having overpowered — everything he represented. Here today she had become the woman she had always wanted to be.

Chapter Eight

The crowd flowed out the front door of the church and made their way around the side, but there was an obstacle in their path this morning. Noreen Fletcher sat in her wheelchair, handing out flyers to anyone who would take one. Maeve dared not tack away in another direction and was almost past when the woman said loudly, 'You won't get away with this, Maeve Fitzgerald. I have an archaeologist coming down from Dublin next week!'

'Oh, she'll buy him off too,' said Owen, lying in wait with his two kids. 'Anonymous donor, my arse!'

Noreen's eyes narrowed. 'I knew the church couldn't be trusted, but there are people with a broader perspective involved now.'

'Your last chance, Maeve,' said Owen. 'I think the price might be going up again any day now.'

Maeve walked on, ignoring both of them. She took the car keys out of her bag and found that her hand was shaking so badly she had to steady herself against the roof to get the key in the lock and get away from them back to Mulcahys'.

She was pacing the hall when Sonny and Maura came in. She followed them into the kitchen.

'Well,' said Sonny, 'that was about as good as telling you to go ahead from Fr Byrne.'

'Yes, but when, Sonny?'

'Oh, it could be another couple of weeks before they get around to inspecting it.'

'We don't have that much time!'

'I can try and hurry them up, but that usually just slows them down. Once we have the go-ahead, there'll be no delays. Pay as you go, as we agreed, and I'll get the work done.'

Jack slid into the room, having heard Maeve's voice. Maura filled the kettle while Maeve stomped heedlessly from one end of the kitchen to the other.

'Damn them!' she rasped through clenched teeth. Then she stopped, looked at her husband, and said, 'Jack, we have Cathal's home phone number, don't we?'

He nodded and she led him by the arm out of the kitchen.

The architect arrived the following morning to be greeted at the front door by Margaret.

'Oh, it's you,' she said coldly, stepping back to the wall.

Cathal was about to slip past her into the hall but he didn't. Instead he grabbed her arm and pulled her outside.

'Listen,' he said, 'maybe you don't like me being back, and I'm sorry that you have to keep seeing me around the place, but this job was a lucky break for me. I'll try and keep out of your way, Margaret.'

She glared up at him. 'I'm the one who told Mam to suggest your name to them.' Before Cathal could reply to this, she went on, 'I'm not a schoolgirl any more, Cathal, so don't treat me like one.' Shaking free of him, she fled back into the house.

Cathal crossed the empty hall to meet his clients in the dining-room, and the three of them left together almost immediately for the site.

Once they reached the hill, the architect roughly laid out the various corners of the proposed multi-sided building with wooden stakes.

'We'll have to terrace up the last bit of the driveway,' he said. 'Then there'll be a few steps up to the porch, with walls sloping in to meet the door itself.'

'Yes, that's right,' said Maeve, looking down at him. 'Then I'm standing in the hall now, and if I turn now, and take a couple of steps down, I'm in the main living-room.'

She paced into the imagined room to find herself confronted

by the smaller segment of mound of the so-called fairy rath.

'So this has to go, or turn itself into a couch,' she said.

'And the other piece of it,' said Jack, 'is right where the south-facing full-length picture window will be.'

Through this as yet non-existent window he saw a yellow machine trundling past the church on the main road, driven by Sonny, with Eddie standing next to him outside the cab.

The three on the hill gathered to watch as the excavator swung off the road and bucked into the field through the gateway. A huge scoop with a row of metal teeth along its lower edge straddled the front of the vehicle, all but hiding its two smaller leading wheels. And behind the large driving wheels on either side of the cab was a second smaller shovel, this one articulated, so that it was folded in against the back.

'It's like some fierce animal on the loose,' said Maeve.

'An ancient war engine?' Cathal suggested.

As they watched it climbing the hill, with Sonny changing gears and switching directions as it struggled with the steepening slope, the loud snorts and jerky movements did seem to give the yellow monster a life of its own, as if they were besieged up here and it was relentlessly rising up to attack them.

It roared up onto the summit, then calmed down as Sonny idled the engine and jumped from the cab.

'Are we ready then?' he asked.

Jack looked at Maeve and nodded.

'Try to give us some fill over here on this side for the driveway up,' Cathal said. 'That's going to be the biggest problem.'

'Fair enough,' replied Sonny.

Eddie sauntered over while Cathal and Sonny conferred. 'This is heavy stuff, what?' he muttered.

'The bulldozer is doing all the work,' Cathal said.

'Oh, now, this place won't be an easy fuckin' thing to build. It's more like something out of James Bond.'

'We'll put in a road first so we can get all the other shite up here,' the architect told them.

'Are you right, Eddie?' asked Sonny.

The two men returned to the digger, and Sonny climbed into the cab while Eddie picked up a shovel and pick from the bucket. The diesel engine roared to life.

Jack put his arm around Maeve and they watched as the steel bucket dropped to the ground. The wheels skidded for a moment, sending up clods of earth, making the first dark ruts, and then the teeth of the bucket tore the soil and roots free, and the machine lurched forward.

After a few feet the bucket was full, but now it acted like a blade, and ploughed the crumbling sods up and out to each side. It reached the first wall segment and Sonny lifted the bucket slightly so that it broke free of the ground and the wheels sped up for the impact with the ancient structure.

The first blow sheared it away and carried most of it a few feet before Sonny stopped and reversed to destroy the rest. Flat stones clattered free of where they had been stacked long ago, and when he drove forward into the remaining piece only the top half dislodged itself, the vehicle riding up over the lower stones and pushing them away behind it.

Cathal shouted and pointed and Sonny nodded back. He drove on, emptied the shovel with a few flicks of the hydraulics, swung the machine around and came back at the stones from the far side. This time what was left gave way; the surprisingly bright and clean stones filled up the steel maw, and the watchers had to hurry aside as the pile of debris was pushed towards them, over the edge of the hill to where it would be needed as fill for the driveway.

The old man who had been in the pub two days earlier stood in the trees, their buds just giving way to tiny new leaves, and watched the spring of water called St Brigid's Well. He listened to its music too against the chorus of birds singing for mates now that the growing season had taken hold. From here he couldn't see the top of the hill, but he must have heard the engine and sensed something, because he ran across the road and into the church car park. Now he could clearly see the yellow vehicle moving back and forth against the sky.

He let out a groan and dug his hands into his hair, and was still standing there like this, with tears in his eyes, when the school bell sounded and children in brightly coloured

anoraks raced past him, shouting and laughing and ignoring
him as if he were just another statue like the blue and white
one looking down from the grotto behind him.

In twenty minutes the hilltop was transformed from a carpet of
grass, cowslips and dandelions to a maze of tyre tracks and
skid marks leading to tipheads of dirt and stones wherever
Cathal wanted them. The second, larger piece of the fairy rath
was even easier, now that they knew it was made of useful
stones beneath its outer mantle of mossy grass. Sonny dug into it
from its north-east end, filled the shovel, lifted it clear and delivered the stones to the porch area. After the first couple of loads,
Jack and Maeve lost interest, and started back down the hill.

'Well, that's the end of that,' said Maeve, folding her arms.

'I guess we've passed the point of no return,' Jack mused.
'We can hardly ask Sweeney for his money back now that
we've altered the landscape.'

Maeve turned to him and, in a voice that had a new-found
hard edge to it, said, 'He still needs to come through with the
planning permission if he wants the rest of the cash.'

On Wednesday night Maeve's last concern was laid to
rest. At Sonny's suggestion, they walked down to Sweeney's.

'Eh, I had a phone call today,' said the little publican,
'assuring me, as yer man put it, that certain matters were all
taken care of and to tell ye to go ahead and the rest would
catch up in due course.'

'Do you mind if we wait till all of this paperwork catches
up before we pay you the rest?' asked Maeve.

'No, no. Whenever you're ready. No rush.' His face broke
into a rare crooked smile as he wiped the inside of a glass.
'That was a stroke of luck, wasn't it?'

Jack and Maeve stared at him, baffled.

'Fr Byrne's sermon,' he added.

'Oh, right,' said Jack. 'Maeve, you were there. What did
you make of it?'

She stared back at him. 'Don't look around. Your girl-
friend is waving at you.'

'Gladys?'

'Yes.'

'Let's go.'

They slid from their stools and hurried to the side door.

Gladys motioned to Sweeney with her empty glass, and he carried her over another vodka and tonic.

'Aren't they only the most beautiful couple, Micko?'

'Oh, they are right enough, Gladys,' he replied, waiting for the money, which she counted out slowly in coins.

'Da da dum, dum dum,' she sang when she picked up the drink, unconcerned that she could remember neither the words of this tune, nor the melody itself. 'Dum dum dum dee, dee-dee, da da da-da, da-da, dee-dee....'

The latest drink went down quickly to help her voice, and when it was gone she stood up to leave, steadying herself on the back of the seat. But long years of drinking her pension like this had conditioned her to walk slowly and carefully, and there wasn't a step of the road home that she hadn't taken a thousand times before.

She shuffled in through her gate and fumbled for the key of her front door. It was dark, and even with the moon up it was pitch black under the trees. As she searched she became aware of thumping noises coming from her house. Then, as she found the key, they stopped. She forgot about them, went up to the door and inserted the key. There was another bump. But now she could tell it was coming not from inside the house, but from the old hen-house behind it.

'It's either rats in it or a badger gone under it looking for them,' she mumbled, then went inside, and took off her coat. She walked into her bedroom, turned on the light and got down on her knees, moaning at her own stiffness. Her hand pawed at the floorboards out of sight under the bed until she found what she was looking for and slid out an old single-barrelled shotgun.

She hauled herself forward on her knees and slid open the bottom drawer of the chest of drawers next to her bed. She groped amongst the corsets and slips she hadn't worn for forty years, found a box of bright orange shotgun shells and took one out.

But this was all an unexpected addition to her usual routine, and the noises had stopped anyway, and she wasn't sure exactly how to get the ammunition into the gun. She got back to her feet, groaning, and fell onto the bed, closed her eyes and forgot about it all, vaguely aware that another day had gone by, no different from the one before it, and the next one would be the same too, so whatever it was she needed the gun for, it didn't matter — it would be gone tomorrow.

Margaret surprised both her parents by appearing in the kitchen early next morning with her clothes on and her hair combed.

'Are you sick or what?' Sonny asked.

'She doesn't want to miss anything,' her mother replied for her.

'Can I help you build this house, Dad?' Margaret asked.

'What? And what in Jesus' name would you do? Begod it'd be a start if you'd help your mother run this place.'

'I do. Mam, have you served Cathal his breakfast yet?'

'I just did.'

'Oh. What about tea?'

'I poured him a cup.'

'Well, maybe he wants more.' She picked up the big teapot from in front of her father, and left.

Cathal was eating his fry standing up at the other table, which was covered in drawings, when she walked in.

'More tea?'

'What, emmm ... yeah.'

'Have you designed a lot of houses like this?'

'Christ, no.'

'And do they know you're only chancing your arm?'

'What? I am not! I know what I'm doing.' He hadn't found that funny at all. 'Those two are the chancers,' he went on. 'A writer and an actress. Now that's just pure hard neck. I hope they pay my bloody bills!'

'Oh, I'm sure they will.'

'Well, I suppose you should know, being so tight with Maeve.'

'Will you be staying here with us the whole time?'

'On and off. Your old man is the one doing the work. I'm just drawing the plans.'

She had poured the tea as slowly as she could, but the cup was full, and she had no other excuse for being there. She made for the door, head down so that he couldn't see how embarrassed she was. But it opened before she got there, and Maeve and Jack came in.

'Good morning!' said Maeve, breaking into a wide smile. 'Jack and I were just hoping we'd catch you both.'

This was news to everyone in the room except Maeve herself, but Jack nodded in agreement.

'Are you terribly busy tonight, Margaret?' she asked.

'No!'

'Because I was just thinking, if you were free, maybe the four of us could go out to dinner?'

They looked at Cathal.

'We all have to eat,' he said.

'Fine. Then let's meet back here at, oh, sevenish, and drive up to the Ballylacken Hotel. I hear they have a great restaurant, and Jack and I are dying to try it. Will that work for you, Margaret?'

The girl nodded, speechless, left, and pulled the door closed.

'Yes!' she mouthed to herself, thrusting the teapot forward into the air so that a stream of tea flew out of it onto the wallpaper, then twirled her way into the kitchen to bang the now-useless object back down in front of her father.

'That woman is a genius, you know!' she announced.

'Where are you off to?' he asked as she headed back towards the door.

'Back to bed.'

'What?'

'I need to rest.'

'That one is gone mad altogether,' Sonny told Maura when the door closed.

Maeve left with Cathal for the site. Jack cleared aside the rolls of drawings, sifted through his own papers, and re-read the last page. It was now Thursday and he hadn't written a word since the previous Friday. He would have to make up some time this week. When had Aaron promised the script to Excalibur? About ten weeks from now. Just enough time to solve every problem and deliver a sequel that would surpass the original.

Forty-five minutes later he was pacing the room, lost in thought, when Sonny and Maeve came in.

'Jack, we need you to sign a few cheques,' she said.

'Can't you sign them?'

'Better if you do,' said Sonny. 'That way there's no complications. You came from America. You brought the money with you. You spent it.'

'Whatever.'

Maeve produced the cheque-book.

'Pay Sonny Mulcahy?' Jack asked.

'Oh Christ, no!' The trawler captain raised his huge hands in front of him to defend himself from this idea.

'We're going to pay for all the materials directly, Jack.' Maeve opened a small notebook. 'We need to put down deposits on concrete. We need to prepay for a few tons of gravel for the driveway. They need to rent a generator, compressor, mixer and some scaffolding. The usual stuff, I suppose.'

'You get caught for the VAT either way,' Sonny explained. 'But this way you can pay me in cash and that'll halve the cost of all the labour.'

'You sure about this, Maeve?' Jack asked.

'Everyone does it,' she replied, with an accepting shrug.

He wrote out the names and amounts to Maeve's directions, accepted a peck on the forehead in return, and tried to get back to his own characters.

Half an hour later the door flew open again and Cathal's beard and dreadlocks appeared.

'Are they gone?' he asked.

Jack nodded.

'Ah, fuck! I have to go into town anyway to meet the engineer, so he can follow me out. I might meet them there. Listen, I told this chap who's going to drill for water to ask for you when he calls. Tell him he can start any time and try and explain to him how to get here.'

'Got it.'

'Emmm ... do you think I should get Margaret something for tonight?'

'What?'

'Flowers, chocolates, I don't know.'

'Why don't you ask Maeve? She's the expert on these things.'

Cathal grunted and vanished, pulling the door behind him.

A truck rumbled by outside, then squealed and hissed to a stop. Margaret stepped into the room, hair the usual mess, clutching a long candlewick robe of some sort over her nightdress.

'There's a man here to see Dad. It's about the house.'

Jack got to his feet, shaking his head at Margaret's sheepish look.

'I couldn't let him in. He's got muddy boots on,' she said.

He followed her out of the room and she returned to her own room, leaving him to deal with the visitor.

At the open front door stood the truck-driver, wearing a donkey jacket over his boilersuit.

'How's she cuttin'?' he asked.

'You're looking for Sonny Mulcahy?'

'I have a load of stones for him.'

Jack walked out onto the porch, told the man how to get to the entrance to the site, left him and returned to his typewriter.

He was just settling back into work when Margaret appeared again, dressed this time, to say, 'Noreen Fletcher is at the door with some man. I didn't say you were here. I said I'd see.'

He wanted to tell Margaret to tell them he had evaporated, and then to do the same herself. But whatever this was, avoiding it now would probably just make it worse later, so he rose one more time and went to the door.

The poet sat in her wheelchair by the lawn's corner bed of roses. Beside her stood a distinguished-looking man in a suit and raincoat.

'Good morning, Jack,' Noreen began coldly. 'Sorry to bother you. Well, no I'm not actually. Is Maeve here?'

'No. She's in town, I think.'

'Oh well, we'll register our protest with you, and you can pass it on.'

'Hey,' said Jack, 'I've been told by anyone I've asked that what we did was perfectly legal.'

'Unfortunately that's true,' said the man. 'But I think you knew that we might have succeeded in getting a judgement to allow us to study that ruin before you destroyed it.'

'And you are...?'

'It hardly matters now. I represent an organisation that tries to protect our ancient monuments from this sort of thing.'

'This wasn't a monument.'

'We'll never know now what it was,' said Noreen. She narrowed her eyes. 'I must say, you're a brave man to build a house there. I'm sure you've heard all the stories of bad luck that comes from interfering with the fairies.'

'Noreen, I don't believe in fairies.'

'These stories — all stories, as you should know — have some basis in truth. People don't just make this stuff up.'

'Look, I really don't want to get into some Jungian analysis with you right now.'

'I must say, I think that was a masterstroke the way you bought off the church.'

Jack smiled. 'Can't comment.'

'I know it was Maeve who gave him the money because John told me.'

'John?'

'Fr Byrne, the priest, remember?'

'Of course. Listen, I'm really very busy....'

The man cleared his throat. 'I have spoken at length with Noreen about this.'

'Don't!' she warned him.

'Now, Noreen....'

'Ah, you're as slimy as the rest of them.' She spun her wheelchair around and headed back towards the road.

'Have you read her poetry?' asked the man. Jack shook his head. 'Very reminiscent of Yeats. And the thing is she really believes in this pagan spirituality.' He lowered his voice. 'She was a brilliant girl. Very high up in the civil service, then on to high finance. Terrible the way she went. But I suppose if these strange ideas keep her going, well....' He nodded condescendingly.

Noreen had reached the road and was rolling past beyond the garden wall. 'Tell Maeve,' she said, 'that I'll be in touch next week, when I've calmed down. I don't know what they have in mind for the old monastery, but I'm not going to let them make a dog's dinner of it!'

'And she is our representative where that's concerned,' the man added. 'That's what I was going to say there when she ran off — we do appreciate that substantial donation towards the upkeep of the cross and all.'

'Hey, we're all just trying to get on with our lives.' Jack shook hands with the man, went back inside and tried to get on with his own life.

His first vaguely welcome interruption came when Margaret appeared with coffee.

'Jack,' she asked wistfully, 'when will Maeve be home?'

'Don't know. Why?'

'She promised to help me with my hair.'

'Aaahh.'

Then someone from the well-drilling company called and asked impossible questions like how deep the water-table was and what diameter sump pump they would want. Jack had to write all of this down, and decided, since Cathal had said it was very urgent, that he had better go over to the hill with the information. But Maeve had the car, so he had to walk, and only Eddie was there, using the excavator to spread the new stones along what would be the first part of the driveway. And he knew nobody's arrangements — probably a deliberate tactic on Sonny's part, to prevent him from slipping away to Sweeney's.

When he walked back to the house, Cathal was there, with the engineer, both of them poring over the drawings and trying to agree on bore holes and samples. This went on for over an hour until Maeve and Sonny returned and began questioning the new man on dates for the plumber and electrician to begin, but this all came down to timing the pour

of the main slab, about which all four of them had formed a
different opinion — already.

And two hours later the day was over. Jack, always ready
before Maeve, stood outside talking to Cathal, the architect
more laconic than ever faced with the task of socialising with
his clients, so that they both lapsed into silence and watched
the sun slip into the water far beyond the bay. The door
slammed behind them and in the gloaming they all sat into
the rental car. Jack drove, which he didn't like to do on these
roads at night, but if he didn't, he would be forced to talk, as
Maeve was now doing.

They reached the Ballylacken Hotel, and followed its tree-
lined avenue to park outside an old-world mansion with
granite steps up to its main entrance.

'Did we make a reservation?' he asked Maeve as he held
the door open.

'Yes, we did. Lighten up, Jack.'

Margaret followed her in, and for an instant Jack thought
he was holding the door for someone else. The girl had her
hair swept entirely back off her face and coiled up on her
head. Her eyes were dramatically made up, and the bright lip
gloss she had chosen gave the rest of her pale face a look of
air-brushed photo perfection.

Cathal slipped in last, but surely, to judge from his surly
look, he had not yet noticed his dinner companion in the
light. The two men followed the women, past the antique-
laden reception area and the oak staircase that led to the
upstairs rooms, and into the dining-room.

'Miss Fitzgerald? Of course, this way!'

The head waiter led them to a centre table, from where no
doubt he would discreetly point Maeve out to the other
diners. And at last, as the four of them took their seats, the
architect, with his well-developed aesthetic sense, sat down
opposite Margaret. And went slack-jawed.

Maeve winked at Jack. 'Champagne to celebrate the start
of our project?' he asked.

The waiter lit the small oil lamp on their table, and now a
warm glow accentuated the girl's throat and set off a beguil-
ing sparkle in her eyes. It was all Jack could do not to join

Cathal in staring at her. Instead he buried himself in the menu that was offered.

They were well into the meal and a third bottle of wine before their younger guests relaxed.

'We could put in the world's shortest cable car, and avoid the driveway,' said Cathal.

'I think you should make it harder to get up,' said Margaret. 'Throw down a rope ladder to anyone you actually want to see. You've no idea what a pain it is having guests every day.'

'Oh?' said Jack. 'So we should move up to the hotel here?'

'Oh God, no!' she exclaimed, laying a reassuring hand on his shoulder. 'Not you two.'

'You mean me, then?' asked Cathal.

'Sure, I never see you.' And she flashed him a demure smile across the table that told all.

Cathal leaned back and eyed her purposefully. 'Do you like the theatre?' he asked.

Margaret shrugged. 'I might if I ever went.'

'Well then, Cathal,' said Maeve, 'you buy a couple of tickets for something you want to see in Dublin and we'll find a way of getting Margaret up there.'

'I could go up on the train for the next set of drawings.'

'Sounds like a deal,' said Jack. 'In fact, I was just wondering, Maeve ... when Margaret's not on important missions to Dublin, do you think she could answer the phone for us, look after some of the details for you?'

'I was just thinking the same thing,' Maeve replied. 'But I wasn't going to embarrass the poor girl into a yes answer until she's had a chance to think about it!'

'You're not as desperate as me,' he added. 'Look, we need to get this done as fast as possible. I just know I'm going to find it hard to be productive until we get into our own place. Are you listening, Cathal?'

He nodded in reply, eating his dessert, eyes reserved for the vision across the table from him, as if she might vanish before he could buy those tickets.

'Speed, man, speed. No delays!' Jack admonished him, and Cathal concurred with still more energetic nods.

Chapter Nine

Gladys Clery had a small pension from a job she had held as a clerk in a clothing factory in Cork city for twelve years. She had started there in 1946, when all the men who would ever return from the war had come back, and hers hadn't, and she had set out to get on with her life. But her heart would not heal, and over the years she became more distant from her colleagues, and instead of meeting them in the pub took to buying the occasional Baby Power on her way home from work, until she overheard a comment on the smell of her breath, and from that day on, the naggin of vodka became her nightly friend.

The pension from the job had kept her going, but now it was hardly worth it, since she was continually harassed by the Department of Social Welfare over her dole and whether she would be entitled to the old-age pension or even any free coal in the winter.

She was still a young woman when she returned to nurse her ailing father in Rathbrack, and many a man had asked her to the pictures and to Saturday-night dances. But her heart was never in it.

When her father died, he left her the house, free and clear, but there was no money, so she started to keep hens. And that filled in her days, with feeding, cleaning, collecting the day-olds from the bus, and selling the eggs. But then, when the supermarkets came along, the price of eggs went so low it was hardly worth her while. And they wouldn't give her the dole until she got rid of the hens.

Now they were talking about not giving her the free coal either. So tonight, as she walked home, she was glad of the warmer weather. It was that last week of the month when she had to watch her few shillings carefully until the next month's money came, and so she had had only two drinks down at Micko's, and he always made a point of giving her an extra sup in the second one when that happened.

She walked through the gate, took out her key and slid it into the lock. And again she thought she heard a noise from behind the house. She didn't remember the night before, but she remembered waking up to find the gun on the floor, and that meant she must have heard a noise then too. There was another bump, too loud for rats.

She took out the gun again, loaded a shell into it and went quietly into the back scullery without turning on the light. There was definitely something moving in the hen-house. She pushed open the door that gave onto the back.

'Who's there?' she asked.

There was no reply. The hen-house was set back in the middle of what had been the chicken run, but she had long ago sold the wire that once surrounded it, and now, as she walked softly over the ground, the only reminders of those days were the poppies that kept springing up from the hard ground every year where she had once fed them. There was another noise.

'Come out!' she demanded.

A face appeared at one of the dark windows, then vanished. Her hands shook, so that the gun waved about as she pointed it at the door. She was afraid to go any closer, but she couldn't stand there in the cold much longer. The vodka had made its way through her and she needed to be rid of it. Maybe she should shoot at one of the windows, but she had only the one shell; the others were still in her corset drawer.

The old door of the hen-house slammed back against the timbers of the wall, and the tramp who had been around the village lately stood there. In her shock, Gladys dropped the gun and wet herself.

'Oh Mother of God!' she exclaimed. 'You're after frightening the life out of me!'

He didn't say anything, just stooped his head low enough to climb down, and took a few steps towards her.

'Was that you in there last night as well?' she asked.

'It was, ma'am,' he growled back.

'And what do you want bothering an old woman for? Go on off with you! I have no money. There's nothing of any value in my house!'

'I just needed a place to stay, ma'am. Just let me get my stick and I'll be on my way then. I mean you no harm at all.'

He turned back towards the doorway of the wooden hut.

'And where will you go in the middle of the night?' she asked.

'I'll find a dry spot under a hedge,' he said back over his shoulder.

'Ah no, there's no need for that. Are you comfortable in there? Sure you're not in my way. And you can use the outside tap if you want to wash in the morning. Ah no, I wouldn't put you out in the dark. You gave me a terrible fright, that's all!' She laughed her crackling laugh as she picked up the gun. 'Janey Mac now, and I almost shot you, you bloody chancer. Go on into bed out of that.'

The bearded man watched her return through the back door of her house, then climbed back into the dark hen-house.

When Gladys arose next morning she felt brighter than usual, and hummed away to herself in a way that she usually reserved for late in the evening when she had had a few to loosen her up. The tramp was out the back mooching around when she got to her scullery, and she laughed again at how he had appeared out of nowhere.

'I'll have a cup of tea and a slice of bread for you now in a few minutes,' she told him when she opened the back door to air the house. He waved at her and continued walking around as if he was lost. The kettle boiled, she made the tea and called, 'Come on in then!'

He took off his two outer jackets, hung them over the ladder that stood against the coal-shed at the back of the scullery, and came inside.

'You put the heart crossways in me,' she said, still tickled by her adventure. 'Go on inside now with that and sit down.'

There was much less of him without all the clothes. He sat down with his mug of tea and plate of bread by her fireplace and looked around the room while he ate, and then slurped noisily at the tea.

Eventually he noticed the old photo of the pilot. He didn't say anything but he looked back at Gladys, eating at a tiny table with one chair, then back at the photo for a long time.

'You're very kind, ma'am,' he said.

She crinkled up her face and shook her head at this rare compliment.

'Is there any bit of a job I can do for you?'

'Oh now, I'm afraid I haven't any money to be paying you.'

He looked at her again for a while .

'But I'll tell you what,' she said, 'if you rake up all them oul' dead leaves from around the side you can stay for another day or two.'

He nodded and lowered his huge eyebrows over his deep-set eyes.

'That's more than fair,' he said. 'You won't regret it ma'am.'

There were no problems with the survey. The hill was solid enough, and with a few acceptable modifications to Cathal's original ideas they could pour a foundation ring beam in the exact shape of the building — two overlapping rectangles with angled doorways set into the inside angles, and chamfered corners with full-length plate-glass windows on the south and west.

All that stood in the way was the building of a driveway that could be used to deliver the materials to the summit. The early part of the following week was too wet to work outdoors, but the forecast was for drier weather, and on Wednesday Sonny and Eddie made a start on the retaining wall that would be needed to build the approach ramp to the front door.

They had already excavated the trench down to bedrock. Sonny had done that sitting in the cab of the digger regardless of the rain, and now he and Eddie used pliers to wire up the steel bars that would stop the wall from cracking later on.

'What the fuck is this?' asked Eddie as a truck filled with unfamiliar apparatus swung in and ground up over the gravel road that now reached all the way to where they were working.

'Ah, that's the crowd to do the well. About bloody time,' Sonny replied and walked over to talk to them.

Eddie finished the last of his wire twisting and pulled off his work-gloves. Without Sonny he couldn't lift the big sheets of plywood that would be used as shuttering, so he lit up a cigarette and blew a slow plume of smoke towards the Atlantic.

'Eddie, get that saw set up!' Sonny shouted when he saw this. The youth nodded, clenched the cigarette between his lips and walked over to the generator. Two pulls on the cord and it coughed to life. He opened the plastic box that the rented saw came in and took out the pistol-grip power tool. Then he scrambled back up on top of the hill to find the end of the long yellow extension cord.

Here it was like walking through a battlefield. They had excavated trenches down to the rock, and had exposed it in other places with tyre ruts and moving the dirt around to reuse it. There were heaps of mud around the edges and wooden posts and brightly coloured tape everywhere, marking out in the real world what the architect had shown his clients on paper.

The first pipes and conduit were already stacked up to be set into the floor slab, and the first shipment of the special metal brackets for the big timber pillars lay under a tarpaulin down by the gate. Eddie found the end of the lead and plugged in the saw, then walked back to where Sonny was now waiting.

'Right, let's get on with this,' said the boss. 'Pick that up and hold it.'

They got the first sheet vertical and propped it in place. After this first awkward panel it would be easier. They marked the pieces that needed to be cut out of the bottom edge so that the wet concrete wouldn't flow out, then laid the plywood on a makeshift trestle, one of them holding it while the other worked the circular saw's disc along the marks.

There was a shout from over on the eastern side of the hill and Sonny went to see what the well-drillers wanted. When he got there, they said they had found water pressure in the hill itself.

'Ah, you're not half deep enough. Keep going,' said Sonny, and watched as they rigged another section to their drill. This went down almost immediately.

'Limestone,' said one of them, and they attached another section.

Eddie worked his way up the inside shuttering, which would be back-filled when the wall had set, nailing it in place until there was no more plywood ready. He had reached the heap of stones that had once been the old rath. Here it was a bit trickier because they had already partly back-filled, and he had to go down on his hunkers and wallop the nails at an angle into the wood.

The stones slid around and he fell back, grabbing at them for support with his left hand. But the rock he grasped was loose, and his hand swung free holding it. He cursed and sat down, and was about to let go when he felt smooth bumps on the stone.

Eddie put down his hammer and took the stone in both hands to look at it. And there, sure enough, was a spiral, or part of one, carved in the flat stone.

The drillers added yet another length. Sonny dug his hands into his pockets, waiting for the outcome.

Down by St Brigid's Well the old tramp leaned on the wall beside the road, and through the branches of the birch trees watched the silvery flow, gurgling over the dark wet rock into the basin, a view that would soon be hidden by new leaves.

He was a man who looked forever angry and the school-children had been warned to stay clear of him. Today was no exception. His brow was thick with creases and he squeezed his heavy stick as he listened to the noise of the machines on the hill.

A couple of young children ran out as far as the main entrance to the church across the road and yelled, 'Yah, Forty-coats! Fortycoats!' and when he turned to brandish his stick at them they ran shrieking back towards the school to work up the courage to do it again.

Eddie picked up another rock. It too was decorated, but with three zigzags next to each other. And another one had half-circles on it. But they were all just pieces of stone. He stood up. It was like a broken jigsaw puzzle. But it was already broken before they bulldozed it away. He shrugged, then decided to tackle the next plywood panel on his own.

They had already marked it, but because it was so big and heavy he decided to bring the trestle to it, and wedged the wooden frame on its side under one end of the ply. This gave him enough clearance to run the saw halfway down and then he would do the same from the other end.

'We found it!' shouted one of the drilling team. 'Water! Ah, this will be much more reliable!'

Sonny Mulcahy nodded.

At the same time the old tramp's eyes widened as the flow out of St Brigid's Well faltered, then slowed, losing the power to spring free of the rock and make noise, until, if there was any seepage at all, it was hidden under the moss and ferns. He grabbed his stick with both hands and roared at the sky.

The children, about to surprise him again from their hiding place behind the pillar of the church gate, ran terrified back to the sanctity of their playground — the car park between church and school, watched over by the grotto.

Over the din of the generator Eddie thought he heard some-one call, or so he said later, but whatever it was that distracted him as he was sawing through the plywood, when he looked around he shifted his weight so that the sheet of ply pushed the trestle over on its side, and Eddie, still holding the saw, fell forward, squeezing the trigger. The spinning steel disc hit the pile of carved stones.

A shard of steel tore free. It hit one of the carved stones further up the slope, made a spark that caught his attention and ricocheted straight back into his right eye.

Eddie screamed, and went on screaming louder than the generator, and stumbled up the hill looking for Sonny. He held his hand over his eye, and every time he took it away there was more blood, and he knew that the metal was in there somewhere, and that he might die.

When Sonny ran to him, he was already a mass of blood all down the right side of his face, and it was flowing down his neck and darkening the collar of his shirt.

'Oh Jesus, Eddie, Eddie,' Sonny cried. He pulled the right hand away and what he saw would haunt him forever. There was a hole in Eddie's eyeball, or what was left of it, and he must have been blinking when the fragment of blade went in, because his lower eyelid was torn down the middle so that the two half-flaps curled outward, and what had been his pupil was now the shape of a keyhole and missing its cornea. And the blood just kept pulsing out and down his face.

Jack and Maeve heard the news from Maura Mulcahy that evening. They called the regional hospital over and over but there was no news, and so they sat gloomily with Maura and Margaret until Sonny came back around ten, haggard, his clothes stained with Eddie's blood, and burst into tears in his wife's arms.

'He'll live,' he said between sobs, 'but the eye is gone.'

'And his brain?' Maeve asked softly.

'Apparently that'll be fine.' Sonny wiped the back of his huge hand over his cheeks and nose and shook himself free of the crying. He sighed, stared into the distance and said, 'And all for the want of a pair of goggles that wouldn't cost more than a couple of quid.'

'I'll put the kettle on,' said Maura, soothingly, 'and we'll all sit down and have a cup of tea. It's really awful, but what can we do now? Our prayers are with the poor lad.'

The story had spread through Rathbrack within the hour. Fr Byrne had gone to the hospital, having been told that Eddie O'Shaughnessy was dying, and when he was satisfied that this was not the case he had driven back to Rathbrack and gone into Sweeney's to inform everyone.

'But he's going to lose his right eye,' he told Micko before things could become too cheerful.

'That's a shame now, Father,' said Micko, shaking his head, then adding quietly, 'You know there's some queer talk going on?'

'What about?'

'Well, you know, the rath and all....'

'Idle superstitious nonsense!' the priest replied, loud enough for the few other customers to hear, even Gladys Clery at the far end under the television. Then he lowered his voice and leaned in to Micko. 'Of course I know you don't believe any of this, because it's you the fairies would be after for selling them the land, isn't it, Micko?'

The publican backed away and gave his familiar jerk of the head. 'Oh now, what they do with the place is up to them after I've sold it to them. Nothing to do with me.'

'Oh, I wouldn't entirely agree there, Micko. Ah no. You knew what they were up to.'

Sweeney had no reply for this.

'You'll do the collection baskets for me at ten o'clock mass this Sunday?' Byrne asked, moving on.

'Oh I will, aye. As usual.'

Fr Byrne left, and the few customers who had been there began drifting away too, denied the drama of Eddie's death and even robbed of the opportunity to speculate on the cause of his bad luck. Gladys had half-followed what was going on. Usually she wouldn't have taken any notice, but tonight, even though this month's cheque had arrived, she had lingered over just a single vodka and tonic, and then she left too.

It was early enough when she got home that she put a few lumps of coal on the fire and turned on the television, an old black and white set in a plywood veneer frame. The old man had raked the leaves and cut back the hedge at the side, but she had not seen him today, and wondered if he had moved on, the way these old fellows do.

The fire burned down and the test card came on, so she stood up and turned off the television. And just as she did so, she heard a soft knock on the door. She went to the back door and opened it, expecting to see the tramp, but there was no one there.

'Hello?' she said, peeping out into the dark. It was almost cold enough for frost, and her breath came in steamy puffs that hung on the air. When her eyes adjusted to the night, she saw that the door to the hen-house was open, so he wasn't in there. Nothing moved. She could hear her own heart beat. And then, as she listened, that beat became a knocking of knuckles on wood again, the same as before. And there was something strange about it, a tap-tap-tap she knew from somewhere.

She backed into the scullery, afraid to turn her back on the night until she had bolted the door shut on it, which she did slowly, as if ... as if she didn't want the others in the house to know. The knocking at the front door stopped, and then started again. Tap-tap-tap.

She remembered now, sliding the bolt on that same back door, forty-two years earlier, the night Derek went away. She vividly remembered the same cold stillness, and not wanting to wake the rest of her family, how he had tap-tap-tapped softly on her window to get in that night.

Gladys Clery stood rooted to where she was and stared at the inside of her front door. Over the years she had dreamed of that night, but it was all washed out, so that she could get through the days. Was that it — that she should be in her bed unconscious now? Or was she asleep? She straightened up her neck and walked stiffly across the room as if to show a watching world that she was up to this. But when she reached the door she hesitated. The taps came again.

She pulled open the door. It was as well she had recollected the sound, because if she had opened that door without a warning the shock would have killed her.

'Derek?' she heard herself say hoarsely.

And there he stood, as he was in the picture she had treasured all this time, as if he had never left, in his blue-grey uniform. And at the sight of her he took off his hat and clutched it under his arm.

'You came back,' she said and raised her hands over her face. But she might as well have tried to hold back the tide, because the tears burst out anyway — tears of joy, where before, all her life, there had been only a well of sorrow.

'Did you miss me?' he asked. And it was the same cocky voice, and all the years were gone and she too was the girl who listened to nobody and would have no one else, but would run shamelessly after Derek and let him take her where he would.

And yet, when she lowered her hands again, they were the same mottled hands that had rooted for the money for a drink in Sweeney's earlier, and now she was unsure.

'Don't worry,' he said. 'I know it's been a very long time.'

His breath too made misty puffs in the cold air and very, very slowly she raised her arm and touched his uniform.

She lifted her fingers to touch his face, but he pulled back.

'I can't,' he whispered. 'I can't be with you yet.'

Despair settled on Gladys, and she felt a fear rising in her, but he smiled at her with all his old charm and said, 'No, don't worry. This will be all right. But to make the magic work, you have to help us, that's all.'

The old woman slumped to her knees and clasped both hands in front of her. She looked up at the young fighter pilot standing in the dark.

'Anything,' she prayed. 'Derek, you know I'll do anything you ask.'

Chapter Ten

The car dealer phoned Jack to say that the Peugeot they had ordered had arrived, and he and Maeve were glad of the excuse to take off for the day, to pick up their own vehicle and return the rental one to Shannon.

'The weeks are really flying by,' Maeve sighed as they turned onto the main road and Jack accelerated past the parish church and over the stream that bounded their property to the south. 'Look!' She pointed and turned back.

'What?'

'Stop, stop!'

He hit the brake pedal.

'Just reverse back over the bridge.'

'But I can't see....'

'For God's sake, there's no one up at this hour of the morning around here.'

He did as she asked, the engine revving loudly as they followed the stone wall back around to a point opposite the church.

'It's that old fellow that's been hanging around,' said Maeve, rolling down her window.

'I thought you said no one was up?'

'I meant normal people.' She leaned out as they drew level with the bearded, white-haired stranger. 'Good morning,' she said cheerfully.

The man studied her face, then lowered himself down to look in at Jack before replying.

'Come on, Maeve, let's go,' said Jack under his breath.

Every American city had its share of these people — unfortunate fringe-dwellers whose lives had gone so far wrong at some point that they could no longer relate to society, or people who just did not have the mental capacity to participate in the world today.

'Good morning, ma'am,' the indigent replied. His voice was gruff, but surprisingly clear nonetheless.

'Are you looking for work?' Maeve asked.

He fixed his intense eyes on her. 'I might be.'

'Well, we're building a house right up there on that hill and one of the workers has ... well, never mind. The point is, they're short-handed right now, so if you go up and see Sonny Mulcahy....'

'And who would I say sent me?'

'Say you were talking to Maeve Fitzgerald.'

'And is that who I'm talking to?' He leaned right in, his gnarled face inches from hers, and she recoiled at the smell of him.

'He'll pay you cash,' said Jack, 'so it won't affect your dole.'

The eyes above the beard now looked across at him.

'Excuse us, we need to be going,' said Maeve, beginning to crank up the window so that he had to pull back. They pulled away and left the old fellow looking after them.

'Do you think he'd be of any use?' Jack asked.

'He's an extra pair of hands, that's all.'

They continued on through the countryside, the tilled fields planted now, but new green leaves filling the branches of the trees and hedges everywhere.

'Jack,' began Maeve after a long silence.

'Yesss?' He too had been lost in his own thoughts, mostly about deadlines and the plot resolution for his script.

'I'm five days late.'

'What?'

'I'm late. And I'm never late.'

For a few moments this made no sense, and then he realised what she was talking about.

'Are you sure?'

'Of course I'm sure. I've been having periods for over twenty years.'

'I know, but ... maybe your body is just now readjusting to the time difference, the moon at this latitude, I don't know....'

'Jack,' — she shook his shoulder gently — 'maybe my body is adjusting to the fact that I'm pregnant.'

He sighed, let the car slow down, and drifted into the edge of the road.

'It's very, very early,' she said. 'Maybe I shouldn't have said anything yet?'

'No, no! This is fantastic, I mean — when do you think...?

She grinned widely at him. 'You don't remember?'

'Uuuh?' This was one of those impossible questions.

'Three weeks ago. On the hill!'

His eyes widened and he smiled back now. 'You really think so?'

'Well, I'd like to think there's some payback for allowing myself to be ravished like that!'

He shook his head knowingly now. 'You mean this is what you were hoping would be the outcome?'

They leaned in together and hugged. 'Yes, yes. This is what I wanted,' she said into his ear. Then she pulled back. 'And you?' she asked. 'Jack, we've talked about this before and you've always said you'd love to have kids.'

'Oh Maeve, yes, no doubts. You know that. It ... just seems like a lot happening at once.'

'It'll all work out, you'll see,' she said. 'This is all just the start of something great.'

'Yeah, well, let's go start with a new car!'

He took off again and they continued their way across the Irish spring landscape. She was right. Not that it needed ever to get any better than this. This was perfect. He grinned foolishly at the road ahead, and she beamed back across at him. Yes, life was perfect that day, and the sun came out to agree with them, and they waved at every child waiting for a schoolbus and even imagined that the cattle and horses they passed were watching them with envy, the whole world thinking — I wish my life could be that perfect.

When Sonny arrived on the site that morning the old man was already there, bending down near the stones at the top of the driveway.

'What do you want?' he asked, suspicious of the fact that the newcomer was in the very spot where Eddie's accident had happened.

'Maeve Fitzgerald sent me,' he answered.

'Maeve sent you here?'

There was a long pause before the old man said, 'I'd have come anyway.'

'Would you now? Can you use a shovel?'

The old fellow nodded.

'And I take it you could use the money?'

The man shrugged at this.

'Don't tell me your whole life story all at once,' said Sonny. 'Right then, come on up here and we'll see if you're any use.'

Over the course of the week they got enough done to cast the driveway embankment wall. The man proved to be a solid worker, with a strength in his arms that amazed Sonny and the other tradesmen who watched him work. He could drive a spade into solid earth without the help of his foot, and when given the job of hammering more shuttering together, he sank the nails home with a single blow each time.

He hardly spoke. When the others took tea breaks he wandered around or sat and played with the stones that were now destined to be buried under the curving driveway that was taking shape all the way from the main road to the top of the hill. And in the evenings he put back on his jacket and coat, picked up his stick and walked down the grass and away through the break in the gorse that dropped down by St Brigid's Well.

His last name was MacHenry, but whenever anyone asked his name he mumbled something that sounded like 'monna-nonna', so they just called him Fortycoats, the name the children had for any lone beggar who passed through the village.

It was some of these children who first heard the woman's

voice. School was over for the day and three of the boys from fourth class had been kept back to write 'I will not talk in class' fifty times each. When they were finished their teacher scolded, 'There you are, the whole afternoon wasted. Wasn't it better when we just caned the likes of you? Get out of here and say a prayer to Our Lady to help you to be quiet and pay attention from now on!'

They jumped down the steps of their prefab classroom into the yard and ran towards the road.

'We're supposed to pray,' said one of them, pointing to the grotto.

'He's not looking. Come on,' said his friend. But the third boy, watching over his shoulder, saw the door of the prefab opening as the teacher left.

'He'll see us!'

They swung right and walked dutifully towards the railing of the grotto, heads down as if they were very sad.

'Is he looking?'

'No, but he'll drive out this way.'

They walked up to the rail and knelt down, listening for the sound of the teacher's car. It droned past behind them and stopped before turning onto the road.

And then they heard the woman's voice. It might have been the wind, but there wasn't any.

'Did you hear that?'

'No.'

'You did, you liar!'

'I don't hear anything.'

The three of them knelt there, shivering in the cold.

'It was nothing.'

One of them blessed himself, and the others copied him. Then they stood up, turned and began walking away. The sound came from behind them again.

'Run!'

The three boys bolted for the village and ran all the way to their homes.

At the end of the second week Sonny paid Fortycoats what he would have paid Eddie for the same amount of time. But then he felt guilty about this, because the man had worked so hard, so he unfolded another twenty.

'Look, there's a bonus for you.'

'What's it for?'

Sonny didn't want to give the fellow a big head, or have him slack off next week, so he deliberately took up the question a different way.

'Oh, you could get a haircut, buy yourself a decent hot meal, or just go on down to Sweeney's there and have yourself a few jars.'

'Fair enough, sir.'

He stuffed the money in one of his coat pockets and shuffled away in the direction of the village.

'Have you money now, before I go pouring this?' asked Micko when the old man gave his one syllable order, 'Beer'.

Fortycoats took out a crumpled twenty-pound note and placed it on the bar.

'Oh, right you be so.'

Around the corner, leaning on the front edge of the counter, Owen Fitzgerald looked at the money, then up at the man's face.

'Been doing a bit, have you?' he asked.

Fortycoats nodded.

'The fishing, is it?'

The man shook his head. Owen frowned. At this time of year there wasn't much else to be doing, so it didn't take long to dawn on him.

'Ah, you're working on this great castle that's going up on the hill, are you?'

This drew a nod. Micko exchanged a pint of Smithwicks for the blue ball of paper, straightened it out and took it to the till.

'Well, I suppose I should tell you to choke on that bloody drink, but sure, you're only trying to make a few bob like the rest of us.'

Micko returned with change. 'Ah now, steady on there, Owen,' he said.

'Oh, begob, will you listen to him,' said Owen to the stranger. 'He's had me as a customer for twenty years and he knows he'll have me for the next twenty. But the sight of a newcomer's money gives him the same pleasure the rest of us get from our wives!'

'Now, Owen....'

'What? Are you going to bar me again, Micko? Did you not feel the sting of the money I wasn't leaving here in the evenings?'

'Ah now.'

'Well, bejasus, I might be the one paying men cash to spend in here if that obstinate bitch of a sister of mine had come to her senses!'

'Now, you should have offered it to her at a fair price in the first place. It's your own doing that they bought the hill.'

'You should have told me what you were up to. You could have had your money, and the land. They would have come around, Micko.'

'Aye, well, you have the land still. Can't you get on with selling it off to others?'

'Ah, that's not where the real money is. I want to develop it. Put in luxury houses.'

'And why don't you?'

'Cash flow, Micko. That's all.'

'Now, I might be able to help you there.' Micko gave one of his twisted leers. 'Don't want to leave that money sitting there in the bank for too long where it might get noticed.'

Owen straightened up. 'Are you serious?'

'Oh, I am.'

Both men stopped and turned to the bearded stranger at the end of the bar. Had he been listening? Two clear grey-blue eyes glinted back at them from between the outsized eyebrows and the uncut beard, but if he had heard, or cared about their illicit investments, he gave no sign. Instead, he raised the large glass of red beer to them and downed half of it in a single swallow.

Cathal drove down that Sunday with final drawings for the foundations. It was a blustery day, with a sea running from the south-west, to pound the rocks beyond the end of the beach, throwing a white spray into the air that could be seen from the Mulcahys' dining-room.

Margaret leaned against the radiator with her back to this view as Maeve, Jack and Cathal studied the dimensions one last time. The architect's eyes drifted up to meet hers as his clients grappled with the lines and symbols. She smiled and raised her eyebrows; he winked in return.

'I tell you what,' he said. 'You two take your time. Make sure everything's where you want it, and I'll take a wander up to the site and just see where they're at.' Cathal stood up. 'Margaret, do you want to come too?' he asked.

There was a biting wind that brought the blood to their cheeks. Margaret dug her hands deep into her pockets and hunched her shoulders against the cold.

They walked on silently, off the main road and up the un-paved driveway, curving left and then right as it rose to the top. Cathal slowed down, taking an interest in the retaining wall.

'This'll work,' he said. 'They just need to backfill in here.'

Margaret wrapped her arms around herself and hunkered down in the lee of the wall, and Cathal sat down on the stones facing her.

'What's this?' he said, picking one of the stones up. 'Fucking hell, this stone's been carved!' He sprang to his feet and looked down around him. 'There's another one. And another. Margaret, come here, help me sort these out!'

'Look at this one!' she said and picked up a flat rock about the size of a dinner plate in both hands. On it was a wavy line with circular indents between each of the crests.

For an hour or more they rummaged through the stones until they had found about a hundred with identifiable patterns. Many of the others showed some signs of carving, but it was like a huge jigsaw that would have to be reassembled to make sense of every vee and whorl.

'How come we didn't notice this before?' Cathal asked.

'Maybe they did, and no one said anything.'

They stood together, looking at the collection of stones they had laid out, and Cathal, hearing Margaret begin to chatter, slid an arm around her.

'Tell you what,' he said. 'I'll run back and get the car and we'll drive up to Ballylacken for a couple of hot whiskies.'

She smiled and nodded, and he ran off down the hill.

Margaret was reluctant to leave the stones and walk down to meet him at the road. But she shook herself and decided that it was just the cold that had her rooted to the spot. This was all the past, all about dead people, and she had the future to think about, her future, and Cathal was the best hope she had of getting away from here where everyone was stuck in the past. She braced herself against the wind and walked down the hill.

Jack had taken to getting up very early in the mornings, before anyone else, and using the quiet time to add a few lines to his all-but-stalled script. As he settled in front of his typewriter on Monday he heard a shot, and wondered what someone would be shooting on a spring morning in Rathbrack. Rabbits? Ducks? What kind of game birds were in season?

There was just one shot, and today he realised that he had heard the same sound every morning last week, just as he woke up, or in the shower. But there was never a second shot. That struck him as odd, but he had other more important issues to think about, and he was sitting in the dining-room, mulling over the previous week's work when Cathal came in.

'Sorry we didn't make it back till very late last night,' he announced, settling himself into a chair.

'Oh, let me see here,' said Jack. 'A night of explaining all about beams and columns or a night out with the lovely Margaret? What a choice. Must have taken about two nanoseconds.'

'There's something you should know,' said Cathal, 'about the site.'

'Not now, Cathal. Tell Maeve.'

'Fine.'

'Look, I'm not trying to be an asshole. I just have this
script to finish and I'm getting nowhere with it. The bedroom's too small to work in and there are interruptions here
all the time. We really need to get that house built and get in
there. Fast.'

'Sorry, Jack. I understand.'

'Thanks.' Jack buried himself once again in his unfinished
plot while Cathal hurried through his breakfast and then left
with a mumbled farewell.

It was another hour before Maeve appeared. 'I think
there's a lot to be said for teenage pregnancy,' she groaned,
looking pale and tired as she sat down.

'Why don't you go back to bed for a while?' Jack suggested. 'Cathal's here this week. He'll keep things straight —
that's what we pay him for.'

She smiled dimly at him. 'This is all perfectly natural, my
dear. It'll go away in a few weeks.'

Margaret arrived with the cooked parts of Maeve's breakfast, and Jack was astonished seeing the two women together.
Now it was Maeve whose hair was unbrushed, and Margaret
who seemed self-assured and was groomed as though on her
way to some office job. He wondered if she and Cathal.... But
that was none of his concern, and he pulled himself away
from the thought and back to his own work.

The two women conferred quietly over some list, then left,
with Margaret slinging a heavy bag of papers over her
shoulder. He heard the doors of the Peugeot slam and was
reminded again of the gunshot.

Maeve pulled into the site's driveway to a scene of chaotic
activity. There were two big, orange concrete trucks ahead of
her — one right up at the top being tended by Sonny and the
others, the second awaiting its turn, its huge conical mixing
chamber rotating slowly. Cathal and the plumber were con-
ferring by a pipe-bending tool on top of the hill, and the
electrician and electricity supply people seemed to be debat-
ing where the meter should go.

They slammed their doors, and Margaret left Maeve to

pick her way up the north slope while she herself followed the drive up past the first concrete truck. The second truck was much higher up, and as she approached it she saw why — the whole driveway inside the wall that had sheltered Cathal and her from the wind the previous day was filled up now with stones, so full they were spilling over the edge.

She passed by Fortycoats, who stared at her without saying anything. 'Ignore them,' Maeve had advised her. 'If you want to be dead sure of getting the man you want, you have to put up with the unwanted attention of all the ones you don't.' And she was sure Cathal wanted her. He had opened up to her, and she was less in awe of him now that she knew how hard he had studied and worked, and that he still lived at home with his parents, and that he was dead scared of the responsibility he had here. And he had listened to her. He had actually listened!

'Is she just up?' Cathal asked, jerking his head towards Maeve.

'It's woman stuff.'

'Aahh. Is she in a mood then?'

'No. Cathal, what happened to all the stones from yesterday?'

'Nothing.'

'Where are they?'

'Right where we put them. But now they're under a few feet of quarry chips. Five tons to be exact.'

'I thought you said they were important, and valuable.'

He looked sidelong at her for a few moments. 'They probably are. But if we'd told Jack and Maeve about them, they'd have had to decide what to do. This way it's better. Look, they were buried for a few thousand years. Now they're buried again.'

They stood and looked at the new stones, only a few feet away.

'I kept a few,' he said. 'I put them in the car.'

She smiled at this. The stones were something they had shared together.

Chapter Eleven

The children rapped on the glass panels with their knuckles until the priest's dark form came to the door.

'Fr Byrne! Fr Byrne!'

'You have to come with us!'

'Now! Now!'

The priest bent down to the crowd of children.

'Is this about the statue of Our Lady again?' he asked.

'It's moving!' they shouted.

'I see and where did it go?'

This stumped them.

'It's still there then, is it?' he went on.

'Yes. But....'

'All right, then, go on home and I'll walk over there in a little while.'

The children — this time there were six or more of them — turned and walked slowly back down the path. Almost every day he had had a delegation with the same story. When the last of them filed out through the gate he slid on his jacket and left. He didn't want them to see him react to their wild ideas, but now he was genuinely curious.

All was as it should be at the grotto. A quarter of a century of Atlantic weather had rounded away the original sharp angles of the plaster rock mound, but the statue itself was in perfect condition — a pale woman with blue eyes, looking skyward, from an otherwise blank oval face, wearing a white robe and sky-blue shawl.

The rockery below her was well tended, and already the

lobelia and alyssum were beginning to flower, which reminded him that the committee should really ensure that there were a hundred or more cut daffodils on the altar this Sunday; they were blooming wild in the fields and going to waste. The ivy could do with a trim, and there were a few rust spots on the railings, but the paint would last another year.

He stared back up at the statue, and now he saw that there was a bit of mould starting in the creases of the robe and there was some bird spatter on the bare feet. Not to worry, he had a catalogue of these statues inside and would order a bright new replacement in a few years' time.

And then he too heard what sounded like the wind, but seemed to take on the shape of words. He fixed his eyes on the face of the statue and tried to concentrate on what he was hearing. But the sound died away, and when it was gone he couldn't be sure he had heard anything.

Surely it was some trick of the wind. But now he understood why he had seen so many people praying in twos and threes in the evenings here. The children were telling their parents and the word was getting around that there was something to be seen or heard. Whatever was behind it, it was good to see the people becoming fervent again. And here was a chance to prove to the diocese that he had what it took to be a parish priest. He would order one of those all-weather devotional candle machines and get one of the electricians working on the Amonson house to wire it in here for him.

He looked up at the construction on the hill. Already they had installed all of the uprights and some of the wooden roof beams, and inside they were busy with the wooden stud partitioning. He hadn't seen much of Maeve other than at a couple of the monastery committee meetings, where she and Noreen were at least speaking to each other again.

'Jack, no, no! Stop!'
  'I can't stop now!'
  'Please, it's too direct. I'm afraid.'
  Jack straightened his back till he was upright, kneeling

back on his hunkers on the bed. Maeve stayed where she was, crouched forward in front of him, her head on the pillow, face down, dark hair everywhere. Jack rubbed her back with his palms, massaging her, though he knew that no cajoling would undo this decision.

He slipped down next to her and she turned her face to him.

'You know this is how a baby sleeps?' she asked.

He didn't answer. To him her posture had none of the innocence of a child. Trust, yes. Love, yes. But adult love. Wanton, come-and-get-it abandon as they shared a bed and a life together as lovers.

Maeve knelt up on all fours and smiled down at him. 'Oh, poor Daddy feels left out, does he?' He glared up at her. 'Jack, I want it too you know. I'm sure it'll be okay later on, but let's not take any chances?'

'I know. You're right.'

She slid in against him, slipped a hand between his legs and closed it around his balls.

'Maybe there's something else we can do here,' she murmured in his ear.

'You're going to rip them off?'

Maeve laughed, then pressed her mouth against his nipple and sucked so hard he winced, and pumped him with as tight a grip as she could with her small hand until his legs stiffened. Then, without letting up, she sat up so that he could see her and she could at least have the satisfaction of seeing what she had wrought.

Jack slept fitfully that night and woke before dawn. Maeve remained fast asleep next to him, so he slipped quietly out of the bed. He was anything but tired and decided to walk up to the house and watch the new day arriving. He dressed, picked up his sneakers and backed out of the room, pulling the door slowly behind him.

For a second, when he looked down the gloomy corridor he thought he must be looking in a mirror, as he watched another figure do the same thing. But when he turned and walked towards the dark image it froze.

'Who's that?' he hissed.

The other figure put a finger to its lips, and came towards

him. And as he came closer Jack recognised the curls that sprang out at odd angles all over his head.

'Morning, Jack,' said Cathal, as he passed by, also carrying a pair of shoes, and disappeared into his own room.

Jack let the front door click behind him and sat down on the step to put on his sneakers. Involuntarily he thought of making love to Margaret, or to someone that young and innocent, then shot to his feet and shook off the idea.

He looked out between the dunes at the ocean. Already the sandy slopes that faced him were brightening and a blue tint was coming over the water. He was too late to catch the dawn from the hilltop. He walked towards the village, looking now and again to his left as the sky in the east paled from the horizon upward.

The unfinished house, with the light behind it, was almost like a postcard of some Greek temple, a silhouette of upright pillars, a few beams in place, and parts of walls rising halfway to the roof. The first birds began to chirp as he reached the monastery and then, as he strolled on, he noticed something that struck him as peculiar. He came to a point where he could see the house through the circular stone ring of the Celtic cross.

His attention was torn from this by a loud bang. It was the familiar gunshot, but it was from somewhere very close by and directly ahead. A flock of seagulls, shrieking at each other for flying room, rose from behind Sweeney's, and Jack ran past the deserted pub to see who had fired the shot that had startled them.

Here he had to choose — either left and up towards the cliffs past Noreen Fletcher's house, or right and the pier, its fishing trawlers lashed together at the deep end. At first he directed his attention up the hill, but nothing moved along the road, and then when he turned and looked out past the bend in the pier, a movement caught his eye in the long shadows of the ships.

Someone threw a white object over the sea-wall. He walked down onto the flagstones, more curious than ever. And then he saw the unmistakable camel-hair coat and fur hat of Gladys Clery, walking away from him, a straw shopping basket in her left hand, and a shotgun, its barrel broken open, in her right.

Ahead of her, an injured seagull, unable to stand or fly, was squawking loudly and using its one good wing to turn itself in circles on the ground. The old lady came up to it, put down the gun, reached into the basket and took out an axe. The bird struggled now with a leg and wing to drag itself away from her, but she easily caught up on it and smashed in its skull with two blows of the back of her axe.

Jack stopped and began to back away, uneasy now. Whatever she was up to, she did it early in the morning when no one was around, and she had a gun, and he was blocking her escape from the pier. Gladys turned the dead bird over on its back and spread out its wings. Then she pounded into the root of each wing with the blade of the axe until she severed them from the body, folded them carefully and put them into her shopping bag, then swung this second carcass by its webbed feet over her head and flung it over the wall into the ocean.

Jack had no time to do anything other than resume his walk out along the pier before she started back towards him with bag and gun.

'Ah, will you look who it is!' she cried as she recognised him, giving him her familiar grin with its revelation of ruined teeth.

'You're up bright and early this morning, Gladys,' he responded.

'Oh but it's a terrible pity to waste the day, isn't it?'

'It is.'

There was no cartridge in the gun, and if she reached for the axe he was sure he could wrestle it away from her before she hit him.

'And how's Maeve?' she asked.

'Great. She's great.' But what if she walked on, then got far enough away to reload and shoot him? If he kept an eye on her he might be able to run to the end of the pier and jump in the sea. Still, he had to ask. 'Gladys, did you just shoot those birds?'

'Aren't they a terrible nuisance?' she replied. 'Far too many of them.'

'Yes, but I don't think you're allowed to just....'

'Your house is coming on fabulous,' she told him, 'and summer only around the corner. Be sure and tell Maeve now if she's looking for anyone to do the housekeeping to keep me in mind. I used to do a bit for her own mother, you know. It's only marvellous to see her back in Rathbrack, tell her.'

'I will.'

He stood and watched the old lady marching away. Maybe she sold the feathers. That must be it. Some kind of black market in seagull feathers.

When Jack returned, Margaret was up and dressed.

'What would you like for breakfast?' she asked. 'A nice mixed grill? Are you hungry after the fresh air? An omelette?'

'An omelette?' Jack repeated. Whatever Cathal was doing, her self-confidence was soaring.

'With mushrooms?' she suggested. 'Or would you like a steak?'

Obviously she had flipped and thought he was Cathal. If she knew the lecherous thoughts he had had....

'Just some of your mother's soda bread and coffee, please, Margaret.'

'You're sure?'

'Yes.'

'Would you like some laundry done?'

Now he just stared disbelievingly. 'Has Cathal been getting you to smoke funny-looking cigarettes?'

'Oh, God. I might as well tell you.'

He was tempted to order her omelette rather than hear whatever she might tell him about her personal life, but she was already sitting down opposite him. 'I'm sure Maeve will be up soon,' he suggested.

'He didn't want to talk to her, just to you.'

'What? Who?'

'Jack, I'm really sorry. It just went out of my head last night.'

'What are you talking about?'

'A man called looking for you. From America.'

Jack sighed. 'Who?'

'Ron Berg something.'

'Aaron Rothberg?'

'That's it!'

Jack looked at his watch. It was after midnight in LA but Aaron was an information junky. Better to call him and wake him than to leave him waiting. He stood up.

'You're not cross?' she asked.

He laughed. 'I should be, but no. I just hope Cathal's not as hopelessly distracted from his work — or wandering around half-asleep up there! Bring me some coffee by the phone, will you?'

The idea of embarrassment must have been born watching pale Irish skin change colour. For such an undemonstrative people, when this feeling took hold of them they were as good as naked. Margaret could not back away fast enough, and far too late she covered her face with her hands and fled to the kitchen, leaving Jack to chuckle his way to the hall phone.

Aaron was indeed awake.

'Jeez, glad you called, man!'

'What's up?'

'Jack, how far are you into that script?'

'I still have another month or two to go.'

'No, no, I mean, what page are you on?'

'Oh, around seventy or so.'

There was a pause at the far end, then Aaron said, 'I'd better come over and see you.'

'What? When?'

'Like, right away.'

'Something's gone wrong, hasn't it?'

'Maybe, maybe not. Look, here's what I want you to do. Wrap up what you have. Add, say, ten pages, and pad it out with screen directions. Anyway, just give me something finished to take back next week.'

'Next week!'

'Yeah. Hey, can't say more on the phone. See you day after tomorrow. I'll call back with flights. You comfortable with that?'

'Yes. No. Whatever.'

They both hung up and it was Jack's turn to cover his face

with his hands. There were only two possibilities here. Either the project had been shit-canned or there was a palace coup in the works at the studio, which would almost certainly lead to the same result.

Cathal and Sonny stood in the hallway of the house looking up at the roof-beams around them. On their left, over the bedrooms, were the familiar crosspieces of a ceiling. Here there would be an attic with skylights. But on the right, over the huge living-room, there would be a vaulted ceiling, and to support that they were now swinging into place a series of huge inverted vees, made of heavy pre-stained timber, bracketed and braced near the apex.

'We'll get the lot of these up today,' said Sonny. 'The roofers can start at the far end tomorrow, and if the weather holds we'll be working indoors a couple of weeks from now.'

'They say there's warm weather on the way,' said Cathal.

Sonny grunted and Cathal was about to leave when he felt the fisherman's strong hand on his arm. He turned to see the weather-beaten face close to his own.

'Are you serious about Margaret?' asked Sonny very quietly.

'I think so.'

'You think so? Well you'd better make your mind up — one way or the other. She's all we have, you know, and I don't want her messed around, by anyone, d'you hear?'

'I do.'

'Then stay out of her room!'

Cathal nodded. Sonny loosened his grip and they both went about their tasks.

The weather remained warm and clear all that day, and the following day started off the same. But in the early afternoon dark clouds rolled up from the south-west, and from the hill they saw the occasional flash of lightning on the horizon. Then, around three, it began to rain, big heavy drops that splashed on the timbers, and, driven by a rising wind, pummelled the polythene that was draped over the first of the internal walls now ready for plasterwork.

'Ah, we may call it a day,' Sonny roared. 'This is a right storm coming. Come on and I'll buy anyone a drink that wants it.' He looked up to the top of the ladder where Forty-coats seemed not to have heard him and was staring into the rain as if looking for something.

The electrician and plumber slammed their toolboxes and ran for their vans, shouting to anyone who wanted to come with them. Thunder rumbled through the clouds above the hill and the downpour grew stronger.

'We're finished here for the day, MacHenry!' Sonny shouted one last time before leaving him.

Cathal was sitting in his car, calculating how many roof-tiles of each type they would need, when the rain began drumming on the metal. He decided that he too would rather be indoors, and reversed down onto the road ahead of the first Toyota Hiace.

Before the little convoy had pulled up outside Sweeney's the sea had gone from deep blue as far as the western horizon to a churning, foaming, dark green that merged with the rain just beyond the harbour wall. The tradesmen scurried head-down to the side door and shouted with relief once inside. There were a few other customers gathered below the tele-vision, pints in hand, watching the horse-racing from Leopardstown, still in bright sunshine far to the east.

Eddie O'Shaughnessy sat with his back to an ocean win-dow that was being slapped now with rain and spray.

'Bedad, that was a short summer, lads, what?' he said as the others tried to avoid looking at the patch and dressing where once his eye had been.

''Tis early in the summer for a storm like this, right enough. A tropical storm they said on the telly,' Micko added, wiping rings of overflowed beer from the counter and awaiting the men's orders.

Owen Fitzgerald was pulling a slurry spreader behind his tractor across one of the big flat pastures near the house when the rain started. He looked behind to see a bright flash of lightning in the clouds carrying the rain in over the sea.

'No fucking point staying out here for that,' he muttered and gunned the tractor towards the open gate and up the sodden cow-path to the milking parlour.

From the tractor seat he could see his black and white herd beginning to huddle in against the hedges of the second field up the peninsula. He thought of going up and driving them down to the lower fields, but they were in no harm, just wet and windswept, and he would be out in the rain for another half an hour or more doing that. The storm would pass over in an hour or so and then he would go up and bring them down for milking.

A day for the high stool, as they say. He jumped down from the tractor and ran to the car, lowered himself into the seat and left. It was either that or sit in the house, with Olivia chain-smoking her way through this, like every, crisis. He was always telling her he should take out life insurance on her because she was sure to croak soon enough with lung cancer.

Noreen Fletcher sat at the table in her cottage, listening to the deafening drumming of the rain on the roof. In front of her she had a lined hardback notebook opened to blank pages, and she twirled the top of a pen between her lips. There was a flash somewhere out the back, followed a few seconds later by a deep roll of thunder.

She hoped the storm would pass directly overhead. Words came and went in her head, but they were all associations that did not lead to anything new. Portent. Majestic. Empty barrel of the gods. Light. Dark. Unseen forces. Madness.

It was for days like this she had come to Rathbrack. Elemental fury. If only she had the strength to pull herself to the cliff-top. But no, she would have to be content to observe from within her stone hut. An encounter with the gods. And then there was another much brighter flash. She wheeled herself up against the small front window. Half-night. Boiling sea. Cauldron. Portent again. No, more, an arrival. An arrival?

No sooner had this thought taken shape than there was a much brighter flash and in the light she saw a face at her window. And then it was gone. But she recognised him — the beggarman who had been around for the past few weeks. Moving from right to left, climbing up the cliff road. Was he the arriving visitor? The pen shook in her hand and she spun back over to the table.

No, not him. He was already here. What was he doing? Why had the gods lit him up for her? An arrival. The thunder from this last flash boomed overhead. The storm was almost here.

Owen pushed open the door of Sweeney's and rubbed his hands briskly together. 'Haven't seen one like this in many a year!' he said cheerfully, and joined the storm-watchers at the bar.

'Sheet lightning they call that when it lights up everywhere,' said one of the builders to Cathal. 'Has to be raining. Spreads the blast around.'

'Are you scared?' asked Eddie.

Cathal, standing next to the maimed crew-hand, shook his head.

'Well, maybe you should be,' Eddie continued.

'What's that supposed to mean?'

Bucketfuls of rain slapped against the windows.

A hand untwisted the baling twine that held shut the gate leading from the field where the cattle were lowing together by the hedge, and a heavy walking stick beat the first few into running into the upper field, where Maeve had dreamt of building her house. The herd followed, stampeding through the opening, jumping up on the cows ahead to push them through the gap that must lead away from the terror of where they were.

And for a few seconds it must have seemed to these beasts that this field was a refuge, because the rain slackened and the wind eased away, and the animals trotted out into the open and gathered together, where they, like the house that was never built, had a view in all directions but back over the rise to the cliffs.

The eye of the storm travelled on, over Noreen's cottage and the village and its pub. The wind and rain closed in on the cattle with a renewed savagery, confusing them because it whipped them from a new direction now. Through her partly open windows Noreen caught the tang of ozone, knew what such a powerful charge in the air must mean, and gripped the edge of her table.

'You should be scared,' said Eddie. 'Because if this is what they did to me,' — he pointed to his eyepatch — 'I'd hate to be in your fucking shoes when the fairies catch up with you!'

The charged air would have cracked the cliff-top in a single bolt of lightning had it not been raining, but now, as it blew in from the sea with the cyclone of wet clouds, it discharged down to earth through the rain, spreading out into a bright flash over the whole upper peninsula and hitting the backs of the standing cattle on the way.

Their howls of pain were lost in the burst of thunder that came instantly now with no distance to travel.

The blast had enough energy to crack the back window as it passed Noreen, and they felt it in their guts in Sweeney's.

Cathal faced down Eddie, but was lost for words as he knew the man had been a rival for Margaret. And then the flash came and pulsed by the windows and Cathal was sure — sure enough that he would later draw with great precision what he had seen — that it was not Eddie that was standing there in that instant, but a warlike savage.

The man had hair drawn back in a plait from his face, was tattooed in zig-zag patterns around his neck and chest, and armed with a stone axe and flint dagger. He was almost naked, and wet, dripping wet, as if he had just run up from the sea. And he too had only one eye.

Like Eddie, his right eye was missing, but this seemed to be no accident. It was highlighted with concentric circles of light and dark face paint, and then rays of bright paint that directed you to look at the empty socket. And while you did that he watched you with his good eye, and you knew he meant for you to be transfixed with terror and that he was going to kill you.

The legs of the lifeless cattle buckled under them. As one keeled over, it pulled down others, until none of them remained standing.

The centre of the storm slipped over the half-finished house on the hill and delivered a sheet of lightning there too before the bad weather moved on inland and the sky began to grow lighter once more out over the sea.

Owen Fitzgerald's herd lay in the wet grass, all of them dead, or so disabled that they would have to be shot, the live ones staring dumbly up at him when he arrived, the rain and wind now almost gone, so that if someone had come on the scene without knowing about the storm, they would have been baffled; it would have been beyond their imagination, to comprehend what had caused this loss of life.

Chapter Twelve

J ack stood in the foyer of the Ballylacken Hotel and looked at his watch one more time.

'Will I try him again, Mr Amonson?' the girl behind the desk asked.

'No. I guess if he's fallen asleep again he needs it.'

'Hey, Jack!'

They both looked up to see Aaron Rothberg trotting down the stairs. He came over, banged the room key down on the wooden countertop and said, 'Say, kid, is there a water shortage or something around here?'

'Oh no,' the receptionist replied.

'That's what kept me, Jack. Took forever in the damn shower.'

'I'm sorry,' said the girl. 'I'd move you to another room but I don't think it'll be any better.'

'Oh well, we'll just live dirty.'

'This hotel is two hundred years old, you know,' she added.

'Jeez, don't you think you should upgrade the plumbing?'

'Yep, he's over his jetlag,' said Jack, winking at the girl.

'The phones do work, don't they?' Aaron put on a look of horror that caused her to laugh.

'Oh yes! And I won't forget to take down your messages, don't worry.'

They left her and walked out into the sun, which was beaming warmly through the beech trees around the hotel.

'So, let's walk and talk,' said Aaron.

'Okay, I'll take you to our beach,' said Jack. 'We'll pick up

Maeve later and come back here for dinner.

They sat into the Peugeot, rolled down the windows and cruised down the tree-lined avenue, the muted shadows of the leaves above them slipping back over the car.

'So they're all out?' Jack asked, resuming the conversation they had begun during the morning's drive up from Shannon.

'Everyone. The execs all got shafted and the new crowd canned all their minions first thing.'

'Bummer. I mean, it's not like they made *Heaven's Gate*....'

'Yeah, but Excalibur hasn't had a blockbuster since *The Steel Blade*.'

They crested one of the many humps in the coast road and met a flight of swallows heading inland.

'And you're convinced they won't do *Steel Blade Two*?'

'Absolutely, Jack. I know these guys. They have their own pet writers, actors, projects they've been touting. They'll keep it in development forever. Just take the money and run.'

'No hope they'll sell it to an indy?'

'Not a chance. Hey, you made a killing out of it.' Aaron gestured to the house on the hill that had now come into view. 'Time to move on. Get the old brain working on a new plot we can pitch to someone else.'

They slowed, then turned off the road onto the sandy field behind the dunes. Jack drove all the way to where the soft sand began, and they climbed out and banged the doors. Theirs was the only car, and the storm the previous day had washed away the usual trail of footprints between the hills, so that the two men left fresh prints behind as they went.

Ahead of them, one wave after another rolled slowly in and broke in a single roar all along the beach, the surf higher than Jack had ever seen it here, the residue of the stormy weather that had come from far out at sea. They were alone, or so Jack thought, until they reached the harder, wetter sand near the breakers, and turned to walk at the ocean's edge.

Now he noticed someone coming towards them from the far end of the beach.

'So no one's even going to read this thing — not any time soon anyway,' Aaron was saying.

It was a woman, or a girl, in a long lightweight dress that

flapped around her in the breeze. Her hair too blew around, so that she had to keep tossing it back from her face.

As they drew closer he saw that she was a tall, slim, young woman, with fair hair — golden when it caught the sunlight — a thick wavy mane. Her dress clung to her hips, but was otherwise loose, coming and going so that it revealed the shape of her legs, and the absence of a bra.

Jack tried to keep his eyes on her face, but it was hopeless. The soft sheer material easily showed the outline of each breast, pressed in by the wind to show the small bumps of her nipples.

'You know her?' Aaron asked.

'No.'

'So it could be me she's smiling at?'

Now Jack met her eyes and it was true — her lips had spread and parted in a wide smile.

'Good afternoon,' said Aaron.

She made no reply and strode on past between them and the sea, her face now in shade, the sun behind her as she glanced sideways at them.

Green eyes. No one who saw her would ever forget that about her. She had penetrating green eyes that could take on a look of rapturous serenity, or one of calculated endeavour, or a beseeching stare, with the slightest movement of her eyelids. And if all of this was not apparent in those first glimpses of her, certainly the promise of it was there.

She slipped past, and both men turned for another look. The light on the left side of her arms and legs shone on smooth pale limbs, and the hair — a rippling cascade falling to half-way down her back — caught the sun at every stray lock and ending, as though within the hair itself there existed a thousand points of light.

She walked on, just far enough to avoid the need for conversation and then swung around, knowing that they would be watching, flinging her hair towards the sun, and fixed an unsmiling, perhaps curious, stare on them.

Jack and Aaron gave a casual wave each and, apparently satisfied with this, she turned back and continued down the beach. She moved too fast for someone lost in contemplation, was too sure in her stride, as though she knew what it was she had to accomplish and, with the power of her beauty on her side, was certain of her own success.

At least that was how Jack chose to view her as he and Aaron resumed their walk and their own machinations about how best to proceed as suppliers to the world of make-believe on the other side of the ocean.

Fr John Byrne was not without his aesthetic sensibilities. It was impossible to dwell on individual faces when saying mass before a crowd of several hundred people, and this Sunday morning his church was full to overflowing, as though this might be midnight mass on Christmas Eve.

Communion went on to the point that he thought they would run out of hosts. If Maeve Fitzgerald was at mass today, she did not flaunt herself in one of her fine outfits. But it was a glorious sunny day outside and he would shed his vestments in time to exchange pleasantries with his parishioners as they left, which would take longer than usual with this large turnout.

Some of the people lining up were entirely new faces and when they said 'Amen' he could distinguish flat Dublin accents, lilting Cork or Kerry ones, and even the timbre that marks out a Northerner. And they just didn't have the look of tourists, he thought, as he finished up the mass.

'Go in peace to love and serve the Lord,' he bade them.

'Thanks be to God,' the congregation replied, then stood while the priest and his altar boys moved out of sight through the door that led to the sacristy.

A few minutes later he was outside and walking towards the far end of the building along the side furthest from the car park, which was clearly full, as the sun glinted on the paint of cars parked all down one side of the main road.

He reached the front entrance as the throng was in full flow down the three steps. A man he had never seen before came up to him, wearing a brown suit and a pioneer pin.

'That was a grand mass, Father.'

'I'm glad you enjoyed it. And where are you from?'

'We drove all the way from Portarlington this morning.'

He could never remember where that was. Somewhere in the midlands. The man's wife and another couple were gathered a few feet away.

'And are you visiting someone in the area?' Byrne asked.

'Oh God, no, Father. Oh, we've never been here before in our lives. We came to see the statue.'

'The statue?'

'Of Our Lady!'

'I see. Well, you just go around the corner there.'

The man hesitated, looked back at his party, then back at the priest. 'We saw it earlier,' he said, then reached into his jacket pocket. 'We just wanted to make a small offering, Father. My wife's sister is very ill. The doctors say there's nothing they can do.' He produced an envelope and handed it over. By the feel of it, it contained several folded large-denomination notes.

'There was nowhere to leave that this morning, Father. But you must be a very holy man that she chose your church. The sister's name is in there. Will you say a mass for her?'

'I will indeed. Be sure and take a look at our beautiful Celtic cross while you're here.'

The man assured him that they would and he and his friends joined the stream of people disappearing from view towards the car park.

He had just begun in that direction himself when someone took a flash photo of him, and then he became aware of the traffic jam that had built up. The parked cars on the road had made it too narrow for two cars to pass on the bridge, and the traffic was backed up in both directions, so no one could drive out the front gate. When he rounded the corner he saw that it was as bad at the side gate, as the cars were backed up past it from the junction with the main road.

And this was just the start of the problem, as most people had yet to get into their parked cars. Instead they were gathering around the grotto between the church and the school. There were women kneeling on the concrete with rosary beads, fathers holding small children up to see over the crowd, a man with a camcorder on his shoulder, and old men blessing themselves and holding onto each other for support.

'What do you make of that then, Father?'

Byrne recognised the voice of Sonny Mulcahy even before he saw him. And with him was one of the parish committee stalwarts, his wife Maura.

'Well, now that I see it, I suppose it was bound to happen. People have heard the rumours, and now they're coming to see for themselves,' he replied.

'And what's the Church's official view on all this?' Sonny asked.

'The Church has nothing to say at present,' said the priest.

Maura nodded approvingly. 'The Catholic Church never comments on these miracles until it's done a very thorough investigation,' she informed them.

'Yes, well, all the same, I think we'd better do something about this parking situation before next Sunday in case another crowd shows up.'

'Oh I think you may count on it, Father,' said Maura. 'We're booked out for the next six weeks, and people pleading with us to give them phone numbers of anywhere else they might get a room.'

'Gridlock in Rathbrack!' Sonny laughed. 'Not much point walking down to Sweeney's either. We won't get in the door.'

'Nothing like a few pints to enhance one's powers of visualisation,' said Byrne, and began down towards the grotto to mingle with this sudden new flock.

'Come in, the door's open!' Noreen called out in reply to a polite knock on her door.

'Hello, Miss Fletcher,' said Margaret, swinging open the door. 'Have we come at a bad time?'

'Oh, Margaret,' said Noreen, recognising the local girl. 'No, not at all. I had the door open earlier but all sorts of people came in asking for directions, and then they seemed put out when I wouldn't go out and point to where the blooming grotto is!'

'We don't want to bother you....' Margaret persisted.

'And who's this?'

'Howya. I'm Cathal Ó Murchú.'

'Ah, the architect. Sit down, sit down!'

'The reason we came...' began Margaret, looking to Cathal for support.

'I've read some of your poetry,' said Cathal. 'And, well, I know you're into Irish mythology and all that.'

'And are you one of the Dublin intellectual crowd who say I've dipped into Yeats and given it all a feminist spin and no more?'

'Emm ... ah, no....'

'Less than convincing, Cathal.' She winked at Margaret, putting the girl more at ease.

Cathal produced a piece of paper he had been holding by his side and placed it on the table. It was a pencil drawing of the strange transformation of Eddie during the storm. He pointed out the various features, explained how it had really been Eddie there before and after, but that he had clearly seen this, and drawn it from memory.

'I can't get it out of my mind,' he concluded.

'He was looking at you with his good eye?' she reiterated.

'Yes.'

'And you, Margaret, anything strange?'

The girl shook her head and slid a hand into Cathal's. Noreen studied the sketch again.

'It's very detailed,' she said. 'Are you sure you saw all this?'

'Does it make any sense to you?' Cathal asked.

Noreen backed her wheelchair away a little so that she could look at both of them.

'I'm not sure we can ever make sense out of these things the way you mean, Cathal. But I'll tell you what my interpretation of this is. There are two possibilities here. Either this fellow is, or was, a hero and what you saw was some sort of representation of what they call his "warpspasm", when he pulls one eye in and sticks the other way out — in other words, goes into a primeval rage that maximises his ferocity — or....' She looked at the sketch again.

'... or, given the connection between this and Eddie, the

permanent sacrifice of an eye, the very deliberate ornamentation, the idea that what we're looking at is half mask, half face....'

The young couple hung on her words. But she was almost afraid to go on, as if she might make some self-fulfilling prophecy, and feared that she had already done that at the instant of this same bolt of lightning. And then she realised what it was that really stopped her.

It wasn't them at all. She too was connected to this. She knew that now. Whatever was unfolding in Rathbrack was a web that now included all of them. She was not simply an observer, sharing her specialist knowledge. She was a part of this and she should rightly fear the consequences.

'Half mask,' Cathal repeated. 'What's he hiding?'

Noreen looked at the picture again.

'I don't think he's hiding anything, really. He's forcing us to hide, to be afraid. She pointed to the missing eye, and her finger shook. 'This was a ritual mutilation. It has to do with inner space. You know the idea of the blind prophet — the belief that people who can't see in this world are always seeing in the dream world, what we can't see — visions.'

'He's trying to be in both worlds at the same time?' Cathal suggested.

'Yes,' she agreed quietly. 'He's calling on the powers of the other world, and he's conquered his fear of pain and death. I don't think any of us would want to meet up with this fellow or his friends. They did this to him to make him fearless, and if you're not from his tribe....'

'This is reading a whole fucking hell of a lot into this,' said Cathal.

'I know,' Noreen replied. 'Maybe far too much. Can I keep this for a while and think about it?' She held up the picture.

'Sure,' said Cathal, standing up. 'I don't need it to remind me of what I saw.'

'What should he do?' asked Margaret as she too rose.

'Now that's a very big question, Margaret. Maybe he should marry you?'

The girl blushed, but Noreen saw that this was not a new thought for either of them, although she was sure they had never discussed it.

'Thanks for your time, Miss Fletcher,' said Cathal. 'I must re-read your stuff.'

They had the door open, their faces in the sun, when Noreen found herself saying, 'I think you should leave Rathbrack. Both of you.'

They looked back at her without saying anything, then pulled the door shut.

'Look,' said Noreen, 'I know the last time we all got together wasn't a great social success, but I just don't see the point in burying our heads in the sand here. You have to agree that it's worth talking this thing through one more time?'

This evening it was a party of five in her living-room: Maeve, Jack, the priest and the second American, Aaron. Now, with the lengthening of the evenings, they ate by daylight, a help-yourself buffet of salad and pasta.

'So, tell us what you really think of this, John,' said Maeve, knowing him well enough now to know that he preferred this familiarity when he was beyond the gaze of his more devout parishioners.

'I'd have to say at this point I don't think this has anything to do with your house or the rath.'

'How can you not see?' Noreen interjected.

'Let him continue,' said Maeve.

'Hundreds of people are saying they see or hear things at the grotto, and if you put any credence at all in that, you'd have to conclude that it is their faith as Catholics that's behind the phenomenon.'

'These people see what they want to see,' said Noreen.

'And are we not all guilty of that?' Maeve asked.

'Sure works in the movies,' said Aaron, drawing everyone's attention. 'I mean, you know how it is, Maeve. Look at all these macho brandnames: Redford, Eastwood, even this new guy, Stallone. All little guys. But the public see them on the big screen, killing everyone, scoring big time, and they create these heroes in their own minds. That's why it's so unpredictable for us. We just never know what they'll see.'

'Yes, redemption,' said Noreen. 'That's what we're all after. Everywhere the Church puts up these statues people eventually attribute healing powers to them. And it's always the mother, never her divine son. The earth goddess....'

'So why don't Americans see moving statues? Where's their Lourdes, Fatima, Knock, whatever?' asked Maeve.

'Only happens in Catholic countries,' said Jack.

'We see flying saucers instead,' joked Aaron.

'Yes, that's right,' said Maeve, taking him seriously. 'And who sees them? Well? The same feeble-minded rednecks who see all these apparitions here. It's usually some teenage girl who later becomes a nun who channels the divine energy.'

'The community sacrifice,' Noreen muttered.

'Speaking of teenagers,' said Maeve, 'Margaret told me about their little visit up here last week.'

'How old is she?' Noreen asked.

'Almost twenty,' Byrne replied. 'She's out of school two years now. Her mother is never done begging me for advice on what the girl should do.'

'She should shack up with the architect and get out of here,' Noreen answered.

'Amen,' said Maeve.

'Jeez, listen to these Celtic women,' said Aaron. 'They really know how to get their claws into you!'

'But we're worth it,' said Maeve. 'Aren't we, Jack?'

Jack nodded, but his attention was on Noreen. 'Cathal left you a drawing, right?'

'He did.' She swivelled around in her chair and slid the paper out from within a notebook, where she had been writing about it. They passed it around — Maeve, Jack, Aaron, Fr John Byrne, and back to Noreen.

'Do you think he really saw this?' Jack asked.

'He certainly believes he did.' Noreen looked around at all of her guests. 'Am I the only one who believes these events are connected?' she asked.

Their silence was answer enough.

'I think we have to be very careful not to intertwine pagan superstitions and the imaginings of creative people with true religion and the presence of God,' said Byrne.

The others groaned.

'I'm sorry,' said Jack. 'I know I'm just a fair-weather agnostic, but to me they are all pretty much the same. I'd say
we sparked off a new interest in the paranormal, which got
hyped up in Sweeney's and now has gotten out of hand.'

'And do you not think we're a bit rich in coincidences
here?' asked Noreen. 'What about Owen Fitzgerald's cattle,
zapped at exactly the moment Cathal saw this?' She waved
the sketch above her.

Jack shrugged. 'And did the lightning storm not inspire
you at all, Noreen? You're a writer.'

'Yes,' she said, nodding slowly at him. 'That's why I'm
being such a bore about all of this.'

'Well, now, don't you see, Noreen?' began the priest. 'Isn't
that what Jack's getting at? We're all looking for meaning and
significance in our lives, so we're susceptible to believing in
coincidences.'

'Ooooh!' Noreen banged the sketch down on the sideboard where it had come from and clenched her teeth.

'It must be hard for you,' said Maeve softly, 'stuck in that
wheelchair. You must always be looking for something to
believe in that will keep you going?'

It was clear that the three men felt Maeve had gone too far
here, because they all tried to butt in at once. Byrne won out.

'And Maeve, have you not spent a good part of your life
looking too? Only to find that whatever it is you were missing is right here in Rathbrack?'

'Now that has a ring of Greek irony,' said Noreen.

'Beats chasing after wacky cults and ... and looking for
symbolism out the window of my stone hut!' Maeve looked
deliberately around the room in case Noreen didn't get it.

'Have you been up to see the house?' Byrne asked Aaron.

'Yeah. Looks to me like it's almost done.'

'If the weather holds,' said Jack, 'we'll be moving in in
about three weeks.'

'So what do you think of all this, Aaron?' Noreen asked. 'I
mean, you're Jewish. You must see this a little differently.'

Aaron leaned back in his chair and folded his arms. 'It's
not acceptable to have a different viewpoint in America any

more just because of your religion. However, I don't see the Catholic Church as holding any higher moral ground than you, Noreen.'

'Oh, I like this,' said the poet. 'Keep going and I'll give you a signed copy of my last collection!'

'Great! I could use something a little above the drivel I wade through every day to read on the plane — sorry, Jack. I guess you have a real problem here in this country, guys. You got this Christianity taking the credit for everything, but you imported that, and it's sitting on top of some older ideas, and the two just don't work together.'

'No one coerced the Irish into Christianity,' said Byrne. 'Not like the Spanish in the New World.'

'Yeah, well, still, your whole religion is based on ours,' Aaron added.

'And we're very grateful to you for bringing us the Messiah,' the priest retorted.

'That's bullshit!'

'No, no. We've been very careful to tell people not to blame the Jews....'

'Now that there aren't any around. Did Pope Pius X say one word against the Nazis in all those years? Well? Did he?'

Byrne had no answer for this, so Aaron continued.

'And they knew. They knew what was happening. So, hey, I'm sorry, but I'm ready to bet that Christianity stole the best ideas they could find here too and then stood by while their new converts did in the people who gave them it all.'

'Dead on, Aaron!' said Noreen, shaking a fist in support. 'We have to put up with St Brigid now, who was a pagan goddess, and their whole calendar is an overlay of the pagan one — May altars, All Saints' Day....'

The sun slipped down over the bay, warming to pink the clouds of a mackerel sky. Its last rays, just above the wave-tops, painted the cliffs at the end of the peninsula with a corn-yellow wash and sent a shaft of light in the four-paned front window of Noreen Fletcher's cottage, dazzling the Hollywood agent and the priest for a moment, before leaving the land in shade, and slowly dying over the ocean.

Chapter Thirteen

'She really is exasperating, with all her half-baked theories, isn't she?' complained Maeve as she, Jack and Aaron reached their car where they had parked it by the end of the pier.

'What about a pint in Sweeney's then to calm you down, honey?'

'Oh God, I'd like to, but I'm not up to it. I'm sorry, Aaron, I just need a lot of sleep these nights. I've completely revised my views on teenage pregnancy now — all women should have their babies when they're sixteen!'

'Sure,' Aaron replied. 'I'm all for that. Just give them my phone number!'

'Jack, give me the keys and I'll drive myself home. You two have a couple and walk — it'll do you good.'

The two men stood politely by while she reversed up the hill, before roaring away from them. When they opened the front door of the pub they were surprised by the buzz on a week night. All of the regulars were there, plus some people who were staying at Mulcahys' to see the statue, and others who appeared to have driven out from Kilcashel because Rathbrack was suddenly a place everyone was talking about. Jack even recognised some of the young staff from the Ballylacken Hotel, carousing away their off-hours down here.

'How are you keeping, Jack?' asked Sweeney, in his usual fashion.

'Hey, great, Micko. The usual. Aaron, are you going to try this black stuff before you leave?'

'I don't think so....'

'Oh, come on, it's your last night!'

'Okay then.'

'Right you be,' said Micko and left them.

Aaron slouched against the bar and looked at Jack. 'You know, there is something I just have to say, Jack. So I'm glad we got this time alone ... oh shit!'

'What?'

'Did Maeve pick up that book that Noreen signed for me?'

'I don't think so.'

'Damn. I'll go back and see if she's still up.'

'Look, we can send it on to you.'

'No, I'll get it. Just hang on here!' Aaron backed away and made for the door again. Jack shrugged and turned back to watch Micko complete the two pints.

A hand grasped his shoulder, and Owen Fitzgerald sidled up to him. 'The missus not with you tonight?' he asked.

'She was but she went home early.'

'Mine is at home drowning her sorrows on her own.'

Jack liked Maeve's brother less with every encounter. 'That was a real shame losing the whole herd,' he said.

'You don't know the half of it,' said Owen. 'They're not covered by any insurance. It was an act of God.'

'Oh, jeez. You mean...?'

'Shhh! Not a word to this bollocks!' Owen hissed as Sweeney returned with the two pints.

'A right gold mine you have going these days, Micko,' said Owen.

'Oh, things are looking up, aye, they are, right enough.'

The publican twisted his head in what would have been a sort of curtsey if he had kept the movement going.

'We should probably put up a sign, start advertising, Micko, what?' Owen continued. 'A lot of these people would be keen on second homes here in the holy land, wouldn't you say?'

'Right enough, if it doesn't all turn out to be a hoax.'

Owen put on a look of disbelief. 'Ah now, Micko. I hear the bishop is coming down to inspect things himself. And another child was cured of asthma last week. Oh, bejasus, I think the future looks very bright indeed for Rathbrack and all who sail in her!'

'Well, there's the man has the best house in the town now,' said Micko, nodding at a strange tilt towards Jack. 'Sure you could turn that into a hotel, Jack.'

'No fear. What I want is some peace.'

Micko winked as though in agreement, and left to ring up the drinks.

'Don't tell him what I said!' Owen muttered. 'I need him to put some money into this project on decent terms.' He grabbed Jack's arm. 'But you're family, Jack. So I'll let you in up front for half what it'll cost him. Is that fair? Are you interested?'

'No. No, I'm not. Not right now. I have my own problems.'

'Ah, fuck it! Well, ask Maeve then. I bet she didn't come in because she saw my car outside?'

'No. But I'll be sure and watch out for it myself.'

'Oh, you're a hard man, what? Listen, Jack, she's not going to let me lose the land. She'll want to make some kind of a deal. How can I put it? She's committed to Rathbrack, even if you're not!'

On that note he slid away again, back to the company of quiet, careful, suspicious farmers, a world of which he still believed himself a part.

Jack surveyed the bar, grown wary himself now lest he might catch the eye of some other nuisance. Eddie was there, but the bearded man seemed to have vanished, as these indigents do. Jack felt a pang of pity for someone so alone that he wouldn't be missed here or anywhere. And then he thought of Gladys and shifted away from the bar to see if she was in her usual seat under the television. He could always send her a drink via Micko when he and Aaron were leaving.

She wasn't there. But sitting in her place was the girl from the beach, apparently alone, her long hair clasped back from her face, legs crossed, again in light, loose clothing, which now, in the absence of a wind, draped itself over her lissom form. Her green eyes stared at a point somewhere on the stained table, but she seemed to feel Jack watching her because her gaze rose to challenge his directly. And then, before he could turn away, she smiled and waved a hand in recognition.

Aaron looked in the window of the cottage, but the lights were out except for a faint glow from the bedroom. He was about to knock on the door with his knuckles when he decided that would create an unnecessary problem for the woman, and he grasped the handle gently instead. With his thumb he pushed down on the latch and the door gave inwards silently.

Noreen was saying something, but he couldn't make out the words — maybe reading her work aloud as he knew so many of them did. He was going to announce himself, but the book was still on the table, only a few paces across, and now he was inside he would only startle her.

'You should feel good about this,' she was saying. 'Oh, yes, really good. You're visiting the sick ... oh, yes, visit me there.'

He reached the table, leaned over and picked up the book, but now as he tiptoed around to go back to the door, he faced into the bedroom, with a view of the back wall of the house.

'More!' she said. 'Oh, God, I miss this so much. You have no idea. Just hold my knees, oooh....'

At the end of the wall, set diagonally into the corner, was a small dresser, and on it was a hinged three-pane mirror whose centre panel reflected the bed which took up the rest of the unseen room. And on the bed the poet lay spread-eagled, her silk blouse unbuttoned, her bra pulled up clear of her breasts, which she fondled with slow back and forth movements of her fingers, while Fr John Byrne, standing in the tiny space between bed and wall, leaned in over her and pulled her knees out past him.

'Look at me, you bastard!' she said in a suddenly clear voice. Aaron let the book slip, but caught it again, and backed away towards the door. 'I'm not just some receptacle for this, I'm a woman!'

'Not so loud,' said the priest and Aaron froze, but he was talking to Noreen. They hadn't noticed him.

'More! Do it harder or I *will* scream,' she said in a quieter but more urgent voice, and as Aaron slipped out the door the bedsprings began to creak and he heard the man's grunts rising and quickening.

'Hi, I'm Jack! Jack Amonson. I think we almost met?'

The girl looked up at him and for a few moments some doubt seemed to flicker on her face, then the wide smile returned.

'Yes, on the strand,' she said.

It was not a familiar Irish accent, but he would have to hear more to place it, or ask her.

'Are you just visiting Rathbrack?' he asked.

To this she made no response, just looked away, then back and pointed to the two drinks in his hands.

'Is one of those for me?' she asked.

'Oh, I'm waiting for someone. Can I buy you a drink?'

'Just water.'

So she worked at looking like this. No wonder she had such perfect skin. Jack placed his two pints on her table, nodded and smiled.

From the bar he looked back once again at the girl, now staring at the Guinness, and he shrugged to himself. True, he wouldn't be doing this if she were not this radiant golden-haired beauty, but where was the harm? And as he looked around at the cast of characters that made up the everyday population here, it was hardly an act of betrayal to engage this lone tourist in conversation.

He returned with her drink and lowered himself onto an empty stool.

'Thank you,' said the girl, repositioning herself with her left hand on the back of the seat, fingers lost in the waves of shining hair.

It was impossible to say what age she was. In her early twenties? There was no ageing at all around the eyes, and, as far as Jack could judge, she wasn't wearing make-up. Maybe she was much younger than that. Here with her family. Too young to drink — not that Micko would either know or care.

'Hey, man, I got the book!' Aaron slid down onto the empty length of seat next to the girl and waved Noreen Fletcher's thin paperback volume of poems in front of Jack. 'So, we meet again,' he said, offering a hand to the girl. 'I'm Aaron Rothberg, and you are...?'

'Áine,' she replied, holding his gaze while he took her hand. The sound of the name echoed in Jack's head, as if she had spoken it from the far end of some narrow tunnel. Awn. Awn. Awn-ya.

'You look familiar,' said Aaron.

'Who do I look like?' she asked very directly.

'Do you act, or model?'

She shook her head and looked back to Jack.

Aaron persisted. 'No, no. Doesn't she remind you of someone, Jack?'

Jack tilted back and to right and left to show his appreciation of this opportunity to study her face. The lighting in Sweeney's was an afterthought, a combination of cheaply shaded bulbs that dangled from the ceiling as a legacy from the building's initial electrification, and chintzy tasselled lamps in pairs around the outer walls between the windows. But here she was also side-lit by the ever-changing glow of the television on its shelf above them.

Áine stared intently back at him. With no movement, and no bright sunlight to accentuate her colouring, it was her bone structure, the shape in the smoky air, that he noticed. And here was one of those faces that would age magnificently. She need not depend on a pretty smile, nor a demure look, nor some intangible innocence that only the very young possess. Were they to make this her death mask, or make one of her fifty years from now, people would equally conclude that this was a face that had embodied a universal image of beauty.

Her eyebrows were heavier and darker than convention might dictate, but that would only add to the expressive power of the eyes. Her nose too was straight and narrow, and not sculpted into the elf-like miniatures offered in Beverly Hills, but even they would never try to improve on her jawbone, a flawless frame that held in place taut cheeks. And with her mouth now closed, it was as if, sealed inside those full lips, and behind those calmly watching eyes, she held the means to make men happy, or not, as she chose.

'I'd say, maybe Hayworth, but with Bacall's eyes,' Jack replied.

'You think so? None of the seventies crowd then — Fonda, Ross?'

Jack shook his head. Aaron shot him a cautionary glance — he was not playing his straight man part the way he should.

'Well, hey, that *film-noir* look is coming back,' said Aaron, undoing the damage and steering them back towards well-rehearsed lines. Jack had seen him do this before at parties, and even in restaurants. For someone very unremarkable in appearance, he had a singular talent for persuading wannabe starlets that a night in the sack with him would be time well spent.

Jack continued to study Áine while Aaron fed her his patter about being a movie producer, always looking for new talent, and how American audiences loved European actresses, and then began shamelessly throwing her name-bait. It was a curious mixture of fact and fiction. Aaron did know Robert Redford, and just about anyone could claim to have met Burt Reynolds, and he could in truth certainly get her face-time with useful people.

But it wasn't working. At first Jack thought Áine simply didn't believe any of this, that it was too improbable a story here in this tiny fishing village, clinging, like a few barnacles, to this windswept shore, and separated by some great gulf of time and space from the world Aaron was describing.

But it wasn't that she disbelieved him. He had been with Aaron when that happened, and they always fired back questions, wanted to know more, because Hollywood was now a kind of universal consciousness, and its icons were the mythological heroes of our time.

This girl just was not interested. She nodded and agreed, as if she believed what he was saying, but yet was not lured

in. As they finished their pints Aaron made one last attempt
to win her over.

'So where are you from?' he asked.

'I told you,' she replied. 'My people were from the North.'

'Yes, but where do you need to get to from here?'

'Home. I just need to go home.'

Now she shifted away from him, as if she had had enough
of this.

'So, listen,' said Aaron. 'I just think you've really got
something, Awny. How would you like an all-expenses-paid
trip to California? Maybe get you a photo shoot or some
acting lessons while you're there? But the thing is, I'm leaving tomorrow, so we'd have to figure this all out tonight.'

She sipped at her mineral water for a few moments as if
weighing up this offer, returned the glass to the table and
placed a hand on Aaron's knee. Jack marvelled at his agent's
ability to prevail in the most unlikely encounters, and when
Áine leaned her face in closer and stroked Aaron's hair with
her free hand he was all set to stand up and excuse himself
for the night.

And then she drew away again and rose to her feet, saying, 'I must go, and you two must have a lot to discuss if
Aaron is leaving.'

Both men began to protest, but she ignored them, and by
the time they were standing she was already near to the side
door. 'Have a safe journey, Aaron,' she said, waving to him,
'and perhaps I'll see you again, Jack?'

'Yes. I'm around. All the time.' But she was gone, slipping
into the doorway and out before he had finished.

'Pity,' said Aaron as he sat down again. 'Jeez, I tell you,
these Irish women are full of surprises.' He picked up
Noreen's poetry and flicked through it. 'You know,' he said,
waving the book at Jack, 'this is more my kind of woman. I
mean she really has it together, knows what she wants, isn't
looking for anything from anyone....'

'Áine wasn't looking for anything.'

'Ah, she led us down the garden path.'

'No, no. You tried to lead her!'

'Whatever. Anyway, I'll see if there's any new drugs or

procedures back in the States that might help Noreen, but I don't think so. I knew another guy with MS and I think he went blind.'

Jack nodded.

'So while we're on the subject of women,' said Aaron, 'how are things really going with Maeve?'

'Hey, fine! She's just having a hard time with this pregnancy, but she's taking care of herself.'

'But she's only three months gone, right?'

'About that.'

'I hope things work out.'

'What do you mean?'

'Hey man, I saw the way you were looking at that girl.'

'Ah for Christ's sake. Now I'm not even to read the menu?'

'Okay, okay. I'm just saying, and maybe I'm way off here, but it looks to me like maybe you're getting a bit tired of this rustic life.'

'I'm not.'

'Hear me out, Jack. This idea of being a tax exile over here is great — you've built this house in Maeve's home town, you're starting a family and all that. But remember your customers are five thousand miles away, and I just don't think you should see yourself as glued to this place. That's all I'm saying.'

'I hear you.'

'Good. So let's have one more of those black beers for the road. It wasn't as bad as it looked.'

Chapter Fourteen

'So why have gas *and* oil?' Cathal asked.

'Makes sense to me,' said Jack, agreeing with his wife.

The architect shrugged. 'So we'll just put a propane tank down here where we already have the concrete pad for the oil; that way it can still be filled by a truck halfway up the hill, and we'll hide it with the landscaping.'

'We need to order that and the furnace right away,' Maeve declared.

'I'll tell Sonny.' Cathal got up and left the dining-room.

Four young Germans chattered away at the other table, two bearded men and two athletic-looking women, all in hiking boots and flannel shirts rolled up to their elbows.

'Getting there,' said Maeve, ticking things off in her notebook.

'So when do you think we can move in now?' Jack asked.

Maeve sighed, and shook her head. 'I know, I know, darling. You can't get a thing done here any more.' She flipped back through the last few pages, then forward again. 'All we really need to do is paint the master bedroom, and then we could, in fact, move into the place.'

'When?'

'Let's see — they're finished the tiling in our bathroom, they've just to put up the mirrors. That means that once the painting is done we can put down the carpet, there'll be no more traipsing back and forth, and then we need to get the bed delivered. The power's on. And the water. We don't need the heat and we can use bottled gas for cooking while they sort out the propane tank.'

'When?'

'Two weeks. At most.'

'Hallelujah! I can finally get some work done.'

'I'm sure Aaron understands.'

'Yes, but he's not the studio.'

She nodded, then asked, 'Did you guys bump into anyone last night?'

'Wow, yes, now that you mention it, I'd forgotten. We met your brother. Well, I did.'

'And where was Aaron?'

'You know. I told you he went back....'

Maeve smirked and put a hand over her mouth. 'I guess I shouldn't be surprised. It's just that they're such opposites.'

'Oh I wouldn't say that.'

'Oh come on, Jack! She's into the earth goddess and the great cosmic oneness, and he's a priest in the service of God the Father. God the Son and God the Holy Ghost, the whole patriarchal bearded messiah thing.'

'So they're both kinda spiritual, right?'

'Yes, well, anyway, what did Owen say?'

'That he's broke — wants us to invest in his little housing scheme.'

'No one in Ireland with a two-hundred-acre farm is broke.'

'Well, you remember Olivia told us they borrowed heavily to build up the herd, and he says the cattle weren't insured.'

'Trust me, Jack. He's saying whatever it is he thinks we'd like to hear. I suppose he said I'd jump at the chance to go after this?'

'Yes. Thinks you'd like to see Rathbrack developed.'

'He just doesn't get it, does he? Why would we want to look out at other people's houses? Jesus, he tried to stop us and now he thinks I'll just roll over and let him put up eyesores when it suits him? It wouldn't surprise me if he killed those cows himself for the money. We got planning permission over his objections, now let's see him do the same thing!'

They should get a dog, Jack told himself as he crossed the road and scaled the low wall that gave onto the sandy flats behind the dunes. That would give him a reason to go walking at night. Not that it was entirely dark. After nearly four months in Ireland he had seen the days go from a dusk that would start in the early afternoon to one that lingered on for hours in the evening.

Yes, a big dog to catch sticks on the beach and lie down on the rug by the fire, and bark at strangers, so that they would all feel safe at night in their new home. But safe from what? Rathbrack was hard enough to find in daylight. There was no crime around here. Surely Aaron had noticed that?

Jack walked on, picking his way along winding trails through the rushes, startling the occasional bird into the air. And that was another thing. He should buy a book about these birds. Learn their names. Maeve was in bed reading by now, if not already asleep. They were visiting Lowry, her obstetrician, tomorrow, and she was not about to give him the opportunity of saying she should get more sleep. And besides, she would be recognised around town.

He felt the cool, fine sand of the dune itself underfoot, and climbed its inland face, throwing up spurts of sand behind each sneaker as he went. He found himself quickening his pace as he neared the top. But when he looked out at the beach, curving away towards the ends of the bay, it was deserted.

Áine was not there. The waves crashed down on the lonely shore again and again, but the girl was not to be seen. He shook his head as if to rid himself physically of this asinine thought and plodded down to meet the oncoming breakers. Like some enormous drum, beating out the rhythm of the ages, the waves thundered relentlessly on. He stood for a while, just listening, and imagined for the first time how the might of the ocean must have impressed the ancient people who had once lived here.

Like all of the doctors in the regional hospital in Kilcashel, Dr Lowry wore a white coat over his shirt and tie. His desk, in the office adjoining his examining room, was hidden under stacks of forms and folders. But he came highly recommended.

'I'm not unduly concerned,' he said. 'At this point everything is fine, Maeve.'

Neither Jack nor Maeve liked this opening statement. Seated side by side in wooden chairs with rounded backs, Jack saw Maeve extend her hand to him and took it.

'You said you had a D and C about ten years ago?'

'Yes' said Maeve.

'Just the one?'

Maeve hesitated, then shook her head. Jack knew she was blushing at the memory, and squeezed her hand.

'Well, in fact,' she said, 'I had an abortion.'

'Why didn't you say so?'

'Because, I didn't know....'

'If an Irish doctor would approve?'

'If my wife's medical history disturbs you, doctor, just let us know and we'll go back to California and have this baby,' said Jack.

'Oh no, not at all!' The man threw both hands in the air. 'My point is that I hadn't noticed, and hadn't been looking for, such extensive scar tissue, that's all.'

'What are you saying?' Maeve asked.

He stood up and walked to his coloured cutaway chart of the womb and Fallopian tubes. 'The embryo is slightly to one side,' he said, 'and that is being caused by the presence of this other scarring here, which is holding back the expansion of your womb on this side. The placenta, I think, is fully functional, but we'll have to wait and see how fast the baby develops. Oh, and there's a better than fifty-fifty chance that we'll have to do a Caesarean delivery'

Maeve threw her hands up to her face and gasped.

'But we are talking a normal baby here, right?' asked Jack.

'Oh yes. If she makes it to full term with no complications — I mean, doesn't lose the baby — then I'm confident it'll be a healthy child. Maybe a little underweight, but that's all. I'm assuming, of course, that there is no other history of congenital defects on either side that you haven't told me about?'

'No.'

'No.'

'Well then, plenty of rest. Avoid stress. Stay healthy your-self, Maeve. You don't smoke, so that's good. And let me know if you've any unusual pains, cramps, whatever.'

Jack looked at Maeve.

'I always preferred one-piece bathing suits,' she said.

'Should we ask him?' Jack reminded her.

'Oh, yes, doctor ... em, what's your advice on having sex?'

Lowry frowned back at her while he thought of an answer to this. Jack was sorely tempted to say — it's not sex with you she's asking about. But he waited and eventually the doctor cleared his throat.

'I'd have to say, proceed with extreme caution,' he said. 'In fact, I'd advise against penetration at all.'

As far as the house was concerned, there was now really nothing for Jack to do except sign the cheques. They had long since chosen and ordered every major appliance, their furni-ture and the paints, woodstains, tiles, curtains and carpets. So Maeve was now busy implementing past decisions. This meant that she was out and about during the day with the car, so that if Jack wanted relief from the pilgrims and tour-ists of the now permanently full Mulcahys' Guest House, he had either to commit himself to the whole day gadding about with Maeve, or take a walk in some direction.

Today, with the promise of being able to work in his own home only a week away, Jack spent a couple of hours read-ing, made a few notes to himself, and left Mulcahys' for a walk to the cliffs.

He had gone into Kilcashel with her yesterday, again, as she was in poor spirits after her visit to the doctor. On the walk from the car park over the bridge to the old part of town, they had dallied at the few boutiques that catered to the women of the area with money. As usual, Maeve was diffident inside and disparaging outside, so he had lost interest as they waited to cross the narrow, busy street, to the last boutique on the tour.

And then the centre mannequin in the window mesmerised him. The sun shone down from behind, leaving a
shadowy outline of the assorted roofs on the walls of the
facing shops. But a gap in the façade allowed a shaft of light
to play directly on the boutique, and he recognised the greyish-
green sleeveless outfit as exactly what Áine had been wearing when he had first seen her on the beach.

'Come on!' Maeve had said, leading the way across. She
might have bought the same clothes somewhere else, but
these shops were hawking exclusivity. And Áine certainly
did not fit the profile of the kind of well-to-do provincial
housewife who, according to Maeve, would shop here.

He was recalling this episode when he spotted her, sitting
on the end of the pier, legs dangling over the edge, reading a
book. Jack was still the far side of Sweeney's, but he waved
anyway. There was no reply, the face mostly hidden by the
long golden hair. Not to worry — there was no escape. Even
if she stood up now, he would be at the near end of the pier
before her.

It was still morning, and as he walked out over the platform of cut granite, past lobster pots and around nets in need
of repair, he saw the sun shining through her hair from the
east, the breeze tickling the ends to life. There were no boats
roped to any of the stone bollards, just the green water rising
and falling below them.

His sneakers made no sound on the solid slabs and his
shadow was thrown to the left, like her own, against the sea-
wall. He should cough or say hello, not creep up like this, but
he didn't. He just strolled slowly to within about ten feet of
her until it occurred to him that she might think him a voyeur.

'Áine?' he said.

She swung around, using her right hand as a prop, and as
she did this the book slipped from her other hand and
dropped down into the sea.

'Oh jeez, sorry,' said Jack, coming up to the edge and
hunkering down.

She laughed, swung her feet back in and stood up. 'Don't
worry. It wasn't very interesting,' she said.

'Oh no, it's my fault. I'll buy you another one.'

'Really, there's no need.'

He straightened up next to her.

'What were you reading?' he asked.

'I was just passing the time. What brings you here, Jack?'

She remembered his name!

'I saw you from over there.'

'You were walking past, then?'

He nodded, still distracted by the book bobbing around on the swell.

'Can I join you?' she asked. There was something about the way she put the question, as if she knew the answer was yes, was always yes, and she was forcing him to say so.

'Well, it's such a great day, I was going to head up to the cliffs.'

'I love the view from up there.'

'So let's go, then.'

She fell into step beside him and they retreated from the pier's end. Áine had no bags — just the sandals, jeans and shirt she was wearing, and again it was her golden hair that held the attention, a veil-like frame to her angelic face. They were walking towards the sun now, and Jack stole a glance at the green eyes at their brightest and saw the beginnings of small freckles across her nose.

'Tell me a bit about yourself, Áine,' he said.

She folded her arms and sighed. 'There's not that much to tell, really. I was born near here and lived here when I was young.'

'But you're still young.'

She smiled at him. 'I'm older than you think, Jack.'

'Oh. So you grew up here?'

'Yes. But we moved away, as everyone does, and I've never returned.'

'You mean till now?'

She didn't answer and seemed to be frowning at the question. They reached Noreen's cottage, and as they passed Jack was tempted to call in, but thought better of it.

'The lady who lives in there is a poet,' he said. 'In fact, that's where we were coming from the other night.'

'Yes, that was the book.'

'You were reading her poems?'

'No. I meant that was the book your friend had!'

'Right!'

They walked on in silence up the steep lane, Áine with her arms folded, Jack with his dug into his pockets. They were approaching the upper field of Owen's farm. So far, Jack had avoided any mention of Maeve, and if Áine had noticed his wedding ring she had chosen not to acknowledge it either.

Even without seeing the ring it was a sure bet she knew he was married. It just showed. He had never known women to get that wrong. They knew when he was married, divorced, and married again. So she must be deliberately avoiding it, allowing him to play out his little fantasy. But why?

The gorse that clung to the tumbled margin between the grassy fields and the sea-battered rocks was all in bloom, great sprays of canary yellow over the thick green bushes.

'Beside yon straggling fence that skirts the way/with blossoming furze unprofitably gay,' Jack recited.

Áine laughed. 'So poetry is not entirely dead in America?'

'Well, it more or less is, but I was a highschool English teacher.'

'Ah!'

He expected her to ask how he got into screen-writing, which would provide him with the answer to his own question. But, consistent with her behaviour with Aaron, she appeared to have no interest in this, and he was left once again to muse on her intentions.

Maybe she had no agenda. Was she even aware that she filled him with desire, let alone intent on pursuing him? Or was she a very cunning gold-digger, content to bide her time while he grew more and more desperate for her? They were alongside the gate that he and Maeve had climbed the day after they had arrived here. Jack stopped and looked in.

'We were going to build a house here,' he said.

'But now you're building it on the hill,' she said, joining him at the gate.

'Yes. My wife's brother wouldn't sell.'

'But he would now?'

'Oh, he desperately wants to, but we're too far along.'

'And why does he want to sell now?'

She had not reacted at all to the mention of a wife.

'His cattle were all killed by lightning here. He needs the money.'

They both leaned on the gate. Some rabbits foraged in the grass, their ears quivering as they sat and chewed on the new spring growth.

'Would you build a house here now, Jack?' she asked quietly.

'Sure! It's still a fantastic location. In fact, he's trying to inveigle me to invest....'

'You don't think the field is cursed in some way by the death of the animals?'

The question was wholly unexpected. He had wanted to see her as an outsider, like himself, and now she had as good as admitted that she too had some involvement in the beliefs that underpinned this strange community.

'You grew up with those superstitions too?' he asked.

She didn't reply, just backed away and folded her arms, and they resumed their walk to the cliff-top. When they reached the edge an updraft whipped at her hair and she narrowed her eyes at this wind as they both peered down at the ocean, steadily carving a new undercut beneath them — a work that could not be measured in human time, the years no more than the ticking of a clock, generations slipping by like minutes, and whole ages the slow movement of its hour hand.

Áine turned suddenly to him and held back her hair that was now blowing across her face.

'What if those cows had been people, Jack?' she asked.

Again she caught him entirely unawares and he had to look back down the hill to refocus before replying.

'I don't know,' he said. 'People are killed in accidents all the time and we drive over those places. We shop where people were gunned down. My God, the world is full of cities that were battlegrounds at some point!'

She shrugged and joined him in looking back inland over the verdant fields where the first dandelions were beginning to flower in the grass, and here and there the leafy hedges were dotted with white flowers. Spring was in evidence everywhere but on the slopes of the hill where the house was nearing completion.

The green tiles and stained timber of the roof did blend in reasonably well as Cathal had planned, but the slopes were strewn with concrete, gravel and builder's debris, and the driveway would remain a bright scar until it was tarmacked in a few weeks time.

'Isn't that your house?' Áine asked.

'Well, mine and Maeve's.'

'Can we walk over there and take a look?' she asked.

'Sure.'

He said it just to please her, but she immediately began picking her way back to the turning space at the end of the lane, and when he just stood there she waved to him to follow her.

They said little as they walked back down through the village. Jack nodded a greeting at the few people who were around, and when they were passing between the old monastery and the churchyard he pointed to the grotto and said, 'I take it you've heard about our talking statue?'

'Statue?' Áine replied.

'That one there, of the Virgin Mary.'

She laughed. 'Is that how they see it — that a virgin has special powers?'

'Well, I'm not Catholic, but I don't think that's the point.'

He wondered was she a virgin, and as she lapsed once more into silence he felt that she knew that she had brought this question into his head. They walked on, turning left on the coast road, and were about halfway to the gate when Áine suddenly moaned out loud, clasped her arms around herself and began to shiver to the point where Jack was afraid she would fall over.

'Áine! Áine, are you okay?' He put his arm around her shoulders and felt her trembling like a small animal that has been badly frightened, 'I think you should sit down.'

But she kept moving forward with tiny steps, and when he tried to hold her back she just looked up at him, her mouth open, her eyes rolled back.

And then, as fast as it had come on her, the turn she had

taken went away. She gasped, leaned a hand on his shoulder, blinked a few times and smiled at him with watery eyes.

'Are you on medication?' he asked.

'No, no. Don't worry. It won't happen again.'

'Are you epileptic, Áine?'

She shook her head.

'Listen,' he said, 'let's go sit in Sweeney's for a while?'

'No, I'm fine. We're this close, let's go on.' The eyes had cleared now and were filled with some fiery resolve. She took his hand and pulled him forward with her.

The building was essentially complete. Jack led Áine up the newly cast steps to the front door, which was open, walked in and said, 'Hello?'

No one replied, but there were voices from his left. He turned right, through double doors that gave onto the huge living-room. Áine followed and looked around her.

Above them there was no ceiling — the wooden beams of the roof were exposed — and the chimney, on the same internal wall as the doors, had been faced with granite all the way to the apex. Large full-length windows gave views to the east, south and west, and another doorway revealed the oak cabinets in the kitchen.

'So, what do you think?' Jack asked as Áine took in the overall design of the house.

'Oh yes, I think I could live here,' she said.

'That's a gas fireplace,' he told her, 'and in here in the kitchen we've got an electric oven and a combination gas and electric hob, and we're looking for a pot-bellied stove for that corner.'

Their steps echoed over the bare floorboards as they walked into the kitchen. Now they heard banging from the far end of the house, then more shouts.

'Let's see who's here,' said Jack.

'I'll wait for you,' Áine replied, hoisting herself up onto one of the counter-tops.

Jack left the kitchen by the far door and followed the central corridor that led to the master bedroom, which took up all of the north end of the house. The first roll of carpet had already been delivered, and the bed itself lay stacked against the wall. In the bedroom there were tools and crumpled packaging on the floor, and on his right, through the open sliding doors that led to the en-suite bathroom, he saw what the commotion was about.

Sonny, Eddie and Fortycoats were all handling a huge mirror into position behind the two matching sinks, and since it was the exact size of the available space they were having problems.

'Just hold it right there!' Sonny shouted.

'I can't!' Eddie yelled, his eye-patch reflecting back at Jack.

'Can I help?' Jack asked.

'Put the flat blade of the screwdriver under his end, Jack!' said Sonny. 'Same as MacHenry has it.'

Jack picked up the screwdriver and looked at Fortycoats' hands. He was bearing the weight of the mirror at his end on the tool and pressing the top in with his other hand. Jack got between Eddie and Sonny and did likewise.

'That's it!' said Sonny and began securing the glass plate to the battens behind it.

MacHenry. At least the guy had a name. A car ground up the driveway outside, but from here it was impossible to see who it was. As Sonny worked his way from one end to the other Jack wondered whether Áine was growing impatient. Hardly. She seemed to be whiling away the time with less to do than he had. Her strange attack came back to him. It had given him a reason to touch her, and now, thinking back on it, he realised that she wasn't wearing a bra.

'Done!' said Sonny.

'Great!' It was Maeve's voice.

Jack released his grip and saw his wife first in the mirror, and then standing in the bedroom holding some bags.

'That was your car?' Jack asked.

She nodded. The fact that she was pregnant was highlighted by the new tent dress she wore, and the way she now stood with her feet apart.

'More kitchen stuff,' she said, holding up the shopping.

'Have you been in there?' Jack asked.

She shook her head and turned back. Jack followed.

'There's someone here I'd like you to meet,' he said, but

when he stepped after her into the kitchen they were alone. He walked into the living-room, but it too was empty.

'You mean the girl?' Maeve asked. He returned to see her unbox a coffee maker. 'She was outside gawking around.'

'Oh, you met her?'

'Yep.'

Jack started for the front entrance, but Maeve shouted after him, 'She's gone.' And sure enough, from the front door there was no sign of Áine.

'Where did she go?' he asked, back now in the kitchen while Maeve assembled a set of knives in their wooden holder.

'I don't know, Jack. Where did she come from?'

'I met her last week with Aaron, in Sweeney's.'

Maeve chuckled. 'Oh, that figures. So she thinks you guys are her ticket to stardom? Let me guess which routine you used on her.'

'No, no, she's not into all that, but I don't think she's well. I was going to drive her....'

Maeve's blue eyes fixed on him. 'Calm down, Jack! She said thanks for giving her a look around.'

'She must have gone by the well, but how would she have known...?'

'She seemed fine to me. Would you get the other boxes out of the car? They're a bit heavy for me — it's all the cups, plates, glasses, anything we'll need on day one.'

'Sure.' Jack turned to go.

'Oh, and I invited that girl to come on Saturday. Hope that's okay?'

'Oh, yeah, fine.' Jack hurried to the front door without looking back, not wanting to explain to Maeve, or himself, why he was grinning so widely.

Chapter Fifteen

By Thursday the bedroom was finished, all of the bath-
rooms were in running order, and the living-room was
clean enough for the house-warming party. They had hoped
to move in on Friday, but Maeve was worried that the paint
fumes might damage her unborn baby, and so they ran the
heat continuously to speed up the drying, which was already
being helped along by dehumidifiers. It was Saturday now
and, come what may, they were moving in today.

They had repeatedly assured Maura Mulcahy that they
were leaving and that, yes, she should rent out the room,
which she did, at twice the rate they were paying, to pilgrims
from Dublin. They ate their entire cooked Irish breakfasts
without remorse, thanked Maura one more time for everything, paid her in cash — over and above what they owed
her — and loaded their personal belongings into the Peugeot.

Maeve had put out an open invitation to everyone who
lived in Rathbrack and, as the afternoon wore on, she, Jack,
Margaret and Cathal took to guessing what the turnout
would be. They had said that the party would start at nine,
but no Irish party ever started on time and it was nearly ten
before the band had finished setting up. Ballylacken House
had done the catering and assigned some teenagers in white
shirts and bow-ties, but they had nothing to do either except
stand around on the back porch smoking while they waited
for guests to wait on.

Jack too was wearing a bow-tie and his tuxedo, and
Maeve, who was starting to blossom three months into her

pregnancy, had acquired a black cocktail dress on her last
Dublin spree, and it camouflaged her tiny bump perfectly.
They stood side by side at their new front door as people
began arriving.

Maeve knew everyone, or at least they all knew her, and,
when prompted, she could say — 'Of course, how could I
forget? Didn't I babysit your brother?' or 'You went to school
with Owen, didn't you?' or 'I remember my father talking
about your family all the time!'

Jack knew some of the faces, but it was only when the
drinkers from Sweeney's began arriving that he started to
recognise names. As the house filled up, the host and hostess
mingled with the crowd and conducted guided tours. Their
books and art had arrived from storage, and photos of Maeve
in various roles lined the corridor, holding everyone's attention and evoking a stream of praise — until Owen arrived.

'Bejasus! The Maeve Fitzgerald mausoleum!' he roared as
he stared at yet another picture of his sister opposite the door
from the kitchen. Olivia tugged at his arm, but he shook her
off. 'And for this we gave up our rath! Now we're just Brack.
Or Maevebrack. Or Rathmaeve?'

'Did you hear why the statue's moving?' asked Eddie as
Jack passed him. Jack shook his head.

'You'd move too if you were the last virgin in Rathbrack!'
The one-eyed sailor and his cronies laughed at their joke, but
Jack's attention was on his brother-in-law, stumbling wildly
from one picture to the next, as if each time he saw his sister's
face it was a worse affront.

'I'm sorry,' said Olivia to Jack as he approached. 'He had
quite a few before we left the house.'

'Owen, can't you give us a break just for tonight?' Jack
asked.

The drunken farmer swivelled around and prodded his
host. 'And as for you, you tight-fisted fucking yank....' His
hand went to his mouth and a brownish liquid spewed
between his fingers.

'Now there's a credit to the community,' said Sonny Mulcahy before Maura pulled him into the kitchen.

'Oh, God, where's the toilet, Jack?' Olivia groaned.

'Here,' Jack replied, trying the door handle, but it was locked. 'Goddamn it! Come on!' He and Olivia each took an arm as Owen now clamped both hands to his face to block a second eruption. They led him through the double doors of the master bedroom, into the en-suite bathroom, and let go.

Owen dropped to his knees and vomited on the toilet seat, then staggered to his feet to turn on the cold tap, and sent another jet of puke at the new mirror.

'I knew we shouldn't have come!' Olivia wailed. 'Just leave us, Jack, and I'll clean this up.'

Jack backed away into the loud music again, passing Eddie and his friends who were clutching paper plates of cocktail sausages.

'It's all Mr Amonson's money paid for this,' he heard Eddie telling the others above the amplified din.

And then he was back in the living room searching out Maeve.

'Oh God, you're only gorgeous looking tonight, Jack!' said Gladys Clery, grabbing his jacket sleeve from where she sat.

'Are they looking after you all right, Gladys?' he asked.

'Marvellous!' Her face wrinkled into a smile and she rocked on her chair like the child's clown that always bounces upright again. 'Oh, didn't Maeve bring back the handsomest man to us after all her travels — and a baby on the way!'

'Would you like another drink?' Jack asked in the hopes that she would release him for this.

'I've given it up!' she told him, putting on a stern face.

'Well, Lent is over now....'

'No, no, I'm off it for good. Blasted stuff was rotting the insides out of me!'

Now that he looked at her, she did look healthier — the eyes less rheumy — but the mind had always been that of a romantic country girl.

'I was just saying to Maeve,' she went on, wagging a finger at him, 'you know, in her condition, with all that she has to do, I'd come up here and clean and cook for ye.'

The party had reached critical mass. The band, in the corner between the south and east windows, was now hidden behind a screen of dancers foxtrotting, swinging and bopping according to their ages. Margaret and Cathal stood wrapped around each other, eyes closed, she with her head pressed into his chest, he nuzzling her long coils of hair.

'Ah, there you are, Jack!'

He turned to see Fr Byrne, and Gladys finally let go.

'John, glad you could make it!' They shook hands and the priest drew him away from the music.

'I have Noreen in the car outside,' said the priest. 'I wonder would you mind giving me a hand lifting the wheelchair up the steps?'

'No problem.' And with that Jack knew he had answered the unspoken question of whether Noreen was welcome here at all after her protests.

When they got out, they found that the poet had managed to stand up with the help of the car door.

'Sorry to be such a nuisance,' she said, smiling warmly, 'but if I let go, I'll just topple over.'

She swung carefully around on one ankle and lowered herself into the custom-made wheelchair. Then the two men grasped a side each and ascended the steps.

'That was easy,' said Jack. 'Just as well you look after your figure so well, Noreen.'

'Oh no, Jack — it's just that I'm still a writer in the starving class.' Before he could reply, she had propelled herself into the living-room, followed by her minder and sometime lover; Jack was left alone at the door of his new house.

There was a full moon overhead, dimming the stars, backlighting the few clouds, reflecting from the tops of the cars parked along the roadside, and causing the water in the bay to sparkle up at him. Nothing else moved. Everyone who was coming tonight was here, singing, shouting and dancing behind him.

It should have been a moment of absolute contentment, a realisation of a dream, an awareness of all he had achieved so far. He had a beautiful wife, worthy of this Camelot, and more, and he had a first child on the way. His career had enough momentum to continue this way for many years, probably to raise his family here without financial worry, and he could think of nowhere else he would rather live. This fecund land, with a life of its own beneath his feet, and with its ever-changing light and weather and seasons was an inspiration in itself.

And yet he was consumed by a desire he had not wished for, wholly unforeseen, but springing from the most basic, most ancient and least controllable urge on earth. A beautiful woman had crossed his path, he had pursued her, and found a nature beneath the skin that drew him on. There was real warmth there, so characteristic of the Irish at their best, but with Áine there seemed to be none of the opposing self-interest that seemed to drag these Celts down.

Or was there? Was he now fantasizing? Perhaps she had been weighing him up, had inserted herself in his path deliberately, and had concluded, when she met Maeve, that the chase was not worthwhile. Or had she simply given in to the impossibility of any affair between them? Jack studied the night sky a few moments longer, shrugged off a cold shiver, and went back inside.

'Where were you?' Maeve asked when he squeezed up to her in the living room.

'Just helping Noreen.'

'She really is a queer fish, isn't she?' said Maeve.

'Hey, what's she supposed to do — hold a grudge forever?'

'But she's never apologised.... I'm sure she still thinks we shouldn't be here.'

'Jeez, come on, Maeve. It's over, the house is finished; we're moved in, and any weird shit that's happening is happening across the road.'

She cast her blue eyes up towards him. 'Oh, I don't know. You've been a little strange lately.'

'Have I? Must be Aaron's visit.' He slid an arm around her waist. 'Would you like to dance?'

She beamed at him now. 'I thought you'd never ask.'

Everyone watched them as they took the centre of the floor. Jack knew that for Maeve this really was a triumph. She was more radiant than she had been on their wedding day, but that had not been a first for either of them and, in its way, today was a more final act, since they were committed now to a place for the rest of their lives. Here, for better or for worse, they would grow old together, and one or other of them would die. The child she was carrying might go on living here, the way people did, if they could, stay in the same place for generations.

The tempo changed and he twirled her around and in against him. He understood now why she could never be happy in Los Angeles. No matter what, they could never have re-created the sense of belonging that even he could feel in this place. People, these people, had lived here from time immemorial and they had imbued the land itself with a personality of its own. It was alive in a way that a wasteland irrigated for the first time fifty years ago could never be.

He met Maeve's gaze as the room and its faces revolved slowly around them. And, in the way that had won her acclaim as an actress, she told him with her eyes, without speaking, that she knew he understood, that it was because of him that she had all this, and that she loved him for it.

Just then he caught a glimpse of blonde hair in the hallway, and, before he had a chance to look again, the music stopped. There was a clash of cymbals, an exaggerated drum roll, and then a screech from the microphone as the singer yielded it to someone else.

Maeve linked her arm in Jack's. 'This is a complete surprise to you, isn't it?' she asked.

'Yes.' He looked over his shoulder and saw Áine now standing in the room. There was a cough over the speakers and he turned back again to see Cathal with the microphone in his hand. Maeve squeezed Jack's arm.

'Ooooh, he's going to do it!' she said, squirming with excitement.

Jack looked back again at Áine who waved demurely at him from folded arms. Why had the music stopped and what was Cathal going to say to her?

'Unaccustomed as I am...' Cathal began in his amplified Dublin accent, 'I just want the whole of Rathbrack to hear me saying this.'

Those who had been talking in the kitchen and hall crowded in and Áine moved forward to make room. Other men looked at her now — Fr Byrne, Eddie, the musicians.

'Margaret!' said Cathal. 'Margaret Mulcahy?'

'She doesn't know either,' Maeve whispered to Jack.

'Here she is,' said someone, and was joined by others in pushing Margaret in from the kitchen.

'Margaret, come here,' said Cathal's voice.

Cautiously, the girl approached her boyfriend. Cathal flicked back his red dreadlocks, put his free hand into his suit pocket, took out a small box, and knelt down on one knee.

'Margaret Mulcahy,' he said, looking up at her, 'will you marry me?'

She stood there awkwardly now, pressing her hands against her reddening cheeks as Cathal opened the box.

'Oh God, you bought it!' she gasped.

'Emmm, yeah, I did. Do you want it or what?'

For a moment she said nothing, then she burst into tears and Cathal stood up and put his arm around her.

'She's not sure!' shouted some wag.

Margaret shook her head to clear her eyes, pulled back from Cathal, took the microphone from him and said, 'Yes, Cathal, I will marry you.'

As they embraced and kissed to cheers and cat calls, the band twanged out a few bars of 'Here Comes the Bride', then slid into the Rod Stewart hit 'I am Sailing'.

The newly engaged couple took the dance floor, and the party buzz resumed.

'Well?' Maeve asked Jack.

'Well what?'

'What did you think of that?'

Jack's mind was elsewhere. 'I guess Cathal doesn't need us as an excuse for coming to Rathbrack any more,' he said.

'But don't you get a real kick out of the fact that it was us, and building this house, that brought them together?'

'I need a drink.'

'It's help-yourself-in-the-kitchen time now.'

'Right.'

That meant it was later than he thought. Long after midnight. But no one was leaving yet. The band was playing. There was plenty to eat and drink. He met Cathal in the doorway of the kitchen with a bottle of champagne and four glasses.

'Peace offering for the in-laws,' Cathal explained.

'Hey, congratulations. Brave move,' said Jack, clapping him on the shoulder.

'Jaysus, if she'd dithered any longer I was going to offer the ring to that blonde over by the door. Do you know her?'

Jack nodded.

'I thought she was a fucking porcelain sculpture. Now that's what I call a real moving statue!'

'Hey, man, I think you've picked a great girl in Margaret.'

Cathal recoiled, shocked that Jack might have taken him seriously. 'Oh Christ, yes!' He winked. 'I suppose we're both brunette men, Jack?'

Before Jack could reply, Cathal had moved on to rejoin the Mulcahys.

'I think this is where you left me,' said Áine's voice close behind him.

Jack turned around as casually as he could. The kitchen was crowded, mostly with younger revellers, perhaps younger than Áine, but when he saw her she stood out, as if she alone were fully lit, and the others seemed to dim. Their voices faded, and if they moved it was no more than some tapestry flapping in the breeze that swirled through a stone window or the wall of a tent holding back the night wind.

'I didn't think you'd come,' Jack heard himself say.

'I had to come. I've been thinking about you all the time.'

'Me too.'

She raised a thin hand and pressed it onto his heart. 'If only there weren't so many people around.'

He wanted to say that he would tell them all to leave. He knew she could feel the pounding going on inside him. He raised both arms to embrace her, the only thought he could now sustain, but the hand on his chest held him back, and slowly as he stared at the green eyes that blazed across at him the madness passed and all the sounds of the party returned.

'Tomorrow, Jack,' she said. 'Meet me tomorrow morning, when all of these people are at mass.'

'Where?'

Her hand slipped away, she leaned in against him and

said softly into his ear, 'At the dunes. I'll wait for you there.'

And then she was gone. Jack stared at the random bottles and wondered how long he had been standing there. The crowd seemed to have thinned, and he felt he should hurry to rejoin Maeve who must miss him. He poured himself a glass of red wine and wandered back around the corner into the living-room.

The music was different now, and a couple of other local musicians had joined the band in the corner, with an accordion and fiddle. Four couples, old enough to have grown children here too, were arranged in pairs, facing each other, and when the music started they began a complex dance in which they exchanged partners, created a circle, danced around each other and deferred to one couple in the middle, with the onlookers clapping to the musical beat and then applauding when the dance was over.

'It's called set dancing,' said Noreen, looking up from her wheelchair at Jack.

'Very impressive,' he said.

'Funny, isn't it,' she said, 'how they're dancing right where the old rath was?'

Jack nodded, struck now by the same thought. And that was where Cathal had proposed to Margaret too.

'Who knows,' Noreen went on. 'Maybe some good will come out of this.'

'Ah now,' said the priest, who had overheard. 'We have to give credit where credit is due. Hasn't the whole parish come alive because of the huge interest in our own shrine to the Blessed Virgin?'

'That and the promise of a tourist bonanza,' Noreen replied.

'I'll bring her back to the fold yet,' said Byrne to Jack, but the look he got in reply silenced him and he returned his attention to his dancing parishioners.

Maeve went to bed long before the crowd began to thin, but Jack stayed up, danced in the céilí for a while, and regaled his guests with much-embellished movie stories. When he finally retired he left a hard core of singers and listeners in the living-room and closed the bedroom door on the strains of Noreen hitting the high notes of an old, old Irish song.

The bathroom showed no trace of Owen's earlier performance, but there were full ashtrays, half-empty glasses and bottles, and all the towels had been used. He undressed by the bathroom light so as not to disturb Maeve, and slid silently in beside her.

Should he keep this tryst with Áine? He lay on his back, closed his eyes and thought about the moonlit countryside all around them. And now a strange, new thought came over him. He was back on the hill with Maeve, when it was all grass, and she slid her long skirt up over her raised knees. She wanted him, wanted to start the baby that was growing inside her now. But Jack was reluctant .

It was bright on the hill, but dark lower down. Dark because it was a wooded land and the canopy of trees created dark places. This forest ran inland as far as the eye could see, south to the distant hills, north into a sunlit haze, and where they were was like a bright green eye set into its westward face.

It was night again, but now they could see nothing from the hilltop, rather it was the other way around. They were being watched. They could be seen, and everything they did was known, known to forces that were malevolent towards them, that coveted what they had, that watched from the woods, watched and waited, and hid when they were hunted, and created the need for vigilance, for the will to defend this place and seek out the danger in the thickest bushes, the darkest corners....

Chapter Sixteen

'Will I leave the curtains closed?'

'What?' He only half heard Maeve's voice, then opened his eyes to see her standing at the foot of the bed. She was dressed in a silk suit he hadn't seen since they left California, and a white hat he remembered her buying for an outdoor wedding somewhere near Santa Barbara.

'I'm going to mass,' she said. 'You sleep on. No big deal, I just want people to know we're not going to lock ourselves up in our ivory tower.'

Jack sat upright and reached for his watch. Quarter to ten.

'Sure, yeah, let's see what the weather's like.'

Maeve strode over to the drawstring and pulled until the curtains were far enough apart to fill the room with light. The sky was overcast again. She looked out and up at the clouds.

'Oooh, maybe I should take the car,' she said.

'You'll never get parking,' Jack muttered.

'True. I'll bring an umbrella.' And with that she disappeared, leaving him to blink at the far wall. Then he dragged himself to the window to study the weather. It might rain — hard to tell.

He showered in their new bathroom for the first time, vaguely aware that the water flowing over him came from within the hill, dried hurriedly, rummaged for jeans and sweater, tied his shoes with fingers that would not stay still and panicked when he couldn't find the car keys.

'Fuck!' he exclaimed, thinking that Maeve must have them, then recalled that he himself had parked the car out of the way beyond the door the previous evening.

He paced to the hallway, but there was nowhere he could have left them there, as it was still devoid of furniture. He had moved the car when the band arrived. He pushed open the double doors to the living-room. The drums and amplifiers were gone. He had shown them where to plug their equipment in. Maybe they knew, but he couldn't phone them, as it would be another two months — at least — before their phone line was installed.

And then he remembered. They had trailed an extension lead over to a socket under the kitchen counter across what would be the dining area. He had left the keys on the counter, of course. He ran to it, shoved the bottles aside, flung the paper plates and crumpled napkins to the floor and found the keys in their little leather pouch.

Now that he had the means to fulfil his quest Jack stopped. He shook his head and stared around at the aftermath of the party. What was he doing? His legs felt weak and in the pit of his stomach there was a cloying, near-nauseous, sensation as his mind returned to Maeve.

And then the memory of Áine standing here, right here, last night, returned, and he ran from the kitchen, out the front door, started the car and reversed it halfway down the hill, into the grass, then forward and out the gate. There were cars parked everywhere. Mass in Rathbrack had become a regular attraction for worshippers from far beyond its own parish.

He turned right, gained speed, then slowed almost immediately, not wanting to miss the opening in the wall that led onto the sandy flat. He found it, swung in and was surprised to find himself having to weave between several caravans, parked at random, and even a couple of tents. The pilgrims were even bringing their own accommodation now.

Maeve had reached the main entrance to the parish church. The newspaper boys had their papers covered in plastic — a sure sign of rain. Already men were gathered around the doorway, and she decided that if she couldn't get a seat she

would go home again. Out of the corner of her eye she saw
the bearded old man standing on the far side of the road and
wondered why he had not been there last night. Had Sonny
and the others not told him about it? People could be so cruel.

Jack felt the first drops of rain on his head and saw the dark
splotches forming in the sand as he walked to the top of the
ridge of dunes.

Every second was now an eternity of indecision, a conflict
that raged in his head, telling him to be glad she wasn't there,
to get in the car and go back home, and at the same time
telling him that she hadn't summoned him here just to dis-
appoint him, that this was an opportunity that would never
come around again.

And then the strangest of all thoughts occurred to him.
What if she had brought him here for some other purpose?
Was he about to be struck by lightning, standing here on top
of this hill of sand, like Owen's cattle? But there was no
rumble of thunder anywhere, just the surf on the beach, far
away now with the tide out.

He saw her. She was hurrying along the inside edge of the
dunes, making her way through the tufts of rushes towards
the car. He waved, then shouted, 'Áine!', and ran down to
meet her.

She was no better prepared for the rain than he was and
he opened the passenger door quickly to let her sit in, then
ran to his own side and sat in next to her.

'I thought you weren't coming,' he said, breathless.

She shook the rain from her hair, pushed it back from her
face and beamed over at him.

'A man of many doubts,' she said, laughing.

'Cold?' he asked, unsure what to do now. She nodded. He
started the engine and turned the knob in the dash to full
heat. Áine put her cold hands on his face and pulled him
towards her.

'You warm me,' she told him.

The green eyes were half-closed, as if to connect with

some dreamed-of longing inside her. Jack put his left arm around her shoulders, his right arm around her ribs, and watched her eyes close completely as he pressed his lips on hers. And he too gave in to the moment, shut his eyes, and felt her soft mouth searching around, unsure in that first kiss what to expect. Her arms tightened around his neck, her lips opened, wet now, and her tongue slipped between his teeth and searched out his own.

The church was completely full. Entire families were already standing in the side aisles. But Maeve too had heard the rain begin. It was only a shower, but she had come this far. She was not going to go back now, or stand for an hour. She walked up the centre aisle, judging by the backs of the heads to left and right how close together people were seated. She found herself running out of rows, and excused her way into the middle of the second seat from the front. With some reluctance the occupants shifted towards either end for her, and then Fr Byrne entered from the sacristy and they all stood up anyway.

Jack felt the flowing hair shifting between his fingers as Áine moved in against him, bent her face into the kiss, her lips chasing his. She made a fist in his hair and he tried to pull her closer, but the car seats defied them, kept them apart. Thin and supple, she twisted in towards him, and holding her waist he felt a gap between the tight sweater and her jeans and slid his hand onto the skin of her back.

It was cool to the touch, so he must feel hot to her and, as if to agree, she pulled free of their kiss, pressed her cheek against his and moaned in his ear. The rain had all but stopped again, but the droplets on the glass, and the mist of condensation from the warm air inside encapsulated them, and created a private world in which no one else could intrude.

Áine backed away enough to study Jack's face. She rubbed his leg slowly with her hand as if afraid to break the spell of physical contact, and he moved the hand on her silky back up onto her ribs and around to her breast. She had no need for a bra; she was taut and perfectly formed, just large enough to produce the bulbous shape below what felt like a small nipple.

As he touched her there she stiffened, closed her eyes and seemed to lose interest in anything else. Seeing her lips part, listening to the short gasps of pleasure, and feeling this freely offered body made Jack's emerging erection grow to the point of pain within the confines of his own clothes. They lunged towards each other and kissed again, more languorously this time, more confident in the pleasure they were creating for the other, and Jack's mind raced at the same time as to how best to proceed here.

His hand rubbed past her navel and she sucked in her waist to leave him free to undo the fly of her jeans, but he thought better of it.

'Not here,' he said. 'Let's see if we can do this somewhere more dignified.'

'You're very kind,' said Áine, as he reversed the car in an arc and headed back to the road.

Her words hovered in his mind, and he wondered once again about her. Had someone been unkind to her? How much sexual experience did she have? He still knew nothing about her. They turned north onto the coast road towards Ballylacken.

Fortycoats MacHenry was untroubled by the rain. When it started, he clambered over the stile in the wall that led to St Brigid's Well, and took shelter in the trees whose leaves were grown almost to their full summer size. From here he could look out at the changing weather, but it was the well itself that interested him. He leaned on his walking stick and peered intently at the hillside, at the layered limestone that had been washed free of soil by the spring that no longer flowed, and at the mossy cliff behind the rock pool that dripped here and there into the lower stream with the rain that seeped out of the growth all around.

Across the road behind him, inside the church, Fr Byrne was starting his sermon. Once again he found himself addressing as many people as could physically fit in the building. He noticed Maeve, close to the front, and recalled the donation she had given him. But now that seemed almost to have happened somewhere else, in some other parish where he had constantly been short of money. Today he was embarrassed by the health of the parish bank account. And he was sure this congregation with all of its out-of-town faces would offer up another record collection. They would never again accuse him of being too liberal to win over a country parish.

Were Maeve to try to persuade him to help her with the same issue today, he simply would not have been interested. He couldn't, and wouldn't, stand up here and give that sermon. No one would care. They wanted to hear about the grotto and how to show their devotion to the Mother of God, not about some long-forgotten fairy fort.

And then he wondered if Maeve knew about Noreen. If she did, she might well have tried blackmail rather than bribery. But that was a very uncharitable thought. He felt himself blush, cleared his throat, and shook off thoughts of Noreen, pagan superstition, and money, and began his homily.

'My dear people, I cannot tell you how proud it makes me to be parish priest of Rathbrack today....'

Jack was relieved to find that none of the staff at the reception desk at the Ballylacken Hotel had been at the party.

'Do you guys have any rooms for tonight?' he asked.

'Let me see now, Mr Amonson,' said the girl nearest the big ledger of bookings. 'We were full last night, of course, with people here to see the statue, but, yes, we have rooms tonight.'

'Is it ready now?' he asked.

'Oh gosh, I don't know if they've cleaned any of the rooms yet.'

'Ah, well, you see this is a friend of mine,' he said, gesturing to Áine, standing a few feet away, studying the old paintings on the walls. 'She just got into Shannon this morning....'

'Oh, right.'

The girl looked up at the boy next to her, who nodded and left, bounding up the stairs. He came back with two keys on big wooden key-rings.

'This is the one Mr Rothberg had, but this is a better one....'

'We'll take it!' said Jack, accepting the second key.

'Room five, right at the top of the stairs,' said the girl.

'You can put it under my name for now ... eh ... her bags are lost, and ... em ... we'll sort it out later.'

The staff nodded at this confused statement and Jack beckoned to Áine, waited for her at the end of the stairs, and wished she wouldn't stare at him as if they were lovers as they climbed the staircase.

Room five was furnished with dark wooden antiques, the largest of which was its double bed, replete with wooden headboard and footboard. Áine made her way to its end, where she noticed herself in the wall mirror.

'My hair!' she laughed in horror.

Jack closed the door, laid aside the key and shook his head.

'Your hair is beautiful,' he said. 'Like the rest of you, Áine.'

She accepted the compliment in silence, neither thanking him as an American woman would, nor denying that it was true as he had come to expect from the Irish.

'Where are you from?' he asked.

'I told you,' she said, taking his hand. 'I was born here.'

'But you've lived in other places too, right?'

She came right up against him.

'I've been away for a long, long time,' she said softly.

Now that he felt her against him he didn't want to talk and seized her head in his hands to kiss her as hard as he could. She pressed in and he clamped her waist to his, then ran both hands over her buttocks and pressed hard so that he felt the points of her pelvis and knew she felt his erection.

Áine broke free and peeled her sweater over her head.
Her raised arms revealed a curly golden down that only
excited him more. And the nipples were fawn coloured, with
tiny creases, like spokes. He fell to his knees, put his mouth
round one of them, then the other, felt them with his tongue
as they hardened instantly, and then undid the metal button
and zipper of her jeans.

Maeve lowered herself to her knees, in unison with the rest of
the congregation.

'Take this, all of you, and eat it: this is my body which will
be given up for you' said the priest, holding aloft the white
host. There was a brief silence broken by the sharp tinkle of a
bell being shaken vigorously by an altar boy.

The people bowed their heads.

The sky brightened over the church and lit the people
through the stained-glass windows. Across the road, Fortycoats too noticed the change, stepped out of the shelter of the
trees and shuffled closer to the spring. Then, unconcerned by
the wet mud underfoot, he too knelt down, as if to pray.

The light streamed through the net curtains of room five as
Jack got to his feet and began to pull at his own clothes. Áine,
without watching him, moved to the side of the bed, sat
down and stripped the lower half of her body.

There were some women, Jack thought, who knew they
could have any man they wanted, and surely Áine was one
of them. But now, as he approached her and she used her
elbows to retreat further across the bed he caught a look of
uncertainty, as if she were afraid that if she lay back she
would lose him.

Years later he would recall that look but he could never be
sure that he had understood it at the time, and had not de-
duced it later. No memory, other than dreams themselves,

fades more quickly and more completely than the memory of sex, so that we are compelled to repeat the act of creation over and over. And yet, though he could never fully recall them, these moments with Áine would haunt him forever.

She knew, of course, when she finally let her eyes drift from his, and saw how hard he was as he climbed on the bed, that she had him, and her demeanour changed. Propped on one elbow, the light behind outlining her sinewy form, she gave one last closed-mouth smile before falling on her back and closing her eyes.

Jack slid a hand towards the cluster of golden hair between her legs, and when he touched her she sighed softly, then pulled his hand away and led him up on top of her. She pulled her feet up under her knees and let them drift apart, moaning as he caressed a breast with each hand, a last gesture of foreplay before he fell onto her.

She had been cool to the touch outside, but now as he entered her he felt a startling heat. Their bodies collided and she bucked along the entire length of hers as if to throw him off if he didn't force himself to stay there. Still with her eyes closed, Áine bared her teeth at this first thrust and let out a grunt that might have been either satisfaction or pain. And when he pressed all the way inside her, again she repeated it, but louder. And again. And with each quickening thrust of his, her voice began to come through in the noisy gasps.

She threw her head from side to side and pounded his back with clenched fists until he grabbed her arms and held them down on either side of her face, and then he felt her flex and tighten around him so that they were locked together, and now he was pulling her up and down with him as if she was squeezing every drop out of him as he screwed his eyes shut for the fireworks of coming somewhere deep inside her.

Áine roared at this, clamping arms and legs around him now, so that as he drove on to satisfy her they bounced to the top of the bed and he felt the wooden bed-head crack as he pounded his skull against it.

The young trainees at the reception desk looked up the stairs
to where the shouting and banging was coming from. The
girl bit her lip and looked at the two boys but they were as
unsure as she was, so she sat there, and they stood there,
listening to the violence in room five at the top of the stairs.

Fortycoats watched the first seepage of water on the face of
the rock. Stone that had been blown dry by the wind and
sheltered by the overhanging grass above it became moist
and began to glisten. A mist sprinkled out of the dark little
canyon to hang in the air, and as the smooth water clung to
the limestone all the way down to the pool below, it was as if
the cleft had grown a soft glaze that was itself an awakening.
The forces now stirring deep inside the hill drove new rivu-
lets out onto the rock until they were quick and powerful
enough to shoot free as little jets that splashed down into the
pool, starting and stopping, but growing in strength.

The lower clouds shredded away and a gap in the higher
white ceiling let the sun play on the south slope of the hill.
Water gurgled out of every crevice as life returned to the
spring, and then a white spray gushed from the midpoint of
the wall and drenched the ferns that had grown up beside the
moss, and was followed by another and another, until the
spring began to flow freely again, quickly filling the man-
made well and spilling noisily over the edge as it had always
done before.

Inside the church, Fr Byrne held the host in front of the
congregation, saying, 'This is the Lamb of God who takes
away the sins of the world. Happy are those who are called
to his supper.'

'Lord, I am not worthy to receive you,' intoned the people,
'but only say the word and I shall be healed.'

Maeve watched the priest, absently, as he consumed the
host, repeating something he must have done thousands of

times and that she herself had seen every Sunday growing up here. The people around her seemed lost in their own thoughts too, of Sunday dinner, or a football match, or the week gone by, or maybe even of life and death and the hereafter.

Having raised the chalice in front of his face with both hands, Byrne lowered it until the rim was level with his lips. He would have swallowed the contents immediately were it not for the fact that he felt a slight movement in the vessel in his hands.

He had poured the wine into the silvery interior himself less than a quarter of an hour earlier. The transubstantiation of the wine into the blood of Christ was complete. He wanted to drink it as he had always done. But as he put the rim to his lips he saw something moving in the liquid.

At first he thought it must be a fly or a wasp that had flown or dropped in as he had raised the chalice at the consecration. But as he slowly lowered the gold cup away from himself so that the contents were less opaque, he saw that it was not a winged insect trapped in the liquid, but a small black creature — perhaps two inches long — that swam and wriggled, searching for some escape from its metal prison.

It was an eel of some sort, a tiny new-born eel. Byrne felt his arms begin to shake. If he simply put the chalice down, the congregation would hardly notice that he had not drunk out of it, but he couldn't. He knew that he was witnessing some unnatural event, that this creature that had invaded his chalice, his church, his parish, symbolised something else.

Stunned now, he felt himself losing his balance and he dropped the chalice. He reached with his hands for the edge of the marble altar as he too fell, but he couldn't hold on. The chalice hit the ground, spilling its contents, and rolled over the dais and on towards the front row of kneeling faithful.

He saw Maeve Fitzgerald looking back at him from beyond it and he knew that whatever had happened had given the lie to the conceit that the magic drawing all these people to Rathbrack sprang from this imported religion.

Chapter Seventeen

'I was having a strange dream when I woke up this morning,' said Jack, lying next to Áine.

'Were you dreaming of me?' she asked.

He shook his head, eyes closed. It was already afternoon and the sun had slipped by, leaving the room entirely in shade. It came to Jack as he held Áine's hand that the two were connected.

Here, with her beside him, he had discovered a sanctuary beyond anything he would have believed possible. Here was an inner peace on which nothing could ever intrude, and he knew it was coming from her. She filled the room with an aura, and if the world beyond the tall rectangle of light that was the window were to fill up with some unseen horror, none of it would ever enter this place.

It was as if the room existed just for them. And the light had been there to shine on Áine, to bathe her, to turn her to pure dazzling gold. Now it had left her, but she was its mistress and she could make it return whenever she liked.

'I still don't know anything about you,' he said.

'You know as much about me as I know about you.'

'No I don't!' Jack sat up. 'You know where I live, where I'm from ... I don't even know your last name.'

'And I know you're married,' said Áine.

Jack sighed. She had broken the spell.

'I suppose I should get back. She'll wonder where I am.'

He began to dress. Áine lay on her front, her head on her hands, and watched him, making no move herself.

'Do you want to stay here?' he asked.

She nodded.

'I mean stay the night?'

Again she nodded, without speaking. He knelt down on the floor next to her.

'Listen, I have to go, but I'll come back tomorrow, okay?'

Her eyes filled up with tears — something Jack had not expected. He stood up. 'Hey, tomorrow then.'

She didn't look at him, just fixed her eyes on some point on the wall, face rigid, as if the tears had come unbidden and unexpectedly to her too and she was willing them back inside as best she could.

Jack left her, his mind churning, and strode past the reception desk, watched by its curious staff. As he drove up and down the hills of the winding road back to Rathbrack, Áine's sadness stayed with him. Perhaps she was sorry she had let him have her so easily. Was she that easy with other guys? He resented the thought of her with anyone else, angrily slammed the gear stick as far as it would go, back, forward, and then shook his head at his own foolishness. Áine was no virgin. No one responded like that their first time.

She was just some kid looking for adventure. There was little enough to do around here. Or maybe ... maybe she was married! That would explain why she was so reticent with information about herself. Still, she didn't wear a wedding ring. In fact, she was entirely devoid of jewellery. Jack wasn't sure she even had her ears pierced.

What if she was very young and didn't want her family to know? That idea startled him. Did they have statutory rape laws in Ireland? Áine could easily be under twenty-one, possibly less than eighteen, but he doubted she was younger than sixteen. What if she was and this was some blackmail scam? She had witnesses, and she sure had a sperm sample.

He crested another hill and Rathbrack bay came into view. And there overlooking it was the house beneath its dark green roof. The house that Jack built. Home. Where Maeve was waiting. With his unborn child. At last the enormity of what he had done welled up inside him. He slowed down.

He had betrayed Maeve, his wife, and the woman he was

sure he still loved. After only two years. And this was no chance encounter. He had arranged it and followed through and intended to see Áine again tomorrow. But he wouldn't. No, he would, but he would tell her that he had made a mistake, he was sorry, and that would be the end of it. Áine must have figured that out. That was why she was crying.

He turned into the driveway. Still, if that was the way she saw it, why had she stayed? And why did she plan to be there tomorrow for him? In fact, what was she up to — she didn't have as much as a toothbrush with her! Would she be discreet or would she blab about him to everyone?

Maeve was in the kitchen, with Margaret and Gladys, all of them cleaning away the remains of the party.

'Oh, there you are,' she said, smiling over as he hovered in the doorway. 'Where were you?'

'Just went for a drive up the coast,' he mumbled. His wife seemed to accept this almost too readily.

'Well, are you going to give us a hand?' she asked.

'Sure.'

It was all too simple.

'Fr Byrne had some kind of heart attack or something at mass today,' said Maeve, handing him a black plastic bag.

'Really? Is he okay?'

'I don't know. He fell, then got up and just sounded terrible the rest of the time, didn't he Gladys?'

'Oh I was much farther back,' said Gladys, turning from the sink where she was scrubbing. 'But he went straight home; and all the visitors wanting to talk to him at the grotto.'

'And did you see any of this, Margaret?' asked Jack, glad of this diversion.

'I don't go to mass, Jack.'

Maeve gave him a sly glance and said, 'It's the only time she and Cathal have the house to themselves.'

Seeing the girl blush, Gladys cackled, then returned to her washing, looked out the window and began to sing off-key:

> 'How would you like to be
> Under the bridges of Paris with me?'

Maeve shook her head at the embarrassed Margaret. 'You'll

miss all that when you're married, you know.'

'She will?' Jack asked. Maeve narrowed her eyes.

'I mean the need for secrecy. Finding a time and place to be alone....'

Now it was Jack who felt his colour rising. And he knew Maeve noticed.

'Anyway, let's hope poor Fr Byrne hasn't anything seriously wrong with him,' she said.

That afternoon, John Byrne sat in Noreen Fletcher's kitchen, hands clasped in front of him, shoulders drooping forward as if he were very cold.

'I just can't get it out of my mind,' he said.

'And who cleaned up the spilt wine?' she asked.

'The altar boys.'

'But they didn't find the eel because there was no eel — is that it?'

'Yes. But I felt it move — and I saw it!'

They both lapsed into silence for a while. The priest stood up. 'I don't mean to burden you with my problems, but there wasn't anyone else I could think of telling.'

Noreen laughed. 'Burden me? I'd have been furious if you hadn't told me! No, no, this is amazing. Messages from the spiritworld!'

'How can you be so ... so casual about this?'

She sighed and shook her head. 'Because, John, I don't believe in the great sky god, with his flowing beard and his judgement day — the one true god with his priests, his all-male priests, running around interpreting it all for the rest of us.'

'Are you saying you don't believe me?'

'On the contrary. The difference is that you look on this as some manifestation of evil, some curse that's hit you. And why? Because it's outside the realm of the Roman Catholic Church's canon.'

'What good can you possibly see in this?'

'We have people flocking from all over the country to listen to a talking statue and it's hailed as a great occasion,' — she wheeled herself to her writing desk, picked up Cathal's sketch and waved it at him — 'and maybe they're pious maniacs who just hear what they want to hear, but now....'

Noreen paused, breathless, and took in a lungful of air. 'But now,' she said slowly, 'I think some of us know that there is another possibility, don't we?'

'I'm not following you.'

'Yes you are.' She stared up at him. 'We both know there is a god, a cosmic being that is beyond our comprehension, that a world of atoms and energy could not exist otherwise. We've gone beyond intellectual atheism, or at least I have. And now, I think, more than ever, that I was drawn to Rathbrack by those spiritual forces that are beginning to reveal themselves.'

She sat all the way back in her wheelchair. 'So, no, John, I'm not afraid, not at all. I intend to piece together these clues.' She was silent for a moment, and then, seeing his dejected look, continued, 'In a way I feel sorry for you, but I envy you too.'

'What?'

'Yes. Like Cathal, you were given a glimpse into their world.'

'Their world?'

'There was no eel. There was no savage. But they exist somewhere else. Here, in Rathbrack, I'm sure, but in some other time. And I want to go there.'

'You're talking madness, Noreen!' Byrne lifted the latch on the front door and backed out. 'Madness!' he repeated as he closed it.

The day went by with more unpacking and more cleaning until finally Jack climbed into bed while Maeve finished in the bathroom. He was dozing off when he felt her sit down and opened his eyes to see her sitting on the edge of the bed with her back to him.

'What are you doing?' he asked.

She held up a plastic bottle and continued some unseen motion with her other hand.

'Oil,' she said. 'I'm oiling myself. You don't want me to end up with stretch marks, do you?'

'Oh. No.'

'Jack, I'm sorry about today,' she said, still working on herself.

Why should she be sorry? What had she done? It was a strange way to broach the subject.

'And I'm going to get a second opinion.' She swung her legs up onto the bed and lay down next to him.

A second opinion. Who had given her the first opinion? And what had they said? He felt her hand slide down over him, settling on his genitals. How could she tell by doing this? He had showered. There was no trace, no perfume, nothing of Áine's for her to find.

'What are you doing?' he croaked.

'I know it's never as good as the real thing,' she said.

Jack sat bolt upright and raised his knees so that her hand was forced away from him.

'What's wrong?' she asked, full of concern now.

'Nothing! What's wrong with you? What are you sorry about?'

'I thought you were upset when I said that about Margaret and Cathal — that you thought I was making a joke about us not having sex, and that's why you blushed in the kitchen this afternoon, Jack!'

'What?'

She sat up beside him, supported on the palms of her hands.

'What did you think I was talking about?' she asked.

'Oh that! Yes, yeah, I just got all confused about your second opinion comment, that's all.' He looked at her and shook his head. 'Look, we're tired. Let's just get to sleep, okay?'

She stared at him for a while, then nodded and lay back down. Jack turned off the bedside light and settled down onto his own pillow.

Again he dreamt of the view from the hill. A wind whipped around him this time and now when he looked down at the forest it no longer held the same menace and he told himself that was because Áine lived there. He was standing where the bedroom had been, or would be, the grass waving back and forth at his feet, facing south. It seemed to Jack that he stood like this for a long time before he realised that this was not the hill the way he remembered it before they built the house, that the fairy rath was also missing.

He began walking towards the place where it should have been, and now he noticed that there were standing stones on the hill, not on the summit, but part of the way down, maybe twenty feet apart, with no obvious function other than to define the space within them. There was a complete ring of them and he was going to walk down and examine them when a movement in the bay caught his attention.

He saw dark shapes on the water coming around the cliffs, skimming fast across the waves — canoes, paddles rising and falling in time to a chant, more and more of them coming into view.

Above the cliffs Cathal sat in his red car, his arm around Margaret, enjoying the moonlit ocean. In the distance he too saw below him what looked at first like a school of dolphins or whales. He got out and walked to the edge, and now he saw the motion of the paddles too.

'Do you see it?' he asked Margaret as she walked up beside him.

'See what?'

'Those boats, like currachs....' He peered over the edge.

It was them! The people with one eye! None of them looked back up, all intent on where they were headed, relentlessly pulling themselves through the water.

'I don't see anything,' said Margaret.

'There!' He pointed. 'Are you fucking blind?'

'Cathal, there's nothing out there.'

He stood up, glared at her as if she mustn't be trying hard enough, looked back, and saw that she was right — they were gone. If they had ever been there.

'Let's get away from here,' he said.

She put her arms around him and pressed herself up against him.

'You're just too sensitive,' she said. 'You have to stop feeling guilty about building that stupid house. If anyone's to blame for wrecking some old grave, it's Jack for paying for it all, or Maeve for bringing him here, isn't it?'

She looked beseechingly at her fiancé, but he just stared out at the Atlantic. 'Or Sweeney for selling them the place, or me for designing a house to build on it, or your father for building it all....'

'Or her brother for not selling her the site up here,' Margaret added. They had been down this path before, had weighed up Noreen's advice. They would be married in November, about six months from now, late in the year, but the earliest they could arrange it. And then she would leave here and live in Dublin with Cathal.

The architect looked back inland at the house where Jack lay sleeping, next to Maeve.

'Well, it's finished now and they're the ones that have to live with it,' he said. 'We get to move on and do other things, don't we?'

Margaret nodded and pulled him into a long kiss.

When Jack awoke, Maeve was already up and dressed. 'Don't wait up for me tonight,' she said. 'I might stay the night in Dublin. Do you want me to ring Margaret and get her to run up here and let you know?'

'Are you taking the car?' he asked sleepily.

She put her hands on her hips and looked down at him. 'No, Jack, I'm going to fly there on my broomstick!'

'Obviously you need to take the car,' he said.

'There's plenty to eat, and Sonny and the others will be in and out if you need them to run an errand for you.'

'Sounds cool.'

She bent down, kissed his forehead and left. He bounded out of the bed as she reversed the car past the bedroom window. How could people live without phones? Maybe they should just buy another car. And he couldn't get someone to take him to Ballylacken and expect Maeve not to hear about it. Why had he said he'd meet her there again today?

He glared at himself in the mirror, denied that he knew the answer to that question, adjusted the shower temperature, threw off his underwear and pulled the glass door closed behind him. As the hot water flowed over him he was unable to hide the truth from himself any longer. He banged a fist against the tiles and let out a roar that reverberated in the steamy cubicle.

He knew exactly why he wanted to see her again today. What he didn't know was what had driven him to want her so badly in the first place. There was a beautiful woman behind every palm tree in Los Angeles, but he didn't try to fuck them all. What was it this girl had? He shook his head furiously under the spray of water.

What did it matter? That was ancient history now that he had had her. It was the most exhilarating sex he had ever experienced and he desperately wanted it again. He massaged the shampoo into his hair, squeezed his eyes shut, and already felt himself growing hard just at the thought of her. She was passion personified — capable of making a man do anything just to have her, and capable of keeping him forever. The fulfilment was equal to the promise. No, it exceeded what could be imagined.

And he must strive to be her equal! If he thought for an instant that there was anything more he could do to please her, that he had left her wanting, not been for her what she had been for him, then he was nothing, didn't deserve to live in the same world as her.

He bolted from the shower and towelled himself so fast it hurt. Then he dressed and marched around the house, looking out the windows, hoping to see Sonny or the painters or the carpet guys, or whoever the hell showed up first and could be persuaded to take him to the hotel. An hour passed. It was nine-thirty. No contractors.

And where was Cathal? Wasn't he going to write a spec for the landscaping this week? Mulcahys'! Jack pulled on a jacket and fled out the front door, straight into Gladys Clery, a straw shopping basket in her hand, a scarf wrapped over her head and tied under her chin.

'Jesus, sorry, Gladys! What are you doing here?'

'Oh my God, you're after putting the heart crossways in me!' she gasped, and then broke into her earthy laugh. 'Didn't I tell you I'd be up a few mornings a week to help ye out with things?' she said. 'But I won't hold you up — you must be in an awful hurry.'

'Yes, yes, I am!'

'Will you be back for lunch?'

'No.'

He turned and walked briskly down the hill, watched briefly by the old lady before she climbed the steps to the front door and went inside.

It took only a few minutes to walk around to Mulcahys', but Cathal was not there.

'Margaret went to Dublin with Maeve,' Maura told him. 'But Cathal is down with Sonny at Sweeney's.'

'Still celebrating the good news?'

'Oh, I've never seen her looking so happy, and she has you and Maeve to thank for it.'

'No, no, you brought up a lovely daughter. Could I use your phone to make a quick call?'

'Of course!'

She left him alone with the black instrument in the hall. Beside it was a typed card with the phone numbers and opening times of places to eat, up and down the coast and back in town. He and Maeve were familiar with the list. Some were only opening now for the summer season and only the Golden Dragon stayed open past nine o'clock. He dialled the number of the Ballylacken Hotel.

'Hello, room five please.'

'I don't think there's anyone in room five,' said a female voice on the other end.

'Oh, well, actually there is.'

'I have no record of anyone staying in it last night.'

'That's because I forgot to fill in the registration.'

'You did?'

'Yes. Never mind. Just put me through to room five.'

'All right. Just a moment!'

There was a click, and then the ringing of the phone in the room. It rang. And rang. And rang.

Jack banged the receiver down, thought about calling again and sending someone up, decided against that, left Mulcahys' and hurried along the road around the edge of the monastery towards Sweeney's. As he passed the high cross, he was drawn to look at it, and suddenly he stopped and retraced his steps. Through the quadrants of the stone ring he could see the house as before.

In itself that was hardly surprising — such a line of sight had to exist somewhere. But now when he swung around towards the bay he realised that the cross had been positioned directly between the hilltop and the water, and what really held his attention was that he was sure Áine's attack had come on her as they passed between the cross and hilltop on the far side.

He should tell this one to Noreen, another thing she could add to whatever wacko interpretation she was dreaming up now. He hurried on, catching sight of Cathal's car parked ahead of him. And there was Cathal, with Sonny and Sweeney, the three of them pacing around by the gable end of the pub.

He waved and they waved back, then waited for him to arrive.

'Are those bloody painters there yet?' asked Sonny.

'They weren't when I left,' said Jack.

Sweeney gave his usual twisted nod that could mean yes or no, and Cathal fumbled with a clipboard and avoided his gaze.

'I just wanted to have a word with you, Cathal,' said Jack.

The architect nodded enthusiastically and stepped over the low wall that separated the path from the high ground behind the beach where Sweeney's was the sole structure.

'I have a lot of the drawings done,' said Cathal, 'I should have something to show you both tomorrow evening.'

Jack frowned. Cathal, believing his employer to be displeased with him, said, 'I don't charge you for all the time I'm down here, you know!' and held up both hands in his own defence.

'What?'

'The landscape stuff. I'll have it done tomorrow. I'm only here this morning to help them get this thing started.'

'What thing started?'

'Sweeney's building a huge extension here — a lounge

with a view of the bay, seating for a hundred and fifty, a stage in the corner, and he wants it up fast.'

'Oh, oh I see,' Jack shook his head and waved his arms in a cutting motion. 'No, no, jeez, Cathal, I know you've put in all kinds of time for us on your own. No problem. No, no. I just need a small favour.'

'Sure.'

'Will you be needing your car today, I mean early in the day?'

'Em, well, no.'

'Any chance I could borrow it?'

'Well, eh....'

'You see, I forgot I've arranged to meet a guy up at the Ballylacken Hotel, and Maeve has the car.'

'Oh!' Cathal plucked at his beard. 'The only thing is, you wouldn't be insured.'

'What?'

'But I'll tell you what. I'll run you up there myself, and sure he can bring you back.' Confident that this solution would appeal to Jack, Cathal took the keys out of his overcoat and rattled them.

'Right! Hey, fantastic,' said Jack.

'Micko's lounge bar won't exactly be a thing of beauty,' said Cathal as he drove. 'He's so tight-fisted he won't go for anything other than a flat felt roof. Like a fucking public toilet it'll be! And as for the foundations, I'm trying to persuade him he needs to put down a really heavy slab, because he's building it on the fucking beach.'

'Well I'm glad you got a new commission right away, Cathal,' said Jack.

Cathal Ó Murchú nodded as he looked out over the steering wheel.

'Me too,' he said in a way that struck Jack as odd.

'Need the money for the wedding?' Jack asked.

'No, no. Christ! Sonny and Maura want to take care of everything. The only daughter, and all that. No, I just can't get that fucking strange face, or whatever it was, out of my mind, and now I'm after seeing something else weird.'

'What did you see?'

'Boats, with those one-eyed fuckers in them.'

Jack looked over at him. 'Coming around the point, below the cliffs?'

Cathal looked over, so shocked he let the inside wheels slip into the ditch, and the engine cut out. Both men sat there silent for a while, their backs to Rathbrack. Eventually Jack spoke.

'So that's kind of a paranormal experience, I guess, but maybe we were both just thinking of the same thing, because we saw a picture somewhere....'

Cathal shook his head. 'Let me show you something,' he said and got out of the car. Jack followed him around to the back. Cathal pulled up the car's hatch-back to reveal the flat stones he and Margaret had taken from the site.

'There's dozens of these buried under your driveway,' he said. 'They're from the fairy rath.'

Jack stared at the carvings. Cathal had taken four very distinct illustrations — waves and circles, chevrons, and two spiral mazes.

'Why didn't you say anything about this?'

'What did it matter? We'd already destroyed the mound. I thought it might make trouble for you, and hold things up.'

'So why are you driving around with them in your car?'

Cathal shrugged. 'Guilty, I suppose. The car corners much better with them in there.'

'Well, why don't you take them somewhere and see if they can carbon date them or something? It looks as if they had lichen growing on them.' Now Jack remembered the standing stones in a ring around the hill, but he had seen only their inner sides. He picked up the four rocks in turn, turning each over. They were carved on one side only, so it was possible....

They pushed the car back onto the road and continued up the hill. As they turned onto the hotel's tree-lined avenue, Jack turned to Cathal and said, 'I don't know about you, but I'm not about to let a few seconds of paranormal experience rule my life.'

'Yeah, you're right, fuck it,' Cathal agreed. 'When I see the likes of Margaret's mother off to say the rosary every night down at the grotto, I think that's real voodoo that was shoved into our heads as kids and that we're trying to shake off, so believing in fairies is taking a giant step backwards altogether, isn't it?'

They pulled up at the hotel entrance.

'Absolutely,' said Jack. 'Thanks for the ride.' He got out and slammed the door.

Inside, Jack recognised the owner seated behind the desk.

'Oh hello, Mr Amonson.' He stood up and extended a hand congenially.

'Hi, good morning,' said Jack. 'I'm here to meet the guest in room five.'

The man turned to look at the key hanging in its assigned place with the others and said, 'No, there's no one in that room.'

'Well, did she check out?'

'Who?'

'The girl — very attractive, blonde.'

'Sorry, I didn't see her.'

Jack smiled. Obviously she was still there. 'Can I just have the key and go up and check?' he asked.

'I suppose so.' The proprietor seemed to hand over the key in slow motion, but once Jack had it, he bounded up the stairs and turned it in the lock of the door. By the time he thought of knocking so as not to startle her, he had already stepped into the room.

It was empty. He checked the bathroom. The towels had been changed, everything neatly hung or folded, unused. The bed was made. There was no trace of Áine anywhere. He stood there for a while, then sat on the bed, lay back and tried to imagine being with her as he had the previous day.

Just one day had gone by. And yet it seemed like forever. He closed his eyes. He ached for this girl, and the realisation that he would not be with her today descended on him with such force that when he pulled himself upright and looked at his face in the mirror he was sure he had aged ten years.

He stood up and looked around the room again. He should never have left. And he had left her in tears. What kind of a man would do that? What had he been thinking? She had said she would wait, but what choice had he given

her? And why if he had the tiniest speck of wit would he
have thought she would wait here? He sighed at his own
stupidity, left, and walked slowly downstairs.

It was a six-mile walk to Rathbrack, but there was no sign
of rain, and Jack had nothing to do for the rest of the day, nor
reason to hurry home, and no prospect of doing any useful
work in this state of mind.

When he finally reached his driveway it was being tarmacked. He skirted past the team of men spreading the black
asphalt around, passed the painting contractor's van, walked
over where the remains of the rath were buried, up the steps
and in the front door.

'Oh there he is now,' said Gladys as he entered the
kitchen. 'You must be famished. I'll make you something.'

She busied herself taking things from the fridge, filled the
kettle with water, plugged it in and then said, 'You don't look
very happy today. Do you miss her already?'

'Yes, Gladys, I miss her.'

'Oh, isn't it marvellous to be young and in love?'

He made no attempt to stop her going on with her
mawkish palaver, just hoped silently that she wouldn't break
out into one of her hideous songs.

Night drew on and Jack found himself alone in his house.
Even with the central heating running, it felt cold, so he
turned on the gas fire and crouched in front of the blue and
yellow flames that lapped up over the fake logs, but after a
while he gave up on this providing any solace and wandered
down to the bedroom.

Lying there in the dark he wondered about all the strange
things happening, and about Cathal, and about Maeve, and
wished that she were here beside him, if only to take the edge
off this loneliness. He told himself that yes, he did love her;
that the memory of Áine would fade; that it was just a single
transgression, never to be repeated; that tomorrow he would
get back to the script he had promised Aaron. When he
finally dozed off, it was into a dreamless sleep.

Chapter Eighteen

Maeve returned next afternoon and sought Jack out working in the bedroom.

'The driveway looks great!' she pronounced as he stood up and they embraced.

'I missed you,' he said, holding her. She leaned in over her little pregnant bulge to press her cheek against him.

'Well, you spent a night alone in this house,' she said softly, 'and nothing terrible happened.'

He held her back to see her face. 'Was this some kind of test?' he asked.

'No! My God, Jack, how can you think I'd do that to you?'

'Hey, it's the first thing out of your mouth....'

'It was a joke, that's all.' She gave him a wry smile and sat down on the side of the bed. 'But I have some really good news,' she went on.

'Oh?' Jack settled back into his chair.

'I saw the doctor again. You'd be amazed how his attitude changed when I talked about a second opinion, or maybe he just didn't know us well enough before, but he thinks if we're careful. He even drew a sort of diagram with different angles — he might as well have said doggy position.'

She raised her eyebrows and made a face at her own explicitness.

'That's great news,' said Jack. 'Wanna practise now?'

Maeve laughed. 'Jack we still have a house full of people. Tonight. Gladys was making tea. Do you want some?'

He shook his head. Having left Mulcahys' where tea was

a staple with every meal he was glad to put the Irish tea-drinking habit behind him.

They made love that night, but so slowly and carefully that when they were finished Maeve summed it up by saying, 'I don't know, Jack. This is more like yoga than sex.'

She was right, but the man in him didn't want to agree, fearing that might prompt her to abandon the attempt again.

'What else did he say about the baby?' he asked.

She sighed. 'Nothing new. It's at an odd angle, so, yes, I'll probably pay for my past indulgences with a Caesarean birth.'

'Did he say that?'

'No! No, that's just me talking. I suppose I just grew up with this notion that, well, life is not about selfish pleasure.' She pulled the sheet up over her bare shoulder. 'And things have gone so well this year that I have this stupid fear it's all going to go wrong. You know, the sun is shining, so it's going to rain.'

'Don't talk like that,' said Jack.

'I can't help it,' she said. 'I'm just being honest with you. That's the price of belonging to a place like this.'

'I don't get you.'

'Well, in America we could just redefine ourselves, and no one cared. But here, at least for me, the whole point is to be a part of the place. You know you can go back just about forever, and someone who was my ancestor lived in or around Rathbrack, and that's true of just about everyone here.'

'What about me?'

She coiled in against him. 'You're the new breed of conqueror, Jack,' she said softly. 'Before you there were the English and the Vikings, and the Spanish and the French marched through here. You took your pick of the Irish women, and your heirs will carry my bloodline forward.'

'Romantic stuff,' he said quietly, but already her breathing told him she was falling asleep. And as he lay there listening to her, he wondered if the rain had not already started.

Three days later they were sitting on the new oak swivel-stools at the counter in their kitchen, Jack re-reading a treatment he was about to send to Aaron, Maeve drinking tea and browsing through a book about pregnancy, when suddenly she began to groan, clutched her stomach with both hands and toppled from the stool.

Jack ran around to her. He had heard a thump as her head hit something while she was falling, and now there was a trickle of blood from her forehead. She was bent double in pain, eyes screwed shut, until he put his arms around her, and then she grabbed his arm.

'Jesus, Jack,' she cried. 'It's some kind of cramp. It's like a knife sticking into me!'

Jack looked up at Gladys. 'Call an ambulance!' he shouted, but the elderly woman just stood there, hands over her mouth, eyes wide, making a whining noise. Then Jack remembered they still had no phone and she would have had to walk to the village, so he gathered Maeve up in his arms and carried her out to the car.

All the way to the regional hospital in Kilcashel she twisted and turned, her face pale and sweaty. He followed the signs for the emergency entrance, and when he began to lift her out of the car some orderlies arrived with a trolley and took over. He walked in with them and explained to a doctor what had happened. He was asked to wait outside while they examined her.

'We're not sure what's wrong with her,' the same doctor told him two hours later. 'But because of her condition we'll keep her in overnight for observation. I talked to Dr Lowry and he agrees. Has she been vomiting much, morning sickness, that kind of thing?'

'No. Not lately. Why?'

'Could be just food poisoning.'

'Hey, we eat the same food and I'm fine.'

'Yes, well, that's why we're keeping her here — just to be sure it's not the baby.'

Jack nodded.

'We've given her something quite strong to ease the pain, Mr Fitzgerald, so you may as well just go home for today and come back in the morning.'

Again he nodded, accepting the name confusion, and,

having looked in at his sleeping wife, walked back out to his
parked car.

This big new hospital was on the far side of the town from
the road that led to the coast, and so Jack found himself in the
single line of traffic that made its way through the town centre.

It was a sunny afternoon, the last of the children straggling home from school in their uniforms, counting the days
to the end of the school year. The trees that lined the river
shook in the breeze, and in the brief glimpse of water over
the wall he saw swans, dazzlingly white against the rippling
brown flow.

He was just cresting the old bridge when he saw her, and
then only because he had looked again to see the swans. At
least it looked like Áine, walking in and out of the shade of
the trees, her back to him, so that really the golden tresses
could have belonged to anyone, but he was sure they didn't,
and desperately he searched for somewhere to pull in.

There was nowhere. The town had been built in the time
of horses, and parking was always scarce — non-existent on
its narrower streets. He had no choice but to follow the flow
of the traffic until he came to a left turn. He sped down this
side street of terraced houses, causing the boys on the road to
scatter to both sides, took the next left turn, which gave onto
a pot-holed street, and came to dead end at the river.

He jumped out of the car and saw her on the far side.

'Áine!' he shouted, both hands cupped to his mouth. She
looked around and he jumped up and down and waved his
arms to catch her attention. She was perhaps a hundred
yards away, and turned and held a hand above her own eyes
to see him. She waved briefly back, and lowered both arms.

'Stay there!' he roared, pointing to the ground with both
hands. He couldn't tell whether she had heard or understood, or really if it was her at all, but at least for now she
wasn't moving so he jumped back into the car, reversed over
the pot-holes, and sped back past the children who shouted
abuse at him for disturbing their football game twice.

But Jack was oblivious to all this, barely heeding the other
traffic as he cut across to the far side of the road and accelerated up over the bridge. He pulled the car towards the centre

of the road so that the oncoming car had to swerve to avoid him, and darted onto the road parallel to the river. As the car slowed, and he finally came up on her, she was looking around as if unsure where he would come from.

He waved her over to the passenger side, ignoring the traffic backing up behind him, and when she sat next to him he even paused to take in her face, every bit as beautiful as he remembered, before driving back into the maze of streets.

It was still light when they reached the house, and would be for hours yet, but there were no cars outside, and Jack searched around for Gladys, to find that she had cleaned up the kitchen and bedroom and left. They were alone.

The days they had been apart seemed never to have existed. All the longing Jack had felt poured into her as she sat on him, clawing at his chest, hair falling over her breasts. Now she looked heavenward, keening at the ceiling, and pressed her hips down onto him with all the force she could muster. And then as she rolled her head around in some ecstasy of her own it was as if somehow time itself slowed down and her hair spun by over him again and again until he was surrounded by a perfumed wind and it carried him away beneath her, as space too gave way to her power over him.

Desire is a hunger, a hunger in the mind, that holds men on a certain course, no matter how devastating. And to know a desire that can never ever be quenched, nor overtaken, nor replaced, is to fall forever into an abyss.

Áine is different this time, not hard and urgent, but all caresses and lingering, and he knows now there is an infinite breadth to her lovemaking, that Áine can always delight him, that there will never come a time when he will not want to be hers.

Áine, and Áine alone, will sate him now, for the rest of his days, and no matter how insistent any other voice, no words that will ever be told to him, no thoughts that he will ever have, no image that ever comes to his mind, will sway him from this beauty.

She will always, always, be there. He will draw all his energy from her. Áine will be the heat and the light, the flame that pushes away the cold, the dark, and all fear, even fear of death itself.

They showered together, but when Jack slid his hands down the back of her wet body she pushed him gently away.

'Please,' she said, 'let me just feel this water on me.'

He kissed her forehead, pushed the glass door open and left her alone with the warm water flowing over her. He watched her as he dried himself. She just stood there, arms clasped over her breasts, her wet hair now a dark veil that clung to her shoulders, her head tilted slightly to one side. It was a familiar image but he could not then think why.

Jack put on his towelling robe and flip-flops and padded down the bare boards of the hallway and onto the new quarry tiles of their kitchen. He wondered what kind of food Áine liked, or whether she would like to go out to eat. Did she drink? Would she like wine?

He was still opening and closing the many oak doors when he heard her singing again. He straightened up and looked across the counter that separated the kitchen from the huge living area that was the entire south half of the house. She was standing there, slowly towelling herself dry, eyes closed as she concentrated on the words of a song, in what sounded to Jack like Irish.

Over the months that he had been here he had learned a fact that he concluded to be at the root of the Irish temperament — no two days were the same. He could take photos out the picture window behind Áine at the same time every day forever and never get two identical shots. The sky, the sea, the vegetation on the far mountains, the growth in the fields, and the sunlight itself would never combine in exactly the same way again.

Out of sight, beyond the western window, the sun was just meeting the horizon, and it struck Áine from that side with a light yellowed by its journey from the far side of the ocean, casting a perfect shadow of her on the opposite wall.

And this body of gold that sang and raised and lowered her arms as if to feel her own heat, and moved around in a languorous, spontaneous dance, was framed by the view southward, across ripening fields and dark blue fingers of sea to the hills whose granite rocks returned yet more of this light from above slopes of purple heather.

This was the hidden beauty revealed. Timeless, momentary and unpredictable. Not if he waited a thousand years would he see this again. Some other unforgettable Irish sunset, yes, but this one — with the sun goddess herself bathed in its light — never again.

Áine opened her eyes, looked over at him and smiled. She made a long skirt of the towel, held out her arms, and faced the sun, so that she threw a cruciform shadow on the wall behind her.

Outside, the fields leading up to the cliffs were already in shade, and, as Áine's shadow was raised to the ceiling by the dying sun another broad flat-topped shadow followed it and it too had arms and a ring with four quadrants of light. The image of the Celtic cross between them and the sea.

Áine's eyes rolled back in her head as they had done that first day, her song died away and she crumpled down onto the floor. Jack ran over to her. This time she had passed out and he scooped her up in his arms, looked briefly out at the silhouette of the cross against the last orange glow between sea and sky, and carried her over to the couch.

She was cold to the touch, so he turned on the heating and lit the gas logs.

What had he just seen? He looked back to where she had been dancing — the part of the room that was over the old fairy ring. The monks had built their cross so that it cast its shadow on the earlier pagan structure, but even they had not dared to destroy it. He stood up and rubbed his temples.

Noreen's words came back to him — 'Don't you think we're a bit rich in coincidences?' she had said. He would go and see her, get her take on this.

Áine stirred, pulled the towel tight around her shoulders and knelt down by the gas flames.

'They stole the sun,' she said.

'Who did?' Jack asked.

'The Christians, with their sky god.'

'Do you know what happened just now?' he asked her, but she was still intent on the fire, and seemed not to have heard. Then she turned to him and said, 'They must decide, Jack. The sun or the cross. It can't be both ways.' She stood up. 'And after tonight you must decide between us. Maeve or me. You must choose.'

The rest of their evening was subdued. He plied her with more questions about herself while they ate, but she remained as evasive as ever, eventually saying, 'Jack, please leave me alone about myself or I won't stay the night.'

'Áine, be reasonable! You're asking me to leave my wife for you.'

The green eyes blazed back at him. 'I have slept with you. You've heard me sing and watched me dance. We've walked and talked together. What more is there to know?'

'A last name would help,' he quipped, but was sorry as soon as he had said it, as she would figure that he wanted it only so that he could investigate her further.

'I want your last name,' she replied.

'I loved your song,' he said, moving away from this subject with all its implications.

Áine smiled widely back at him. 'I learned that as a child, a long, long time ago. We all sang it, to the sun, to come and ripen the crops again tomorrow.'

He held back from all the questions this raised, offered her more wine, which she declined, and suggested the bedroom again with movements of his eyes, which she accepted by standing up and silently leaving the room.

They made love all night, dozing in each other's arms while he recovered, until, finally, with the birds beginning to chirp outside the window, they fell into a real sleep, and awoke to the hammering of the carpet-layers at work in the other bedrooms.

It was another sunny day. Jack checked the kitchen for Gladys, but her loyalty was to Maeve, not to him, and the old lady was not there today. He could see Sonny's car down by Sweeney's, where they had now demolished the wall and dug trenches for a foundation. It didn't look as if they were following Cathal's advice for a single heavy slab, but what the heck — there was hardly a straight, plumb, level wall in the whole of Rathbrack.

He walked confidently out to the car with Áine, drove down the hill and headed back into town.

'Have you decided?' she asked, fixing her green eyes on him as he drove.

'Yes.' She waited while he took in a deep breath. 'I'll meet you in town tomorrow night. I just need tonight' — he paused, turning to her — 'to tell Maeve.'

She put a warm hand on his as he changed gears, leaned into him and kissed his cheek. Then she slumped back in her own seat, as if she were exhausted from the effort of winning him over. Or the tension of not knowing. Or both.

Chapter Nineteen

He dropped Áine where he had picked her up the previous day, and drove on to the hospital. Maeve was still in bed in the maternity wing, awake, but looking tired.

'Oh, Jack, I'm glad you're here,' she said. 'I'm just waiting for Lowry. They wanted him to look at the blood tests.' She held out both hands to Jack and he sat down on the bed next to her. 'You didn't bring me any clothes,' she said.

'Oh, jeez, sorry, I just didn't think....' He knew she hated to wear the same clothes twice, but she smiled back at him now as if she didn't care.

'Jack, I'm so afraid I'm going to lose this baby.' Tears formed in her eyes. 'Oh God, I was thinking, what if it ever came to a choice between my life and the baby's?'

'Maeve, stop torturing yourself.'

'But if it ever did, Jack, promise me you'd tell them to save the baby, and not me.'

'But Maeve, I don't think I would.'

They were interrupted by the white-coated obstetrician.

'Good morning, Maeve,' he said, all but ignoring Jack. A nurse scurried in behind him and asked Jack to wait outside.

He stood at the window in the corridor, lost in his thoughts. He was doing something thoroughly abominable leaving her like this. Should he stay and tough it out till the baby was born? Would Áine agree to that?

But there would never be a right time. And Áine had been pretty clear that she wanted him to decide now. He had never been in this position before. In his previous marriage it had been the other way around. And what about the baby?

He knew that it was his child too, but it was not growing inside him, and he knew that if he were asked to give up his own life for this unborn foetus he would almost certainly refuse. What if he were required to die to save both Maeve and the baby? Morally, that would be much harder. He shook his head. This was a marriage he was ending, not a life.

The nurse cleared her throat behind him. 'You can come in now,' she said. Jack followed her back into the room where Maeve was now sitting up on the edge of the bed.

'You'll be very pleased to know,' said Lowry, 'that you probably saved your wife's life and certainly the baby's by bringing them here when you did.'

Jack stared at Maeve.

'My hero,' she whispered.

'I don't get it,' said Jack.

'She ingested something highly toxic,' said the doctor. 'According to the lab it was definitely organic, and if we hadn't given her a muscle relaxant when we did, and it had run its course for maybe as little as another half an hour....'

'So why am I not affected?' Jack asked.

'Something I took that you didn't?' Maeve suggested.

'Well, then it's not in the water, and we've been eating the same stuff,' said Jack.

'Anyway,' said Lowry, 'there's nothing more we can do here. I've given you a prescription for a couple of different things to help. Get plenty of rest and be careful. Another attack like that could prove fatal.'

Jack left Maeve in the car while the chemist made up the prescriptions, brooding as he waited on how he should explain himself to her. And all the way home he tried to bring himself to tell her, but he had no idea how to begin.

She brightened up immediately when they reached the house and she saw the progress that had been made. Already they were laying the under-felt in the living-room, the floorboards where Áine had sung and danced now hidden.

'We just need some plants to take the harsh look off the corners and it'll look like this house has been here for years,' said Maeve brightly. 'And we'll have the phone in, in what, about three weeks?'

Jack left her to take her medication and carried his typewriter into the study.

'Maybe it was the paint fumes,' she said, passing him on her way to the bedroom to rest. He nodded as he fed a blank page into the roller. Then he was seized by the thought that she would notice Áine's presence somehow. He had tidied up and straightened the sheets, but surely some clue would give him away. Too many used towels? Blonde hair in the shower?

Maeve reappeared in the doorway and clasped either side of the door jamb. He looked up at her, staring quizzically back at him. She knew.

'It's a girl,' she said.

He nodded stupidly, got slowly to his feet, glanced at her, then back at his typewriter.

'I guess that's not what you wanted?'

'Aaaahh....'

'Oh come on, Jack, think about it — a little baby girl!'

'The girl is a baby! I mean the baby is a girl!'

'Yes, yes!' she said.

'Oh that's great! Great!'

'Sorry, I didn't mean to interrupt. I just forgot, they told me that last night.'

'No. Yeah. I was thinking of something else.'

'See you later,' she said, and was gone.

Jack collapsed back into his chair, flopped his arms on the typewriter and laid his head on them. One thing he knew for sure — he was not cut out to have sordid little affairs. All or nothing. He would not have his mind corroded by keeping in place a whole fabric of lies. He would be honest about this, would tell her what he had decided, and leave.

But he couldn't just leave her like this. He stood up and stared out the window. He was reminded of his first sight of Áine on the beach. Something had changed, changed completely, with her arrival, the day after the storm, with the huge breakers rolling in.

He no longer loved Maeve. He could barely stand to be in her presence. Everything she stood for now repulsed him. She wanted this house. He didn't. It was like a prison now. He just wanted to be free — free to be with Áine all the time.

Then an idea occurred to him and he sat down again and spun the paper down to starting position. He typed:

> I, Jack Amonson, owner of the property situated at Rathbrack Hill, Rathbrack, being of sound mind, do hereby quit all claim to this property, the house and the land, in favour of Maeve Fitzgerald.

He looked at what he had written with some satisfaction, then decided that it should probably be witnessed if he wasn't going to be around. He typed in his own name as the signatory and Noreen Fletcher as the witness.

Maeve was rested enough by dinnertime to help Jack prepare a light meal, which they ate in the kitchen. She noticed the empty wine bottle from the previous night and chastised him for drinking alone.

'A girl, Jack,' she said lifting her glass to him.

'Is that what you wanted?' he asked.

'It would have made no difference at all to me,' she replied. 'You know it's the man who determines the sex of the baby, the XY chromosome thing — not us at all.'

He nodded diffidently. Maeve had grown used to seeing him preoccupied with his work and made little of it. She went away and returned with two of her decorating books.

'Now that we know it's a girl,' she said, 'do you want to help me pick out the look for your little princess's room?'

For two of the most miserable hours he could yet remember Jack discussed cots, bedspreads, borders, curtains and the conflict between primary colours and pastels. Maeve made lists of possible combinations, of the pros and cons of the ideas in her books, and of the numbers of the paint samples that appeared to match the photos or items of furniture.

'I kept wanting to tell her,' he said to Noreen when he drove down to see her later. 'I just don't know how.'

'Yes, well don't expect any sympathy from me there,' said the poet. 'If you're going to slink away with another woman, the more gutless Maeve perceives you to be the better.'

'Is that how you feel about Byrne?' he asked.

'Ah, touché! Well, no, no I don't. I just feel sorry for him. He really thought Christianity had a monopoly on God, and then in one flash of truth he lost it all. By the way, where were you that morning, Jack?'

'With Áine.'

Noreen stiffened in her wheelchair. Light from the west filled her cottage as it had Jack's living-room.

'What makes you so sure,' she asked, 'that this was all happening to Áine, and not being caused by her?'

Jack looked across the table at her. You wouldn't ever say she was pretty, but she had one of those triangular faces that age well, and short hair that lent emphasis to her eyes — and these, he felt, would never lose their icy, penetrating stare.

'You're such a goddamn conspiracy theorist,' he said. 'You should get together with Aaron and come up with a new book on the Kennedy assassination.'

'I have my own ideas on that,' she said.

Jack threw up his arms in exasperation. 'But this girl....'

'When did you first see her, Jack?'

'With Aaron. On the beach.' He paused. 'The day after the storm.'

The light was waning, the sky outside the back window near to night, but still there was a glow over the bay.

'Don't do this, Jack,' said Noreen softly. 'Leave, yes, but take Maeve, not this ... this girl.'

'Meaning?'

'She's not what you think she is.'

'Look, Noreen, give over on this. I don't believe in fairies. I never have and I never will, okay?'

'How can you be so sure?' she asked.

'All right, all right. I'm open to the possibility of the paranormal. As you say, just too many coincidences. But I know this girl — this woman. We're lovers. And if she has any part in this, I can tell you I believe — with every single fibre of my being, Noreen — that she's an innocent victim in it.'

'I hope you're right,' the poet replied slowly.

'Even if *you're* right,' he said, 'I'd kill anyone who got in my way.'

Noreen sighed and shook her head. 'Oh Jack, Jack.'

He stood up.

'Are you in a hurry back?' she asked.

'No. Maeve's asleep. Sedated.'

'And this bout of food poisoning, Jack. Don't you see, they're trying to kill her?'

'Here we go again,' he said.

'Well, if you're not in a hurry, how about wheeling me to the end of the pier and back?'

'Sure, but that's as far as it goes, okay.'

She laughed as he stood up and opened the front door for her. 'You cheeky yank!' she said as she passed him and he took hold of the chair's handles.

From the end of the pier the monks' design was obvious. And now, as they watched, the shadows of the church and gravestones crept up the hill, and the Celtic cross, above all, made it to the summit. Or, as it seemed from where they stood, the light retreated up the hill from this advance, but could not be seen to go anywhere else, and might well have simply vanished underground into the hill.

Jack saw Áine again in her unforgettable dance, glistening, the hair both light and dark, and heard the humming that became words. In the long Irish twilight swallows darted back and forth over the harbour, feeding on the midges. Beyond, the extension to Sweeney's took shape, the concrete pillars now in place, with spikes of iron rising out of them.

'My money at work again,' said Jack.

'They're still at it,' said Noreen. 'How can they see what they're doing?'

Jack peered into the gloaming and made out two figures, gesticulating as if they were having an argument, one circling the other. And then Micko must have been told by his customers, as he so often was, that they weren't paying to sit and drink in the dark — the lights in the pub came on, lighting up the two distant characters as if they were on a stage.

It was Áine, arguing with Fortycoats.

'That old guy is back,' said Jack.

'MacHenry,' said Noreen. 'And I take it that's Áine?'

They watched as Áine appeared to make some point, then shied away again, then shook her head. At this the old man raised his walking stick as if to hit her, but he didn't and lowered it slowly again.

'Holy Shit!' shouted Jack. 'Hey you, Fortycoats!' he yelled across the water. 'Get your hands off her!'

They heard him and turned. Then Áine looked back at the old man, sank to her knees and prostrated herself in front of him.

But Jack was already running back along the pier. He galloped past the front of the pub, hearing flashes of conversation through the windows, and then crashed into Fortycoats who stepped out from just beyond the gable wall.

Jack grabbed the man by his over-sized coat and shouted at him, 'What were you doing to her?'

But he had underestimated the old man. Fortycoats raised his right arm and delivered a smack to the side of Jack's head that sent him careering against the side of a parked car.

By the time he straightened up, Fortycoats was already crossing the street with his back to him.

'What were you doing, asshole?' Jack persisted.

'Ask her,' came the reply.

Now Jack turned his attention to Áine, still on her knees, with her eyes fixed on the old man.

'Are you all right?' he asked, coming over to her. Áine got to her feet, smiled at him and allowed him to embrace her. 'What was that all about?'

'He doesn't want me to go with you,' she said.

'What?' Jack shouted, his head throbbing from the blow.

'He thinks you won't bring me back.'

'No, I mean, what's it got to do with that old fucker?'

She pulled back from him, her eyes wide, a look of shock on her face. 'He's my father,' she said.

Jack stared back at her. So many thoughts now rushed through his head that he had no hope of sorting them out. 'Wait here. I'll get the car,' he said.

She nodded and folded her arms tightly about herself as if she were very cold.

'Jack!' Noreen shouted, seeing him reach his car as she herself reached the inner end of the pier. But if he heard, he ignored her. She waved as the lights passed over her, but he screeched back down past the pub and jammed to a halt. She heard him rev up again when Áine had got in, and saw the lights on the hedges as he sped around the coast road, and his tail-lights vanished over the brow of the first hill.

She had also seen the old man cross the street and march down the road that led to Fitzgerald's farm and Gladys Clery's house. She knew that she could wheel herself along this level road, so she decided to follow him. He hadn't been around lately, but she remembered his face in her window on the day of the storm, and now with his connection to the girl, her curiosity overcame any fear that he might turn on her.

But as she pulled herself along the dark road without catching sight of him ahead of her she found it difficult to control her active imagination. The beech trees that ran down both sides — the closest Rathbrack came to a wood — were now a leafy canopy that broke up even the starlight. It was so dark that she was not even sure which side of the road she was rolling along, let alone how far she had come, until she saw the light in a window of Gladys's cottage.

Noreen drew level with the house and slowed down. All the lights appeared to be on, and she could see directly into the living room through a gap in the hedge.

And there was Fortycoats — dancing with the old woman! At first, Noreen was taken aback, but then she smiled at the idea of these two crazy old people comforting each other. They held her attention for a long time as they waltzed around the room, in and out of her view, throwing their joined shadow towards her or onto the back wall when she couldn't actually see them.

If they were playing music, she couldn't hear it. And as she watched she noticed an energy to their movements that she would not have associated with people their age. They had real rhythm, their heads rose and fell, and their steps were just too perfect.

People had been commenting on the change in Gladys, how she was no longer seen in Sweeney's, how she was out and about early in the mornings, in good humour all the time, and not just when she'd been drinking.

With difficulty, Noreen managed to wheel herself around behind the house. The back window threw its light onto the old hen-house, revealing something very strange — there were bird feathers hanging over the edge of the roof into the light. And now that she focused her attention on the roof she saw that it was entirely covered in white bird wings, tacked in place so that they overlapped like shingles with pointed ends. There must have been a few hundred of them.

Noreen gasped. She had heard from Jack about Gladys shooting seagulls, but she had never ever suspected that this was what was behind it. No part of the original hen-house roof was left uncovered, and the wing-tips hung like icicles over the eaves. White feathers. A roof of white feathers.

A fear beyond any she had ever known came over her. Any lingering doubts about Cathal's drawing, or John Byrne's eel, or Jack's description of Áine fainting vanished. She knew what she was looking at, and now it all made sense — appalling, unreal, pagan, even primeval, sense.

She backed the wheelchair towards the front of the house again, her hands shaking so badly when she lifted them from the wheel rims that it was hard to get a fresh grip. And she began to wheeze. Silently she cursed herself for believing this had all been mischief with no plan behind it. She bumped into the unseen gate and it rattled.

Noreen froze, her eyes darting between the back of the house and the front door. If she could only stop hyper-ventilating ... but the fear wouldn't go away, and now she didn't want to see what was happening in the house, never wanted to look on that face again.

She couldn't feel her hands. And when she did bring herself to look up, everything was blurred. It became harder and harder to breathe — took a conscious effort. One of her legs shot out of the footrest in spasm. She was having an attack, and she was over a mile from her house and the tablets that saw her through these. With a superhuman effort she spun the wheelchair round, gripped the wheels hard, and pushed the chair forward as far as she could without toppling out, then slid her hands carefully back so that her fingers stayed locked around the hand ring and did it all again.

All her ideas about God being a woman withered. Whatever lay behind the creation of the cosmos was not to be brightly contemplated over a cup of herbal tea. Even the Christians had gone too far in their belief that they could appease God. But the pagans who were here before them....

Her other leg now shot out from under her, so that she had to bend double to work the wheelchair. And she felt her neck muscles tighten, making it almost impossible to move. Now she was all but blind, just blurry spots dancing around in front of her, and all she could do was feel her way along the road by the grass and nettles rubbing against her arm.

'Derek! Derek! Derek!' said Gladys over and over as they danced around her living room.

'We're alone at last,' said the fighter pilot.

'Yes,' she said, tightening her grip on him. 'They took the donkey and trap into town and they won't be back till all hours!'

'Didn't I tell you I'd come back?' he said.

'And didn't I say I'd wait till the end of time for you, darling?' said the young girl whose father laboured on Fitzgerald's farm and grew vegetables down the side of the house and whose mother raised hens for their eggs.

Her dark hair fell down past her shoulders in smooth waves, her blue polka-dot dress clung to hips that had filled out in the last year, and she wantonly pressed against his blue-grey uniform the breasts that no man had ever seen. He knew it was time for her and kissed her until she broke away and led him, both hands clinging firmly to his, as if he might go away again, into her bed. Gladys giggled with delight when he fell on the bed next to her. She felt his hand slip under her skirt and onto her thigh and she sighed with the contentment of a child who has discovered some new, wholly unimagined pleasure.

'You'll help me again?' he asked.

'Anything, Derek, anything.'

Chapter Twenty

'Do you need to go back for your clothes?' Jack asked.
'No,' said Áine. 'Just take me somewhere away from Rathbrack for tonight.'

They were now well inland. Jack was finally calming down enough to broach the subject of Fortycoats. 'I guess at least I know your last name now. MacHenry, right?' he said.

Áine looked out her window for a while without replying, then she smiled at Jack. 'Does it matter to you?' she asked.

'No,' he said. 'No, not at all. But if I'd known, I might have been kinder to the man.'

'Or less kind to me?'

There was a petulance about Áine tonight that he had not noticed before. He knew nothing about her relationship with her father, but he suspected she was probably ashamed of the old man. She certainly hadn't mentioned him before. All he really wanted to do now was reassure her.

'We all have dark things hidden in our past,' he said, 'and we all have family we love who don't accept us or can't see things our way, or don't treat us very well.'

'But he had to do what he did to me, Jack.'

'What did he do?' Jack asked.

'I can't tell you that now.' There was a sadness about Áine's voice as she answered this, and the memory seemed to send her into a kind of trance. She just sat there, staring ahead of her, while they drove on and on through the night.

While she was like this, Jack began to wonder for the first time about Noreen's comments. Had the storm brought

Áine? Hadn't Fortycoats first appeared when they began work on the site? Didn't Noreen suspect Fortycoats of complicity in the death of Owen's cattle? And hadn't that given them a final opportunity to change their minds about building on the hill? Was Áine part of some strange plot to get him away from the hill, and where did Maeve fit in in all this?

'My name is not MacHenry,' said Áine.

'Then what is it?' he asked.

She swung around to him, tossed back her hair, leaned forward and kissed his cheek.

'Áine is my name,' she said into his ear. 'MacHenry is *mac an rí* — the son of the king — but I'm not the son of the king. That's my father's name, not mine. I'm the daughter of the sun. Haven't you seen the sun in my hair and on my skin?'

'Yes, I have,' he replied. Her voice was so soothing next to him, he wanted to pull over and close his eyes, but he was afraid to break the mood, and he drove on.

'And haven't you felt the heat of my body?' she continued. 'Do I not arouse the flames of passion in you?'

He nodded. She was arousing it all now. She stroked his hair and blew on his face. 'Where are you taking us, Jack?' she asked.

'Anywhere you want to go,' he answered. 'How would you like to go back to California with me?'

She drew away at this question.

'Hey, if you don't like it,' he said, 'we'll come back, live in Ireland.'

'Oh, Jack, we have no need of any paradise in the west, over the ocean. I am the sun that will shine for you forever if you stay with me.'

She was too much. They came to yet another striped pole with signs telling the distance to various towns, but Jack did not know which, if any, of them, would have a hotel.

'Any ideas?' he asked.

'Turn right if you want to cross the Shannon,' she said.

They swung onto this winding secondary road.

'So you do know your way around,' said Jack, 'Then what part of the country do you think we should try?'

'Rathbrack,' she answered without hesitation.

Jack cleared his throat. 'That's going to be a bit awkward, don't you think?'

'Why?'

In that one word all the warmth drained from her voice.

'Because Maeve is there,' he said calmly.

'Maeve will soon be gone,' said Áine. Now there was a hardness to her voice. 'You brought me to your house, Jack. Do you not want me there with you now?'

'Yes, but that's not really possible now. Maeve is there.'

'Maeve cannot stay there!'

'Okay, okay,' said Jack. 'We'll live somewhere around Rathbrack. I'll get used to it, if that's what you want.'

Áine banged a fist on the dashboard. 'That's not what I want! We have to live in your house on the hill!'

'No!' Jack insisted. 'Anywhere else but there. We can build another house just as picturesque on some other hill.'

Áine dug her hand into his hair, shook his head and screamed, 'Maeve can't live there. She will be gone! But you and I must go back there. Will you do this for me?'

Jack grabbed her wrist, but she had two free hands while he had only one.

'Áine, Áine,' he said, trying to calm her. 'That hill has a strange effect on everyone. Let's talk about this.'

She broke both hands free and pounded his left shoulder. 'No, no! You have to agree to this!' she cried.

Jack turned to her to push her away, and as he did so, the road curved sharply to the right. He felt the left wheels leave the road and bump their way through soft ground, and then the margin fell away and it was impossible to pull the car up onto the road again. He braked, which made it worse, then accelerated in the hope of pulling right under power, but instead the rear wheels went off the road and the car fish-tailed around and slid backwards down a grassy slope and into a stone wall.

The engine stalled, the metal creaked for a few moments and there were scrapes and thumps behind them as more of the rounded granite rocks fell under the weight of the car. And then there was just the sound of their breathing and the headlight beams shining up at the sky through a thin mist.

'Áine are you all right?' Jack asked, his own heart still pounding.

'He was right,' she murmured as she pulled at the door handle.

'Áine.' Jack laid a gentle hand on her shoulder, but she shrugged free and heaved the door open, then got out before it could slam closed again under its own weight.

Jack scrambled out his side and pulled himself up to the road. But Áine was nowhere to be seen. He cupped his hands and shouted her name.

She must have been tempted to reply because he saw her face when she turned towards him from the field beyond the wall, but she said nothing and when she turned away again it was difficult to see her.

Jack slid back down the slope and clambered over the broken wall as she must have done, then chased after her.

'Áine, you don't understand!' he yelled. 'I'd like to get Maeve to leave for you.'

Ahead of him, the thin figure in the gloom stopped and turned to him again. He ran up to her, breathless now, and looked into her eyes.

'Look,' he panted, 'Maeve is pregnant. How can you ask me just to throw her out?'

'Forget Maeve,' said Áine. 'And her unborn child. Tomorrow they will be gone.'

'What do you mean gone?'

'My father will have her killed.'

Jack's breathing came in visible gasps. He took a step back from Áine, and now she fell to her knees in front of him, reached out and wrapped her fingers tightly around his wrist, this time with both hands.

'For the last time, Jack,' she said, 'I beg you to say you will take me back to Rathbrack and that I can live with you as your wife on the hill. I promise you everything your heart desires. I will bear you a healthy child, from my perfect womb, and not a sickly one like Maeve. And I promise you, you will never see me grow old, and yet we will live a long time and be content, and I will sing and dance and be your lover' — she paused — 'forever.'

As she held onto him, the mist that rolled slowly by above them became the cover of an immense tent, and the wind that made it billow was held still by this power she had over time. He looked longingly into the green eyes that wanted to lure him down to themselves, and he knew then that Áine, kneeling in front of him as if she had sprung from the soil then and there on the dark grass, was a creature from some other world.

Now he believed that Maeve truly was in harm's way, and in a voice so weak it seemed hardly to penetrate the endless dark cavern between earth and cloud he said, 'We can't go back there, Áine. Today I gave the house and land to Maeve. It isn't mine any more.'

Áine let go and howled, then covered her face and burst into tears. Unlike him she did not want for strength. It was deafening listening to her, as if somehow her voice resonated in this vast space. She sobbed on and on, and when he backed away she threw herself on the ground face down and pounded it. He felt the energy through his legs. She rose to her hands and knees and clawed furiously at the earth as if she wanted to be back inside it, then looked up at him again, her mouth wide open, eyes red with tears. She pointed at him and said, 'Jack Amonson, you defiled me!'

'You seduced me, Áine,' he heard himself answer.

'No! Maeve seduced you into doing what you did. But we gave you every warning. You came here from outside, and your wealth gave them the power to destroy me.'

'You're destroying yourself,' he said.

'You fool!' she shouted. 'You still don't see who I am, do you?'

'The daughter of the sun,' he repeated from the car.

At this she got to her feet again. 'Oh, yes, Jack. I am that. From childhood they knew I would be a great beauty and that's why I was chosen.' Her voice had grown not weary but languid again. 'But it's what I have become.' She held out her arms. 'I *am* Rathbrack,' she said. 'I am the spirit of the hill of judgement. Behold! Now you see what no one has seen before!

Áine's hair became a veil of light that spread down over her. The shirt and jeans she had been wearing became a white gown that rippled around her. Jack reached out to see if this was real or if he was having some kind of hallucination brought on by the accident, but he was too far away. She held out a hand to tell him to stay back, but he so desperately wanted to touch her again, he reached as far as it with his fingertips. And when he touched it, it was as if he had put his fingers in a flame, or scalded them. He recoiled with a gasp of pain, and when he looked again she was already backing away from him.

'You can never have me now, Jack,' she said, with a power coming through her girl's voice that reminded him of thunder. 'You will never forget me,' she told him, 'and no other woman will ever make you happy again.'

Áine spoke now as if from a distance, although she was still close to him. 'And because I am Rathbrack you must never, ever return there to me. If you do I will haunt you all the more. You cannot help them now, Jack. They too have made their own doom.'

The cloud that had hung above them dropped to ground level, swirling by like the breath of some giant and, as Áine dissolved into a pillar of light, Jack stumbled around trying to see her better until she seemed to come and go in the mist, and then he fell and scrambled to his feet a few times until he saw two lights. He pushed on towards these through the mist until he saw that they were the two beams of the headlights shining into the sky. He had circled around and was back near the broken wall and the crashed car.

Dawn came to Rathbrack through a thin haze, the chatter of unseen birds growing with the light. Noreen sat hunched forward in her wheelchair, freezing with the cold. But at least her sight was returning. She saw that she had made it most of the way back to the village, before giving up. Ahead was the shadowy form of the old cross.

She doubted she would be able to push herself all the way home, but at least if she got to the end of the street she could pull herself along the walls of the terrace of cottages. And yet she could not just haul herself home, crawl into bed and be free of what she had seen. The sun rose and the mist thinned enough to cast shadows.

Noreen waited until it was fully daylight, then turned herself around and began back towards Gladys Clery's. She would take a look at this house of white feathers in the morning sun. But she had not gone far when she heard a door slam shut ahead of her. There were no other houses here, so again she stopped and waited.

The valley was still in shade, but she saw the silhouette of someone joining the road from the right and coming towards her. She sighed with relief when she saw a handbag and not a walking stick and knew it was Gladys. Noreen wheeled herself slowly forward.

'Ah will you look who it is!' said Gladys as she approached.

'It's such a lovely summer morning,' said Noreen. 'I thought I'd visit the countryside.'

'Oh another glorious day! Aren't we only blessed with the weather these days?'

Gladys looked better this morning than at any time in the three years Noreen had lived in Rathbrack. She was still a stout old woman, but there was a firmness about her now. Her cardigan sat well on her shoulders and she moved with none of the slouchiness that came with her excessive drinking. Gone was the old scarf, and even her hair had some life to it.

'You're looking very well, Gladys,' said Noreen as the older woman came up to her.

Gladys unashamedly preened herself. 'It's love that does it,' she said. 'That's what you need, Noreen. Get a fine man for yourself there and you'll feel ten times better.'

'A man!' Noreen replied, widening her eyes. 'And who is this man that you've found, Gladys?'

Gladys looked dreamily up at the sky the way they did in the movies. 'There was only ever the one man for me,' she replied.

'And he's come back to you, has he?'

'He has!' Noreen could see that Gladys was caught up in

the memory. 'And he's as handsome as ever.'

'After forty years?'

Gladys pushed away this unwanted question with a wave of her hand. 'True love,' she said, 'is for all eternity.'

'I see.'

'Nothing will ever come between us again.'

'And what about this roof of white feathers on your hen-house, Gladys? Why did you do that?'

'What are you talking about?'

'You know what I mean!'

'I have to be getting on. Maeve Fitzgerald is not well and I must get up to look after her.'

'Fortycoats MacHenry told you to do that, didn't he?'

'I don't know what you're talking about,' said Gladys again, this time with her back to Noreen as she walked on.

'He made you build the house with a thatch of feathers to summon Áine, didn't he?' Noreen called after her.

Gladys quickened her already sprightly pace away from the woman in the wheelchair. For a while Noreen sat there, unable to piece together what was happening now. And then it all came to her. Gladys was their instrument! She tightened her grip on the wheel rims once more and propelled herself after the old woman.

Jack jumped down from the cab of the tractor that had given him a lift as far as a village crossroads and ran to a phone box outside a sweetshop that doubled as a post office. Dial tone! One. Zero. The mechanical dial took an eternity to send out the pulses, and then the phone rang and rang and rang.

'Operator,' said a surly voice at the far end.

'Hello, yes, I need to make a call to a guesthouse and I need to reverse the charges.'

'What's the number?'

He recited what he hoped was the right area code and number for Mulcahys'. There was silence. Then ringing. Then silence again.

'There's no reply,' said the operator.

'Okay, okay, I want to try another number. It's an Owen Fitzgerald and he lives in Rathbrack.'

'Do you have his address?'

'No but he's the only one!'

'Hold on and I'll see.'

Again there was silence.

'There's no reply there either,' said the voice.

'Ah shit! Fuck, fuck!'

The line went dead.

'Hello?' Jack tapped the cradle a few times, then banged the receiver down. It was too early. That was all. He stepped out into the cold morning air again, folded his arms and paced around.

Gladys let herself in the front door with the key Maeve had given her.

'Hello? It's me!' she said. No one answered so she walked into the kitchen and put her handbag up on the counter, humming to herself. She filled the electric kettle with water, picked up the red enamel teapot and rinsed out the old leaves that were in it. Then she went back over to her hand-bag, fumbled in it and found a small brown-paper bag, its top rolled tightly all the way down to stop the powder in it from spilling.

Gladys remembered buying sherbet in bags like this as a child. She brought the bag back over to the teapot and kettle and then her brow wrinkled as she tried to decide whether to put the poison in the kettle now or wait till she scalded the teapot and then put it in with the leaves. And for the life of her she couldn't remember what she had done the last time. 'Use all of it,' was all he had said.

Gladys had her back to the door, and with the carpet in the hall and corridor now laid she didn't hear Maeve walking down from the bedroom.

'It's you, Gladys! I thought it was Jack,' said Maeve from the doorway.

The old lady let out a gasp of surprise. The paper bag

dropped from her hand onto the counter by the kettle. She stared at it for a few seconds, then swung around in the same place so that it was still hidden from Maeve.

'Oh God, Maeve, you shouldn't sneak up on a person like that. You're after putting the heart crossways in me!'

'I'm sorry, Gladys,' said Maeve, leaning against the door-jamb for a few seconds before moving to the kitchen table to sit down. 'You're here very early,' she said, as she spread out a sheet of paper on the oak table.

'Sure, wouldn't it be a sin to sleep in on a day like today, Maeve?'

'I suppose,' her employer replied, still intent on the piece of paper. 'Gladys, why would Jack sign over the house to me? I found this next to his typewriter. And where is he?'

She looked up at the old woman who appeared startled to be asked these questions. And of course, so she should be — they had nothing to do with her. Maeve shook her head. She was still not fully awake.

'I suppose he went out before you arrived,' she said. 'Probably gone into town for something.'

The kettle began to boil over behind Gladys. She jumped at the sound, let out a sharp cry, and grabbed hold of the sink to steady herself.

Maeve laughed. 'My God, Gladys, you're making me nervous. What's wrong with you this morning?'

'I didn't get much sleep last night,' the old woman said, turning back to the window to switch off the power. 'Will you have a cup of tea, Maeve?' she asked, without turning back.

Maeve stood up. 'I think I'll go back to bed for a while and read.' She stretched, then rubbed her palms lovingly over her bump. 'But bring me down a cup, would you?'

'Oh, I will.'

Noreen was thankful that they had surfaced the driveway as she pushed her way forcefully up the hill. But she soon found it hard to grab the wheels before they began turning the wrong way, and for every quarter turn forward she slipped

back nearly as much. And she was exhausted. She turned the
wheels side on to the slope, cupped her hands and shouted,
'Maeve! Maeve!' but there was no response.

Again she took to pulling herself up the hill, sorry that she
had not gone straight to someone's door and sent them on
her behalf. Below her she saw a yellow schoolbus arriving
with the first load of children who poured into the
schoolyard. Damn John Byrne anyway! It hadn't occurred to
her to try the new priest, if there was one living there yet.

She had taught herself not to depend on anyone, had refused to accept this illness, had tried to alter its chronic
course by changing her whole life around. She might as well
have stayed in Dublin and proved that women do make
better stockbrokers. It was less stressful than what had be-
fallen her here.

Noreen came to the one level part of the driveway and
coasted around the little hairpin bend to the final ramp. But
now there was no hope of pulling herself along. She thought
of shouting again, but worried now that she would just alert
Gladys.

The only hope she had of getting up this steep part was to
pull herself backwards, using her feet as brakes every time
she let go the rim. But to do this she needed to slide most of
the way out of the chair. It worked the first few times, but
then her feet caught on a stone that she hadn't seen, and
instead of pulling herself along she pushed the wheelchair
out from under her.

Noreen fell awkwardly to the ground, and before she
could catch her lightweight chair it rolled clear of her and
trundled over the concrete embankment out of sight, down
into the long grass. There was nothing for it but to try to
continue on her hands and knees.

'Oh, God, somebody help me!' she moaned as she fell on
her face again after a few more yards.

She was lying there, willing her spastic legs to work when
a feeling came over her that they would, that her prayer had
been answered. She rolled over and sat up, then drew her
knees up under her, lowered them one at a time, then raised
them again. Shakily she pulled herself to her feet. She could

stand at home for short periods of time. Could she walk?

Noreen moved one leg warily ahead of the other. She gasped at the realisation of what had happened. She tried the other leg. It too worked. True, her hamstrings were in pain and her upper leg muscles had badly atrophied, but she had her balance and her muscle control back! She took the last few paces up onto the parking area and turned around to see how far she had come.

She was no longer alone. Sprinting up the hill to meet her was Margaret Mulcahy.

'Noreen!' she shouted. 'Jack called to say that Maeve is in real danger. We need to get her away from here!'

It was all too much for the poet. 'Yes,' she said, grasping the younger woman's shoulders. 'It's Gladys. She already poisoned Maeve and now she's going to do it again and....'

'I know, I know,' said Margaret. She too had a key to the door and she left Noreen, took the steps two at a time, and bounded into the house.

Gladys carried the large mug of tea carefully down the corridor, knocked twice on the door and pushed it open. Maeve had propped herself up with pillows, and smiled back at her. Her cheeks were wan, while Gladys's cheeks glowed with health as she strutted across the room. The spinster's eyes shone, clear and full, while Maeve's were sunken with tiredness — dim and watery above dark crescents of lifeless flesh.

'Now, there you are, pet,' said Gladys, placing the tea on the nightstand next to her. 'Is there anything else I can get for you?' Even her voice had gained a modulation it had never had before.

'No, thanks, Gladys. I think you need to do a washing. Check the basket in the bathroom, would you?' Maeve's own voice was a hoarse monotone, and that above all the actress could not abide. She reached for the tea that would perk her up, watching Gladys as she turned and walked with a peculiar stiffness towards the bathroom.

Maeve turned to Jack's side of the bed as she raised the mug to her lips and filled her mouth with the hot tea. And then it dawned on her — what had been troubling her since she awoke — he hadn't slept in the bed last night! There were no creases. It was still as Gladys had made it up! She wrapped both hands around the mug and stared. And those few seconds while she pondered her husband's whereabouts saved her life.

The bedroom door burst open and Margaret flew into the room, saw the drink in Maeve's hands and rushed over to her. The girl let fly with her right hand, sending the cup spinning towards the window, its brown liquid spiralling out, and smacked Maeve's cheek with the end of her blow, so that she spluttered and spat out the first gulp again.

The empty mug hit the window pane, cracking the glass.

Outside, Noreen looked up to the source of the noise. After a few seconds Margaret's face appeared at the window, looking down on her, and she saw the girl nod, saw the relief in her face that she had saved her friend.

All of the new-found strength in Noreen's legs vanished, and she toppled over, unable to stop herself. She lay there, helpless, and cried, and was still crying when Margaret ran by to retrieve the wheelchair, shouting, 'She's fine. She didn't drink any. Gladys broke down. She's telling Maeve everything!'

Noreen said nothing, just watched her tears forming on the dirt below her face and trickling slowly away. Directly beneath them, buried under gravel, and sealed in with asphalt, lay the stones that had once been the rath of judgement.

Chapter Twenty-One

The sun rose somewhere beyond the Cajon Pass and lit the Los Angeles basin, swiftly and predictably, as if a giant hand was sliding a brightness control to maximum. The headlights of the traffic on Interstate Ten winked out, and the cars, like some fantastic school of silvery fish swimming upriver, closed ranks and moved slowly together towards the Harbor and Hollywood Freeways.

Jack Amonson lay on his back beneath a single sheet in Aaron Rothberg's bungalow in Santa Monica, vaguely aware of this reality around him. He had been feverish again during the night, and when he tossed left and right now he pulled the sweaty sheet with him. The mini-blinds held back most of the light outside, and in the half-dark he went on dreaming.

Over and over he had seen this same scene. He stood on Rathbrack beach and the men with one eye paddled their canoes directly towards him. And as they drew closer to the surf they tilted their good eyes forward and whooped, working each other into a war frenzy.

Jack stood there, unable to move, as always, and waited. The dream ended as the line of canoes rode the surf to the shore, pushed along by the breakers, the warriors free now to put down their paddles and pick up crude weapons, roaring above the ocean as they shook spears and clubs at him.

But today the dream did not stop there. Now he heard the keels of the boats grinding onto the sand, and saw the men leap out from both sides. They charged forward from per-haps twenty or so of these war canoes, and when Jack looked

from right to left he saw that he was not alone on the beach,
that he was part of a long line of defenders, unleashing
arrows and running forward to meet this threat.

These were thinner, taller people. Although fast and athletic,
they lacked the ferocity of the invaders. They found themselves in an unwanted fight, and it was only when the first of
them were hacked down, their heads clubbed in with stone
axes, that the others grew angry enough to hold their own in
this life-and-death hand-to-hand combat.

But no one came to Jack's assistance, and four of the canoe
men surrounded him, yelping as they danced around. For the
first time since these dreams had begun he turned and faced
inland, as in his earlier dreams, and saw Rathbrack as it must
have been before the forest gave way to farms.

He saw the ring of standing stones around the hill, and
now, gathered within the upper space they defined, he saw a
throng of people, some standing, some sitting, mothers with
young children, older people, and on top of the hill, with no
one around her, a woman he was sure was Áine.

'Jack!'

He flailed around with his arms to keep the one-eyed savages at bay, but one ran in behind him and hit him on the
back of the head with his stone axe. Jack staggered and the
others saw their chance. They screamed and yelled, went for
his legs until they got him to his knees, and the last thing he
saw before his sight dimmed with the pain of the blows was
Áine, her white gown flapping around her, her hair cascad-
ing over what he saw was a cloak of white feathers as she
looked down from the hilltop on the carnage on the beach.

'Jack! For God's sake, man!'

'What? What?'

He shot up into a sitting position, thinking the savages
had left him for dead but that he wasn't dead. Yes, his head
hurt from the sudden movement, but now as he saw Aaron
standing above him he knew that it hurt from all the drinking
and not a real hatchet.

'Maeve's on the phone for you.'

Before Jack could protest, Aaron handed him the cordless
phone.

'Jack?' he heard his wife say.

Aaron stood by the bed until Jack replied, 'Yeah, it's me.' Then he left, pulling the door closed behind him.

'Oh, Jack, it's just wonderful to hear your voice.'

'Well, I just woke up so I can't sound that great.'

'But you do.' There was a pause. 'Just to have that little piece of you with me means so much.'

Jack groaned loudly.

'Jack, please don't hang up on me !'

'This is hopeless, Maeve.'

She didn't say anything and he knew she was crying.

'I can't go back there,' he said softly. 'It's not you, Maeve.'

'It's been five months,' she said. 'You have to get over this, Jack. Aaron says you're still not doing any better.'

'Are you in the house?' he asked.

'Of course I am. Where else would I be?'

'Were you thinking about me for long before you called?'

'Jack, why are you asking me these questions? Yes, yes, I think about you all the time. How many times do I have to tell you that I still love you, that I forgive you for whatever you did? Jack, this is your baby daughter I'm about to have and I want you here with me....'

He heard a distinct sob. She could have spared him that. She was acting out.

'You should have come over while you could still fly,' he said. They had had this conversation more times than he could remember.

'I know, I know. I was too angry and I'm too stubborn. But I will go over, Jack, after the baby's born. I told you that. That's a promise. I just need you to be here to help me through this. Please, Jack, I'm begging you!'

He hated for her to be like this. 'Are you alone?' he asked.

She sighed. She was used to this question. 'Yes. But Margaret is all but living here now. In fact, she has moved out of home because they've been renting out her room.'

'Isn't that a bit heartless?'

'It was her own idea. Makes it easier to be with Cathal.'

'Is he around?'

'Not tonight. Sonny spotted his car up here a few mornings,

and, well, they've only three weeks to go to the wedding.'

Jack stood up and paced around, the phone held to his ear. 'I can't believe how you've all just swept what's happened under the rug.'

'Jack. Five months. No one's seen Fortycoats since. Or the girl. Gladys is home, but she's being closely watched. It's over. Whatever they were up to didn't work, and they're gone.'

'And Owen?' Jack asked.

'He's in England. He lost in the High Court. He knew he would. I think he has a job. I gave him some money, but I don't think he'd ever go to America. He couldn't handle it, Jack. He's never lived anywhere but Rathbrack.'

'Can you see the sea?' he asked, sitting down on the bed.

There was a pause while she carried the phone to one of the windows. She had interrupted his dream with her phone call, but she had saved him from being beaten to death this time, no longer just watching and waiting. Now he was filled with indecision, and when she spoke again he knew that she sensed that at last she was getting somewhere.

'Yes, Jack, I can see the ocean. The bay is very calm. It's overcast. Very still.' She paused, but he didn't say anything. 'One of those bottom-of-the-sea days, Jack, as if we're way down here looking up at the surface of the real world.'

Jack shook his head at this reference to the underworld. 'What's the sea doing?' he asked.

'The tide's coming in now,' she answered. 'You know, I can tell when it's high and low tide from here now just by looking at the rocks.'

'Any ships?' he asked.

'No. Oh, yes — way, way out I see one.'

'We never bought that telescope,' he reminded her.

He was sure that made her smile.

'I'll buy it for you for Christmas,' she said softly.

Jack closed his eyes. He couldn't say he still loved Maeve, though he was sure he could rekindle it if he tried. But there was this rift between them now. He believed and she didn't.

'Maeve, just give me a little bit more time....'

'Oh, Jack, there is no more time. The baby's due in less than two weeks, and then Margaret and Cathal....'

'I'll be there,' he said, surprised with his own decision .

'Thank you, thank you, thank you,' she said, over and over, until he said he had to go and hung up.

'You're doing the right thing,' said Aaron as he poured them both a cup of coffee in his kitchen.

'What do you think happens to people who dream that they're dead?' Jack asked.

'Ah, everyone has the occasional nightmare about being shot or falling out of a plane or whatever.'

'But suppose it just goes on and on?'

'I don't know, Jack. I guess if it wears down your will to live, you eventually come down with cancer or something.'

'Yeah, I think that's what'll happen.' Jack stood up and pushed open the back door to look out at the hibiscus, still flowering in this endless summer.

It was impossible, standing here under the California sky, to believe in inviolable covenants with the past. Roots here ran no deeper than the sprinkler system just below the surface, and there were few buildings older than the oldest people. And this was the future — a place with no past where people and whole societies could effortlessly absorb every new idea — this was what the rest of the world craved.

Yes, he would go back to Maeve. He would break Áine's taboo, but just this one time, and then leave again with his wife and baby daughter and bring them here, where the past held absolutely no significance. He turned back around to Aaron, already engrossed in his day planner, and asked, 'Any chance of a ride to the airport later on?'

'You got it, Jack!' said his friend and agent, holding up a resolute fist and nodding his approval.

That night he flew from Los Angeles to London and took a connecting flight back to Shannon. He remembered Maeve holding his hand as they descended towards the Irish coast, all those months ago — her pleasure at the sight of the fields. But now as he flew back over the breadth of the island he

saw nothing. A blanket of cloud sat between the plane and
the land below, one that ran to the horizon in all directions.

On the final approach to Shannon the aircraft dropped
through this thick layer and only then did he actually believe
that he was there. He understood Maeve's elation, and more.
He knew why he didn't have the same feelings when he
returned to Iowa. He was not looking at an artificial state
created to manage the plunder of a land that had hitherto
known only the comings and goings of nomadic tribespeople.

Ireland had been settled for millennia, and the blood of
those first people ran through the veins of its inhabitants
today. He had been away five months, hardly a heartbeat in
the span of consciousness of this island. That thought tem-
pered his joy with a great, dark nameless fear.

In Rathbrack, Maeve looked up at the same cloud cover in
the windless sky. Another day like yesterday.

'Do you think he'll come?' asked Margaret.

'If this was the old Jack, I'd bet my life on it.'

Some gulls soared by outside the south window, screeching as they rounded the house, as if complaining about this
new obstacle on the hill. The two women walked from the
living-room back into the kitchen. Two of the gulls fluttered
into view, fighting in mid-air over a piece of food.

'This waiting is just terrible,' said Maeve.

'I know.' Margaret watched the two birds. Whatever they
were fighting over fell and they both spiralled down after it.
'This is what fishing is like,' she said. 'Really boring.'

The baby kicked. Maeve put one hand over her womb
and the other on the table to steady herself.

'I know what we'll do,' she said. 'Get the big bucket out
from under the sink. We'll drive down to the dunes and walk
around to the rocks. I remember we used to gather mussels
underneath the overhangs where the gulls can't get them.'

'Are you sure you're up to it?' asked Margaret.

'Oh sure. We'll be careful. Bring a couple of knives too.'

Jack sat behind the wheel of his rental car and studied the map. But he knew the way to Rathbrack. And he desperately wanted to go there. The rational man wanted to do the right thing by his wife, and the man who was haunted by dreams wanted to see the real Rathbrack one more time and try to put the dreams to rest — any way he could.

He started the engine. Áine had told him he would only make everything worse if he went back, but maybe she was tricking him, just as they had tricked Gladys. What if they didn't want him back because he knew too much? What if she really meant he would make things worse *for them* and not for the real people alive today?

Visions of Áine flooded his mind before he even reached the Limerick road. Always he saw her dancing with the sun streaming through the west window of the house. But now he was back in bed with her. And he could physically feel her arms and legs around him, her face rubbing past his. And besides, all she had really asked was that he do exactly what he was now about to do — take Maeve away from her hill.

The thought occurred to him that if he cuffed Maeve around, threatened her, maybe she would leave and Áine would return. And then this nauseated him so much that he pulled over and stood up out of the car. Surely it was just jet-lag? Besides, Áine had not offered any possibility of forgiveness. She had said that if he ever came back to Rathbrack she would haunt him forever. He got back into the car.

Maeve steadied herself as she walked along the broken ridge of wet rock, skirting the tide pools with their purple sea anemones, barnacles and periwinkles.

'I'm not so sure about this,' she told Margaret, now coming back towards her twenty feet below.

'Just throw me down the bucket,' said the younger woman. 'You were right, I can see tons of them under here.'

Maeve dropped the bucket onto the pebbles in Margaret's

path. 'I feel I cheated you into coming here to do all the work,' she said, settling herself down onto the spine of the rock.

'Ah, don't be silly, Maeve. Wow, these are big ones.'

'Restaurant size?'

'Oh, I'd say so.'

'We'll shave their beards off and boil them in garlic,' Maeve declared as she watched the swell lapping by into the bay. 'But be careful of your nails, Margaret.'

'I'm just going to take the really big ones,' said the voice below. 'And I'll try over where I climbed down. I saw more across from there.'

'Be careful,' said Maeve, listening to Margaret's boots crunching by.

In this light the mountains south of the bay were no more than dark humps, but it would be impossible to imagine the view between the peninsula and the hill without them. The one was a frame for the other.

Sweeney's extension was an appalling eyesore. Maeve had thought of complaining at the time, but it was too much of the pot calling the kettle black, and she had too much else on her mind. Noreen was no help. She had withdrawn from any involvement in the area. And the new priest was not as interested in aesthetic matters as Fr Byrne had been.

Cathal too was embarrassed by the way it had turned out. He called it a giant public toilet. Seen from around here it was at its most hideous, with its flat roof and its row of cheap windows that belonged on the bedrooms of semi-detached houses. These and the ugly black plastic drainpipes were its only features, really, as there wasn't even a door on this side.

Margaret scrambled over the seaweed and rock near the water's edge and carried the bucket up into the next little canyon. She disappeared from view and Maeve heard the scraping of the knife as she hacked the shellfish from their anchorage.

'How are those ones?' Maeve shouted.

'What?' Margaret replied.

Maeve stood up and began to pick her way back past the high-water mark. She would find another perch from where they could see each other.

She was almost back up to the grassy trail when the wave

struck. Behind her she heard the undertow, far too loud, and when she turned the water had already built up into a face that towered over her.

They would say later that it was a random occurrence, something that happened perhaps once a century. NATO sonar had picked up the seismic disturbance, and experts would agree that it had been the exfoliation of a large section of the underwater cliff that forms the edge of the continental shelf. A slab of rock the size of a football field had fallen away and plummeted from the shallow sea bottom off the Irish coast to the depths of the Atlantic, three thousand feet below.

Some of the waves it formed when it crashed through the water would cancel each other out, as when a ship sinks, and others would radiate in such a wide arc before reaching a distant shore that they would hardly be noticeable above the incessant surf there anyway. But as surely as when a stone drops in a pond, or a motor boat speeds across a still lake, whatever wave it did produce would travel all the way to the edge of that body of water.

The giant wave began to break, from right to left, as Maeve watched it, rooted by the sight of the impossible glassy green face. The foam cascaded over the rocks like a river in flood and spat smaller waves up the channels on both sides of her. The sea spumed as if it were actually boiling as the water found itself with nowhere to go, and then two roaring waves collided, making a geyser that fell on Maeve and slapped her to the ground.

As she fell, she tried to protect the baby, but the water was too powerful for her arms and somersaulted her forward, breaking her left arm when she tried to use it. And then it was over, and the sea was draining back down around her on all sides as if someone had flooded the field above her. She sat up, wincing with the pain in her arm, and rubbed her right hand over the child inside her, deathly afraid, praying it would kick, but there was no movement. None.

Now the wave had reached the beach, rolling almost to the dunes before breaking over them and then over the low wall onto the road by the monastery, and finally it surged into the harbour, carrying the water up onto the pier to break over the sea wall. But only a tiny fraction of the water spilled away like this; the rest turned back on itself, broke in the side door of Sweeney's and ran the length of the seaward wall of the old and new parts of the building, before spending itself in a rip-current that took the water back out into the bay.

As it subsided, as all waves do, it pulled in its path all the sand and stones its impact had loosened. The torrent of seawater that had been scooped up in the arm of the pier burrowed effortlessly under the blocks of Micko Sweeney's new extension, and when the water was gone the wall that had caused Maeve's earlier displeasure lurched down into this new trench. The plaster inside cracked free of the end walls and sprang away in whole sheets from the twisted and splintered ceiling beams, some of it falling to the floor while more flapped from one edge, held by the remaining nails.

It was a Thursday morning in late October. The pub was not yet open, and Micko was upstairs. The water that swirled over the old carpet looking for a way back out knocked over the new wire rack of postcards of the grotto and the Celtic cross. It had seeped away to a depth of a few inches before Micko came down, and it took him a while to comprehend the force that had torn away the wall of his new lounge.

Margaret did not drown. She was killed instantly when the water fell on her and pushed her head-first into a rock that shattered her skull. Her dead body tumbled over the now-submerged rocks and was swept onto the beach along the course of the wave and flung through a gap in the dunes. She was barefoot when they found her, and later on one of her boots was found on the pier.

Jack was just past Ballylacken when the fire engine with lights and sirens on came up behind him. His heart sank as he pulled over. Whatever had happened it hadn't even waited for him to arrive. Slowly now — what was the point in hurrying? — he drove into the village where there were more flashing lights, police cars, and an ambulance.

He saw Maura Mulcahy, surrounded by other women, her face buried in her hands, while a crowd stood around staring and pointing at the bay. The new priest ran across from the schoolyard, a small box in his hands, and climbed into the ambulance, watched by the children, their faces pressed to the windows of their classrooms.

Then a second ambulance hurried noisily in around by the church. Jack's hands shook on the wheel as he watched it join the first one. The back doors of the stationary ambulance opened and two paramedics in dark blue sweaters jumped out. And then he saw them helping Maeve down, wet, covered in a blanket over wet clothes, one arm cut free of them and held up in a sling. He jammed on the brakes, forgetting the clutch so that his car stalled.

'Maeve!' he shouted, as he ran to her.

She broke free of the two men when she saw him.

'Oh my God! Jack, Jack!' she cried back. 'Oh Jesus, Margaret is dead, Jack! They didn't want me to go in the same ambulance with her.' He embraced her awkwardly over her bulge and they stared at each other.

Maura Mulcahy tried to follow the priest, and when the other women held her back she pounded the metal doors with her fists and wailed, 'Give me back my child!'

'Is this your wife, sir?'

'Yes.'

'We must get her to the hospital immediately or she may lose the baby.'

'I thought I had lost her, Jack,' said Maeve. 'Oh my God, you don't know what it means to see you now. Here.' She had cuts on her forehead too, and by the sound of her voice she was in severe shock.

'Come on, Maeve. They have to get you to the hospital. I'll go with you.'

'You're going to see me through this, Jack, aren't you?'

'Yes,' he replied, as the men from the second ambulance wheeled up a chair for her. He would stay by her side, but he was unsure what good it would do. She had cheated death twice now, it seemed, and he feared that being near her he would only pull her down with him.

Chapter Twenty-Two

Jack took a taxi back to Rathbrack that night. His rental car was still parked outside Sweeney's. He had Maeve's keys, but she had parked the Peugeot at the far end of the dunes and he was much too tired to search for it.

As he stood outside, the loud buzz of conversation came out to him through the open windows, and the cars lined up and down both sides of the streets told him too that the pub was crowded. He wondered whether Sonny was there. He should offer his condolences, but what could he say?

Besides, he was exhausted. He hadn't slept for two days — not since Aaron had woken him from his last dream. And when Maeve came out of shock they were going to deliver the baby. He thought about her, lying there now, unconscious, with a drip in her good arm. She needed this baby more than ever to get over the nightmare of what had happened today.

The streetlight nearest the front door of Sweeney's shone down on the fine sand that had been deposited by the wave and smeared into a hundred interwoven footprints by the comings and goings here since. Everyone knew what had happened. He had seen it reported briefly on the evening news on the television in the hospital. But there was no angry mob here to deal with him. No one even connected this with the talking statue, let alone the house on the hill.

He was tempted to walk around to Noreen, but again his need for sleep was too pressing. And now that he was here he wanted to see the house his money had built. So he drove up the smooth avenue and carried his bag up the front steps, and into the hall. He switched on all the lights as he went, marvelling at how Maeve had completed the furnishings exactly as they had planned.

At first he told himself that it was because she had always expected him back. He walked around the living-room and looked back at the fireplace, then up at the open frame roof work. And then he paced over to the southwest corner where there was now a grand piano. That was a new idea.

A doubt crept into his mind. A couch ran the length of the west window. This was where they would have placed the telescope. And if she had expected him back, wouldn't she have bought the telescope or left room for it here anyway? He strolled down to the bedroom. The walk-in wardrobe was filled with Maeve's clothes. There was nothing of his there.

She desperately wanted him here now, but at some point she had written him off. He sat on the edge of the bed. She had invested too much of herself in this house now just to walk away from it. And if she was not prepared to believe in the powers she was up against, and to submit to them, then he had no idea how he would persuade her to leave.

Wearily he kicked off his shoes, peeled off his outer clothes and slid into the bed. Right now he just needed sleep.

He closed his eyes and drifted down the hill and out over the dunes to where the men on the beach were still hacking each other to death with nothing more lethal than bronze daggers. Áine's people were taller than the one-eyed invaders, their bows and axes more finely made, and they carried sturdy leather shields, but they still lacked the ferocity of the horde that was pushing them back from the beach.

And he was one of them again. He ran forward with them and pulled back behind their line of shields when the face from Cathal's sketch led the men from the sea towards them, hurling axes and spears that thudded against the leather.

There were perhaps two hundred in each army, but Áine's people included young boys and older men; the attackers were made up entirely of this professional caste of fighters with the missing eye as their mark.

He couldn't understand any of the words being shouted

back and forth, but in the next clash he saw that the defenders would surely lose. Their objective was to push the
invaders back to the sea, to force them off the beach and into
the water. But the attackers stood their ground, and every
time they could separate a few of the others they encircled
them with overwhelming numbers and beat them to death.

Stone on bone, as in his dream before. But now he was far
beyond that. He was immersed to the point that he was being
jostled when he failed to follow the tribe's direction. He
wanted to tell them that they must become as vicious as their
enemy, cull whom they could from the horde, chase them
down and hack them to pieces too. But he couldn't speak.

It was as if he was now cursed by all the months of saying
nothing, of going along with Maeve's ideas, of being no more
than an observer in the argument over spirituality between
Noreen and the Catholic priest. This was his fate for his part
in desecrating her hill — to see over and over this brutal
ancient drama and be helpless to alter its course.

The light began to fail. The fair-skinned defenders clung
to the top of the ridge of dunes and the invaders left them
there and retreated to their boats over the sand. Both sides
had reached a point where their men were too weak to inflict
any decisive harm. Jack watched in sick fascination as the
savages picked up some of the dead bodies of his people and
carried them away with them.

They set fire to one of the canoes and gathered around it,
but before they had torn the meat from the first corpse he
was caught up in the long file of his fellow fighters picking
their way back through the marsh that separated the dunes
from the hill. And now, at last, as they began back up the
slope of the hill, he saw its strategic importance.

This was a land of thick forest and impassable bog. Meadows
existed only on the margins of the two, or on hills such as
this. And these bronze-age people had neither the technology
nor any great inclination to change the landscape. Halfway
up the hill they walked past the ring of standing stones and
he saw now what had been hidden from view in earlier
dreams, but what he had long suspected — the outer faces
were carved, like the ones Cathal had shown him.

Women and families ran to the surviving men, and they dispersed into the crowd camped up here, sitting down to eat around small fires. Jack was left alone to stare back down at the single huge fire now blazing on the beach. He could hear the savages shouting, invoking whatever power would come from eating the bodies of their slain enemies.

They had come from somewhere else down the coast in those canoes and he was sure that this battle was one more act in a conflict that would decide which people would dominate Ireland for generations if not centuries to come. Once more the invaders were probing for a way inland. To access the rich hunting grounds of the wooded hills they would have to pass by the hill, or overrun it.

A hush rippled through the site. It was now fully dark, the fires reflecting on the inner sides of the stones, so that to be within the circle was to be a part of an oasis of light. Everyone's attention turned to the summit, and there, once again, was Áine, standing silently in her white garb. But it was not Áine who held the people's attention. Next to her stood someone else who shouted gruffly and who seemed to be putting an argument to some of the others.

Jack drifted in closer, and in a way he was not surprised when he caught sight of the face of their priest-king — Fortycoats! Grey and bearded, but younger-looking than the tramp in Sweeney's, he raised his arms out of a long cloak and pointed at the men, then at the fire on the beach. The others gesticulated toward Áine, who glared sullenly back at them.

They closed in around her, but the king pulled her back from them. Widespread shouting broke out and all of the men, women and children gathered on the flat summit to listen or participate. Áine was a prize. She had stood there all day to be seen by the warriors and to be given to the best of them, but no clear champion had emerged.

Her words came back to him — 'They knew I would be a great beauty.' And she was. She seemed to float above them. The people between Jack and Áine began to squat down on the ground, and he saw that she was standing on a wooden platform, which had made her so easy to see during the day, and now, exactly as on the evening he had seen her sing and dance, her voice rang out into the night, she shed her feathery cloak, and her body rose and fell with the same sensuality.

All Jack's memories of her flooded back to him. He saw her coming towards him the first day, saw the very look she had given him in Sweeney's, the light on her face as her hair came and went with the movement, the pliant legs, bending and stiffening, the green eyes flashing.

Was this what she meant by what she had become? That she embodied their culture, was there to prove to them that what they had achieved, their art and their ideas, were worth fighting and dying for? He prayed that she would look at him. Just one look and he would fight to the death for her.

The night seemed to pass far too quickly. Áine could not possibly have been performing for all those hours, and yet she was just chanting a lament to the stars when the first blue ribbon of light in the east outlined the tops of the trees.

She stood there, glistening, as he had seen her before, the sleeveless robe clinging to her breasts and hips. Her hair too hung differently, the wild cascades now pulled down close to her head with the sweat and the morning dew. Around him, as her last words faded away, there was silence.

She turned to the east, raised her fists over her head, and spoke some more words to the light. Then she fell to her knees, clasped her hands together and bowed her head. Jack tried to go to her, but he couldn't move. He told himself that was because it was a dream, but he knew it wasn't. He knew that he had been warned not to return, but he had, and now all his strength drained away and he watched in horror as she lay down on her back on the wood, her head to the north, arms and legs outstretched.

The king rose from the watchers who began a kind of synchronised humming. In one hand he held a sharply pointed knife and in the other a rock. Jack felt himself shake with rage, but he was powerless now. Áine's father stood over her and placed the knife over her heart.

The eastern horizon grew pale along its entire length, and then yellow where the sun was readying itself. Colour returned to the world and Jack prayed for night, for an eclipse, anything that would stop this. But relentlessly the disc of light rose from beyond the trees until it was fully present and banished the last of night beyond the ocean.

Jack saw Fortycoats raise his arm as he had that last day before he had tried to take Áine away from here. The rock crashed down onto the top of the hilt and drove the knife through her. Her body convulsed as a jet of her blood flew up into the air in front of the sun, catching the light as it broke into red droplets that seemed to fall slowly, slowly, to earth.

Jack broke free of whatever spell had held him in place and jumped to his feet. He heard himself shouting, 'No!' and reached out a hand, but as soon as he took a step forward the ground wobbled under him and he tumbled forward off the bed and crashed heavily onto the floor of the bedroom.

He sprang up and looked around, but he was alone. He dashed to the window. It was late morning. The tops of the dunes looked oddly smooth where the wave had broken over them. Two official-looking vehicles were parked on the sand, but everything was as it should be. Or should be now.

He shook his head and looked around, confused. It was always the same after these dreams, but this time it was much, much worse. He tore off his underwear and staggered into the shower. But even this was a memory of Áine.

As he stood there, with the water flowing over him, he realised that this was the water from inside the hill, the hill of judgement, and that even now, after however many millennia had passed, it was not without some tiny residue of her blood. Hadn't Maeve told him that they used blood in the mortar of the early monasteries that were still standing?

He was still brooding on this, towelling himself dry, when the phone rang. He didn't know where it was. There had been no phone when he left. But, predictably, Maeve had had an ivory one installed to match the lampstand beside the bed.

'Hello. Is this Maeve Fitzgerald's husband?' It was a woman's voice.

'Yes.'

'Dr Lowry wants to deliver your wife's baby this morning, but she's refusing unless you're here.'

'I'll be there in about half an hour.'

'Right so. I'll tell the doctor that.'

She hung up. Relieved to be given some purpose to pursue, Jack drank some apple juice from the bottle in the fridge, finished dressing and left for the hospital.

'This is not going to be very pleasant for her,' Dr Lowry announced as soon as Jack arrived. 'But she was feverish last night and I'm worried about the consequences if we wait.'

'What does Maeve want?'

'She wants you to decide.'

Jack shrugged and pushed open the door to Maeve's room. She was propped up, much as he had left her the previous night. She smiled from behind her lank hair that wouldn't stay off her face and held out her good arm to him.

'What did he say?' she asked, as if unaware that the doctor was standing behind him.

'It's up to you, Maeve,' said Jack, taking her hand and pushing back her hair.

'Then you'll be there!'

'No, no, Maeve. If anything went wrong....' said Lowry.

Jack turned to the doctor. 'You didn't say she asked for me to be present.'

'I thought I explained to her.'

'Jack,' said Maeve, tugging at him. 'I want you to see her being born. I won't, so it's important to me that you do, that she sees you the instant she comes into this life.'

Jack turned to the doctor. 'Come on, I'll stay in the background, out of the way,' he urged him.

The doctor nodded without enthusiasm. 'Maeve, if this will help to relax you, then if he sits well clear of us....'

Jack felt her squeeze his hand, before he was led away by a nurse who tied a gown, mask and hat on him.

'Wasn't it very sad about the girl who was killed by that wave?' she said as she brought him through to the delivery room, where the anaesthetist was setting up.

They wheeled Maeve in noisily, and transferred her to the table. She turned her head and he waved at her. Lowry appeared, checked through his instruments with one of the nurses, nodded to the anaesthetist, and the team closed in around Maeve, blocking Jack's view.

'Jack?' she asked in a weak voice.

'I'm here, Maeve. Everything's fine. You just relax.'

'Hold me, Jack....' she said, her voice trailing off. The anaesthetic had taken effect.

In the moments of silence that followed Jack stared at the table to concentrate all his thoughts on his wife lying there, but as hard as he tried, his visions kept returning until eventually it was dawn and the king was leaning over Áine and the red blood burst up into the light again. And then there was a baby's cry and the vision changed, and it was his newborn daughter, still red with afterbirth, that they were holding up in the glare of the operating theatre beams.

The midwife carried the child to a scales, called out — 'Five pounds, twelve ounces,' and wrapped the infant carefully while the others kept their attention on Maeve. Jack stood up and the midwife presented him with the child.

'She's very small,' she said, 'but she has a healthy cry.'

Jack held the child in his arms. He was always amazed when people said the child looked like this parent or that parent. This baby bore no resemblance to anyone but herself. She was perfect in her own way, her little crinkled pink face getting used to this world, to the air and the light.

'You'd better take her,' he said. 'I know nothing about babies.'

'Oh, they all say that,' she said, 'but you'll soon learn. It's all ahead of you now.' She took the child again and pushed her way out through the double doors.

When he had finished with Maeve, Lowry came over, to Jack.

'That was very quick,' said Jack. Behind the doctor they were transferring Maeve again to the trolley that would take her back to her room. She moaned and shook her head, but her eyes remained closed.

'Maeve will be fine,' said the doctor. 'But she's had a difficult pregnancy, and she's given birth to a very small baby.' He shook his head. 'We've added another scar to her womb today. I doubt she'll be able to take another baby to term.'

Jack sighed and ran his hands down his face. 'Listen, doctor, we're just delighted with the baby we have. I don't think she has any thought of another child right now.'

'Well, let's not break this news to her until she's fully recovered,' advised the doctor. 'I have to run. They can contact me over the weekend if there are any complications, and I'll look in on her on Sunday.'

They shook hands and he left. Jack was ushered out the other door, peeled off his garb, and went to sit by Maeve.

She came around quickly, but dozed off without saying anything, and it was two more hours before she awoke again.

'Where is she?' she asked.

'Who?'

'The baby, Jack!'

'They took her to the nursery,' he replied.

'You saw her. You held her?'

'Yes. She's really beautiful.'

'Who does she look like?'

'You, Maeve. I think she'll look like you.'

'Dark hair?'

'Em, she weighed in at less than six pounds. She doesn't have any hair yet.'

Maeve groaned. 'What did I do to deserve all this?'

Jack wanted to tell her, one more time, but that would just increase her guilt about Margaret. As if she was following his thought, she asked, 'When's the funeral?'

'I don't know. Want me to find out?'

She nodded, eyes closed, and he left her, hoping she would fall asleep again.

No one in the hospital could help him, so, very reluctantly, he called Mulcahys' from the foyer of the hospital. It was crowded here with afternoon visitors and when the phone was answered he could not make out the voice at the far end.

'Who?' it asked.

'Jack Amonson. Maeve's husband.'

He heard voices in the background as if the Mulcahy home was filled with people, as it surely was, and then the voice of Sonny himself.

'Jack? Oh, Jack, you've heard the news then?' the fisherman sobbed.

'Yes, yes, Sonny.'

'Oh, God, was it Maeve told you?'

Jack shook his head. 'I'm here Sonny. I'm with Maeve. We wanted to know about the funeral.'

'I thought the sea would never take my daughter,' said Sonny. Jack swung around to hear better and as he did he thought he caught a glimpse of the back of Fortycoats going down the main corridor, but there were too many people in between to be sure.

'I'm so sorry,' said Jack. 'I just don't know what to say.'

'All this time that I had no sons, that was my one consolation,' Sonny cried. 'What have we done to bring this down upon ourselves?'

Jack gritted his teeth. Why were they all asking him? He wanted to say, 'You bulldozed a fairy rath'. But instead he said, 'I'm sure she's gone to a better place, Sonny.'

'Oh, she is,' her father sobbed. 'The funeral will be on Sunday, Jack. At two o'clock. And damn that new priest. He says the bishop will be here then to say prayers at the grotto and tried to make us have it tomorrow. Bloody blow-in!'

'I'll certainly be there.'

'Would you do one more thing for us, Jack?'

'Of course, Sonny, of course.'

'Would you take the back end of the coffin?'

'What?'

'Look, there was never anyone as good to her as Maeve and yourself. And she has no brothers, and all Maura's are too old to do it for us.'

'I've never....'

'Cathal, Eddie, myself and yourself, Jack. She couldn't ask for more.'

Jack felt his throat lump up. 'Yes, Sonny. I'll do it.'

He wandered around the grounds of the hospital for a while and then returned to Maeve. The staff sought him out again and told him that Maeve and the baby could go home some time over the weekend. They agreed that they would keep her till after the funeral and then he would pick her up. They even helped him arrange for a private nurse to look after the baby in the beginning, what with Maeve's arm.

That night he stared out the window of Maeve's room at
the passing traffic, telling himself he was here because he
wanted to be with her, but knowing too that he was deathly
afraid to go back to that house again. Preoccupied as he was,
he didn't notice the old man who slipped out the main entrance until he was clear of the lights, and then it was only a
silhouette of a man with a walking stick, his other arm hidden.

Yet he was sure when he did see him that he had seen a
ghost. He had to know. He dashed out of the room and down
the three flights of stairs, dodged orderlies, and bounded out
the main door. The man had been heading for the pedestrian
entrance, so Jack followed this, out to the road, saw that the
path towards town was deserted and ran into the dark in the
other direction. But the lights of passing cars showed him
that there was no one walking this way either.

If it was him, what had he been doing in the hospital earlier? Was he out to finish Maeve? Or harm the baby? Had he
enlisted another Gladys? Was some nurse right now injecting
Maeve with a lethal dose? Jack tore at his hair. And had he
been carrying something in the arm that was hidden? He
dashed back the way he had come, on past Maeve's room to
the nursery.

'I need to see my baby,' he told the young nurse on duty.

'They're all asleep,' she replied.

'Show her to me now!' he rasped.

'Baby Fitzgerald, isn't it?' she asked, standing, flustered.

'Yes.'

He started to follow her into the room but she told him to
wait and went quietly in herself. A few seconds later she
came back out with the baby.

'Does your wife want to feed her?' she asked.

'Yes, but she's not up to it right now.'

'It's all right. She's fine.' The nurse smiled at the baby in
her arms. 'Do you want to hold her?' she asked.

Jack shook his head. 'Will you be here all night?'

'Yes. Eight to eight.'

'Just keep a close eye on her, please?'

'Oh, I will.'

Chapter Twenty-Three

He spent the night in Maeve's room, dozing in the arm-chair. Again the dreams came. Over and over he saw the blood on the sun. But Áine never looked at him. Once he thought she did, but she was looking past him, and when he turned to see what had drawn her attention he saw the invaders crossing the marsh in three long files.

Later that day he visited Noreen.

'They're the Fomorians, Jack,' she told him.

'They gathered at the bottom of the hill and began a war dance,' he continued. 'But the others just waited, perfectly still, holding their weapons, with their backs to Áine.'

'The hill of judgement,' Noreen interrupted. '*An brei-theamh* — the judge; *breathach* — judicial! How could we have thought all these years that it was *breac* — trout?'

He shrugged.

'They anglicised it to Rathbrack, I suppose,' she went on, answering her own question. 'They lost the Irish language and then some idiot had to make a road sign and came up with that.'

Jack nodded. 'I guess no one realised all those years ago what the implications of losing your language would be.'

'Or the ones who did wanted the outcome they got. Go back to the battle, Jack.'

'This is the first time I've seen this. But the Tuatha De Danann, as you call them, had a colder fury about them.'

'They wanted to die, to be with her,' said Noreen, visibly shaken at this idea.

Jack nodded. 'There was no fear of death at all about the

way they fought this time. If any Fomorians came forward to taunt them, they picked them off, relentlessly, then fell back.

'And they just waited until the Fomorians were so agitated they had to rush the hill. Then the whole place became a killing ground. The women and children pelted the savages with stones, or tried to trip them up and crack their heads open. I don't know how many times they stormed the hill, but every time they were beaten back.

'One guy got as far as Áine, but they stabbed his other eye to pieces and cut his head off just for looking at her body. Fortycoats himself did that. It was just a slaughter, with the Fomorians becoming weaker each time until they knew they couldn't win and turned back towards the marsh.

'The Tuatha De Danann came after them. I don't think they were expecting that, because then they scattered. Every man for himself, which was really stupid because we could see them from the hill and we sent a big enough party to the beach ahead of them to start burning their boats.

'A few of them made it to the woods, but the young children kept track of them and led the men after them later in the day. I don't think one of the Fomorians survived. We could hear the wolves that night — on the beach, all around, eating the carcasses, calling to their packs.'

Noreen sighed. 'I've been wracking my brains all these months to put the pieces together. And now it just about fits. John Byrne once told me that the church is built on drained ground, that they diverted the flow out of Brigid's Well around the church and then into a culvert to the harbour. That would mean that the church is in the path of the flow of the sacred well, and the statue was pointing to the well or the hill itself. We've unconsciously re-venerated the same sites.'

'But we've destroyed whatever it was they built on the hill,' said Jack. Noreen's cottage was a gloomy place on a wintry day. She kept a small fire going, but that just made the rest of it look all the darker.

'Not *we*,' she corrected him. '*I* tried to stop you.'

He threw his hands up at this. 'Don't you think they've exacted their vengeance? I'll spend the rest of my life blaming myself for Margaret's death. And they ruined Owen's life....'

'Yes, they drove Maeve's people off the land. And they maimed Eddie. And they took Margaret as a sacrifice for what Sonny did. And what Cathal did. They've wrecked your marriage and your writing career. And they were going to kill Maeve, but you and I interfered, didn't we?'

'And who was our instrument?' Jack asked. 'Who actually physically saved Maeve?'

'Margaret. I know. I've been brooding on that for the past five months, and I haven't slept since she died.' Noreen stared at the fire.

Jack stood up and hunkered down by the flames. 'I think you're right. This is not over.'

'The eel in the chalice,' said Noreen absently. 'There would have been eels living in the marsh of course, but I still don't know which way to interpret that.'

'The eel?' Jack asked.

'You didn't know about that?'

He shook his head.

'John saw an eel in the chalice the morning after the party.'

It came back to him — Gladys, Maeve and Margaret cleaning up; the priest falling on the altar. And now he was back in room five in Ballylacken House. Áine moaned and thrashed her head from side to side. And then the spring in the hillside burst into life again.

'I thought it was a symbol of death,' Noreen went on. 'When Cúchulainn's mother gives him his last drink of wine, it turns to blood and he can't drink it. I thought this was similar. But maybe it has something to do with the well.'

'I'm sure it does,' said Jack.

'Why?'

'I just know. I was making love to Áine right then.' He straightened up. Noreen was quiet for a while. Finally she said, 'You're going to take Maeve and the baby away from here, aren't you?'

He nodded. 'If she'll go.'

'She has to, Jack. She has to!'

He left and walked back down to his car. A bitter wind whipped about the village; the sea churned in the harbour and the rusting trawlers clanked and rattled at their moorings.

He was about to drive away when he saw Cathal's red car outside Sweeney's. He turned off the engine again, got out and walked slowly across to the door of the pub.

Cathal sat alone at the end of the bar, his head in his hands, oblivious to Jack's approach. In front of him was one of those stubby glasses — just bulb and foot, as if they forgot to give it a stem — with a good measure of whiskey in it. Micko gave Jack his usual queer nod, but said nothing, just absently wiped whatever was nearest to him.

'Cathal? Cathal, it's me, Jack.'

The hands slid away from the architect's face to reveal red, sore eyes, the whites bloodied from crying, the lids swollen from the drink and sleeplessness.

'Cathal, I don't know what to say.'

Cathal shook his head, as if he were the one now looking at a ghost. 'You came back! I told Margaret you wouldn't. That you had more sense. That you'd seen them too!'

Jack sat up on the stool next to Cathal and put a hand on his shoulder.

Cathal leaned into him, tears welling up in his eyes. 'They took her, Jack, didn't they?'

Jack raised his eyebrows momentarily, as if that might be possible, but he couldn't — or wouldn't — say. Cathal reached for his drink and swallowed it in a single gulp. 'Buy me a drink,' he demanded in a voice already badly slurred.

'Sure.'

But before Jack could call to Micko, Cathal shouted, 'Hey, Micko, my fellow murderer and I would like two more. And have one yourself. You're up to your neck in this too!'

'Right you be,' muttered Micko Sweeney, and presented each glass in turn to the optic below the Black Bush.

'Ah, the good stuff. Impress the yanks, what?' said Cathal. 'Are you hoping for a fucking tip?'

'Terrible tragedy, Jack, wasn't it?' said Micko, delivering the three drinks.

'It was.'

The three men raised their glasses. 'Here's to you, Margaret,' said Cathal in a hoarse voice. He took one sip of this drink and then broke down and let his head fall into his arm on the counter, sobbing loudly. 'It's not fucking fair,' he bawled. 'Why did it have to be her? It should have been us!'

'Ah now,' said Micko.

Cathal sat up again. 'You sold him the place!' he roared.

Micko looked at Jack. 'His head is full of all this old codology about the fairies,' he said.

'Do you believe in an afterlife, Micko?' asked Jack quietly.

'No more, no less than the next man,' the publican replied.

'Then you'd agree that graves are sacred places?'

'I would,' said Micko, nodding emphatically, eyes darting between the two men on the far side of his counter.

'And yet you sold me a sacred site....'

'Well now, there was no bodies of any sort turned up when ye were building the place, did they?'

'No, but people died on that hill. Your ancestors, maybe.' Jack finished the shot of whiskey and banged down the glass. 'You make me sick, Micko. You and all the people like you. You have a way around everything. You and Owen Fitzgerald and Sonny Mulcahy. Just one crooked deal after another. But you're worse than any of them. At least they fished or farmed here, but all you do is dole out booze to people with ruined lives. And business has never been better, has it?' Jack took out a five-pound note and slapped it on the counter. 'That's for the drinks, Micko, and it's the last you'll see of my money.'

'That's telling the bollocks,' said Cathal, perking up a bit.

'Come on, Cathal, I'll take you back to my place to get some rest.' He reached out a hand but Cathal brushed him away.

'Oh no!' he said. 'I'm not going back up there.'

'Well, I'll take you up to Mulcahys' then.'

'No, you go on, Jack. I'll have one more and walk up.'

'She's gone to a better place, Cathal,' said Jack, backing away. 'I'm sure of that.'

The bleary eyes looked at him to see if he was serious, the architect nodded, and lost interest in his surroundings again.

The hospital was crowded with visitors: whole families in from the countryside to visit relatives; bored children running up and down the corridors; husbands with bunches of flowers for their expectant wives or eager to visit the new mother and child.

A nurse intercepted him before he could get to Maeve's room. 'Oh, Mr Fitzgerald, we've had to sedate your wife again!'

'What? What happened?'

'We brought the baby to her and she said it wasn't hers. There was a terrible scene. She screamed and shouted for you.'

'Oh, Jesus.' Jack pushed on into her room to find her now-conscious but groggy, eyes drooping, barely able to manage a faint smile.

'They say I have post-natal depression,' she told him as he pushed the hair back from her face. 'Get our baby, Jack, I want to try feeding her.'

'I don't think that's such a good idea,' said the nurse.

'Bring the child here to us,' said Jack, shaking his head.

'If you'll stay in the room with her.'

'Yes, yes!'

The nurse left and Jack sat down by Maeve and squeezed her hand.

'What'll we call her?' he asked.

'Margaret,' said Maeve.

Jack let go and got to his feet. 'No, no! Well, let me think about it.'

'We could make that her middle name, I suppose,' said Maeve, sleepily. 'I had a whole list of names, but I can't remember where I put them now.'

The nurse returned with the baby in her arms. 'Now, Maeve. Do you know how to do this?'

'Women have been doing this forever,' she said and reached out in slow motion, it seemed to Jack, and took the child. The nurse continued coaching Maeve in how to support the baby's head, and together they positioned the child's mouth over her right breast. Maeve winced for a few moments at this first effort but the child instinctively suckled her anyway.

'There now, she knows exactly what to do!' said the nurse, straightening up. Jack couldn't tell whether she meant the mother or the child, but she strode away satisfied and left the threesome together, so Jack sat down on the bed next to Maeve and watched her.

'How does it feel?' he asked.

Tears welled up in her eyes. 'I just can't feel anything for her, Jack!'

'You will,' he said.

'I can't! I can't!' she replied, more insistently.

'She's a beautiful little baby,' said Jack.

'I know,' Maeve sobbed, 'and she has your blood type and she's the only little six-pounder in the nursery and there isn't any mix up, but ... I can't do this!' Her voice rose. 'Please, please, take her away!'

'Steady on,' said Jack.

'No! Take her away from me! Jack, this is not my baby!'

Jack pulled the little baby gently away, and she began to cry in his arms.

'See, she wants more,' he said.

Maeve pulled herself more upright with her good arm and directed her blue eyes at him. 'Take her out of here!' she roared, loud enough to bring the nurse back again. 'I want *my* baby!' she bawled before more staff arrived and they injected her with something that knocked her out cold.

Jack followed them wearily out of the room and went up to the nurse's station.

'Oh, you're here,' said a voice behind him. He turned to see the young nurse from the baby's nursery in a coat and scarf behind him. 'I hear you're looking for a private nurse for a few days.'

'Yes!' She was a pretty girl, with a more rounded face than Margaret, but very Irish, winter-pink, with thick, dark hair.

'I'm free all next week. I'm just a temp here.'

'Okay, you're hired. Meet you here tomorrow at about six o'clock.'

'Right so.'

She was gone before he even found out her name, but at least that was another problem solved. And yet there it was again — he was a sucker for a pretty girl. And they knew that. The Tuatha De Danann knew that sending Áine would work on him. And once again he slipped into the debate between free will and destiny that would occupy his waking hours for the rest of his life.

Jack had no idea what to expect from a Catholic funeral. But it was easy enough to sit, kneel and stand when everyone else did, and when the mass was over he copied what Eddie was doing on the far side of the coffin. The four men hoisted the oak box onto their shoulders and carried it slowly down the church, Jack anxious that his new black coat was not so loose on the shoulder that the coffin would slip off.

He had never been close to Margaret. He remembered her transformation though from the sullen teenager who sometimes served their meals, to a self-confident, sensitive, elegant young woman. What would she have done as Cathal's wife? Gone on with her education? Become a part of his business?

All of the faces in the church bowed down and no one spoke, so that there was just the scuffling of their shoes as they followed the priest. They reached the front door and he saw the gleaming hearse outside.

Around at the grotto the bishop continued with the rosary over the new public address system, while the throng that had gathered to stand in the freezing wind mumbled their responses through chattering teeth. They were sliding the coffin into the back of the vehicle before they heard the bishop calling for a few moments silence in respect for 'the girl who was tragically drowned'.

Rathbrack had never seen so many people in one day. The entire parish was crammed into the church while another thousand or more visitors were gathered outside.

An hour of confusion followed. Some of those who had been outside intended to break away and join the funeral cortège to pray by the graveside. Others inside wanted to join the bishop's prayers to the Virgin Mary in recognition of this as a holy place of pilgrimage, and to hear the testimonial of the nun who been cured of lifelong deafness in one ear.

As with every Irish occasion, people were arriving late for both events, and the road in from both sides of the hill was jammed with traffic looking for parking spaces. Visitors were discovering that the main street led either to the pier, where cars were parked randomly, blocking each other, or up to a dead end at the cliffs where they were fearfully making U-turns and trying to get the oncoming traffic to reverse back down.

And there was a third crowd, drawn by the newspaper reports of a tsunami. They were parked all over the dunes, looking for evidence of the phenomenon. Sweeney's was closed as Micko was at the funeral, but crowds milled around waiting for it to open, studying the damage to the building.

Jack looked up at the angular walls and roof of the house on the hill and imagined the scene from there — as Áine would have seen it. But if they had left that mound — whatever it was — alone, none of this would be happening.

Darkness was falling as they lowered the coffin from their shoulders at the waiting grave. Sonny Mulcahy wept openly for his daughter, his wife so spent with grief that she could stand there only with the help of what Jack took to be her brothers. Cathal was ashen-faced, his red hair a wild mess. Eddie blessed himself, over and over, and Jack heard him more than once thanking God that he had escaped so lightly.

It was after seven when Jack finally returned to the maternity ward for Maeve. The private nurse was there with the baby sleeping in her arms, coo-cooing attentively to her. Maeve was dressed, her coat over her shoulders.

'Where are you taking me?' she asked drowsily.

'Home,' he said. 'For a few days, until you're well.'

'You want to take me away from Rathbrack, don't you?'

'Maeve, we talked about this just a few days ago.'

She stood up. 'I can't go without my baby, Jack.'

'Of course not. We'll bring the baby.' He picked up her hold-all and followed her out. The nurse fell in behind them and he sat her in the back with the baby.

Micko opened his doors to a thirsty crowd and was glad he had hired Eddie to help him. Cathal slid in and found a niche for himself next to the window. He stared at Eddie.

'You must hate me,' he said.

'I should,' said Eddie. 'But what's the point hating a man who hates himself?'

Cathal snorted. 'You were standing right here when I saw you become one of them.'

'I was. And do you remember what I said?'

'I do. And you were right.' Tears came to him again. 'I can't go on without her. Forty, fifty empty years ahead of me. Just like poor old Gladys.'

'I saw her at the funeral today,' said Eddie. 'She sings to herself all the time up in her little house, you know. And dances.'

'Oh God!' Cathal covered his face and Eddie left him to his dark thoughts.

Noreen had gone to the church but not the graveyard, where she would just have been a nuisance. This bitter cold made her stiffer than ever and she was sure to have been short taken in the middle of nowhere, so she had wheeled herself home. She slipped down now out of the wheelchair to stoke the fire, and then pulled herself up onto a chair by the table.

Jack's words from the previous day had rattled around in her head, troubling her. In one version of the Ulster cycle, Maeve, Queen of Connacht, is advised by a tiny eel to marry, which she does, but she marries a weak man, and so remains in command of the army that ultimately attacks Ulster. The eel that spoke to her was a person, a pig-keeper transmogrified. A cow drinks him and then gives birth to a bull of enormous strength.

But a different story had unfolded here in Rathbrack, one that had not been passed down and then recorded by the monks, or if it had, the manuscript had been long since lost.

What mesmerised Noreen now was the power from within the water. Somehow, this eel was a symbol of life, life springing up from a female source, magic in the water that came from the spring in the side of the hill. She had gone over this a hundred times in her mind, becoming more and more sure each time. The bishop and his followers were so intent on the virgin mother of their all-powerful male god, that they missed the whole point.

She closed her eyes and saw Áine dying as Jack had described, but there was more because Áine was still there. Not just her spilled blood, but all of her — as she herself had said — was in that hill, and that was her spring and her well! Noreen sat up, pulled herself back into the wheelchair and rolled across to where she had left her heavy sweater.

Eddie had served Cathal his third neat whiskey when Micko came around behind the semi-comatose architect and tapped him on the shoulder.

'Get off!' said Cathal, brushing him away.

'Could I just have a word with you, for a second, Cathal?'

'No. Fuck off!'

'Ah now. Just for a tick — I want to show you something.'

Cathal shrugged. 'Suppose I'd better humour my only client.'

'Oh, good, good. This'll take your mind off things maybe.' Micko led him through the packed premises to the door that adjoined the extension, and unlocked it.

'This place is fucked, forget it,' said Cathal as they closed the door behind them and turned on the lights, some of which still worked.

'Well, I'll agree it'll need a lot of work, fair enough, but....'

Cathal blinked at this and tried to clear his head.

'Hold on a minute. Did you bring me out here to talk about this dump again?'

'Eh, well, what I was wondering was whether you think it might be safe enough to let people come in here, just for a while. It's very crowded.' The publican's small frame twitched as he finished this. And before Cathal spoke he knew he had made a mistake.

'Can't fit them in, is that it?' said Cathal, pushing him. 'Never had it so good, as Jack said!'

'Right you be,' said Micko. 'We'll leave it so.'

'Oh no, we won't fucking leave it!' He pushed Micko towards the stage in the far corner, blocking him every time he tried to escape back to the old pub.

'Ah now,' said Micko, 'that won't get you anywhere!'

'And where did the money come from to build this?'

'Eh ... proceeds.'

'Proceeds? Proceeds of what?'

'I've been at this all these years.'

'No, Micko, that's not fucking true. You got the money to build this place by selling the rath to Jack and Maeve.'

Micko was afraid now. He took harder and harder blows from Cathal until they reached the stage, then he tripped backwards over it.

'Say it's your fault she's dead, Micko. Go on! Say it!'

'Ah now, Cathal. It's no one's fault.'

This was too much for the architect. He leapt onto the little publican, picked him up by his clothes and thrust him against the damaged wall. The whole structure shuddered, the beams creaked and there were snapping sounds in the roof.

'Safe is it? The foundations are washed away, because they were only sand, and you think it's safe?'

Cathal lifted him clear of the ground and shoved him back against the wall again.

'It's not safe, Cathal, it's not, you're right!' Micko was shouting now too. But they were at the furthest point from the old building, itself jammed with people trying to shout over each other, and no matter how loud he shouted, he would not now be heard.

'You're going to fucking admit your part in all this if I have to beat it out of you, Micko!' Cathal roared, spitting whiskey and phlegm at the other man.

The architect pulled the publican back from the wall and pushed him back again with all his might. This time the wall of concrete blocks moved away with Sweeney. Cathal let go and staggered back. But Micko lost his footing and tumbled backwards, along with the falling wall. And the wall was pulling all of the roof-beams down with it. Cathal looked up, saw the light fixtures coming apart, the fluorescent tubes shattering, and he fell flat on the ground.

As Micko fell backwards, he saw the lights ripping out, their glow replaced by blue sparks, and when he felt the thump behind him of the blocks hitting the sand, he made the fatal mistake of scrambling into a sitting position. When the collapsing ceiling finished its hinged fall, the blow broke his neck and the life went out of him in a last parody of his twisted nod.

Cathal was much luckier. The window booths stopped the ceiling from reaching him and he was already out from under the debris when the crowd came pouring in through the door.

Noreen reached the stile in the stone wall on the far side of the road from the church — so much for wheelchair access. She gripped the top step of this notch, pulled herself up out of the wheelchair, and then let herself topple over the stile onto the muddy grass inside. She should have brought her stick. Now she would have to crawl along, slow and painful going with her knees frozen up.

But at last she found herself lying in the dark below the basin that held the water tinkling down from the cleft in the hill. She pulled back so that she could look up and see the silvery cascade, the flow just enough tonight to allow a single sliver of water to arc free of the rock wall.

With a great effort she forced her knees to bend, knelt and joined her hands.

'Áine, I believe. I do truly believe,' she said. 'I didn't understand that he was your father. Please, please forgive me!'

Nothing happened.

'I know that it's your power that's helping people at the grotto and I'm here to tell you that I want to help you!'

Still there was only silence.

'I will do whatever I can to restore your hill, Áine. Anything. They don't understand, but I do. And I will help you.'

Again, for a long time there was only silence. And then there was what sounded like a rustling of dead leaves and the splashing of the water changed, slowing down in some way. Or was it Noreen's sense of time that was being altered?

'Do you believe?' asked a girl's voice.

Noreen looked frantically around.

'Yes!' she said as emphatically as she could with the fear spreading through her.

The spring began to glow with a light of its own.

'*Drink the water,*' said the voice.

Noreen wanted to reply that she couldn't reach, but something held her voice back. And then the tingling in her legs that she had felt on the driveway that day returned. Slowly, she pulled one knee forward, reached up and grasped the rim of the basin. And now, when she pulled with her arm, her leg supported her, and when she was erect the other leg fell obediently into place.

She leaned her face into the pool and drank the near-freezing water, then pulled back to see a girl's ankles in front of her. She followed the glowing white robe up its length and saw Áine, with hair like fire, looking back down at her. But this was a wraith, not a thing of flesh.

'*Destroy the house. Now! Before he brings her back,*' said Áine's voice without her face moving.

'Yes, yes!' whispered Noreen, falling back to her knees before this pagan goddess. 'I will.'

'*Now!*' the voice commanded, and then the image faded.

The poet got to her feet and walked around in circles a few times. She had complete control of her legs. She was cured of an incurable illness. And she knew that if she did as Áine had asked she need never worry about her MS returning again.

Knowing it was possible to climb the hill from the well, she found the trail up through the gorse without much difficulty. A crescent moon was rising, high enough now that it lit her way to the house.

She tried the front door and marvelled that it was open, then switched on the hall light. How was she to do this? She walked into the living-room, then the kitchen, and tested the gas stove. She must burn it down. She had made a promise.

She would have done this without the gift of health because she knew now that the chaos would not end until it was done, but they had cured her! She laughed as she stood in the dark kitchen, laughed at how simple it had been.

She remembered that the house also had a gas fireplace. She would fill the house with gas and then ignite it, and no matter how fast they came, it would be a ruin when they got here. But how would she do it without blowing herself up?

Chapter Twenty-Four

Noreen twisted one of the knobs on the cooker to its fully on position. Nothing happened. She looked closer at the cooker and saw that it had two gas rings and two electric rings. She tried another knob. The built-in lighter clicked and the gas burst into a blue rosette of flame. She turned it off again, then half on. Now the gas hissed without lighting.

She walked into the dark living-room. The light from the kitchen cast long shadows, but the chimney blocked the light from most of the room. She grew accustomed to the gloom and searched around by the fireplace, where she found the valve handle that allowed the gas to shoot out a series of holes in a pipe below the grate. She turned this as far anti-clockwise as it would go and felt the cold jets of propane blowing directly out into the room.

Now what she needed was some kind of timing mechanism. She returned to the kitchen. The electric oven had a timer but she had no idea how it worked. Could she put something in it that would burst into flames when it heated up? No, she would have to leave the door open, which would probably mean that the temperature wouldn't rise enough. Already she could smell the gas.

She should have thought this through. Or she should wait till tomorrow, but then they would be back with their baby.

She returned to the cooker. There was a copper saucepan on one of the rings. She opened the cupboard doors above her until she found a bottle of vegetable oil. This would catch fire — it had happened to her before. She emptied the oil into the pot and turned both electric knobs all the way on again.

It was a very unpredictable timer. How long would it take for the oil to reach flashpoint? Maybe ten minutes or so. She felt the pot to be sure it was heating up, backed away, turned on the two gas rings, pulled the door to the hall closed behind her so that the gas would concentrate better, and left.

There was nothing more she could do. Would this look like an accident or would they know it was arson? She would go back to her wheelchair, wheel herself home, and not reveal her cure for a few weeks. She hurried back over the wet grass towards the well and picked her way through the spiny gorse.

Jack's misgivings grew as they approached Rathbrack. He saw the Tuatha De Danann carrying their own dead back to the summit and laying the bodies over Áine. They added logs and branches until they had made a pyre half of limbs and half of fuel, Áine now completely hidden at its centre. Forty-coats cried and tore away pieces of his clothes and lumps of hair until his scalp bled.

They came around the bend by the church and as they slowed for their own gate, Maeve said, 'I think that was Noreen Fletcher's wheelchair.'

'Where?' Jack asked.

'Back by the well.'

'And was she there?'

'No. Jack, go back and see....'

'Let's get you and the baby settled, then I'll check it out.' He looked in the rear-view mirror where the nurse was rocking the child gently. 'Did you see anything?' he asked.

'No.'

They turned into the driveway.

Noreen had seen the car go by, but cars passed on the coast road all the time. Surely they wouldn't notice a wheelchair well in from the kerb on this dark evening. She dropped down by the spring, the one place from where she could not see the beams of Jack's car as he ascended the driveway. Here she paused again to give thanks for her cure while the people on the hilltop got out and climbed the steps to the front door.

'It's open,' said Jack to Maeve who was ahead of him.

She turned the knob and pushed the door open, then switched on the hall light. Jack ushered the nurse past him, and followed them in.

Cathal bent over and retched again as Eddie held him steady.

'You didn't kill him,' said Eddie. 'The wall fell on him.'

'Yes I did,' said Cathal, straightening up. 'Just as surely as I killed Margaret.'

'Give over,' said Eddie. 'Get out of here now and I'll deal with the guards.'

Cathal nodded and staggered to the door and out into the street. No one understood what had happened, and those now streaming out the front door of the old pub to see what had caused the loud crash saw only the undamaged front wall of the extension.

He looked for a few moments at the house on the hill as he fumbled for the car keys.

'If I thought for one moment it would bring you back,' he mumbled, 'I'd tear the place to pieces with my bare hands.'

The architect sat into his car, wiped the tears from his eyes, and pulled out onto Rathbrack's dark street. The car was pointed toward Mulcahys', but he would never go back there now. He turned in a half circle and drove slowly past Noreen's cottage. Everywhere held memories of Margaret for him, and there was only one way he could be with her again.

The car was reluctant to accelerate at first, but as he climbed past the field where the cattle had died in the storm the moment Eddie had become a Fomorian, he felt a surge of speed. He was going faster and faster. He sped past the 'No Dumping' sign, onto the grass and over the rim of the cliff.

'I love you, Margaret,' he said aloud as the car tilted forward. For an instant he saw the house in his rear-view mirror, lit by a sudden flash from within itself, before the headlights picked out first the sea and then the buttresses of rock below, like those on the far side of the bay where she had died.

The car struck the upper edge of an escarpment and Cathal flew forward through the windshield, breaking his neck, back and legs as he somersaulted into the sea. The car tumbled forward after him. The boot opened as the roof crumpled, and the carved stones were pitched out onto the sloping rock.

His corpse rose and fell on the surf a couple of times before a wave pulled it clear of the rocks, then lifted it and pounded it, over and over, against the same place, where it would be discovered next day with every major bone broken.

'What's that smell?' asked Maeve.

'Gas,' said Jack.

Beyond the closed door of the kitchen smoke rose from the hot vegetable oil. It bubbled, then spattered hot droplets onto the glowing ring next to it.

'Must be a leak,' he called, walking through the open doors into the living-room. He heard the hiss from the nozzles of the gas fire, but before he could react, the kitchen exploded.

The blast blew open the door to the hall, knocking Maeve over backwards, into the nurse and child, and throwing all of them to the floor. The two women screamed, drowning out the baby's cry. Jack spun towards them, seeing the debris that was flying from the kitchen into the living-room.

'Get out of the house!' he heard himself say.

He stooped down to help Maeve up, but she was already scrambling to her knees.

'The baby,' she said. 'Get the baby.'

Already the sound of the explosion was gone and pieces of broken furniture, glass and pottery lay everywhere beyond the wrecked door to the kitchen. Patches of burning oil clung to doors and walls and relit the gas rings.

The nurse scrambled to her knees and picked up the child.

'No! No!' Maeve screamed. 'I want my baby!'

'She's all right,' said the nurse.

Jack saw Maeve shake her head as she pulled herself up on one arm.

'She is,' he said. He had been protected from the force of the blast by the chimney and couldn't tell how badly the others might have been hurt, but he wanted right now just to reassure Maeve and not have her panic.

'Give her to me!' Maeve shouted, stretching out her good arm to the nurse.

Jack reached Maeve and lifted her to her feet, but she shrugged him off.

'Let's get out of here!' he shouted.

'No! This is my home!' Maeve replied. Her eyes blazed at him. 'You did this, didn't you?' she yelled.

'No, Maeve. It's some kind of leak. Let's get out of here and I'll turn off the main gas valve at the tank, okay?'

He tried to take her arm but she backed away. 'I'm staying here,' she said.

'For God's sake, Maeve!' He turned to the nurse. 'Take the fucking child out of the house!' he roared.

'Give her to me!' Maeve screamed even more loudly.

The nurse was trembling. She held the baby at arm's length for whichever of them would take it. Jack reached out, but Maeve backed into him and winded him with her good elbow. She scooped the child out of the other woman's arms and pulled back from them.

The nozzles in the fireplace continued to send their invisible fuel all the way to the far side of the huge room where it had now spread out around the walls in a dense cloud and drifted slowly back towards them.

And then this much larger mass of gas reached the kitchen and was lit off by the nearest splashes of oil still burning on the floor. This time, instead of an explosion, a plume of blue flame billowed through the large room. The burning gas expanded and rose, found more oxygen, and became a ball of fire that outgrew the room.

Now Maeve was protected by a wall, while Jack was thrown to the ground. The nurse bolted from the building just in time to avoid the jet of flame that engulfed Jack, scorching him as it set fire to the paint and varnish all around.

'Maeve!' he roared, but there was no reply.

He pulled himself up and lunged through the hall, filling with smoke now as the roof and floor timbers began to burn.

Noreen was already halfway across the churchyard, passing below the pale statue in the grotto, when she heard the first blast. She looked back to see the light in the hall, and gasped as she saw its reflection on the roof of a car at the front door.

She stood up and put her hands over her mouth, and was still standing there, unsure what to do, when the second blast came. From where she stood she saw the entire south half of the house light up inside. It flickered and dimmed, but it was obvious the burning continued. A figure fled through the front door, followed by smoke.

Should she interfere? The last time she had interfered her disease had returned after only a few brief moments of remission. Would that happen again? The flames dimmed, then grew brighter again as the gas was replaced by burning wood and paint. Maybe there was no one else in the house.

She would do time for arson. They would not let her off as lightly as Gladys. But that was not it. No, she would not go back on her promise. She would not be the cause of another death like Margaret's. She would not defy the spirit of the hill. She sat into her wheelchair and continued on past the school without looking back.

Jack's eyes stung and he felt dizzy. He reached where Maeve should be standing, but she was no longer there.

'Maeve!' he shouted again. There was no reply. The crackling of the burning wood covered the sound of her movements. Then he heard the child cry, but it was a moan that seemed to come from everywhere in the house at once.

No matter which way he turned the sound was ahead of him. He pushed into the master bedroom, the furthest part of the house from the fire, and he was sure that the child was back behind him.

He went into the kitchen where smoke was seeping down from the light fittings and a line of flame was climbing the cabinet doors below the breakfast counter.

'Maeve!' he shouted again.

Then he saw her at the far end of the living-room. She was kneeling at the edge of the rath. Around her the flames climbed the pillars and spread in along the roof-beams to meet at its apex.

It was the funeral pyre alight, with hundreds of people kneeling around it as the Tuatha De Danann cremated their dead. He walked in closer and saw the looks on the mourners' faces as they watched, and the sacrifice that had been made for them was seared into their memories forever.

'Give me back my child!' Maeve shouted again. But now she was pleading. She banged her fist on the ground in frustration. Jack saw the baby in its swaddling on the couch a few feet nearer to him. Sparks showered down next to the child.

He picked her up and as he did so Maeve noticed him and swung around.

'You found her!' she exclaimed.

'Yes, yes!' he answered. 'Now come on, let's go!'

Maeve stood up. The flames roared above her as the air began to find ways out through the roof tiles and the fire sucked in the new draughts it needed through the broken kitchen windows. Every beam and pillar was blazing, Cathal's design outlined in orange fire.

He reached out a hand to his wife and saw her smile as she came closer.

'It is my baby, Jack, isn't it?' she said.

'Yes!'

'It couldn't be anyone else's, could it?'

He wanted to say no, but he hesitated. He saw the eel in the chalice, just as the priest had done. He heard Áine again saying she would bear him a child. And he saw the shadowy figure leaving the hospital, holding something....

'No, Jack! Tell me it's not true!' His wife shook her head slowly from side to side.

'Maeve, it's over,' he heard himself say. 'Let's go, or the child will die!'

But she was beyond listening to him. She stepped back into the fairy rath, and as she did so the central roof-beam burned free of the last of its brackets and fell slowly away from the southernmost apex above them.

'Maeve!' Jack roared above the flames, but she shook her head and moved away even further.

'I'll never leave!' she shouted, and as she did so a flaming support beam fell between them.

Jack dodged the next one and backed away drawn more by the sound of the nurse shouting to them than what he could see through the smoke. More and more of the roof collapsed, working its way back towards the fireplace, the only part of the house not on fire.

When he reached this stone upright he waited a few seconds, then sprinted with his head down over the child for the front door, and ran through it into the night to hear the rest of the roof crashing in behind him. He handed the baby to the nurse, ignored the cars that were now arriving from the village, and ran around the house to try to save Maeve.

But it was hopeless. She was buried under the burning beams and now as the window frames twisted and the glass broke he was just looking at billowing black smoke from the burning floorboards. Twice he tried to climb in, but even when he could see with the light of the fire he couldn't make his way to where she must be.

He stayed there all night, wrapped in a blanket they gave him, refusing to leave, and watched as the firemen picked their way to Maeve's remains in the early light, smoke meandering up into the still air from different parts of the ruin.

And he saw it ending the same way five thousand years before. The funeral pyre collapsed and the people began pulling up the ring of stones from around their hill and breaking the slabs into smaller pieces. With these they built a circular wall around the ashes, and packed the gaps with sods and smaller stones, so that when it began to rain what was left was not all washed away.

Jack felt the rain on his head and finally turned away to walk slowly down the driveway past the line of emergency vehicles.

Aaron said nothing for a long time after Jack had finished telling his story. He walked to the balcony window and looked out at the cathedral spires that rose above the dark Mexican city.

'Then you knew all along it was Noreen?' he asked without turning back.

Jack nodded at the reflection in the glass doors. 'Still an open case, isn't it?'

'Yes,' said Aaron.

'So you've been back?' asked Jack.

'Several times. I thought I might pick up your trail. Find you, be of help.'

'Has Rathbrack changed much?'

The Hollywood executive turned back around. 'It's all different,' he said. 'They did build houses on Owen Fitzgerald's land. He would have made a fortune. They've even built a new school the other side of the church.

'And Sweeney's?'

'You mean O'Shaughnessy's. Sonny Mulcahy bought it for Eddie — or gave him the money anyway — as a settlement for his eye. Eddie never rebuilt the extension. The concrete slab is still there. But there are other bars and restaurants too. It's a very trendy place to live now.'

'And Noreen?'

'She bought Gladys Clery's place. Let the old woman live in it till she died, about five years ago, then moved over there herself. She's done great things with it. You know I got a lot of her work published.'

'Really?'

Aaron shrugged. 'In fact, I tried to persuade her to come to the US. I, ah, kinda wanted to take up where that priest guy left off.'

'Well that explains why you were so hesitant.'

'I guess Noreen has no choice in this?' said Aaron tersely.

'No.'

'She won't even see it as blackmail. She really believes all of this stuff,' the entertainment mogul added.

'And you still don't?'

Aaron shook his head. Jack looked at his watch. Deirdre
was crossing Plaza de Armas now. He saw her, in his mind's
eye, from behind, as if following her, in her school uniform,
shoes moving swiftly over the dark flagstones.

'I wouldn't have thought you'd end up in somewhere so
intensely Catholic, Jack. And after all you've said tonight....'

'Hey, I'm not one of them.' Jack reached for the tequila
bottle again. 'I think the Christian veneer is even thinner
here,' he said as he refilled his glass. 'So much so, they just
might hang on long enough to make the jump from organised
religion back to their own sacred beliefs again without the big
gap in the middle that ate up Maeve and me.'

'That's why you're sending Deirdre to Noreen — to teach
her spirituality?'

'Deirdre has to go back,' said Jack flatly.

The intercom buzzed.

'Dad, it's me! Is he here?'

Jack stood up and pressed the release button again.

Aaron stared at the door. Jack opened it and stood
watching his friend. Neither spoke as they waited for the girl.

Her feet tapped on the floorboards as she hurried up to
meet her father's friend, who would take her to Ireland, to
the very place she was born.

Jack watched Aaron's face as realisation, however reluctantly, came to him. Deirdre reached the doorway and
paused, as if unsure whether she should join the two men.

'Then it is all true,' said Aaron softly.

He looked at Jack, a look of intense pity now, then back at
the writer's daughter. The golden hair was pulled back
neatly into a pony tail, but there was no need to see it cascad-
ing loosely, or to imagine the willowy figure inside the school
uniform. The green eyes that shone back at him were enough.

'You poor bastard,' said Aaron, shaking his head. Jack
nodded wearily, closed his eyes and saw the three of them
that day they had first passed her on the beach in Rathbrack.

And again, as he did a thousand times a day, Jack recalled
Áine's last words before she faded into the mist — 'You can
never have me now, Jack. You will never forget me. And no
other woman will ever make you happy again.'